## DATE DUE

| | |
|---|---|
| MAY 1 2000 | JAN 3 1 2019 |
| MAY 2 9 2000 | JUL 2 1 2022 |
| OCT 6 2000 | |
| NOV 2 3 2000 | |
| MAR 6 2001 | |
| JUL 1 2001 | |
| JUL 3 1 2003 | |
| OCT 2 4 2003 | |
| FEB 2 3 2004 | |
| JUL 2 0 72 2004 | |
| SEP 0 3 2004 | |
| SEP 0 2 2005 | |
| OCT 1 2 2006 | |
| SEP 2 7 2013 | |
| DEC 7 - 2013 | |
| JAN 1 0 2014 | |

BRODART, CO.                    Cat. No. 23-221-003

# Kindred Bond

## DEBORAH RANEY

**BETHANY HOUSE PUBLISHERS**
MINNEAPOLIS, MINNESOTA 55438

*Kindred Bond*
Copyright © 1998
Deborah Raney

Cover illustration by William Graf
Cover design by the Lookout Design Group

Unless otherwise identified, Scripture quotations are from the King James
Version of the Bible.

Published by Bethany House Publishers
A Ministry of Bethany Fellowship International
11300 Hampshire Avenue South
Minneapolis, Minnesota 55438
www.bethanyhouse.com

Printed in the United States of America by
Bethany Press International, Minneapolis, Minnesota 55438

**Library of Congress Cataloging-in-Publication Data**

Raney, Deborah.
    Kindred bond / by Deborah Raney.
    p.   cm. — (Portraits)
    ISBN 1–55661–999–5 (pbk.)
    I. Title.  II. Series: Portraits (Minneapolis, Minn.)
PS3568.A562K56    1998
813'.54—dc21                        97–45450
                                                    CIP

To my husband, Ken,

who keeps romance in my life

in the truest, most sacred sense of the word.

# Portraits

DEBORAH RANEY is an at-home mom, speaker, and author of several books. Her first novel, *A Vow To Cherish*, was a winner of Excellence in Media's Angel Award for its sensitive depiction of one family's struggle with Alzheimer's disease. Deb and her husband, Ken, have four children ranging in age from elementary school to college. They make their home in Kansas, where they are active in their church and community.

# One

*T*he morning sunlight played off the leaves of the old locust tree bowed low over the flagstone patio. Yellow shafts of light cast dappled, ever changing patterns across the wrought-iron table and the breakfast tray it held.

Claire Anderson absentmindedly stroked the sleek gray cat ensconced in her lap while a gentle breeze rustled the pages of the newspaper she was reading.

The *Hanover Falls Record* was a newsy little paper, full of local gossip and scrumptious-sounding recipes, but it contained very little of interest to a newcomer to the town. Still, Claire was determined to become familiar with the goings-on in this little Missouri community in the foothills of the Ozarks. She was still getting used to calling Hanover Falls *home*.

In five short days she would begin the first real job of her career. Claire had struggled to put herself through school, alternately working and attending university classes. After almost seven years of being tied to a rigid schedule of work and study, she had landed her first teaching job at the town's small elementary school. She felt a growing excitement knowing that the life she had dreamed of was finally becoming a reality.

She gazed with satisfaction at the secluded backyard of the little house she had rented just two weeks ago and could scarcely believe her luck. The house was everything she could have asked for. It was tiny—no more than a cottage, really—but with its cozy living room with a brickwork fireplace, the large, sunny kitchen, and the shady flagstone patio where she now sat enjoying a leisurely breakfast, it was perfect for her. Even Smokey, the cat she had inherited with the house, was part of the fulfillment of the dream she had envisioned for her life in this little town.

The house was sandwiched between two larger Tudor-style houses on Brookside Drive, one of the town's oldest streets. The "brook" of Brookside Drive was more of a muddy creek than the babbling stone-bottomed stream its name called to mind, but its murky waters fed a small copse of birch trees, a hedge of tall pines, and a surprisingly beautiful array of blooming weeds and wildflowers.

The house was owned by Millie Overman, a delightfully spunky widow of eighty-eight, who had recently been persuaded by her two daughters to move into the town's senior citizens' apartment housing. Claire had spotted Millie's advertisement offering the house for rent in the classified section of the first copy of the *Record* she had picked up, and by the day's end she had signed the contract without so much as looking at another place.

Smokey, a huge silver gray tom, was almost ten years old and had been Millie Overman's dear companion. But the apartment where she was moving had strict rules and "no pets" was at the top of the list. Millie, in what Claire was discovering to be her indomitable way, had written Smokey into the rental contract, requiring the renter of the house to care for Smokey "as long as aforementioned renter inhabits the house or as long as Smokey shall live." When Mrs. Overman had pointed out the clause in the carefully typed document, Claire had suppressed her amusement and earnestly assured her new landlady that she would consider it a privilege to share her home with the cat.

Now Claire nudged Smokey off her lap, folded the front page, and laid it aside. She took a cautious sip of tea from the steaming mug in front of her, set it back down on the crumb-strewn tray, and opened another section of the newspaper, shaking it out to straighten the wind-creased pages.

As she glanced at the first page, a vaguely familiar face stared back at her from a three-column photo. She tried in vain to think why the man seemed familiar to her. Had she met him recently? She looked more closely at the photograph. Dressed in a dark suit and tie, the man wore a wide smile, though Claire thought the smile didn't quite reach his eyes. Even in the black-and-white photo, his eyes seemed to hold a hint of sadness. Beside him in the photograph stood a woman Claire recognized as a teacher she had been introduced to at a faculty luncheon just the week before. Claire and the woman had joked about their shared surname and how commonplace and uninteresting a name they each had inherited. "Well, at least it puts us first in line every time!" Becky Anderson had quipped.

Claire scanned the brief caption beneath the picture:

MICHAEL MEREDITH, ADMINISTRATOR OF RIVER-VIEW MANOR, ACCEPTS A CHECK FROM REBEKAH ANDERSON, PRESIDENT OF THE HANOVER FALLS CIVIC CLUB. THE CLUB RAISED ALMOST $5,000 FOR THE NEW SENIOR CENTER THAT IS SCHEDULED TO BE COMPLETED NEXT SUMMER.

Michael Meredith's name wasn't familiar to her, but Claire couldn't shake the feeling that she should know him. Perhaps she had seen him at Riverview Manor. The facility he administrated was part of the complex of residential care homes where Millie Overman now resided. Claire had been introduced to many people from the school and the town over the past few days, and she was struggling to keep all the new acquaintances straight. Still, she felt she would have taken special notice of this man with his dark good looks and deeply clefted chin. Maybe he just looked like someone she knew.

Claire let the paper fall to the table, dismissing the subject. Sighing heavily, she leaned her head against the back of the heavy Adirondack chair and closed her eyes. She would be glad when the first week of school had come and gone. Though she was excited and anxious to begin her new career, she was apprehensive, too. It was a bit frightening to think she was finally about to embark upon the career for which she had spent seven long years preparing. She was just now beginning to realize how much she was depending on this new job to fulfill her desire for happiness . . . to redeem some of the loneliness that had marked her childhood and adolescence.

Growing up in a home with a distant, sickly mother and a preoccupied father, Claire had become somewhat of a loner. Life seemed to be less complicated that way. The few friends she had made in college graduated long before she did and moved away to begin their own lives. For a while she had kept in touch with a couple of her roommates, but eventually they drifted apart and she lost track of them.

When Claire was sixteen, her mother died after a long illness. The ensuing hospital bills had drained the family's bank account. Then, when Raymond Anderson died suddenly during Claire's second year of college, she discovered that not only was there no insurance money, but proceeds from the sale of the family home barely covered the debts he had piled up. Left virtually penniless and terrified of running up a debt of her own, Claire had worked at various jobs, taking only as many classes as she could afford to pay for and sitting out several semesters to work full time. Difficult as it was, Claire was proud of the fact that except for the first year—when her father and a small scholarship had helped with the bills, along with an occasional check from her grandmother—she had put herself through school.

The only things that had urged her on and helped her keep her eyes on her goal over the stressful years were Nana's love and support and fond memories of Raylene Emerson. During Claire's senior year in high school, she had served as a student aide in Mrs. Emerson's third-grade class. Never having been around small children, Claire was fascinated by their exuberance and simple trust. She found that she adored working with young children. Mrs. Emerson, a mother of four young sons, took the lonely teenage girl under her wing during that year. Claire baby-sat for the Emerson boys and found their mother to be a wonderful listener as she worked through her grief over her own mother's death and her guilt at the anger she felt toward her parents. As the year wore on, Mrs. Emerson had encouraged Claire to pursue a career in education and even helped her obtain the small scholarship. Claire had lost track of her mentor over the years, but she thought of her often and silently thanked God for the woman who had been such a powerful influence in her young life. Claire hoped that someday she would be able to let the older woman know what an inspiration she had been during that difficult time.

Claire reached for her mug and drained the last of the now tepid liquid. She replaced the cup on the tray and stretched her arms over her head. The warmth of the sun made her drowsy, and as she drifted off, her memories melted into dreams.

They were standing in the middle of the vast cemetery in the St. Louis suburb where they had always lived: her father holding her hand, squeezing it too tightly; her mother kneeling, weeping at a tiny grave marker in front of a hard-packed mound of rich brown earth. Beside it a second identical marker shadowed a patch of sparse yellow-green grass. Claire had always liked the little stone capped with a miniature statue of a lamb. *Now the little lamb will have a friend*, she thought. She wished her mommy wasn't always so sad when they came to this place. They came nearly every Sunday afternoon, unless it was raining. Claire thought it was such a pretty place with all its shady trees and pathways. And almost always a sea of flowers dotted the pillars of stone, large and small.

She remembered a few weeks ago when there had been many people here with them. They had lowered the little white box into the hole in the ground. Her parents had not allowed her to look inside the box, but her five-year-old mind understood that this place was where her baby brothers had gone when they died. Though she had only been three when the first baby, Michael James, had died. She didn't remember him, but there was a small picture of him on the dresser in Mommy and Daddy's bedroom. Claire would never say so out loud, but she didn't think he was very cute. Even in the tiny picture, she could see that his face was all red and wrinkled, and his eyes were scrunched shut so tightly they were merely slits.

Now this new little stone stood beside the first one, though there were no pictures of this baby to remember him by. Daddy had told her that this baby's name was Ryan—Ryan Alan. Unlike little Michael, Ryan had never even come home from the hospital.

She wished the babies hadn't died. Then maybe her mommy wouldn't be so sad all the time, and she would have someone to play with. But as she looked around the cemetery, she thought that if *she* died, this would be where she would want to be—among the leafy trees and the pretty rocks lined up in tidy rows. This was how she thought heaven must look. She could almost see Jesus walking among the gravestones, His long purple robes flowing out behind Him just like the picture in the little pink Bible she carried to Sunday school whenever she visited Nana.

That's where she had been when baby Ryan died—at Nana's house in Lee's Summit. Nana had hugged her and told her that the baby was in heaven with Jesus and that she would get to see him someday if she would only ask Jesus into her heart. But Nana had cried bitterly when she told Claire this, and that made Claire feel sad—and a little frightened. If heaven was such a wonderful place, why did everybody cry whenever someone went there?

Being in the cemetery now made her feel happier. Claire pulled her hand from her father's grasp and reached out to touch the new lamb, relishing the feel of the smooth, cool stone under her small hand.

Her mother wiped her eyes and blew her nose. She rose awkwardly, steadying herself with hands outspread on the grass, while the heels of her black pumps sunk farther into the soft earth. Claire heard her mother's deep intake of breath and recognized the same shudder she sometimes heard in her own voice when she had been crying for a long time.

It used to make Claire sad whenever Mommy cried so hard, but now she was used to it. It seemed that Mommy cried almost every day now. For a time Claire had supposed that all mommies were that way—until the night she slept over at her friend Gretchen's house. Gretchen's mommy always seemed to be happy. Mrs. Gaylord let them have pizza and ice cream for supper, and she didn't even get angry when Gretchen's brother spilled his Pepsi on the carpet. After supper Mrs. Gaylord had played games with Gretchen and Claire, laughing and smiling and sitting right down on the floor beside them. Mommy never played games with her. . . .


Smokey's loud *meow* woke Claire from her light sleep. The cat stretched his full length, scratching at the back doorpost.

"Smokey!" she yelled, jumping up from her chair. She hurried to let the cat in before his claws damaged the freshly painted trim around the door. She had to smile as she noticed for the first time the deep indentations that matched Smokey's scratching pattern perfectly. The marks had been camouflaged by a fresh coat of glossy forest green paint, but there was no mistaking how they had come to be there. "I guess you can't teach an old *cat* new tricks, either," Claire said wryly, letting the big tomcat inside before she went back to carry in the remains of her alfresco breakfast.

# Two

*B*ye, Miss Anderson. See you tomorrow." The little girl waved shyly from the doorway, then turned and raced down the hall, her thick blond ponytail flying behind her.

"Good-bye, Lacey. Good luck at your soccer game tonight. . . ." Claire's voice was overtaken by the bustling, crowded hallway.

Sighing with satisfaction, she turned back to the empty classroom and began to organize the papers stacked haphazardly on her desk. The third week of school was nearly complete, and Claire was finding her job more fulfilling than she could have ever imagined. During the first few days, there had been some tense moments when a project didn't work out quite as smoothly as she'd hoped or when discipline problems reared their inevitable heads. But all in all, teaching was turning out to be a wonderful experience. Even after such a relatively short time, she felt she was beginning to know each of her students individually and to have some solid insight as to how she could best help each of them to learn. Best of all, she had a strong sense that she *was* a teacher. It felt like the thing she had been born to do.

Marjean Hammond, the elementary school principal, had been very supportive and helpful, as had the other teachers in the school. With fewer than three hundred students in the building, there was much freedom for the teachers to work together and for Claire to try some rather innovative methods of teaching. She was proud of the fact that she had already lined up several townspeople to come in and speak to her class during an upcoming social studies unit. Each success in the classroom made her feel that she could begin to relax a bit and rely on her education and her instincts to carry her through.

Though there always seemed to be work to take home—papers to grade or lesson plans to complete—she was finally beginning to be able to leave the mental stress of her job behind at the end of each day. She had *dreamed* school—while awake and sleeping—that first week, nearly driving herself crazy as she tried in vain to put names with her students' faces. Sometimes she even got out of bed in the middle of the night to check her files for the information when it simply would not materialize in her mind. Now she was surprised there had ever been a time when she didn't immediately recognize that charming lisp as Brianne Sizemore's or the carrot red hair and freckles as belonging to Jarrod Hamilton. She thought with a smile of Mimi Harrold's pixieish face and Talisha Jackson with her meticulous cornrows and her keen sense of humor. Even ornery Lucas Crockett had captured a little corner of her heart. She thought of them as *her* kids now, and it was a wonderfully fulfilling thought. Some days she almost felt guilty that they were paying her for the privilege of teaching these children.

Often the smells and sounds of the classroom reminded her of that special year when she had helped in Raylene Emerson's classroom. She cherished those remembrances, realizing they were among the few happy memories she had of her youth.

Claire had deposited her first paycheck into a new bank account at First National of Hanover Falls and made—with no small measure of satisfaction—a sizeable contribution to her savings account. She had also budgeted a small amount from each paycheck for decorating the house. Her first weekend shopping excursion netted a great buy on new throw pillows for the comfortable sofa her grandmother had given her. The soft blue and yellow stripes of the new cushions tied the faded blue of the sofa and the living room's aging floral wallpaper together perfectly. With the lamps turned low and the soft glow of candlelight, the room looked almost elegant. She didn't need much in the way of furnishings, having saved a few pieces from her parents' home, but she did have her eye on a tall oak bookcase she had spotted in an antique shop downtown.

As the rooms of her first home took shape, Claire realized with pleasure that it was beginning to take on the homey, welcoming ambience of Nana's house. Claire still missed her grandmother's cozy little home. Katherine Anderson had lived in Lee's Summit near Kansas City for more than fifty years, until she had been forced to move after falling and breaking her hip three summers ago.

Millie Overman often reminded Claire of her grandmother. Though physically there was little resemblance between the two women, Claire's landlady had Nana's spunky, fun-loving personality. And they seemed to share the same intuitive nature—a fact Claire wasn't certain she welcomed. Millie had managed to wheedle more personal information out of Claire than she ever meant to relinquish. Millie was also coming dangerously close to making a pest of herself. Claire truly appreciated the woman's generosity in offering helpful information and advice about both the house and the town of Hanover Falls. But the woman had taken to calling Claire on the phone several times a week with flimsy ruses that were nothing more than excuses to check up on Smokey. It wasn't difficult for Claire to see that Millie missed her home and her pet terribly. When she was a bit more settled, Claire resolved to invite Millie over for dinner.

However, Millie beat her to the punch. The phone was ringing when Claire came home from school on Friday. Dropping her burden of books and tote bags on the kitchen floor, she hurried to pick up the receiver.

"Hello?"

"Claire? How are you?"

Claire recognized the gravelly voice immediately. "Hi, Millie. I'm fine. How are you?" The older woman had insisted they be on a first-name basis from the moment Claire's signature had dried on the rental contract.

"Oh, I guess I'm about as good as one can be when they've lived on this good earth for as long as I have," Millie answered with a sigh. "How was your day, dear?"

"It was good, thanks."

"Well, I'm glad. Listen, Claire, I won't keep you but a minute. I wanted to invite you and Smokey over for supper Sunday night." Before Claire could get a word in, the landlady hurried on, "Now, I know they say they don't allow pets here and all, but surely they couldn't object to a little visit."

Claire's voice held a genuine smile. "I don't think they'd mind too much. And thank you for the invitation, Millie. Smokey and I would love to come. Can I bring anything? Besides Smokey, I mean."

"Oh, heavens, no. But now, don't expect anything fancy. There's not enough room in this little cubby hole they call a kitchen to make much more than soup and a sandwich. But I'll see what I can rustle up."

"I'm sure whatever it is will be delicious. Please don't go to any trouble. And thanks for the invitation, Millie. What time should I . . . uh . . . *we* . . . come?"

"Is six o'clock too early?"

"Just right. We'll see you then."

ॐ ॐ ॐ ॐ

Claire spent most of her Saturday pulling weeds and clearing out the beds of languishing summer flowers. Along the sidewalk and near the back door, zinnias were beginning to bloom in bright bursts of orange and yellow and burgundy, utterly changing the face of the backyard. In summer the gardens surrounding the flagstone patio had worn shades of pink, from pearl to fuchsia. Now Claire was delighted as the yard began to don its bright fall wardrobe. She would have to remember to tell Millie how much she was enjoying the rewards of the older woman's labor.

On Sunday morning she attended church at a small nondenomi-national church near the elementary school. In her systematic, or-ganized way, Claire had meant to attend each of the seven churches in Hanover Falls before deciding on a church home. But since arriving in the town more than a month ago, she had found excuse after excuse to sleep in on Sunday morning. The truth was, it was very difficult for her to walk into a gathering alone. She had never liked meeting new people. It made her feel vulnerable, on display. But entering the small sanctuary this morning had not been nearly as difficult as she had imagined.

This church reminded her of the one she had attended in the small college town where she had lived for seven years before moving to Hanover Falls. Now, as the organ swelled with the notes of a familiar hymn, Claire realized how much she had missed the time of worship and fellowship each week.

She was embarrassed but pleased when, in the middle of the ser-mon, a familiar little red head peeked over a pew a few rows in front of her. The boy waved vigorously in her direction. After the service, Jarrod Hamilton's parents introduced themselves along with the par-ents of several other third graders. Everyone seemed so friendly and welcoming. Already she felt this might be a place she could call her church home. One of the first things Nana would ask her when they spoke on the telephone would be "Have you found a church yet?" This time she might have an answer for the grandmother who had introduced her to the Lord so many years ago.

Claire's heart swelled with gratitude as she thought again how different her life might have been had Nana not taken her under her wing when she was just a little girl.

At twenty-five, Claire was just beginning to comprehend the emotional battles her mother had fought over the years and the various problems that had plagued her parents' marriage. For the first time, she understood that her mother's and father's failures as parents had little to do with her. As she grew older, she was piecing the events of her childhood together and realizing that her mother's health problems had probably stemmed from severe depression, which had truly been beyond her power to control. Her father had been consumed with her mother's needs and therefore had been unable to recognize the struggles of his young daughter.

Myra Anderson had suffered from a serious clinical depression most of her life and she died—of a broken heart, Claire often thought—during Claire's sophomore year in high school. The woman never fully recovered from the deaths of her babies, and her mental anguish had manifested itself in a variety of physical ailments. Claire remembered how stunned she had been to read in her mother's obituary that she had been only forty-one years old. Tired eyes, hollow cheeks, and a defeated demeanor had made her seem two decades older.

Claire's relationship with her father had remained cordial, though never close, until his death of a heart attack five years ago. His sudden death had come as a shock, yet Claire realized somewhat guiltily that Nana's death would grieve her far more than had either of her parents' deaths. Though she sometimes wondered if she would always hold some bitterness toward her parents, she had tried to forgive their shortcomings. She didn't think she would ever understand the concept of "forgive and forget." How could she forget mistakes that had changed her life and formed the very person she was? Yet, in spite of the heartache of her past, with Nana's guidance she had found a sustaining security and peace in her growing faith in God.

Claire drove home from church feeling content and hopeful for what the future held for her in Hanover Falls. She fixed a sandwich for lunch and spent the afternoon sprawled on the sofa in the living room reading a new mystery novel she had checked out from the town's tiny library. She relished simply spending time in her own little house.

As it neared six o'clock, she changed into slacks and a sweater and tried to tame her unruly strawberry-blond curls into a barrette. She coaxed Smokey into the backseat of her old car and headed across town to the Riverview Manor Apartments.

The apartments were part of a large health-care complex that sat on the banks of the Gasconade River at the edge of town, adjoining rolling patchwork fields. The promise of fall could be seen in the squares of plowed earth and fields of milo just beginning to turn amber.

The apartments were arranged in pods of six to eight units with miniature courtyards within each pod. The grounds on the outer edges were lush and green with newly planted grass and the beginnings of professional landscaping. At the center of the acreage, however, was a wide, uncultivated scar of dark earth that marred the entire layout. This spot was the freshly broken ground for the new senior citizens' center. Claire had read in the paper about the fund-raising efforts for the center, and on more than one occasion, she heard Millie's complaints about all the blowing dust and debris the building site generated.

Parking in a space designated for visitors, she pulled Smokey from where he cowered in the backseat and secured the heavy tomcat in her arms. Taking her cues from directory signs along the pathway, she headed in the direction of Millie Overman's apartment.

Millie answered the door with a happy shrill. "Smokey!"

The cat leapt from Claire's arms and weaved himself back and forth between Millie's legs, purring loudly. Millie stooped to scratch his upturned chin, and Claire saw tears form in the frail woman's eyes.

"He's missed you, Millie," Claire said quietly, surprised by her own emotion at the reunion.

"No more than I've missed him." Millie cleared her throat and stood to her full five feet three inches. "Thank you for taking care of him, Claire. He looks good. You must be feeding him well."

"Well, I'm just following your instructions," she demurred. "I've always wanted a cat, and Smokey is just the kind I would have chosen.

I wish I could have known him as a kitten."

"Oh, he was the cutest little ball of gray fur you could imagine. And so frisky! He would chase a ball of yarn for hours." Millie ran her hand affectionately over the scruff of the cat's neck. "But you're getting old now, aren't you, Smokey Boy? Yes, yes, we're getting old, aren't we?"

While Smokey explored his first mistress's new apartment, Claire helped Millie set the table. Contrary to her caveat, Millie had fixed a huge supper of roast beef with mashed potatoes, gravy, and all the trimmings. Claire savored each bite, reminded of dinners at Nana's house.

Millie had just placed a generous serving of warm apple cobbler in front of Claire when the doorbell rang. She excused herself and hobbled to answer the door. Before she reached the foyer the bell chimed again. "I'm coming, I'm coming. Give an old woman a chance, will you?" she groused good-naturedly.

From where she sat, Claire's view to the door was blocked, but she heard a deep male voice greet Millie. "Hello, Mrs. Overman. I hope I'm not disturbing you." Claire heard the visitor inhale deeply through his nose. "Mmm, something sure smells good in here."

"Hello there, Michael. If you'll promise to remember to call me Millie, I'll invite you in for a bite to eat."

"Oh no, no. Thank you for the offer. It does smell wonderful, but I've already eaten. I just stopped by to see if you've finished that questionnaire I dropped off the other evening."

"Oh my . . . I'm afraid I forgot all about it."

"It was the survey about the apartments," he reminded.

"Yes, I *know* which one you mean," she snapped. "I just forgot to fill it out. Now, I wonder what I did with that. . . ." The sound of a desk drawer opening and papers being riffled floated into the small dining room where Claire sat picking self-consciously at her cobbler.

"Do you need it right now?" Millie called out to the entryway.

"Well, we'd like to have them all turned in by tomorrow evening, if possible. I can give you another copy if you like."

"Maybe you'd better do that. I can't find a thing in this place," she said, exasperation in her voice. "Now, in *my* house I knew right where everything was. If I was home I could put my hands on it just like that." She snapped her arthritic fingers to prove her point. "But then, if I was home I wouldn't be filling out that stupid survey, now, would I?"

Claire heard the smile in his voice. "No, I guess not, Mrs. Over— Millie," he quickly corrected himself.

"Good for you," Millie teased, her good humor returning. Then, almost as an afterthought, "Michael, come on in for a minute. There's someone I'd like you to meet. You can at least have some apple cobbler, can't you?"

"Well, if you twist my arm. . . ."

Their voices grew closer, and feeling as though she'd been caught eavesdropping, Claire hurriedly wiped her lips with her napkin and turned in her seat toward the visitor.

Recognition struck her much as it had that morning on the patio when she saw his picture in the newspaper. This was the man from the photograph in the *Hanover Falls Record*. Millie was making introductions, and Claire pushed back her chair and started to rise.

" . . . and this is Michael Meredith," Millie was saying. "Michael is some bigwig here at the apartments. I can't ever remember your title," she said, disappearing into the kitchen.

"Please, don't get up," he told Claire, gesturing politely for her to remain seated. "I'm the administrator of Riverview," he explained. "It's nice to meet you, Claire. So you're one of the new teachers?"

"Yes. I teach third grade. This is my first year of teaching."

"Well, I would imagine that is quite a challenge."

"Oh, it is that, but it's a fun challenge. I really am enjoying it. *And* Hanover Falls. This is a great little town."

"Yes, it is. I'm still kind of a newcomer myself. I've only been here two years now, but it feels as much like home as anywhere I've ever lived."

There was an awkward lull, filled only by Millie rattling dishes in the kitchen.

"I'm renting Millie's house on Brookside Drive," Claire offered to fill the silence.

"Ahh, so you're Smokey's new mother?"

She smiled, and as if on cue, Smokey sauntered into the room.

Sheepishly, Claire looked in the cat's direction. "I hope it's okay if he visits once in a while."

"I won't tell if you won't," he said, winking at Millie, who had emerged from the kitchen just in time to see that she'd been caught red-handed.

While Millie fussed over Michael Meredith, pouring coffee and setting a large serving of cobbler in front of him, Claire watched him from the corner of her eye. In a crisp white dress shirt and red silk tie, he was the epitome of "tall, dark, and handsome." His dark, almost black hair fell in thick waves in front, and though cut short, it sprang up in ringlets at his neck. He wore the faintest shadow of a beard, as though he had forgotten to shave that morning, and his chin sported a deep cleft. His smile showed white, even teeth. The eyes above the smile held an expression Claire could not quite put her finger on. Sadness, perhaps. She was certain now that she had not met Michael Meredith, for she would have remembered this man. And yet, in person even more than in the newspaper photo, he reminded her of someone. . . .

"Here, Claire, let me warm your coffee," Millie insisted, hovering over Claire's chair. She poured another inch into Michael's cup as well and bustled into the kitchen and back out with the warm pan of cobbler. She spooned a second generous serving onto Michael's not-yet-empty plate. With Millie's back turned, he gave Claire a conspiratorial smile that said "let's humor the old girl, shall we?"

But Claire held up a hand as Millie headed toward her plate, spoon in hand. "Just a small helping for me, please, Millie. It's delicious, but I ate too much of that wonderful roast beef."

Michael took a sip of coffee and wiped his mouth. "So you're feeling at home here, are you, Claire?"

She tried desperately to think of a witty, clever answer but felt suddenly tongue-tied under his gaze. "Oh yes . . . very much so," she managed.

"Do you have family here?"

"No. I'd never been here before until the day I interviewed."

"What made you choose Hanover Falls?"

"To tell you the truth, I didn't have terribly many schools to choose from. I really wanted third graders and there was only one other opening in the area. My grandmother lives in Kansas City, and I didn't want to be too far away from her," she explained.

As they talked, Claire relaxed a bit and began to enjoy their conversation. With Millie interjecting amusing anecdotes, Michael versed her on some of the more colorful characters who inhabited their quaint village.

It was after eight o'clock when he looked at his watch and exclaimed, "Look at the time! I really need to get going."

He pushed back his chair and reached down to give Smokey one last scratch under the chin. "Will you be home tomorrow evening, Millie?"

"I plan to be."

"I'll have Ollie stop by to pick up your questionnaire. You've met Ollie, haven't you?"

"Oh yes. Who hasn't met Ollie? That little man was a big help when I moved in."

"Ollie—Oliver Moon—is Riverview's jack-of-all-trades," Michael explained to Claire. "He's somewhat of an institution around here. As I understand it, he came to work here as a young man many years ago when his mother was a resident. He must be fifty-five or sixty now. Ollie has some mental disabilities, but apparently he made himself so indispensable that he's been here ever since. You'll see him around town, if you haven't already, Claire. He's hard to miss."

Millie and Michael laughed at what was apparently an inside joke.

"Well, I'll have my form all ready to go when Ollie comes by," Millie assured him.

"I think he works the late shift on Monday nights, so it might be after seven before he gets here. Will that be all right?"

"That'll be fine. I'm not planning to go anywhere."

"Well, thanks again for that delicious cobbler," he said, moving toward the door. "It was nice to meet you, Claire."

"You too," she nodded.

Claire followed them to the entryway and stood at the door with Millie as Michael walked down the pathway toward the main parking lot.

"He is such a nice young man," Millie exclaimed as he disappeared from sight.

"Yes, he is," Claire agreed, moving to help Millie clear away the dishes. The older woman chattered away as they worked. When the dishes were done, Claire pleaded an early morning ahead of her. Thanking Millie again for the delicious meal, she gathered Smokey into her arms and headed to her car.

On the short drive home, she replayed her conversation with Michael Meredith over and over. His striking good looks had intimidated her somewhat, and yet she was drawn to him. And it wasn't just his appearance. The man seemed to be completely unaware of just how attractive he was. It was a sensitive, vulnerable quality about him that she found intriguing. He seemed sincerely interested in her life, and it was clear that his affection for Millie was genuine.

She turned into her driveway and parked the car in the garage. After making sure Smokey had food and water in his bowls, she went inside to get ready for bed. She washed her face, brushed her teeth, and climbed into bed, suddenly exhausted.

But as sleep crept upon her, the happy thoughts of her evening at Millie's were displaced by an unwelcome memory from her childhood. The scene wove itself into her subconscious and churned her thoughts into disquieting dreams that she would have called nightmares were it not for the truth in them.

"Kitty!" Her mother's voice drifted up the stairs and broke in on her childhood game of playing house.

Claire's given name was Claire Marie Katherine—Marie and Katherine for her two grandmothers. But when she was a tiny baby, Daddy had nicknamed her "Kitty," and it had stuck. Now everyone called her Kitty.

"Kitty!" her mother called again, louder this time.

She laid her baby doll in the cradle, gently patting its cotton-stuffed tummy. "Mommy will be right back, Susie. You go to sleep now," she whispered to her favorite doll.

She ran into the hallway just as her mother reached the top of the stairs. "Here I am, Mommy. What's the matter?"

"Oh, Kitty! There you are. Nothing's the matter, sweetheart. I . . . we have wonderful news. Come downstairs. Daddy and I have something very important to tell you."

She followed her mother down the staircase, only mildly curious. Her mother sometimes made a big deal out of seemingly little things, and Claire had learned not to take her too seriously.

In the living room Daddy was sitting on the sofa, still dressed from the office in his suit and tie. "Hi, pumpkin."

"Hi, Daddy," she said politely, turning her eyes toward the floor. She loved her father, but she feared him as well. Though at times he was one of her favorite playmates, she also knew the wrath that awaited her if she was careless or naughty. Her father rarely spanked her, but she would have much preferred a spanking to one of his frequent lectures.

Daddy patted the space beside him on the sofa, and she climbed up to sit primly at his side, hands in her lap, while her mother took the rocking chair nearby. Now her curiosity was roused. If Daddy was here, it must truly be something very special.

Her father cleared his throat. "Kitty, you know that for a long time now we have been hoping for a little brother or sister for you."

Claire waited expectantly, not daring to speak. Daddy didn't mention the baby brothers she'd had—and lost.

Raymond Anderson took a handkerchief from his breast pocket and wiped his brow before he continued. "We always thought that a new brother or sister would be a baby. We've always talked about you being a *big* sister, Kitty. But you see, we have been given the opportunity to take in a little boy who is eight years old. Adopt him. You remember what adoption means, don't you, darling?"

Claire shook her head solemnly. They had talked about this before.

"You're going to be a *little* sister, Kitty!" her mother interjected. "You'll have a big brother to look out for you. Oh, I always wished *I'd* had an older brother, and now you'll have one, Kitty. Isn't it wonderful? His name is Joseph."

"When . . . when will he come?" she asked, bewildered.

"We will go get him next Friday afternoon," her father said.

The next week had been busily occupied getting ready for the day when Joseph would become part of their family.

Daddy moved the cradle out of the nursery and they painted the walls a bright sky-blue. Claire and her mother shopped for a new bedspread and curtains and even pillowcases with Joseph's name monogrammed on them. Then Mommy let Claire choose new linens for her own bed. Claire had never seen her mother so happy. She seemed to smile more than ever these days. And they hadn't been to the cemetery for two Sundays in a row.

For the first time she could remember in her short life, Claire had let herself feel happy—truly happy—and secure with the kind of joy that bubbled up inside her when she least expected it. It was an emotion she had never dared to feel before. It was *hope*.

She hadn't known then that this was merely the calm before a ravaging storm.

Claire woke with a start and sat straight up in the bed. As she had done so many times before, she consciously pushed the memory away, not wanting the rest of the story to play itself out in her dreams.

She heard Smokey meowing at the back door, and grateful for the distraction, she slid out of bed and padded down the hallway to let him in.

# Three

Claire awoke on a cold morning in November to the season's first frosting of snow on the ground. Autumn was her favorite season and she hated to see it end too abruptly. Though Hanover Falls was not officially on the tourist maps as part of the Ozarks region, Claire thought the city could boast at least equal beauty to anything farther south.

The week before, Becky Anderson, the fellow teacher who shared Claire's surname, had invited her for a drive deep into the heart of what the locals called the "mountains." They had driven almost to the Arkansas border, where the Ozarks were indeed resplendent with autumn foliage. Unfortunately, the roadways were equally resplendent with traffic. Claire decided that the tourists' view had nothing over the scenic panorama of her own backyard.

The plants and flowers she had carefully tended had faded long ago, but the trees made up for the loss of other foliage. The locust tree was aglow with an almost iridescent yellow, and the birches and other trees on the property added various shades of gold and brown and claret to the autumn palette. This morning's dusting of snow added its own beauty.

Claire dressed warmly for school in tan corduroy slacks and a new sweater she had been anxious to wear. At least that was one good thing about the change in the weather. She was glad for a chance to bring some of her warmer clothes out of storage and add them to her meager wardrobe.

The snow was still coming down in fine, soft flakes as Claire maneuvered her car cautiously over powdered streets. As she drove, she contemplated how she might incorporate the newly fallen snow into the day's science lesson.

The halls were buzzing with excitement when she walked through the front doors. Parents on their way to work and anxious to get a head start on the weather had dropped many children off earlier than usual. The students fed one another's excitement until Claire's class-room was near a frenzy by the time the bell finally rang.

She decided to forgo any attempts to calm them down and instead allowed each of them to share their stories of getting to school that morning.

"My brother and I had a snowball fight," Talisha Jackson offered.

"You shoulda seen my dad!" Lucas Crockett exclaimed. "He was shovelin' the driveway and he fell down and slid halfway across the street on his . . . his *backside*." Embarrassed, he snuck a glance at his teacher to make sure his choice of words was deemed appropriate. When Claire smiled her guarded approval, he trumpeted, "It was awesome!"

"That's nothin'," Brianne Sizemore lisped. "My mom thpinned our car around in thircles in the middle of the road. We just about didn't get thtopped in time before we hit a big truck!"

Everybody had a story to top the previous one, and Claire knew that the discussion was serving to bind the class together with a mem-ory they would all share long after this day was over.

Claire was telling her own tale of Smokey's antics in the snow that morning when the principal, Marjean Hammond, stepped into the room.

Claire excused herself with a discreet warning to the children to keep the noise down and went to the door with a questioning look on her face.

"Sounds like you're having fun," Marjean said with a smile.

"The natives were restless. I decided we might as well get it out of our systems. I'm afraid this may be the highlight of the year for my class so far." Claire grinned wryly.

"Well, it gets better. The superintendent has just decided that we're going to go ahead and dismiss school at ten o'clock. The fore-cast is for a couple more inches, and we don't want to wait until it gets dangerously slick out there." Marjean motioned toward the wall of windows that framed the wintery scene.

"Oh, this will be fun news to deliver." Claire rubbed her hands together conspiratorially. "You wouldn't want to stick around and help with crowd control, would you?"

"I'm afraid you're on your own there. I get to call some parents who will be considerably less happy about the news." Marjean waved to the now curiously silent children and breezed out of the room.

It was almost eleven-thirty before Claire had delivered the last of her third-graders to a parent and battened down her classroom in the likelihood there would not be classes the following day. The sky had grown darker, and though the wind remained calm, the snow continued to fall steadily.

Claire was pulling on her gloves near the front door when Becky Anderson came down the hallway. "Hey, Claire, got everybody accounted for?"

"Finally," she sighed.

"Do you feel adventurous? Norma and I are going to slip-slide out to Happy Chef for some of their great chili. Want to come along?"

"Sure . . . Why not? Sounds great." Claire didn't know Norma Blair—one of the kindergarten teachers—very well, but she had gotten to know Becky over the past weeks when they served on a parent/teacher committee together. Their long drive through the Ozarks the week before had sealed their friendship.

Becky was a plump, pretty, likeable mother of two preschoolers. Her husband traveled often during the week, leaving Becky alone with the adorable, ornery boys. Claire knew it was a stressful situation, but Becky seemed to handle it with good humor.

"I called my baby-sitter and told her not to put the boys down for naps yet. With any luck I'll get two glorious hours to myself this afternoon—and lunch with the girls to boot!" She tossed her blond hair off her shoulders and laughed.

Norma, a petite, attractive grandmotherly woman, came bustling down the hall, and the three navigated their way across the parking lot and piled into Becky's van. Apologizing for the fast-food wrappers and Sunday school papers that littered the well-used minivan, Becky revved the motor, and while the car warmed up, Claire and Norma got out and helped her scrape the windshields.

Half an hour later the three were in animated conversation over steaming bowls of soup and bottomless cups of fresh coffee. The restaurant was crowded with downtown businessmen and women on their lunch breaks. There was a spirit of community in the casual din-

ing room as friends and acquaintances shouted greetings to one another across the room, commenting on the weather. The unexpected
storm seemed to have everyone in high spirits, and no one seemed in
a hurry to get back to work.

While Claire listened to school gossip from her co-workers, Becky
was interrupted by a hand on her shoulder.

"Hey, Becky."

"Michael! How's it going?"

Claire glanced up from her bowl of chili into the eyes of Michael
Meredith.

"It's going good. Isn't this something?" he asked, glancing toward the snowy panorama outside the restaurant's windows. "Hi,
Mrs. Blair." He recognized Claire and gave a friendly nod in her direction. "Hello there."

Becky jumped in. "Oh, I'm sorry. Claire, this is Michael Meredith.
Michael is the administrator of Riverview Manor, the nursing facility
out on Broadway. Michael, this is Claire Anderson. Claire teaches
third—"

"Yes, we've met," Michael interrupted politely. "How are you,
Claire?"

"I'm fine. School's out," she said with levity. Her voice came out
an octave too high and her palms had grown moist. *Why does this man
unnerve me so?*

Not seeming to notice, Michael turned to Becky. "Ah, I see. I
thought maybe you were all playing hookey."

"Well, I guess I sort of am . . . hookey from parenting, anyway,"
Becky said, explaining her baby-sitting arrangements for the day.

There was a lull in the conversation, and Michael scanned the
crowded restaurant. "Well, I guess I'd better get in line for a table.
Nice to see you all."

"Hey, listen," Becky said suddenly. "Are you by yourself? You're
welcome to join us. It may be a while before you get seated in this
madhouse. We're just about finished, anyway. You ladies don't mind,
do you?"

"No, of course not," the other two women chimed in unison.

"Well, if you're sure you don't mind. It does look like tables are
at a premium today. And I'm kind of in a hurry. I'm supposed to be
back for a one-thirty meeting."

He glanced at his watch and pulled out the empty fourth chair from their table.

"So, Becky . . ." Michael's voice held a teasing note. "That wonderful civic club of yours wouldn't have any more money they don't know what to do with, would they?"

Becky was always ready to banter. "Hey, buster! We're still recovering from that last fund-raiser. You guys cleaned us out!"

"Well, I guess it can't hurt to ask," he said, feigning embarrassment. "Seriously, Becky, we really do appreciate what the club raised. It's made a big difference."

"Well, I don't want to speak too soon, but we have talked about the possibility of another fund drive for the center. It probably won't be until spring, though. Things just get too busy for everyone until after the first of the year."

"Oh, I understand. But, hey, that would be great. Really, I *was* kidding." He turned to Claire. "Becky's club raised almost five thousand dollars for the new senior center that's going up near Mrs. Overman's apartment," he explained.

"Oh, I remember reading about that in the *Record*," Claire told him. "Millie Overman is the lady I rent from," she explained to Becky and Norma. Turning back to Michael she asked, "Did Millie ever get that questionnaire turned in?"

He laughed. "Let's just say she did so under duress. I didn't get the pleasure of tabulating the answers, but I expect she ripped us to shreds."

His playful bantering put her more at ease. While Becky and Norma discussed a situation at school, Claire turned her full attention to Michael Meredith.

"Poor Millie," she said. "I don't think she's adjusting too well to the move. Especially leaving her beloved kitty behind. I thought I'd die when Smokey walked into the room the other night. That wasn't a problem, was it—having the cat there for a visit?"

He laughed at her sheepish expression. "No. The only thing I'd worry about with that particular woman is that she'd try to turn that little rendezvous into an extended visit."

"Well, Millie would have to fight me for custody of Smokey," Claire joked. "I'm getting pretty attached to him. I've always wanted a cat."

"Humph," he grunted. "I can't say that I see what all the hype about cats is. Give me a dog any day. A dog . . . now there's a pet worth the trouble."

"You obviously have never held a purring cat in your lap on a cold winter night," she said with mock offense, a flirtatious edge on her words.

"And you obviously have never had a dog bring your paper and slippers to you on a cold winter morning."

She threw him a suspicious glance. "You're kidding, right? Your dog can't do that."

"Oh, I never said I was talking about *my* dog. Shoot, I don't even *have* a dog!"

They both laughed, and at Becky and Norma's questioning looks, Michael filled them in on the debate. As the four of them laughingly discussed the pros and cons of dogs and cats, the waiter brought the women's checks. Norma excused herself to get her coat, and Becky asked Michael about the progress on the construction of the senior center. He spoke animatedly, obviously enthusiastic about the project.

Surreptitiously, Claire watched his face. In a dark suit and tie he was undeniably handsome. The fairy-tale description "dashing" came to mind, and she had to confess that his presence made her heart beat faster. But somehow their brief visit had made him seem more approachable.

Michael's lunch arrived and the women said their good-byes and bundled up against the cold.

When they got back to the van, Becky asked dramatically, "Is that not the most gorgeous man you have ever laid eyes on?"

"Rebekah Anderson!" Norma chided. "The last time I checked, you were a married woman."

"And a very happily married one, Norma, but I'll tell you what—it's hard not to notice a man like that. And he's such a sweetheart, too. Not a bit stuck on himself. Hey, Claire. How do you know Michael?" she asked suddenly.

Claire explained their meeting at Millie's apartment.

"Well, if I were you I wouldn't waste any time going after that one. He's single and available, you know. At least I think he's still available."

Claire felt herself blush. "Becky . . ."

Norma laughed, and from her perch in the front passenger seat, she playfully smacked Becky in the arm. "You are hopeless, Becky."

She turned to Claire in the backseat. "Don't you pay one bit of attention to this woman, Claire. She likes to think she has the gift of matchmaking, but I happen to know her success rate leaves a lot to be desired."

Claire smiled, grateful for Norma's intervention. "Thanks for the warning, Norma."

Claire lit her first fire of the season in the fireplace that night while the snow continued to fall softly. It was heavenly being curled up in front of a warm fire with a good book and cup of hot cocoa, knowing that she didn't have to get up and go to work the next day. Mozart played softly on the stereo, and her own personal lap warmer purred with a contentment that matched her own.

She had loved sharing the first snowfall with her students this morning. Her friendship with Becky had deepened, and she made a new friend in Norma today. And, she had to admit, she met a man to whom she was more than a little attracted.

For the first time in her life, Claire began to think she might truly have found shelter from the haunting memories of her childhood in this little town and its people.

# Four

Michael Meredith closed the drawer of the large oak file cabinet and locked it. Trying unsuccessfully to ignore the nagging concerns that pelted his mind, he dropped the key into his pocket and reached for his coat, which hung on a hook on the back of his office door.

The papers in the file he had just put away seemed, on the surface, to be in order. And yet—if one was looking for discrepancies—there were several entries in the medical chart and nursing charts of this patient's file that might conceivably be interpreted as contradictory.

He had studied the file carefully this afternoon and had almost convinced himself that everything appeared in order, but now his earlier doubts resurfaced. He couldn't be too careful. It would never do to have anyone question the information in a patient's file—especially a patient who had died only one week after entering Riverview.

Impulsively, he went back to the file cabinet, unlocked it, and once again removed the file in question. Tucking the folder into his briefcase, he headed for the parking lot.

He drove the few blocks to his apartment over streets slick with the powder of the season's first snowfall. Deep in thought, he parked the truck in front of his building. As he gathered his briefcase and gloves and started to get out, he noticed the young couple who lived in the apartment next to his unloading groceries from the trunk of their car.

He stepped down from the pickup and slammed the door, tucking his briefcase under one arm.

"Hi, Brett, Alicia. Can I give you a hand there?"

"Hey, good timing, old buddy. You bet." Brett McGinn unloaded two bulging grocery bags into Michael's free arm and went back to the car for the last two bags.

"Thanks, Michael," Alicia McGinn said, flashing him her sweet smile. "How have you been? Haven't seen you for a while."

"Oh, I've been around. Working late, though. I'm pretty swamped at the office. How are you guys?"

"Doing great," she answered as her husband unlocked the door to their apartment and led the way through the narrow entry to the kitchen.

"Especially great now that the cupboards will be full," Brett chimed, putting the groceries on the counter and tweaking his wife's cheek affectionately.

"Yeah, and two days from now you'll have eaten everything not tied down," she lamented cheerfully.

Brett rubbed his stomach and began rummaging through the bags. He pulled out a package of cookies. "Well, let's get started." He tore open the package, stuffed two Oreos in his mouth, and offered the bag to Michael.

"Oh, you . . . you're impossible!" Alicia punched Brett's arm playfully.

Michael waved away the proffered cookies and observed the newlyweds with a mixture of wistfulness and melancholy. The obvious joy they took in each other's company was a delight to watch, and yet it was as though he was no longer in the room. They had eyes only for each other. He couldn't help but wonder if he would ever be part of such a relationship himself. He hoped that his future included the love of a wife and children, but well into his twenty-ninth year, he was beginning to fear that he might always be alone. Now, watching the newly married couple, he deeply envied the warm camaraderie they shared—the way each so obviously *belonged* to the other.

Even the McGinns' meagerly furnished apartment was warm and cozy in contrast to his own. The kitchen bore the unmistakable signs of a woman's touch: ruffled curtains at the window, an artfully arranged basket of fruit, flowers on the table. The very air held a feminine fragrance.

Looking for a graceful exit, he deliberately repositioned the bag of groceries he had carried in. "Well, see you guys around."

"Bye, Michael," Alicia called over her shoulder as she began to put boxes and cans into the cupboards. "Thanks again."

"No problem." He backed out of the kitchen, suddenly feeling like an intruder.

His own apartment was dark and chilly when he let himself in a few minutes later. He turned the thermostat up a notch and switched on the television set as he walked through the living room on his way back to the bedroom to change out of his suit and tie.

Comfortable in jeans and a ragged sweatshirt, he went back to the living room and plopped into the recliner in front of the TV. He flipped absentmindedly through the channels. Nothing really interested him, but maybe the noise would keep him company and keep his mind from brooding dark thoughts.

In spite of himself, he found his thoughts on the McGinns and the happiness they seemed to have found with each other. Once—it seemed a very long time ago—he'd thought he had found that kind of love.

Her name was Michelle. He met her in college and uncharacteristically asked her out the day his roommate introduced them. They went ice-skating and he fell for her almost immediately. She was pretty and fun and caring—and she shared his newfound faith in God.

They dated that whole semester and he fell more in love with her each day. He had been so sure that she felt the same about him, so sure that she was the one. Though he never told her, he had planned to ask her to marry him—the very night she told him she would like to date others. As it turned out, she had a particular "other" in mind: a long-time boyfriend from her high school days. The last Michael had heard, Michelle had married her old beau and they were happy together, living somewhere on the West Coast.

He had been a little gun-shy since then. He had had the occasional date, but never had he fallen for someone the way he had for Michelle. Looking back, he knew it was for the best that she had broken things off when she did. He was a wonderful man, she had told him, but she realized now that she had always loved Chris. She was sorry, but she knew he would find someone new and then he'd realize that she was right.

It had hurt, but he was a survivor. He was long over Michelle, rarely thinking about her except to acknowledge that he had known a little of what love could be—enough that he knew he longed to find it again, longed to have it returned. But the prospects in a small town like Hanover Falls were slim. He had met the new third-grade teacher,

Claire Anderson, and had to admit he was attracted to her. She seemed quiet, even shy. He had always liked that in a girl. Maybe he would give her a call . . . perhaps when things settled down at the office a bit.

The worries about his job surfaced again as he thought of Riverview. He had only recently begun to feel confident in his job as administrator of the Riverview Manor complex. When he had been thrust into the position just over a year ago, it had been a stressful adjustment. Complicating matters was the fact that the woman who had been hired as his assistant was as green as he was. Beth VanMeter had been employed as a social worker for the county Social and Rehabilitation Services for a year before coming to Riverview. An ambitious young woman, she was now beginning the master's program at SLU in St. Louis and was away from her office at Riverview more than she was there.

Besides the various departments in the nursing-care center, Riverview encompassed the assisted-living wing and the separate retirement homes and apartments. Beth VanMeter worked more closely with the nursing home, while Michael's main responsibility was for the apartments and the assisted-living unit. But with Beth gone much of the time, he had been called upon more and more to troubleshoot problems in the nursing-care center. The additional headaches brought about by the ongoing construction of the new senior center and the necessary fund-raising had nearly been the straw that broke the camel's back for Michael.

Then gradually, over the past couple months, things had finally begun to fall into place. With much trial and error, he was learning the intricacies of the system and was finally becoming comfortable in his role as administrator. He had just begun to feel that he could catch his breath. And now . . .

Deliberately, he pushed aside the disquieting thoughts about his job.

He went into the kitchen and rummaged in the refrigerator. After fixing a sandwich and pouring a tall glass of milk, he took the light supper into the living room. A police drama caught his attention and slowly the complex plot of the program drew him in, making him forget, for tonight at least, the lonely feelings his encounter with the McGinns had dredged up—and his deepening concerns about the file in his briefcase.

# Five

*T*he winter's first snowstorm seemed determined to make an impression. By Thursday night five inches of snow had fallen, and all the schools in the area were closed again. On Friday morning, though the ground was still blanketed, the sun came out, turning the fields and village into mounds of diamonds that sparkled against an ice blue sky.

School resumed on Friday, but again the children were so enchanted with the newness of this early advent of winter that Claire felt the week had been nearly wasted—at least as far as academics were concerned. For the first time during the school year, she assigned the children homework. Their groans and good-natured grumbling rang in her ears as she gathered her things and headed for home that afternoon.

She was in the middle of fixing herself a sandwich for supper when the phone rang. Hurriedly wiping mayonnaise from her fingers, she picked up the receiver.

"Hello."

"Claire?"

"Yes?"

"Hi. This is Michael Meredith. We visited at the Happy Chef Wednesday?"

He spoke it like a question, as though she wouldn't remember talking with him only two days ago. "Yes, of course. How are you?"

"I'm fine, thanks. Listen, I was wondering if you might like to go to dinner with me some night this weekend. We could take in a movie afterward if you like or . . ." He let the question hang in the air.

Her palms began to perspire. She hadn't dared to hope he might call her. Willing herself to calm down, she answered with what she hoped was mild indifference. "Oh, well, sure. That would be nice." It was a bit easier to pull off when she wasn't looking into those smoldering eyes.

"It might be kind of short notice," he said, "but would tomorrow night be all right? Say about six o'clock?"

"Tomorrow would be fine. Do you know where I live?"

"As a matter of fact, I do. Mrs. Overman—Millie—has all but drawn me a map to her house, and I remember you told me you were renting from her. Brookside Drive, right?"

She heard the smile in his voice. "I forgot you have connections with my landlady."

He laughed. "Oh yes . . . she's quite the character."

"I'd have to agree with you on that."

"Well, I'll see you tomorrow night then?"

"Six o'clock—I'll look forward to it."

Claire had dated a few young men in high school and a few more in college. It was a ritual she was not altogether comfortable with, and one that now seemed a bit adolescent for a woman nearing twenty-six. Yet she was definitely interested in getting to know Michael Meredith better.

She tossed and turned that night, but it was a refreshing change to lie awake agonizing over what she should wear to dinner and a movie with a handsome man, rather than lying in bed trying to shut out the foreboding and all too-familiar nightmares.

సౌ    సౌ    సౌ    సౌ

At exactly six o'clock Saturday evening a dark green pickup truck pulled into her driveway. Nervously, she answered the doorbell and ushered Michael into the living room. She was relieved to see that her choice of corduroys and sweater had been just right. He was dressed casually in khaki pants and a navy sweater over a turtleneck. He waited by the door while she gathered her coat and purse.

Outside he offered his arm and helped her navigate the icy sidewalk and driveway. He opened the door on the passenger side for her and she climbed in.

"I guess this isn't exactly the perfect vehicle for taking a lady out to dinner," he began, "but actually . . . well, it's all I've got," he finished lamely.

"Oh, I think it's a pretty truck." The pickup was spotlessly clean inside and waxed to a shine on the outside except where it had been newly splattered by the salty slush from the highway.

He laughed heartily, and when he caught her quizzical expression, he told her, "I've *never* heard my truck described as pretty before."

"You obviously haven't seen *my* clunker," Claire said. "I'm *not* picky about vehicles." She drove a little Japanese import that had rolled over a hundred thousand miles long before she bought it.

"Well, that's a good thing." As he backed out of the driveway he told her, "I thought we'd drive to Boyd City if that's okay. There's a nice Italian place there, if you like Italian. . . ."

"Sounds delicious. I'm hungry."

"Good. And hopefully Boyd City will have more to choose from than 'The Muppets' and 'Freddy Krueger' in the movie department."

Claire laughed. Those were, in fact, the only two movies playing at Hanover Falls' tiny outdated theater.

Michael turned the truck onto the highway, and they drove the forty minutes to Boyd City, talking animatedly about movies they had seen and books they had read. Claire was enjoying herself immensely, all her worries about what they would say to each other forgotten.

After they were seated in the crowded but quiet restaurant and the waitress had taken their orders, their conversation turned to their respective jobs.

"I've only been administrator for a little over a year," Michael told Claire. "I was an assistant for ten months before that. I was offered the administrator's position just before the corporation made the decision to develop the land. That project includes the complex where Millie lives and the new senior center."

"What an undertaking," Claire breathed. "That sounds scary."

"Believe me, it *was* scary. I was flattered by the promotion, of course," Michael told her. "I was still working on my masters at the time, pretty much inexperienced in this field. But I probably never would have taken the job if I'd known then what it would turn into. Mr. Stoddard, the previous administrator, moved to Texas just weeks after he announced his retirement, and I was left pretty much on my own. It's been a challenge."

He ran a hand through his hair, and a look of frustration crossed his face. "It can be a real headache at times," Michael continued, "especially the financial end of things. In some ways I'm still learning the ropes, but for the most part it's been very rewarding to be part of this organization. I feel very blessed to have come on board when I did. It was . . . well, it was an answer to prayer for me."

It was the first time Michael had made reference to his faith.

"You're a Christian?" she asked, not feeling the least bit awkward posing the question.

"Yes. Since I was in college. And you?"

She nodded. "My parents never attended church, but my grand-mother took me to her church whenever I visited her. She shared her faith with me every chance she got. But I didn't really make it my own until I was seventeen. I sometimes think I still have a lot to learn, a lot to overcome—" She stopped short, afraid she had revealed more than she wanted to explain.

"Oh, well," he said almost apologetically, "I think we all have a lot to learn. We don't become saints overnight."

Their plates had been cleared away and they were enjoying second cups of coffee when Michael looked at his watch and took in a sharp breath. "Uh-oh, if we're going to make a movie we'd better get going. Did you want more coffee?"

She held a hand over the empty mug in answer. "I've had my limit for the week," she said wryly.

Michael then helped her into her coat, and they tromped across the snowy parking lot to the truck.

The movie they decided on was a remake of an old western. Claire had always enjoyed westerns, but this version was too explicit for her taste.

On the way back to Hanover Falls they talked about the film, and Michael apologized for its graphic nature. "They just don't make them like they used to, do they? They don't leave anything to the imagination anymore," he sighed.

"No, that's for sure. But don't apologize. It's certainly not your fault—unless you haven't told me about the fact that you moonlight as a movie producer."

He laughed. "You know," he told her, a faraway look coming sud-denly into his eyes, "sometimes I wonder what my grandparents would think if they could come back and see some of the things that we just take for granted nowadays. The bad things, I mean."

"You must have been really close to your grandparents."

He nodded. "They were the finest people I've ever known."

"Are you close to your parents?" she wondered.

He hesitated for the slightest moment. "Yes. Oh yes, my parents are wonderful, too. My grandparents were missionaries to Brazil for most of their lives. My mom was raised there in fact—in Brazil. When Grandma and Grandpa finally retired, they came to live with us. I'm not sure they knew it at the time, but they had a pretty good mission field in me."

"You were quite the rebel, huh?" she teased.

But his reply was serious. "I was a rebel of the worst kind. I . . . maybe I'll tell you about it sometime."

Claire couldn't see his face in the darkness of the truck's cab, but he became deathly quiet, and she wasn't sure how to respond. Finally he broke the silence. Claire could sense by the tremor in his voice and the detached tone of his words—almost as though he were talking to himself—that what he was telling her was important to him.

"My grandparents meant the world to me, Claire. They are the reason I am where I am today. I just hope I can give back to my residents at the manor—listen to me," he chuckled, interrupting himself. "*My* residents. Anyway, I just hope I can return a tiny part of the love and encouragement Grandma and Grandpa—and Mom and Dad, too—gave me. Because I wouldn't be here today if it wasn't for them. Literally . . ."

His voice trailed off and Claire waited, curious, for him to explain. But he kept silent, and for some reason she was afraid to ask him what he had meant.

They drove several miles in silence. Then, as though he suddenly remembered she was sitting beside him, he asked politely, "So what about your family? Where did you grow up?"

"Well, Kansas City mostly. Except for kindergarten, all of my school years were spent there. My parents aren't living. My mom died when I was in high school, and Dad passed away about five years ago."

"I'm sorry," he said softly.

She waved his sympathy off.

"I was born in St. Louis," she went on, too cheerfully, wanting to change the subject. "We lived there until I was about six. Everyone is always saying it's such a nice city, but I really don't remember much about it. And I've only been back once or twice since we moved away."

He fell silent again, and trying to draw him out, she asked, "Have you ever been there—to St. Louis?"

"Yes. I lived there for a while."

"Oh? Then you know the city pretty well?"

"No, not really. I was just a kid." His answer was strangely abrupt and he turned away from her to concentrate on the road in front of him.

The easy flow of conversation they had shared all evening came to a confusing halt. He retreated into silence again, and she was suddenly afraid to ask any more questions.

As they entered the city limits of Hanover Falls, Claire watched his face as the glow from the streetlamps rose and waned, illuminating his profile. He was silent again, pensive, not responding to her. The sorrowful, almost haunted look in Michael's eyes had disappeared as they visited in the restaurant earlier this evening. Now it was back, but instead of intriguing her, the foreboding darkness that crossed his face made her wary, almost frightened to be with him.

She longed to go back in time . . . to take back whatever she had said that had made him withdraw. But not knowing how to undo it, she said nothing.

They pulled into her driveway, and he came around and opened her door and walked her to the front door of her house in silence.

"Thank you for the evening," she said. "I had a very nice time."

"I did, too. I'm glad you could go." But the warmth was gone from his voice. He was merely being polite now.

A heavy awkwardness hung between them. "Well," she said finally. "I guess I'd better go in. Thanks again for everything. Good night."

"Good night," he said.

Then the roar of the truck indicated he was gone, leaving her to wonder what had gone wrong, what she had done to ruin the evening. Depression creeping up on her, Claire washed her face and got ready for bed. Confused and deeply disappointed that the evening had ended as it had, she crawled under the quilts. She would never understand men. What had she done? What had she said to cause him to shut down like that? Was he uncomfortable because she had told him about her parents' deaths? Sometimes people didn't know how to react when Claire revealed that she had lost her parents at such a young age. But no, she felt sure his "I'm sorry" had been warm and genuine then. It was after that when he had become distant. What could she have said? They had been talking about St. Louis. . . .

Her own memories of that place and that time in her life were not happy ones. Unbidden, the old feelings washed over her as they had on so many other nights.

She was back in their big house on Madison Street in St. Louis. Every room was festively adorned for the holidays. It was a special day. Her mother and father had gone downtown to get her new brother. Nana was staying at the house with Claire until her parents returned.

She sat at the dining room table with her grandmother playing her special domino game—the one that had animal pictures on each tile, so that even if you didn't know your numbers you could match the pictures. Over and over they mixed the tiles up and turned them all facedown to draw for a new game. Finally Claire tired of the game and began to make domino chains, standing the tiles on end, one next to another, forming a big S that meandered the length of the table. Claire watched with fascination as one domino knocked over the next in a noisy chain reaction. Nana leaned back in her chair and clapped her hands. Above the clatter of dominoes they heard a car pull into the driveway.

Nana nervously scooped the dominoes into a pile and began putting them back in their wooden box. Claire ran to the window and watched as her father opened the car door. A strange boy climbed slowly from the backseat.

Claire had never seen her brother before, but already there was a picture of him on the bookcase in the front room beside Claire's new kindergarten picture. Joseph Matthew Anderson and Claire Marie Katherine Anderson, side by side in a little hinged frame. Just like the pictures of Gretchen and her brother that sat on the piano in Gretchen's dining room.

Would she fight with Joseph the way Gretchen argued with her brother? Claire knew Gretchen loved Tim. Sometimes she saved a piece of candy or a cookie for him when she and Claire got to bring treats home from a birthday party. And Claire thought Tim loved Gretchen, too. Sometimes when they all played baseball in the Gaylord's big backyard, he would pound his sister on the back and tell her, "Way to go, Gretch! Great catch."

Claire had looked at Joseph's picture often in the days leading up to this one. She imagined the boy in the picture to be tall and talkative. He had a big smile and curly hair, just like Ronnie Mason, a fourth grader at her school. She imagined that her brother would be full of jokes and laughter the way Ronnie was.

But when her brother walked in through the front door that afternoon, he was nothing like Ronnie Mason. He was tall and slender—and that was where the resemblance ended. His hair had been shorn so close that his white scalp showed through, and his ears stuck out from the sides of his head. The smile from the picture was gone, and with it, all Claire's hopes for jokes and laughter and a brother who might one day clap her on the back and tell her, "Great catch, Kitty."

Her father called Claire from the doorway, and with Nana's nudging, she came into the living room and stood there shyly waiting for the boy to say something.

"Kitty, this is Joseph. This is your new brother."

"Hi," she said bashfully, burying her chin in her chest.

He just stood there glaring at her.

"Joseph, this is your sister. Can you say hello to Kitty?" her father asked patiently. "Joseph?"

No reply.

Claire's mother had gone into the hallway to put her coat away. Nana stepped into the silence and put an arm around the boy. Ignoring his cringe at her touch, she stepped away from him and said, "I'll bet you're hungry after such a long trip. Why don't we see what we can find to eat in the kitchen. Come along, Kitty, Joseph. Let's have a little snack."

Claire caught the worried look her grandmother gave her father as she ushered Claire into the kitchen. Joseph followed behind, head bent. He ate the juicy slices of apple and the hunks of yellow cheese that Nana put in front of them, chewing noisily and wiping his mouth with the back of his hand. He said nothing.

And so it went. At first Joseph would not answer when they called his name. He sat stiffly on the sofa in the living room, blatantly ignoring them, defiance in his steel gray eyes. But as the day wore on and supper came and went, hunger finally won out and he heeded their beckoning. He came to the huge table in the dining room and sat, methodically spooning into his mouth the thick stew his new mother had reheated for him. Raymond Anderson had not allowed him to eat until he acknowledged them, and by the end of the week, the boy seemed to have settled reluctantly into the routine of their household.

Claire wondered how it would feel to be in a strange new place, to have everything familiar taken away. And she felt pity for this strange boy who was now her brother. But after a month Claire knew that she did not love Joseph. Not the way she had thought she would love a brother. She didn't even like him, really. He was silent and sullen and not like any of the other boys she knew.

Sometimes he was mean to her—knocking over her dollhouse for no apparent reason or grabbing her baby doll out of her arms and running away with it. No, she didn't think she could love him. But she couldn't hate him, either. Sometimes she walked by his bedroom in the evening and heard him crying. And then she truly felt sorry for him. He always seemed so sad. Once she had gone in to ask him what was wrong, but he had quickly wiped the tears away and, reddening with anger, ordered her loudly out of his room.

And then that awful afternoon.

Claire sat up in bed. She put her head in her hands and rubbed her temples furiously, as though she could keep the thoughts from coming. She reached for the lamp beside her bed and turned it on, silently begging the light to chase away the dark thoughts.

# Six

November had come and gone, and Claire's good intentions of inviting Millie Overman for supper remained just that—intentions. The old woman's phone calls had abated somewhat, and Claire felt mildly guilty that she hadn't done a better job of keeping her landlady apprised of Smokey's well-being.

Claire thought Millie would be pleased, for Smokey had grown a long, sleek winter coat that he meticulously groomed in front of the fireplace each evening. He was fat and—if the volume of his purring was any indication—very happy.

The first week in December the teachers held an early Christmas potluck luncheon, and Claire collected half a dozen new recipes from fellow teachers. Becky Anderson had talked her through the instructions for a delicious chicken dish, and Claire felt brave enough to try it out on company.

She called Millie and invited her for the following Friday evening. Millie was delighted with the invitation and offered to bring a loaf of her homemade bread.

Friday night Claire was struggling to open a bottle of salad dressing when the doorbell rang fifteen minutes early. She wiped her hands and pushed back a wayward strand of hair before going to the door.

"Hello, Millie. Come in and get out of the cold. My goodness," she said, sticking a hand out into the night air, "it feels like the temperature has dropped twenty degrees since I got home from school."

Millie was bundled from head to toe, and Claire took her coat and the fragrant offering of yeast bread and helped her find a seat by the fire where she could remove her boots and several layers of sweaters.

"Oh, this fire feels wonderful! I was beginning to fear I'd turn into a block of ice before I got here!"

Claire carried Millie's wraps and boots to the back entry to dry. When she came back into the living room, Millie was standing with her back to the fire surveying the room.

"Oh, honey . . . you have the house looking so nice. It's so good to be home—to be *here*, I mean." She didn't apologize for her gaffe, and Claire pretended she hadn't heard.

"Do you really like it?" Claire asked. "I'm having so much fun decorating, but I don't have much confidence—or much money, for that matter—when it comes to decorating." She looked around the room, trying to see it with an objective eye. "I do like it, though. It's such a cozy house, Millie. I can see why you loved it so much. It reminds me of my grandmother's house in Lee's Summit. Actually, Nana doesn't live there anymore," she explained. "She's in Kansas City now, in an apartment complex sort of like yours. Her house in Lee's Summit—the house I remember as a child—was bigger, but a lot like this one."

"Well, you've done a wonderful job, Claire. I like it," Millie said decidedly. "Now where is that pussycat hiding? Surely he's not out of doors on a night like this?"

"Oh no. The last I saw him he was asleep at the foot of my bed. I'm surprised he's not out here. He usually enjoys the fire in the evening."

"I certainly remember." Tears came to Millie's already clouded eyes, and Claire left her to her memories while she went to retrieve the cat.

She scooped Smokey up off the bed and carried him out to the living room to deposit him in Millie's welcoming lap.

"You two visit awhile, and I'm going to finish getting our supper on," Claire told her.

It was a special evening and Claire wondered why she had waited so long to make it happen. Millie praised the cooking until Claire was almost embarrassed, and after the dishes were done, the two women sat in front of the fire and Millie gave Claire a brief history of the old house.

"My dear Samuel was born in this house—right there in the room where you sleep, Claire. When Lydia—that's our oldest daughter— was born, Samuel's parents decided we needed the space more than they did, so they built a little house over on Hudson Street. By the time our girls were in school, this house didn't seem so big anymore, but back then it was a mansion to us." A faraway look came into her eyes as she said, "We had some happy, happy days here. Samuel died here, too. Didn't want to go into the hospital even though he knew he was dying. He wasn't even seventy years old." She clicked her tongue. "Too young for a good man to die. Too young . . ."

Claire listened sympathetically until Millie became cheerful again. After visiting for a while longer, Claire offered to make tea. She was carrying mugs of hot spiced tea out to the living room when Millie said, "Our young advisor—or administrator or whatever in the world he's called—tells me that he took you out to dinner not long ago."

Claire tried not to show her surprise at the comment. "You mean Michael Meredith?"

"Well, of course, Michael. Have you been seeing him?" Millie asked in her most innocent, grandmotherly voice.

Claire cleared her throat in an attempt to buy some time, not sure how much she wanted to tell Millie. "Uh . . . no . . . we just went out that one time. I've been awfully busy getting ready for our Christmas open house at school." Truth was, Michael hadn't called her again. She had tried not to think about it.

"He hasn't called you, has he?" Millie said, voicing Claire's thoughts.

"No, Millie, he hasn't."

"Well, I'll just have to put a bug in his ear."

"Don't you *dare*, Millie!" Claire was aghast at the mere thought.

"Well, you don't have to get snippety about it."

"I'm sorry. It's just . . . well, I'd just rather he called on his own, that's all," she finally sputtered.

"Ah . . . so you *would* like to go out with him again, though?"

"Mil-lie!"

"I'm sorry, honey." Millie put a blue-veined hand on Claire's arm in apology. "I'm just being an old busybody. I can't help it some-times."

"It's okay. But could we please just talk about something else?"

"What we need to talk about is getting this old woman home."

It was said in good humor, so Claire knew Millie wasn't upset. But she was grateful for the change of subject.

"Are you sure you wouldn't like me to drive you home tonight?

I could bring your car back sometime tomorrow when the weather has warmed up a bit and then I'll just walk home."

"Heavens, no. I'm a tough old bird. I'll be fine. What you can do, though, is help me with the fasteners on my boots." She held her crooked fingers up for Claire's inspection. "These old hands just don't cooperate with me like they used to."

Twenty minutes later Claire called Millie's apartment to make sure the old woman had arrived home safely.

"Oh yes, dear. No problem at all, but thank you for thinking of me. And thank you again for that lovely supper. It was a very nice evening."

"I enjoyed it, too," Claire said with sincerity. "Good night, Millie."

"Good night, dear."

With Millie safely accounted for, Claire walked through the house, turning off lights and putting the teacups in the sink to soak.

She looked around her house and thought about all the lives that had been lived in these rooms. In a society where no one seemed to stay in one place for long, it seemed amazing that Millie's husband had been born and died in the same room. And rather than frighten her, it seemed comforting to think about Samuel Overman's gentle death in the room where she now slept. It spoke of a continuity of life that Claire had never known.

It had been an enjoyable evening, and Claire had a feeling that Millie had gone from being merely her landlady to being her friend.

    &#x218b;    &#x218b;    &#x218b;    &#x218b;

Claire was discovering that her biggest challenge in the classroom was finding time for the day's lessons. Between releasing her students to practice for the Christmas program and having them make the obligatory Christmas gifts for the parents, she was struggling to stay on schedule with the academic work.

After one especially frustrating morning, Claire was pleased that the afternoon geography lessons had gone well and they had even managed to get a bit ahead in the book. She decided to use the last half hour of class to finish up the gift projects they were working on.

Claire had inherited the idea for the craft project from the teacher whose place she had taken. According to the other third-grade teachers, this particular craft was a long-standing tradition at Hanover Falls Elementary, and there were sure to be some disappointed children if they didn't get to make the candle holders "like my sister made last year."

The project involved punching a pattern of decorative nail holes in old tin cans to create a rustic votive candle holder. The tins were first filled with water and frozen to keep the hammer and nail from smashing the can flat.

Most of the children had completed the hole-punching step of the project and were ready to rub the outside of their can with black shoe polish to give it an antiqued look. However, several of the students weren't quite so dexterous with a hammer as the others. Claire was hoping this would be a good opportunity for the children to learn the value of working together to help one another finish the project on time.

Before she could orchestrate the choosing of partners, several of the students had already paired off. They seemed to be taking the task seriously, so although she would definitely not have linked up Jarrod Hamilton and Will Frederick, for the time being the two seemed to be getting along. Perhaps there was hope for these seemingly bitter rivals. *It is, after all, the season of miracles*, Claire thought wryly.

She was wiping off Brianne Sizemore's shoe polish-covered hands when a howl of pain pierced the air. Claire whirled around in the direction of the screams to see Jarrod holding his thumb and jumping around in circles on one foot. Will Frederick had flushed a deep shade of red and was craning his neck for a peek at Jarrod's wound, all the while insisting to Claire's as yet unasked questions.

"I didn't do it. I swear, I didn't do it!"

"Yes, you did!" Meg Brayton shouted. "I saw you with my own two eyes."

Several other girls agreed with Meg's observation, and the hammer hanging limply in Will's hand was the "smoking gun" that convinced Claire that the girls were telling the truth.

"Shh . . . hush!" Claire admonished all of them. She managed to calm Jarrod down and determined that his thumb had been smashed quite severely. It would probably cost him his thumbnail. Already blood was collecting under the nail, turning it the blackish-purple color of an eggplant. Claire knew from experience that the injury would be very painful.

She left her students whispering their various eyewitness accounts of the incident to one another while she walked Jarrod to the school nurse's office.

He had calmed down sufficiently to answer her questions as they walked down the hallway.

"What happened, Jarrod?"

"Will hit me with the hammer as hard as he could," the boy whimpered.

"He surely didn't do it on purpose?" She wasn't at all confident of her implied assumption.

"Yes, he did!" Jarrod practically shouted. "He bet me I couldn't pull my finger out in time before he hit it. And then he didn't even say 'on your mark, get set!' He just slammed the hammer down." The boy grabbed his thumb as though it had been smashed anew and the tears started again.

They had arrived at the nurse's doorway. "Jarrod, you stay here with the nurse, and I'll talk to Will."

Claire explained to the school nurse what had happened, and by the time she got back to the classroom, it was nearly time for the final bell to ring. The students were quiet and cooperative and had the tables cleaned up before it was time to go. When the bell rang Claire quietly asked Will to stay after for a few minutes.

He hung his head but he couldn't conceal the defiance in his eyes.

"Will, Jarrod's finger is hurt pretty badly. I want you to tell me exactly what happened."

"I don't know. I was just standin' there and all of a sudden he starts screamin' like crazy." He scuffed the toe of his shoe on the floor. "I didn't do it. I swear I didn't! I didn't do *anything!*"

"Will, I heard some of the other kids say that they saw you do it." She gave him a chance to confess.

"Well, they're liars!"

"Will, look at me."

He peered up at her from under long, shaggy bangs.

"Will, Jarrod told me that you bet him he couldn't pull his finger out before you hit it. Is that true?"

Silence.

"Will?"

"Well, he shouldn't of made the bet if he didn't think he could win!"

"So are you telling me that you *did* hit Jarrod's thumb with the hammer?"

"It was an accident. I didn't do it on purpose!" He started to whimper.

Claire had the strangest desire to pull the little boy into her arms and hug him. Oh, how she could relate to his anguish over the web of deceit in which he had tangled himself. And yet, he had told a serious lie . . . one that was meant to absolve himself of responsibility for hurting another student. She couldn't let him get away with it. She couldn't.

*But I got away with it, didn't I? All these years later and nobody ever knew the truth. Except Gretchen and Tim—and I don't even know where they are now. They've probably forgotten all about it. But I haven't. It follows me everywhere I go. It haunts my dreams, it caused my brother to—*

She forced herself back to the present. "Will, I think we need to tell Mrs. Hammond about this. We'll call your mom and dad and see what they think we need to do."

She walked Will to Marjean's office and together they called his parents. She would help William Frederick do the right thing so that he wouldn't be haunted by his lie the way she had been haunted by hers.

That evening she drove slowly away from the school toward home, replaying the events of the afternoon in her mind. Distractedly, she carried her things into the house and plopped into a chair.

For the first time, Claire forced herself to willingly think about the lie—*her* lie—that had conceived the darkest secret of her childhood.

Joseph had turned nine the week before. It was early in June but already the weather was scorching. Her father was home from work and had set up the plastic wading pool in the backyard. They had invited Gretchen and Tim and Mr. and Mrs. Gaylord. Nana was there, too, Claire remembered. Nana had brought presents, and so they were turning the afternoon into a belated birthday celebration for Joseph.

Her father was cooking steaks—and hotdogs for the children—on the patio grill. Her mother was in the kitchen fixing cold drinks for everyone. Myra Anderson had been very sick—in bed for so many days that Claire could scarcely remember her any other way. But today she was up and dressed in a pretty pink summer shift. She was thin and her hair hung limp against her neck, but she was smiling a little.

Like always, Joseph sat off by himself away from the other children. He was wearing the new bright green bathing trunks Nana had bought him, but he had not been in the water once. Tim and Gretchen, and even Claire—though she knew better—had tried to get him to join in, but he just sat on the corner of the sandbox with elbows on his knees, mindlessly drawing circles in the sand with a crooked stick.

The other three children splashed and played while the grown-ups sipped drinks on the patio. After a while Claire noticed that most of the water had splashed out of the pool, making soggy puddles in the grass. With her wet hair dripping into her eyes, she tiptoed over the gravel drive around the side of the house and turned on the faucet to which the garden hose was connected. The end of the hose was lying near the pool where they had used it to fill the pool earlier in the day.

As soon as she had cranked the faucet as far as it would go, she hurried back around the house and grabbed the end of the hose, surprising Tim and Gretchen with an icy blast of water.

"Hey!" they squealed in unison.

"Kitty!" her father hollered sternly from the patio, "put the hose down."

"But, Daddy, we need more water. Look. It's all splashed out."

"Well, all right, but leave the hose in the pool." He turned back to his conversation with the adults.

Claire still wasn't sure why she did what she did next. Maybe she was showing off in front of Gretchen and Tim. Perhaps she was a bit jealous of the pile of birthday presents waiting for Joseph on the picnic table on the patio. Maybe she was just trying to get *some* kind of reaction out of her brother.

Whatever it was, she did it . . . did it almost without thinking. She picked up the hose, and putting her thumb down hard over the nozzle, she turned and aimed it in Joseph's direction. The full force of the water hit his bare chest, drenching him with its cold spray.

What happened next seemed to unfold in slow motion. Joseph arched his back and opened his mouth. A wild howl, like that of a wounded animal, came out. As one, Joseph and her father jumped from their seats on opposite sides of the yard. Joseph was closer and he reached Claire first.

With the stick from the sandbox still in his hand, Joseph tried to grab the garden hose from her. But the wet hose slipped out of his grasp and the stick sliced across Claire's bare arm, opening a long ragged gash. Bright red blood oozed from the wound, mingling with the water and running in red rivulets down her hands and onto her legs. Claire had never seen so much blood. She thought surely she was bleeding to death.

Claire's father got to the pool just as she started crying. By now Joseph was standing horror-struck, looking from the stick in his hand to the blood covering Claire.

"My arm! My arm!" she screamed in panic. "He cut me! He cut my arm."

"No! I didn't mean to. I was just trying to . . ."

It was the most Claire had ever heard Joseph speak in one sentence. In any other circumstances, she would have been awestruck to hear him become so vocal. But now she was too furious to care . . . and too terrified by the bleeding wound on her arm.

Her father held her in his arms, trying to calm her. He knelt down and reached into the pool to splash water on the gash. With the worst of the blood washed away, the cut was not nearly so gruesome, but now his white shirt was damp with a mixture of blood and water.

"Joe, what happened?" Raymond Anderson asked calmly, looking into the boy's eyes.

"She started it!" he shouted vehemently.

"No!" Claire protested. And for the first time in her life, Claire told a deliberate lie. She looked at the rage on Joseph's face and knew he deserved to be angry. But then she looked at her father's face and she knew she had disobeyed him. He would be so disappointed in her. And she knew she would be punished. Besides, Joseph had hurt her. "I didn't do anything! I didn't do *anything*!" she repeated, as if to persuade herself.

Raymond Anderson turned to Joseph. "You go straight up to your room, young man."

Joseph stood there, as though about to speak in his own defense.

"Do you hear me? Get to your room this minute!" Now her father was losing his temper.

Gretchen and Tim stood at the center of the pool like statues, watching the little family drama unfold. They had both seen exactly what happened, and Claire knew it. Now they bent their heads, obviously embarrassed to be in on Claire's deceit. But neither of them said anything.

Nana ushered Joseph hurriedly into the house. Claire's father started to lead her to the house when her mother came through the back door carrying a tray of fresh drinks. When she caught sight of the blood-stained shirt and Claire's stricken face, she turned pale and let the tray slide precariously onto the edge of the picnic table.

"Oh no!" she breathed. "What happened? Oh, Kitty darling . . ."

From that moment Claire was the center of attention. Her mother bandaged the wound, cooing comforting words to her "baby." But all the while, Claire's mouth was set in a tight, angry line.

Joseph was finally allowed to come down for a hotdog. But the party had been spoiled. He opened his presents in silence, mumbling perfunctory thank-yous, and instead of playing with his toys afterward, he piled them into his arms and retreated to his room.

The Gaylords and Nana left before it was dark, and that night, her arm swathed in a cocoon of gauze, Claire slept between her parents in their big bed.

Claire shuddered. What had transpired after that was too much to think about tonight. Feeling drained of every vestige of energy, she forced herself to get out of the chair. She trudged wearily into the kitchen to grade geography papers.

# Seven

*A*lmost two weeks went by and the questionable file languished in a deep compartment in Michael Meredith's briefcase.

The day after he brought the file home had been one fraught with problems at work. While the staff of the nursing home scurried to fill out admission forms and help three new patients settle in, a long-time resident of the assisted-living wing fell and broke her hip. Beth VanMeter, the assistant administrator, was in St. Louis in classes for the day, and Michael was pulled from one crisis to the next without so much as a coffee break.

By the following Friday night, he had all but forgotten the questions the file had aroused. But at home on a Sunday afternoon, as he sat on his bed sorting through his briefcase in preparation for the upcoming week, the slim folder materialized from the leather recesses of the attaché case.

He felt as though he had been punched in the stomach when he opened the file, and the problem stared him in the face once again. Regardless of the hectic weeks he'd had at work, he could not justify putting this off any longer. He knew he needed to look over the information again and make a decision. It was really quite simple, he told himself. Either the papers were perfectly in order and could be filed away forever, or the information warranted further investigation.

Sighing, he laid the folder aside on the bed and hurriedly returned his other papers and office supplies to the briefcase. He snapped the case shut and set it on the floor in his closet, then picked up the importunate folder and carried it down the hall to the makeshift den in the apartment's second bedroom.

As he leafed through the file folder for the second time in as many weeks, the telephone rang.

Absently, he picked up the receiver.

"Hello."

"Hey, baby brother!" His oldest sister's bright voice brought instant cheer into the room.

"Sarah! Hi!"

"I figured you'd be out playing in the snow or something."

"Yeah, right. When was the last time I had time to play?" His words surprised him. He hadn't meant for them to come out with such bitterness.

"Working pretty hard, huh?"

"Oh, no harder than anyone else, I suppose. Don't mind me. It's just been a rough week."

"You want to talk about it?"

"It's really no big deal." He hoped he was telling her the truth. "So what's up at the Iverson house?" he asked, deliberately changing the subject.

"Nothing too exciting. Mallory lost a tooth and Eli swallowed the two dimes we put under her pillow," she laughed.

"Are you kidding? He swallowed *both* of them? Did you have to take him to the doctor?"

"No. He's fine. He . . . well, let's just say everything came out okay in the end. It gives a whole new meaning to the phrase 'diaper change,' though!"

Michael roared at his sister's wry telling of the story. Sarah was a CPA who had put her career on hold to raise the three active children she had with her husband, Evan. Michael had always thought Sarah had missed her calling as a comedian. She could always make him laugh.

"Have you talked to Mom and Dad lately?"

"Mom called Friday. They were getting ready to go out to Uncle Warren's for an early Christmas, so we didn't talk long, but it sounded like everything was fine. You know how Mom is, though. She wouldn't tell you if she was calling from her deathbed."

"I really need to call them," he told her guiltily. "I phoned a couple weeks ago, but Mom wasn't home, and you know how it is to try to talk to Dad on the telephone."

Jim Meredith had become quite deaf over the past few years, and though Michael's mother had seen to it that he owned the best hearing aid money could buy, she didn't seem to have much control over whether or not her husband put the thing in his ear. Michael's parents lived near Evan and Sarah in Springfield.

Talking to Sarah made him homesick for his family. It was a two-hour trip, and he hadn't felt he could afford to take more than one day off at Thanksgiving, so he had stayed in Hanover Falls and missed the family's traditional get-together.

"I should try to get back more often," he said, thinking aloud.

"Well, you'll be home for Christmas, right?"

"Of course. I wouldn't miss it."

He visited with his sister for half an hour, then talked in turn to Evan Jr., Mallory, and Eli.

When Sarah came back on the line, she asked him teasingly, "So brother dear, have you met any nice women in that little Podunk town of yours?"

Michael recognized her serious sisterly attempt to pry personal information out of him and said, "Hey, I happen to like this little Podunk town."

But Sarah wasn't going to let him off the hook. "Quit changing the subject, Michael. Answer the question."

He laughed. "I've met a lot of nice women, thank you very much. Trouble is, most of the ones I meet are a little old for me. Like about fifty years too old." He hoped his joke would sidetrack her.

She laughed but persisted. "You know very well what I mean. Have you had even one date since you moved to Hanover Falls, Michael?" She knew he hoped to marry one day, and she was clearly exasperated with his failure to produce the requisite girlfriend.

Not really ready to talk about his feelings, but wanting to get his sister off his back, he told her about his date with Claire Anderson. "And if you must know," he concluded, "we had a very nice time."

"Michael, that's wonderful! Have you asked her out again?"

He smiled at the eagerness in her voice. "Well, it's only been a couple weeks. Give me a break. I'm working on it."

"A couple weeks! Good grief! She gave up on you a long time ago." Sarah growled her frustration. "Men!"

"All right, all right, I'll call her. I'll call her."

"Hang up and do it right now! I mean it."

He hung up, laughing at her motherly admonition.

Maybe he *would* call Claire. They truly did have a good time together. He smiled to himself as he thought of Claire with her unruly strawberry curls and those expressive hazel eyes that had captivated him from the first time he'd met her that night at Millie Overman's. She had made him feel so comfortable, so at ease with himself in her presence. Conversation had flowed easily between them. Until . . .

He remembered again how he had clammed up when their conversation had come too close to things he didn't wish to talk about. He knew exactly when he had closed himself up to her that night. It had happened a dozen times with a dozen women. Why couldn't he get past it? He was who he was. Any woman who might ever come to love him would have to know and understand that. He knew in his heart that Michelle *had* understood and accepted who he was—sordid past and all. She had not rejected him for any reason other than that she had realized she was already in love with someone else. He knew that. Oh, at first he had been devastated. But God had used the experience to strengthen him in a miraculous way. For the first time in his life, he had understood that not every rejection was a direct reflection on him, on his character, his worth.

But Michelle was the only woman he'd ever come close to loving, and sometimes the old fears and doubts came back to haunt him. Was he a faulty human being, undeserving of love? Imperfect, certainly. But, no . . . He shook his head to clear away the condemning thoughts. He should have conquered this long ago. He would not allow the negative feelings to overcome him.

Putting his head in his hands he prayed, "Oh, God, I don't want to go through these doubts again. I have so much to be grateful for. I know my worth is because of you. And I sit here daring to question you. Forgive me. I have no right to feel sorry for myself. Help me not to dwell on something I can't ever change."

He raised his head, and his eyes rested on the ominous folder from Riverview. *Well,* he thought, opening the folder, *I guess here is something bad to take my mind off of something worse.*

He spread the various documents out across his desktop. The papers in his possession were copies, made by the nursing director in order to avoid any undue delay in processing and finalizing the original documents.

His first vague misgivings had surfaced when Vera Johanssen, the director of nursing at Riverview, had nervously asked him to look over the medical charts of a certain resident of the manor's nursing care unit.

The seventy-six-year-old patient, Frederick Halloran, had been admitted to Riverview's skilled nursing unit about a month earlier. Though Halloran was elderly and his cancer was terminal, the disease was not in the final stages. According to notations on the medical chart, the man's doctor had expected him to live anywhere from eight months to two years.

Halloran had died barely a week after his admission to the nursing unit. And though his death had been unexpected, the attending physician attributed it to natural causes.

Entries made by a charge nurse the day before Halloran's death indicated that he had been quite despondent since his arrival. *Patient says medication is not relieving his pain. He continues to be severely agitated, moaning and loudly vocalizing his wish to die. Noon meal refused*, the large, fluid handwriting on the chart spelled out. According to Nurse Johanssen, the information had been corroborated by several other nursing staff on that shift.

Michael himself knew it to be true. He rarely spent time on the nursing-care wings. By mutual agreement those areas were Beth VanMeter's domain, while Michael concerned himself mainly with the apartments and the senior center. But Beth had been away much of the week in question, and that afternoon he had taken a quick tour of the skilled nursing unit in her absence. He had clearly heard Frederick Halloran's tortured cries of "Oh, God! Oh, God! Let me die. Please . . . somebody help me!"

He remembered because the cries had torn at his heart. The man's agonized pleas echoed the words Michael's own grandfather had screamed from his deathbed. He had been barely twenty when his grandfather died, and it had horrified him to see the man he loved and respected in such pain that he seemed not to be in command of his mind or body. His grandfather had always been a tower of strength, had never for a moment been out of control. But on the day of his death, he had been reduced to a helpless animal, yowling for mercy, begging to be released from the agonizing snare of cancer.

Michael had wanted to leave his grandfather, to run outside, clap his hands over his ears like a frightened little boy. But he had stayed. He had prayed for strength and had sat in anguish by his grandfather's bed until death finally, mercifully, granted him peace.

He remembered how grateful he had been the day of Halloran's rantings, that his job did not require him to sit at the bedside of this dying man and relive all over again his grandfather's death. So disturbed had he been that day that he had asked Vera Johanssen about the man, asked if there wasn't something that could relieve his pain. Michael recalled Vera's reply that the patient had been given the maximum dose of pain medication and unfortunately in a few cases, pain seemed to persist in spite of modern medicine. He had memorized the man's name and lifted it to heaven, asking for mercy on behalf of one who could no longer ask for himself. He remembered thinking what a blessing death would be for Frederick Halloran. Little did he know that the events of that afternoon would haunt him far beyond the day.

Michael pushed away the disturbing thought and adjusted the desk lamp to examine another page in the folder. There were no new orders for medication. However, a scribbled entry by an LPN on the evening shift that same day indicated that Halloran, unaccountably, had eaten a light supper and was "resting comfortably." He had been discovered dead in his bed at nine o'clock that night when the evening shift made rounds.

According to Nurse Johanssen, it certainly wasn't inconceivable that an elderly cancer patient could die so suddenly and unexpectedly, yet she had confided in Michael that something about this particular case raised a red flag in her mind.

Vera Johanssen was as level-headed and experienced a nurse as Michael had ever known. He trusted her judgment and, in truth, was more troubled by *her* feelings of disquiet over the situation than he was by his own inconclusive findings from the charts that lay scattered across his desk now.

Frustration rose in him as he wondered what, if any, action he should take in this matter. There was nothing concrete to work with here, and yet he couldn't help feeling that the circumstances warranted at least a cursory investigation.

Frederick Halloran was dead and buried now. There had been no autopsy and no questions had been raised by his family or other staff members. It was tempting to let the matter rest. No nursing home administrator wanted his reputation or that of the institution he represented tainted by the stigma of an investigation or even rumors of suspicion. And yet, as a licensed health-care provider, he had a legal and moral obligation to report any valid suspicions involving the health and well-being of the patients in his center.

When a director of nursing felt something was amiss, it could not be summarily dismissed. Even if it was merely an obscure hunch on her part. And now that he had combed the files himself, he had to admit that while vague, the discrepancies he had come across this afternoon filled him with a chill of foreboding.

Although he was highly reluctant to involve any personnel beyond his assistant administrator and the director of nursing, he nevertheless decided it would be prudent to visit with the nursing staff who had cared for Halloran during his last hours—to clarify details and put his mind at ease. He made a mental note to set up informal meetings the following day.

He rubbed his temples to combat the beginnings of a headache, carefully put the papers back in their folder, and switched off the lamp. There was nothing more he could do tonight.

᪥   ᪥   ᪥   ᪥

"Yes, I heard Mr. Halloran yelling that afternoon, but like I said, Mr. Meredith, he had calmed down considerably by the time I took his supper tray in." Cynthia Harper shifted self-consciously in her chair. Harper was a licensed practical nurse who had worked at the 150-bed nursing-care center for the past four years. Beside her, looking equally nervous, sat Geneva Grayson, a registered nurse who had been at Riverview almost as long as Vera herself.

Vera Johanssen had called the nurses off the floor to speak with her and Michael Meredith about Frederick Halloran. The four of them sat in Vera's office away from the curious glances of the nurses' station. Michael had discussed the situation with Beth VanMeter at length this morning, and they had agreed that it was important to keep the initial inquiries very low-key, thus Beth's absence from this meeting and from the one they'd had earlier this morning with two other nurses who had attended Halloran on the night he died.

"I remember he even joked with me a little about the 'baby food' we were feeding him. He was on a soft diet and had pureed beef on his tray," the LPN explained.

"And you didn't see him again before you went off duty?" Michael asked.

"No. I'm just part-time. I work the three-to-seven shift, so I went home shortly after supper trays were picked up," she said somewhat defensively.

"I see." Michael smiled at the petite middle-aged woman, wishing to put her at ease. "Vera tells me you worked as a hospice nurse for quite a number of years before coming to Riverview. Would you say this is fairly common—for a patient to die this many months ahead of the doctor's prognosis?" By seeking her expertise he hoped to make the meeting seem less an interrogation.

She cocked her head to one side and scratched at the wiry blond hair now streaked with gray. Her voice was so soft that he had to strain to hear her. "Well, with the type of cancer he had, it is usually a long, drawn-out death. But if there's one thing I've learned in twenty years of nursing, it's that there is no such thing as a 'normal' death. Especially with the elderly. I've seen everything from a violent struggle for that last breath of life, to people literally falling asleep and just never waking up."

"I see. Well, thank you for your help, Cynthia," Michael said. "I do appreciate your input." He turned to Geneva Grayson. "Do you have anything to add to what Cynthia has said?"

"Not really. To be honest, I don't remember the patient very well. He was only here a week. Cynthia apparently has a much better memory than I do." She gave the LPN a sidewise glance that Michael could not interpret but which seemed to border on disdain.

"I can understand how you might not remember a patient who was only here for a short time, but"—he indicated the file before him—"based on the information here, do you feel there was anything untimely about this patient's death?"

The older nurse shrugged. "Not necessarily. I wouldn't say it was unheard of for a patient to die a week after admission. Is that what you're asking?"

"Well, my question has more to do with his death in relation to the medical prognosis. His doctors seemed to feel he had at the very least . . ." Unnecessarily, Michael paused as he referred to the medical chart in the file folder. ". . . eight months to live."

"Not meaning any disrespect, Mr. Meredith, but I don't put much stock in doctors' predictions. If I had to guess, I'd say they're wrong at least half the time. And of course, the will to live is a huge factor."

"That's what I wanted to know," he told her, satisfied with her answer.

"Do you have anything else, Mrs. Johanssen?" he asked Vera.

"No." Vera turned to Nurse Harper, and there was an uncharacteristic coldness in her demeanor. "But if you think of anything else—anything at all—please don't hesitate to let me know." Addressing both nurses she said, "Of course, we'll want you to keep everything we've talked about today strictly confidential. We've talked with the others who were on duty that night as well. We're simply trying to make sure the details in his records are very clear," she finished evasively.

Geneva Grayson raised a questioning eyebrow but replied dutifully, "Yes, of course, Mrs. Johanssen."

"Of course," echoed Cynthia Harper.

Vera Johanssen nodded, dismissing the women. When the door closed behind them, Michael looked questioningly at Vera.

"Does everything sound on the up and up to you?" he asked. They had heard the same general account from each of the four members of the nursing staff they had questioned.

"Yes, it seems so," she admitted. "I apologize if I caused you to worry needlessly, Michael. You don't know how I dreaded even saying anything in the first place. But finally . . . well, it wouldn't quit nagging at me. I felt I should let you know my concerns."

"You did the right thing, Vera."

The nurse opened her mouth to speak and then closed it again. She cleared her throat, apparently debating whether to voice her next thoughts.

"What is it, Vera?"

She sighed. "Oh . . . it's nothing. Nothing," she said firmly, shaking her head.

He looked at her skeptically. "I want to be sure about this, Vera. There was obviously *something* about this situation that was disturbing to you in the first place. I don't want to dismiss it lightly."

They sat in silence for a long minute.

"Vera, think about this before you answer." He posed the question in slow, deliberate words. "After talking today with the employees involved with this patient, are you completely comfortable with all the information we heard concerning Frederick Halloran's case?"

"Yes, I think so," she answered with reserved conviction.

"And you're satisfied with the information in here as documented?" He slapped the slender file folder softly against his knee.

"Yes, I am."

"Are you comfortable closing this file permanently then?" he reiterated, anxious to have her full agreement.

"Yes." Her assent seemed more confident now.

He stood and reached for the doorknob. "All right. And please, Vera, don't apologize for bringing this to my attention. I know it has weighed heavily on your mind. And I also realize that the timing couldn't have been worse." He opened the door and she preceded him into the hallway. "This has been a hectic month for you, hasn't it?"

Brushing a strand of snowy hair from her forehead, she sighed. "That's putting it mildly. I can't remember the last time we had so many dismissals and admissions in quick succession."

"How many new ones this month already?"

"I'm not even sure. I've lost count. Five or six."

He smiled sympathetically. "Well, hang in there. And, Vera, I do appreciate your conscientiousness. You did the right thing in coming to me about your concerns. I want you always to be able to do that."

"Well, I promise to try not to go *looking* for trouble," she said almost sheepishly.

"That," he laughed, "would be greatly appreciated."

As they reached the nurses' station, a young aide motioned for Vera. He dismissed her with a wave of his hand. "Thanks for your time, Vera."

"No problem." She turned her attention to the papers the aide held out to her.

As Michael turned a corner onto the hallway that led to his office, he heard a commotion at the end of the hall. A tiny man in blue coveralls was fighting with a heavy industrial mop and bucket. His white-blond crewcut was almost invisible on his squarish skull, and over the clatter of the wooden mop handle Michael could hear the familiar garbled muttering.

"Having trouble there, Ollie?" Michael asked.

The elflike figure turned slowly and a snaggletoothed smile spread over his smooth-shaven face. "Nah . . . nah . . . I got, Murmuff. I got."

Michael couldn't help but return the sturdy little man's smile.

"Murmuff" was the best Ollie could do with Meredith. Michael had learned early on that Oliver Moon understood a great deal more than it might appear. A serious speech impediment made him seem more seriously retarded than he actually was, but every employee of Riverview knew that in spite of his mental deficiencies and his diminutive size, they could count on Ollie to do the work of two men.

"Well, you let me know if you need any help there," Michael told the man.

Back in his office, he tossed the file that had stirred up so much anxiety onto his desk. He was relieved that their concerns had apparently been unfounded. Opening the folder a final time, he took out the copies Vera had made. He ran them through the paper shredder and into the waste basket, trying as he did to discard his worries as well. But a tiny scrap of doubt clung tenaciously to his brain, refusing to be dismissed.

# Eight

O n the eighteenth of December, Claire turned out of the school parking lot and headed toward the south end of town to her landlady's apartment. Her rent check wasn't due until the end of the month, but she was trying to tie up all the loose ends before she left Hanover Falls the following Wednesday to spend Christmas in Kansas City with her grandmother.

On the seat beside her was a small, gaily wrapped package. She was pleased with her gift for Millie. She could scarcely wait for the old woman to open it. Over the past few weeks she had brushed up on her skills with her 35-millimeter camera—a high school graduation gift from her father—and she had snapped pictures of Smokey in various poses: washing himself by the fireplace, curled up asleep on the sofa, lapping milk from a dish. The photos had turned out surprisingly well. She'd had the best ones enlarged and had arranged them in a pretty album. She was certain Millie would be delighted with the gift.

As she pulled into the circular drive, she looked across the field at the new senior center that was rising from the once empty lot at the center of the complex. In spite of the cold, snowy weather, the construction crew was making rapid progress on the building. Claire had watched with interest over the past few weeks as the structure took shape. It was projected that the building would be finished by late spring, and Claire could imagine that by summer's end the landscaping would be well-established, attractively integrating all the buildings of the Riverview Manor complex. It amazed her how quickly such elaborate architecture could spring up from a field of dirt.

Claire got out of the car and grabbed her purse and Millie's package. She had just turned the corner into Millie's courtyard when Michael Meredith stepped out of the entryway door.

"Hello, Claire."

Claire felt herself blush, suddenly self-conscious at running into him unexpectedly. She hadn't seen him since their date several weeks ago. His warm smile quickly put her at ease.

"Millie said you were coming," he told her as they walked toward each other on the long walk. "Just a warning—she has quite a spread of Christmas goodies in there." He rubbed his stomach pointedly.

Claire laughed and groaned. "Oh great, just what I need. Between that and all the Christmas parties at school, it'll take me till Easter to get back in shape."

"Well, you've had fair warning."

"Thanks a lot," she said.

They passed on the walk, smiling at each other, and Claire reached for the door.

"Hey, Claire . . . wait a minute."

She let go of the door handle and turned toward him.

"Would you . . . are you free for dinner tonight?"

"Tonight?"

"Yes. I know it's a school night and terribly short notice, but . . . well, you have to eat anyway. I promise to have you home at a decent hour." He grinned, seemingly self-conscious, waiting for her reply.

"Well . . . sure. That would be nice."

"Great! We'll just go to *Amigos*, if that's okay. Nothing fancy." He glanced at his watch. "Could you be ready around six-thirty?"

"I'll be ready." Claire headed down the hallway to Millie's apartment singing to herself.

❧    ❧    ❧    ❧

They sat across from each other in a wide booth at Hanover Falls' only Mexican restaurant. Candles dripped and flickered in old wine bottles on the tables, and a scratchy sound system played mariachi music.

From the minute Claire climbed into Michael's old truck that evening, they recaptured the easy, comfortable friendliness she had felt at the beginning of their first date. They were both in good spirits, laughing and teasing each other.

After conversing animatedly through appetizers and huge plates of sanchos, beans, and rice, the conversation turned more serious as they nibbled on sopaipillas and sipped hot coffee.

"Claire, I know the last time we went out I . . . I kind of shut down on you when we started talking about our childhoods." He sighed and leaned closer, elbows resting on the table, hands clasped in front of him. "In case you haven't guessed, my childhood was not a very happy one—at least not the early years. I'll tell you about it sometime."

"It's okay, Michael," she said around a mouthful of honey-filled confection. "You don't owe me any explanations." That was true enough, but he had certainly aroused her curiosity.

"No, I . . . I want you to know. It's not all *that* tragic," he said with a reassuring smile. "But tonight I don't want to talk about the past. I'd rather talk about happier things—like the wonderful family I have now."

Claire wasn't sure how that comment fit with his claim of an unhappy childhood, so she simply asked, "Does your family live around here?"

"In the Springfield area mostly. One sister lives in Michigan, but my parents and another sister are in Springfield. My other sister lives in Billings."

"Oh, Montana. I hear that's a beautiful state. I think I'd like it there. The wide open spaces and—"

He cut her off, laughing and shaking his head. "No, she lives in Billings, *Missouri*."

Claire flushed, embarrassed at her misunderstanding. "Oh, sorry. I didn't know there *was* such a place."

"It's southwest of Springfield. It's tiny—probably only about a thousand population."

"Wow. Even smaller than Hanover Falls."

"Yeah, you big city folks wouldn'ta heard of it way up there in Kansas City," he said in his best southern drawl.

"Quit it," she laughed. "Kansas City isn't *that* big."

"Oh, but much more sophisticated than Springfield . . . or Billings, for sure."

"Besides, I've decided to adopt Hanover Falls as my new hometown," she said, choosing to ignore his wisecrack.

"You really like this town, don't you?"

"I do," she said, turning serious again. "I like the feeling of belonging. The people here are so friendly. And I'm sure it doesn't hurt that I love my job."

"What made you decide to be a teacher, Claire?" he asked.

He leaned closer and her heartbeat quickened at his nearness. *Oh, but he is handsome!* Feeling a rising excitement that they were together again, that he seemed genuinely interested in her, that she found him so easy to talk to—Claire began to tell him about her mentor.

"I'd never been around little kids much before, being an only child. It was like discovering a whole new world. And . . . well, I was good at it. The kids seemed to love me as much as I loved them. After that, I never doubted that teaching was what I wanted to do with my life," she concluded.

"When you think about it, it's pretty amazing the way God puts people in our lives. You probably never dreamed what it would lead to that first day you helped out in her class."

She laughed. "That's not the half of it. I didn't even want to be there. The only reason I took that aide position—or so I thought at the time—was that I'd already gotten all the credits I needed to graduate. I figured it would be a good way to kill fourth hour."

Michael laughed. "It kind of makes life exciting, doesn't it—never knowing what seemingly insignificant event in our lives will end up changing it completely!"

"I never thought about it that way. That's neat."

"Do you still keep in touch with her?"

"Mrs. Emerson? No, and I feel bad about that. After Dad died I kind of lost track of everyone in our neighborhood. I don't know if she's even teaching there anymore. She knew I was studying to be a teacher, and I'm sure she knew that it was because of her influence. But I never really told her how much she meant to me. I hope I get a chance to do that someday."

Claire suddenly felt shy, as though she were revealing things that were too personal. But as she looked into Michael's eyes, the warmth she saw there stirred her to go on. "I guess the most important thing Mrs. Emerson did for me was to show me for the first time what it might be like to have a mother."

Michael raised a questioning eyebrow.

She hesitated. "I hope that doesn't sound disrespectful. My parents were . . . I don't know. Remote is the word, I guess. I know now that my mother suffered from serious, debilitating depression along with a lot of other health problems. She lost two babies in infancy, when I was very young, and I always thought that was the reason for her problems. But I wonder now if she had problems even before that."

"Your father didn't explain what was going on with your mom?"

She shook her head. "It wasn't something we talked about. Everything was always hush-hush in our family. Mother spent a lot of time sick in bed and . . . I'm not sure, but I think she may have even been institutionalized a few times. Like I said, we never talked about it. I think I told you she died when I was sixteen."

"That must have been awful. I don't know much about girls, but it seems like that would be a tough age to lose your mom."

Claire nodded. "I know my mother couldn't help the fact that she was . . . sick. But still, I . . . well, I needed a mother."

"It was a pretty good plan God had—of mothers, I mean. Too bad it's gotten so messed up."

She just nodded and was grateful when the waitress came with their check. Michael paid the bill and helped Claire into her coat. They drove back to her house, each absorbed in their own private thoughts.

When they pulled into her driveway, he parked the truck and turned to her. "Well, it looks like I did it again."

"Did what again?"

"Ruined the evening by getting so blasted serious."

"I'm the one who should be apologizing. I didn't mean to get morose on you."

"Well, I started it by asking all the wrong questions."

She smiled. "Let's not argue about whose fault it is, okay?"

"Okay, but I don't want you to think I'm always Mr. Negativity. I can be quite a funny guy, given the chance."

She laughed. "Well, as Becky Anderson would say: 'I know you're funny, but looks aren't everything.' "

Now it was his turn to laugh.

Their laughter seemed to bridge a chasm between them, and feeling brave, she turned to him suddenly. "I make a mean cup of hot chocolate. Would you like to come in for a minute?"

"I thought you'd never ask."

All talk of the past was left behind, and they spent the rest of the evening sitting in front of a warm fire, nursing mugs of cocoa and being entertained by Smokey's acrobatics with a roll of red Christmas ribbon.

When he said good-night at the door, Michael asked her if she would go with him to Hanover Falls High School's last basketball game before the Christmas break. The game was the following Tuesday night in nearby Boyd City. Claire had intended to spend the evening packing for her trip to Nana's. But she told him yes without hesitation and then fell asleep worrying about how she would ever accomplish everything she needed to do before she left for Kansas City.

❧    ❧    ❧    ❧

As Claire drove toward Kansas City, she breathed a fervent prayer that her little car would make it there in one piece.

She looked out on the wintery scene along the roadside and was filled with happy thoughts about her new life in Hanover Falls. But as the miles carried her closer and closer to the one tie she had to her childhood, Claire found herself reflecting again on the most confusing time of her young life.

She remembered sitting perfectly still at the top of the stairway in the dining room, afraid even to take a deep breath. From her perch she could see her mother at the kitchen table, her hands clasped tightly in front of her, her lips pressed together in a grim line. Her father paced the length of the kitchen, speaking angry words that Claire didn't fully understand.

"Myra, you can't blame the boy for every little altercation. These things are to be expected. Besides, it was an accident."

"Ha!" her mother spat sarcastically.

"Myra, it's only natural that it will take a while for all of us to adjust. For six years now Kitty has been accustomed to being the center of attention. It's not all bad that she should have to share the limelight with someone else now. This whole . . ." He grasped for a word and finally spat out, "This whole ordeal will be good for her in the long run. You'll see."

Claire's mother sat, unmoving, and her father continued, his voice impassioned now. "Joseph has had a rough life, Myra. You can't expect him to just fit in without some sort of struggle. He's having to find his own place in the scheme of things. It can't be easy for him. Put yourself in his place for a minute. Think how you'd feel."

Through clenched teeth Myra almost growled at him, her words clipped and measured. "I'd feel mighty grateful that someone had taken me in and given me another chance at life. I hope I'd have the common courtesy to eat the food that was put before me and to give a civil answer to the questions that were asked of me. He can't even do that, Raymond! He's been here six months and he still can't even do that!"

"He's barely nine years old, Myra. For crying out loud! He's a *child*."

"He's three years older than Kitty. You don't see her balking at the meals that are put before her. You don't see her treating me with total disrespect. You don't see her *slashing* other children with sharp sticks." She spat this last accusation out and waited for him to find a defense. "Well? Do you?"

Now his voice turned gentle, pleading. He went to stand behind Claire's mother and put his hands on her shoulders. "Myra. Joe hasn't had all the advantages Kitty has had. Don't you see? He doesn't un-derstand that the things we are asking of him are for his own good. It's . . . it's going to take a while before he can fully trust us. We've got to give him time. We've got to give him a chance."

Her mother put her head down, and from her vantage point on the stairs, Claire could no longer see her face. But she heard the fa-miliar sound of her mother's sobs, and she knew that her father would not argue anymore.

With her head buried in her arms on the table, her mother's muf-fled words floated up the stairwell to Claire's ears. "I just can't take it anymore, Ray. I can't take it. It's too much. It . . . it was a mistake. I see that now. It was all a huge mistake. I want things back the way they were before . . ."

Claire was used to her mother's crying. Ordinarily it hardly had any effect on her, but somehow she knew this time was different. What mistake was her mother talking about? Did she mean *Joseph*? Would they . . . *could* they send him back?

For a fleeting moment, she thought about going to Joseph and warning him about the conversation she had overheard. But it was a silly thought—maybe even cruel on her part. The words she imagined saying to him sounded threatening: "You'd better start acting nice or Mommy and Daddy are going to send you away." She pushed away the frightening thought that if they knew the truth, it might be *her* they sent away instead.

She stood and crept silently to her room, her mind a maze of troubled thoughts.

Had what happened after that truly been her doing? Had the consequences of that thoughtless deceit been so far-reaching that even now it made her tremble to think about it? And if so, then how much worse had it been for Joseph? How much more had he suffered?

Hot tears stung her cheeks, and nearly blinded by their flow, Claire pulled the car off onto the shoulder of the road. With her head bent over the steering wheel, she wept.

Looking down through a veil of tears, she pushed back the loose sleeves of her coat and the sweater underneath it. Her arm still bore a faint, thin scar from that day. It wasn't something she thought much about. But now she stared down at the pale silver-white line on her forearm. She traced it with a finger and thought how insignificant it was compared to the scar which that incident had gouged into her heart. And for the thousandth time, she prayed for forgiveness.

In Claire's mind it seemed that things had happened very quickly after Joseph's ruined birthday celebration. Her next memories were of her mother hovering tearfully and protectively over her, while her father made hushed phone calls and packed up Joseph's few belongings.

Her thoughts traveled back to the day they had taken her brother away. She remembered it now as though it were yesterday.

Though only six, Claire was aware of all the hurt and confusion in her home. As she peered from behind the filmy, pink rosebud-strewn curtains in her bedroom upstairs, she watched as the ladies from social services carried Joseph's two small bags down the front sidewalk to the waiting car.

Joseph followed dutifully behind them, his head erect, his jaw set in that sullen way he had about him. Claire's windows were closed, but she could hear the faint crunch of gravel under his feet as he walked on the driveway to the waiting car.

Her father came off the front porch and into Claire's view to stand behind Joseph. He put his hands on the slender shoulders and turned the boy toward him. Then he knelt in front of Joseph. Claire couldn't hear his words, but his face held an anguish beyond Claire's comprehension. Joseph kept his face turned to the ground, expressionless. Finally, her father rose awkwardly and put his hand gently on the boy's head.

Joseph ducked out from under the gesture of affection and climbed into the backseat of the car. The social workers nodded wordlessly at Claire's father. One of them slammed Joseph's door shut and went around to the passenger side, while the other got behind the wheel and started the ignition.

Joseph gazed out the tinted car window. The darkened glass reflected the house and the huge elm tree in the front yard, but behind the distorted reflection Claire could make out his face. He stared toward the house, but his eyes seemed empty, spiritless, and too care-worn for a boy of only nine.

Downstairs she heard her mother's muffled sobs. Over and over her mother moaned. Not Joseph's name, not the name of the living son she had banished—but the names of her dead infant sons.

"Michael, Ryan . . . my babies . . . oh, my babies . . . ."

As the car backed out of the drive and turned onto the street, Claire parted the curtains and pressed her face to the window, unable to believe this was really happening. The flutter of curtains apparently caught Joseph's eye because he looked up suddenly toward the eaves. Small and alone in the backseat, he looked across the distance full into her face. The utter sadness and dejection reflected in the dark pools of his eyes pierced her heart and forced her to turn away, trembling.

Her father stood on the driveway for a long time afterward. She watched him from above until, shoulders sagging, he trudged slowly back to the house—a house so silent it frightened her.

Claire stared straight ahead at the ribbon of highway spooled out before her, awestruck at the clarity of the memories that had materialized.

She remembered she had gone to stay with Nana Anderson the next day. Though Nana seemed cheerful enough, Claire could tell she had been crying. She remembered hearing snippets of hushed tele-phone conversations Nana had with Claire's father. They were talking about Claire's mother. Her grandmother's voice sounded tired and sad as she whispered the word *hospital* and a big word that Claire hadn't understood then: *institution.*

A few days later Claire had a nice talk on the phone with her father, but when Nana took the phone from Claire and began talking to him, her voice became angry. Claire had been frightened to see Nana so upset. She ran into the back bedroom, but she could still make out her grandmother's words.

"How can you do this to the boy, Raymond? It doesn't make sense," Nana had said. Her voice rose until she was wailing. "He'll never get over this. It will destroy him. Can you live with that, Ray-mond? Please, son. I beg you . . . please don't do this thing."

Somehow Claire knew that Nana was referring to Joseph. But no-body told her anything, and she was too afraid to ask what they were going to do to her brother.

When her father came to pick her up at Nana's several weeks later, her mother was in the front seat beside him, looking pale and even thinner than before, but wearing a pretty new dress and bright red lipstick.

Claire's sorrow over saying good-bye to Nana had outweighed her joy at seeing her parents again, but she went dutifully to pack her things. When their car backed out of Nana's driveway that afternoon, Claire sat silently in the middle of the backseat looking straight ahead.

The next weeks were a jumble of disjointed memories.

The house in St. Louis was sold, and in a matter of days they had loaded all the furniture and all her toys and clothing into a big moving van.

"We're going to Kansas City," her father had told her. "It's a beautiful town, Kitty. We'll be closer to Nana, and you'll be there in time to start first grade in our new neighborhood."

"Will Joseph be there, Daddy?" She knew he would not. She knew he was never coming back. She had seen Mommy throw his per-fectly good monogrammed bed linens in the trash while they were packing. But the words were out of her mouth before she could think why she had asked.

Her father's face reddened in anger. But as he knelt in front of her, his expression softened. "Kitty, darling—No. Joe . . . Joseph won't be coming back. Not ever. He . . . he went to another home. A foster home. Perhaps . . . perhaps he'll be happier there. We made a mistake. But we're not going to speak of it again. Do you understand me, sweetheart? We will never speak of Joseph again. Do you understand?" he repeated.

Claire had nodded solemnly, not understanding at all.

      ❧    ❧    ❧    ❧

Now as evening fell, Claire drove toward Nana with a sense of urgency. Soon she saw the lights of Kansas City twinkling in the winter twilight. She mulled the memories over in her mind, feeling confusion and depression seep into her spirit. At times like this she wondered if she had inherited her mother's dark moods, the tendency toward depression. It was a frightening thought.

But she determined she would not let her holidays be spoiled by thoughts of the past. "Oh, dear God," she cried out, "help me to put these troubling things out of my mind. I want to celebrate your birth and I want to be happy—for Nana's sake. Please fill me with your Spirit and your joy. Amen."

She reached down and turned on the radio. Every station was playing Christmas carols back to back, and as the strains of "Joy to the World" filled the car, she slowly allowed herself to feel the warmth of the true Spirit of Christmas. She would get through this holiday as she had twenty-five others before it.

She had spoken with Nana on the telephone the previous night, and though she had offered to get a hotel room, her grandmother wouldn't hear of it, assuring Claire that her tiny apartment—one large L-shaped space, really—was more than roomy enough for an overnight guest.

Claire's excitement grew as she imagined telling Nana all about her life in Hanover Falls. She felt silly when she realized that she was talking to herself, rehearsing aloud just how she would tell Nana about the children at school and about her new church and Becky Anderson and Millie and Smokey.

And Michael.

She and Michael had had a wonderful time at the basketball game. They had laughed all the way to Boyd City and back, talking of their college days and of mutual friends in Hanover Falls. The subject of painful childhoods had not come up once.

Claire had noticed many curious glances and knowing looks as she and Michael tripped over feet to find a seat in the bleachers among the Hanover Falls crowd. She had to admit that it was fun being seen on the arm of the town's most handsome, eligible bachelor.

*Yes*, she thought, *I'll tell Nana about Michael.*

# Nine

*K*atherine Anderson peered over her reading glasses and looked her granddaughter up and down. Claire smiled at this familiar appraisal by her beloved Nana.

"Well, Kitty, I do believe life in Hanover Falls becomes you," the elderly woman finally declared.

Grandmother and granddaughter sat side by side on the firm sofa in the tiny apartment. Nana's room was decorated with a miniature Christmas tree and various homemade ornaments, many bearing the faded childish signature of Kitty Anderson.

The door opening onto the wide hallways of Elmbrook, the Kansas City retirement home where Nana lived, revealed festoons of greenery and holly berries along the ceiling and huge foil-wrapped pots of poinsettias flanking every doorway.

Even Nana herself was decked out for the holidays. She wore a crimson skirt and sweater set, and her yellow-white hair had been freshly permed and arranged. Despite the deep lines in her face and the rheumy-aged eyes, Claire thought her grandmother was still a beautiful woman. Tall and slender in her youth, her bearing was still regal, even though the broken hip had left her posture crooked.

Claire returned her grandmother's smug smile and sighed with contentment. "I really am happy, Nana. I love my job, and the people I work with are so nice. The house is perfect. I even have the silly cat I've always wanted."

"A kitty for Miss Kitty," Nana quipped.

Claire laughed, happy to see her grandmother so lighthearted.

"And my kids . . . oh, I just wish you could meet them, Nana."

"I feel like I already know them from the things you've told me in your letters, honey."

"Oh, I just remembered! I brought our class picture to show you." Claire went for her purse, and when she settled back on the couch beside Nana, her grandmother exclaimed over each child.

"And here . . . that's Lucas," Claire pointed out.

"I would have guessed him in a minute from the ornery gleam in his eyes!"

"He keeps me on my toes all right. Oh, Nana, being a teacher is even more fun than I thought it would be. It . . . it's like I'm *finally* where I belong," she blurted out.

A faraway look came into her grandmother's eyes. "Oh, Kitty, I'm glad you've found some happiness. I wish things could have been different for you."

"It's okay, Nana," Claire said, knowing exactly what her grandmother was referring to, and feeling the weight of regret herself. "I'm doing fine. I think I'm happier than I've ever been in my life." And Claire knew it was true.

"Now, Miss Kitty," Nana said, a twinkle coming into her eyes, "why do I suspect that this happiness I see in your eyes is not entirely due to an old tomcat and a passel of third-graders?"

Claire grinned. She never had been able to keep a secret from her grandmother.

"Oh, Nana, I've met someone. He's . . ." She paused, wanting to say just the right words that would let Nana know how special Michael Meredith was. "He's handsome and sweet and . . . he seems to understand me so well."

"Sounds like my little Kitty is in love," Nana teased.

"I don't know about that, Nana, but I do know that I like him a lot. And I think he feels the same way about me. I've never felt like this about anybody before."

"Sounds like my little Kitty is falling in love," Nana repeated in the same playful sing-song voice.

"Do you really think it could be love, Nana? I've known him such a short time, and yet . . . in some ways, I feel like I've known him forever."

Nana patted her granddaughter's knee affectionately. "Don't be in too big a hurry, sweetheart. If this is right, the good Lord will let you know plenty soon enough. In the meantime, you just take it slow—and enjoy every minute of it.''

Claire fell asleep that night on Nana's uncomfortable sofa bed, a whirlwind of thoughts blowing her dreams first in one direction and then another. She awoke often during the night and lay awake listening to the soft sound of her grandmother's breathing. Then her mind would turn to thoughts of Michael Meredith and the bright hopes she had for their friendship.

It was a special Christmas with the person Claire loved most in the whole world, and she dared not spoil it by thinking of how few Christmases she might have left with her grandmother.

☙  ☙  ☙  ☙

On New Year's Day Claire made the four-hour trip back to Hanover Falls in bright sunshine and a bitingly cold wind. At times she had to fight the steering wheel to hold her car on the road in the strong crosswinds. But it was the sunshine, not the bitter wind, which reflected her spirits.

The first day back in her third-grade classroom was much like the day of the first snowfall. Not much schoolwork was accomplished amid all the exchanging of news. Everyone had brought a favorite Christmas gift to share at show-and-tell, and each child wanted a turn to tell about his or her family celebration.

Claire was delighted to see her students again, but when she pulled into the driveway at home that evening, she realized that getting back to the workday routine had exhausted her. Still, she wanted to visit Millie and find out how her landlady's holidays had been spent and thank her for caring for Smokey while she was gone.

Though Millie had recently sold her car and reluctantly given up driving, she had insisted on looking after Smokey while Claire was in Kansas City. She told Claire that her daughters' families would be visiting daily during the holidays, and she was certain they would be more than happy to drive her over to the house to feed Smokey and allow him some time outdoors. Claire had half suspected that Millie would spirit the cat away to her apartment for the week, but judging by the cat food scattered across the garage floor and the little clumps of fur clinging to the sofa, it appeared that Smokey had remained on the premises throughout the holidays.

By afternoon, the winds had died to a breeze and the sunshine was so inviting that, in spite of her exhaustion, Claire decided to walk the mile and a half to Millie's apartment. The succession of school and church parties and the rich food she had eaten in Nana's dining room had taken their toll, and Claire was determined not to let the extra five pounds take up permanent residence on her hips.

She set out with a heavy coat, stocking cap, and mittens, but by the time she had walked half a mile she had shed the cap and mittens and unzipped her coat. The sun dipped quickly toward the horizon, but the exercise warmed her and flushed her cheeks.

The Riverview complex had just come into view when Michael Meredith rounded a curve of the long, winding drive that led to the entrance. He, too, was on foot.

"Claire! Hi!" He gave her a light, spontaneous hug and stood back to smile into her face, suddenly looking boyish and uncertain. "How was your Christmas?" he asked, burying his hands in his coat pockets.

His nearness sent a thrill through her and she could scarcely keep herself from falling back into his arms. The pure joy she felt at seeing him again took her by surprise.

"My Christmas was great . . . really great," she answered, out of breath from more than just the brisk walk. "How about yours?"

"Perfect. My youngest sister, Betsy, was back from Michigan, so my whole family was together for the first time in three years."

"Oh, how nice. I'll bet you hated to come back."

"Not really. It's always kind of good to be home. Here, I mean." His arm swept to embrace all of Hanover Falls.

"You know, I thought the same thing. It really did feel like I was coming home this time."

"Well, after all, you told me you were going to make this your new hometown."

"It's kind of a nice feeling," she laughed, delighted that he'd remembered.

"Uh-huh." He smiled knowingly. "Are you on your way to Millie's or just out for a walk?" he wondered.

"Millie's. Have you seen her since the holidays?"

"I ran into her in the hallway ten minutes ago, as a matter of fact. But I'm afraid you won't catch her at home. She just left with one of her daughters to go out for supper."

"Oh. Well . . ."

He patted his stomach sheepishly. "I wish I could tell you I was trying to walk off some of the Christmas cookies and pies I've inhaled over the past month, but the truth is, I was on my way to get some pizza. They have a Tuesday night buffet at Mario's—all you can eat. Could I talk you into coming with me? They make a great pizza," he added, noting her hesitation.

Mario's was a tiny hole-in-the-wall pizza place downtown. Claire had always thought of it as a teenagers' hangout and had never eaten there, but Michael made it sound like the most appealing place in town.

"Oooh . . . I really, really shouldn't," she groaned. "But it does sound good."

"Let's go." He flashed a wide smile and abruptly took her arm. "We'll walk and work off all the calories before we get there," he said, playfully turning her in the direction of downtown.

The sun had disappeared below the horizon, and the air was growing chillier. Reluctantly, Claire let loose of Michael's arm to zip her coat and put her mittens and hat back on. They walked briskly, their breath forming wispy clouds in front of their mouths as they recounted their holidays to each other. Michael told her about his family's Christmas Eve celebration in Springfield, laughing over the antics of his sisters' children.

"You should see my youngest nephew, Claire. He is the cutest little guy I've ever seen. For some reason he really took a liking to me this visit. He actually cried when I left yesterday," he boasted.

"Now, which one is this? Eli?" Michael had talked a lot about his nieces and nephews.

"Right," he said, sounding impressed that she remembered. "He's Sarah's youngest."

"How old is he?"

"He must be . . . oh, two or maybe three. Whatever age they start speaking clearly. Well, *mostly* clearly. He still calls me 'Unco Mike-o.' " He formed his mouth into a toddlerlike pout as he laughingly pronounced the name.

"Unco Mike-o," she repeated. "How sweet. You know, that's the worst part of being an only child," she said wistfully. "I'll never get to be an aunt."

"Oh, I'd never thought about that, Claire. I'm sorry. I hope I wasn't rubbing it in."

"Don't be silly. I'm enjoying your nieces and nephews vicariously. How many do you have altogether, anyway?"

"Nine. My sisters each have three kids. Mom told me this weekend that she's counting on me to contribute my three and make it an even dozen."

Claire flushed at Michael's reference to his future children. She was glad it was nearly dark and glad he couldn't read her mind and know the thought that popped immediately into her head. She was beginning to think she would love to be the one to bear those children for him.

When they reached the downtown business district, Michael sniffed the air. "Mmm. I can smell the pizza from here. Do you smell that?"

Grateful for the change of subject, she followed his lead and inhaled deeply through her nose. "Yes, sir!" she teased, smelling only the sharp scent of wood smoke from a chimney. "Smells like pepperoni to me."

"Come on!" He grabbed her mittened hand and took off in a slow trot, half dragging her toward the restaurant. Their laughter was carried on the clear night air, and Claire thought she, too, would float away with the lightness of the joy she felt.

When they emerged from the cozy pizza parlor an hour later, the temperature had dropped almost twenty degrees. They stood on the sidewalk outside the restaurant and buttoned up against the cold. Claire was grateful for her hat and mittens.

"Here." Michael took off his woolen scarf and wrapped it around her neck. She lifted her chin to him and their eyes met. "You look cold," he said, as though suddenly embarrassed by his actions. But his gaze didn't leave her face.

"Thank you," she whispered, touched by the tenderness of his gesture.

Finally, uncomfortable under his scrutiny, she looked down and brushed at some imaginary dirt on a mitten.

He cleared his throat nervously and pulled on his own gloves, the spell broken. But he took her hand and started in the direction of her house. "Come on, I'll walk you home."

The biting cold was forgotten as they walked, mitten in glove, deep in conversation. When they reached her doorstep, Claire pulled off a mitten and dug in her coat pocket for her keys.

She turned to thank Michael for the pizza and for walking her home, but before she could say a word, he took her face in his gloved hands and leaned over and kissed her lightly. "Good night, Claire. I'm glad you're home."

He turned and headed briskly toward the street, shouting over his shoulder, "I'll call you."

She stood, openmouthed, staring after him, too surprised to squeak out a reply. When he had disappeared in the shadows between streetlamps, she unlocked the front door and went inside.

Still dressed in all her cold weather gear, she flopped down on the sofa, heart pounding, hands trembling. She relived their evening over and over again, committing every word, every touch, every expression to memory. She could still feel the strength of his hand enveloping hers, the warmth of his lips against her own. What was happening to them? It was almost frightening to realize they had entered strange new territory in their friendship tonight. Strange and new . . . and wonderful.

Overly warm and drowning in a sweet drowsiness, she took his scarf from around her neck. She held it to her face and breathed in the hint of his aftershave that lingered there.

"Oh, Michael," she whispered.

# Ten

$\mathcal{M}$ichael called Claire the next evening. Their conversation was playful and easy, but neither of them mentioned the kiss. Before she hung up the phone they had made plans to spend the following Saturday together.

Though it took some persuading, she finally talked him into going antiquing with her. On Friday night she balanced her checkbook and decided that with the money Nana had given her for Christmas and if she pinched pennies the rest of the month, she could just afford the bookcase she'd had her eye on since her first visit to Ozark Antiques, a charming shop on the square downtown.

When Michael picked her up early Saturday morning, she warned him to make room in his pickup and to be prepared for hard labor.

"Oh-h-h, now I get it," he joked. "You're just using me for my truck."

"*And* your muscles," she added, squeezing his biceps with an impish grin.

The day was cold and sunny and they grabbed donuts and coffee before heading to the square.

Hanover Falls had several antique and specialty shops on the courthouse square downtown that drew shoppers from the surrounding communities. Saturdays usually found the square crowded with groups of talkative women and reluctant husbands pushing strollers. Often the courthouse lawn was dotted with craft booths and food vendors offering funnel cakes, homemade fudge, and coffee or hot chocolate. The whole atmosphere had the air of a county fair Claire had attended with Nana once when she was small.

They poked around in the other shops for an hour until Claire became impatient. Ordinarily she could spend an entire morning shopping here, but she was chafing to get the bookcase home and see how it looked in her house. Michael teased her about her impatience but didn't complain when she steered him toward the west side of the square.

Inside the musty smelling shop, she strode purposefully past the merchandise displayed in the front of the store to the back wall where "her" bookcase had sat since the day she first discovered it. It was an old lawyer's bookcase—oak, with four glass-doored sections stacked one atop another.

"Isn't it beautiful, Michael? Can't you just see this between the windows on the south wall in my living room?"

He had to agree that it was a nice piece, and all the nicer because it was in such good condition. Even the original brass pulls were intact and only slightly tarnished.

The proprietor approached Claire with a smile of recognition. "Ah, you brought help with you today. Does this mean you're finally going to take this thing off my hands?"

"Today's the day!" Claire told the woman, barely containing her excitement.

"Great! Let me wait on this customer," the owner said, nodding toward an elderly gentleman who stood at the front counter, "and I'll be right back to help you take it apart."

While they waited, Claire paced anxiously back and forth in front of the wall where the bookcase stood.

"You're like a little kid at Christmas, Claire," Michael teased.

"I've been saving for this a long time, Michael. Now don't give me a hard time about it," she said with a feigned pout.

He raised his hands in defeat, and she laughed and ran her hand over the smooth, golden oak for the tenth time.

The proprietor emptied the bookcase of the glassware that had been displayed inside, and together Claire and Michael lugged the heavy sections to his pickup, carefully covering them with the old blankets and towels Claire had brought.

When they unloaded the bookcase at Claire's house and started reassembling it, Michael discovered several missing screws and drove back to his apartment to get his tool box.

By noon the bookcase was in fine repair, smelling of fresh lemon oil, and filled with Claire's growing collection of books. She had ar-

ranged a few old framed photographs and a mantel clock she had inherited from Nana on top. They nestled among the trailing leaves of
an English ivy plant Michael had bought for her at a flower shop on
the square to celebrate her purchase.

With the tail of her flannel shirt she wiped at an imaginary smudge
on one pane of glass and stood back to admire the total effect. "Oh,
I love it. It's just perfect."

"It does look nice," Michael agreed, surveying Claire's handiwork. "Just right for this room."

They went out for a late lunch. Later that evening Claire lit a fire
in the fireplace, and they sat on the floor in front of the new bookcase
listening to music on the stereo, eating popcorn, and laughing over
a half-hearted game of Scrabble.

Nana had taught Claire to play the word game at a young age, and
she was an adept and competitive player. Spelling was not Michael's
strong suit, and more than once Claire accused him of making up a
word. Yet his convincing definitions kept her from challenging nearly
every word he spelled out with the wooden tiles. As a result he ended
up winning the game by ten points.

"Oh! I knew I should have challenged you on that last word," she
pouted when he finished totalling the score. "I can't believe you beat
me with a word like 'boxile.' "

"Hey," he gloated, "this game isn't just about being a good
speller. I used to always beat my mom at Scrabble, too. She finally
wouldn't even play with me anymore. Now we like to play Spades
when the whole family gets together. Ever played that?"

"I hate that game," she said adamantly.

"Spades? How can you hate Spades? It's a great game."

"I can never remember how to keep track of all the points."

"Too much math involved, huh?" he teased.

"Well, at least I can spell," she dished back.

"We all have our strengths. How about Spoons? You know how
to play that?"

"We used to play it in the dorm sometimes. It's a contact sport as
I remember it."

"It is when my mom plays." He laughed and launched into the
story. "You have to know my mom. She's about five five, barely a hundred pounds, as meek and mild as they come. But she is a *killer* when
it comes to that game. You do *not* want to get in her way when she

goes for a spoon. Dad is the only one in the family who has the guts to fight her for it. And that's just because he's determined enough to wrestle her down." Michael's voice was full of affection, and it was obvious that he found joy in the memory.

Claire smiled, too, enjoying his pleasure, but she was confused at the same time. "Michael, I hope you don't mind my asking, but I'm having trouble putting this together with the unhappy childhood you've hinted at." Hastily she added, "If it's something you don't want to talk about, I understand."

He took a deep breath and shook his head. "No. No, I don't mind. The truth is, I'd just as soon get it over with. My past is a big part of who I am, and I want to share it with you—if you want to hear it."

"Of course I do." She was almost afraid to breathe, afraid to break the spell of this intimate sharing.

"Well, I guess I'll start with the kicker."

He took another deep breath, and Claire had a sudden vision of a diver poised to plunge into a pool of icy water.

"I was adopted into the Meredith family," he said simply. "In this day and age, I know that's not such a big deal, but . . . I guess I always feel like an imposter, like I'm not really being honest with people until they know that about me. I'm not sure why I feel that way, really. I suppose it was the circumstances. You see, I was ten years old before my parents adopted me."

Now Claire felt like the one who had been immersed in icy water. Fighting to hide her astonishment, she asked, "Then you know your real—your birth parents?"

"I never knew my father. I'm not sure my mother even knew who he was. I'm told she had a lot of problems . . . alcohol, mostly. I don't remember her really. I have a vague, fuzzy picture in my mind. I'm not sure how accurate it is."

Claire listened with fascination as his story unfolded.

"I was probably three or maybe four when I went to live in the first of a long succession of foster homes."

"Oh, Michael," Claire whispered, suddenly overwhelmed with sorrow for the little boy he had been.

He ignored her reaction and went on, speaking in a monotone, almost as though he were in a trance. "I was definitely one messed up kid. I don't think anybody had any hope for me." He had been staring into the fireplace, but now he turned to Claire and brightened visibly. "Then Mom and Dad Meredith came along and—well, here I am." He held out his hands as if to say "ta-da!" and Claire couldn't help but laugh.

"You turned out great," she said, her voice quivering with emotion.

"Well, it's a little more complex than all that, but in a nutshell, the Lord had His hand on me. In the nick of time He reached out and put me in a family that just wouldn't give up on me." A shadow passed over his face, and his voice was filled with emotion as he told her, "I've been through some pretty bad stuff, Claire. I'm talking drugs, violence, the whole gamut."

"It doesn't matter what you were then, Michael—"

"It *does* matter, Claire," he interrupted. "I am who I am today because of the things I went through then."

"I didn't mean—"

"I know, I know. And I appreciate your forgiving spirit. But I just want you to know what you're getting into if you . . . well, if we're going to be . . . friends."

"Do you still see your birth mother?" she asked, filing his reference to their future together in a separate compartment of her mind.

He shook his head. "I don't even know where she is. It's not something I think about a lot. Like I said, I don't really remember her. I've never had any real urgency to look her up the way some people seem to. Mom and Dad are truly my 'real' parents now. I hope you can meet them someday, Claire."

"They sound pretty special."

" 'Special' doesn't do them justice. They were . . ." His voice trailed off and he shook his head, apparently unable to come up with a word he felt was worthy of his adoptive parents. "They never gave up on me, Claire," he said finally. "It's strange. I look back not so many years ago, and I know it was me who did those things—the drugs, the alcohol, the rebellion—but it all seems so unreal. Sometimes I can hardly believe that was me."

" 'If anyone is in Christ, he is a new creation,' " she quoted.

"I *am*, Claire. I am a totally different person. I hope you believe that."

"I do, Michael. I can see it." She turned toward him and gently put a hand on his arm. "Thank you for trusting me to hear all this."

"I'm kind of relieved that you know—and that you're still sitting here beside me."

"Why would you say a thing like that?" she admonished, a bit uncomfortable with this vulnerable, uncertain side of Michael.

He waved his hand as though he could shoo his words out of the room. "I've had a lot of rejection in my life, Claire. And I've struggled through a lot of feelings of inferiority as a result. But that *is* in the past. I'm sorry about that comment. Bad habit." He attempted a smile.

"Don't apologize," she told him. "I asked. I want to know. But, Michael, no matter what your past was, it doesn't change who you are now. Of course it affected you. Pasts are sort of notorious for that." She smiled and looked into his eyes, trying to read his reaction. "What I'm trying to say is that I think I know you well enough by now that I can see that whatever horrible things you did, you've more than made up for them."

"If I can correct your theology just a little," he said carefully, "there was nothing *I* could do to make up for my mistakes. That was all taken care of two thousand years ago."

"Oh, of course you're right. I just meant—"

"I know what you meant, Claire. Thanks for your vote of confidence. God has done some serious construction work right here"—he patted his chest—"but once in a while, for some stupid reason, I get in there and try to tear things down again."

They continued to sit together on the floor—the game board and tiles scattered across the rug forgotten—and talk about the struggles of their childhoods. Claire felt such understanding from him. He, of all people, knew what it was like to grow up lonely and alone. He seemed to understand her as no one had before. And she felt she understood him as well.

Though his early years had been far more tragic than her own, she was envious of the warm family relationships he now had with the Merediths. Claire thought they sounded like wonderful people. Strangely, in spite of the fact that she had never met them, she loved them deeply for loving Michael as they had.

As the hour grew late, their conversation turned light again and they simply enjoyed being in each other's company. Michael made her laugh with his stories about some of the residents at Riverview. His affection for the elderly people in the center was obvious, and she could sense he was good at what he did.

At midnight Michael kissed her good night—only after she had secured his solemn promise for a rematch of their Scrabble game.

༅  ༅  ༅  ༅

All through January and February Claire and Michael spent time together. Sometimes they drove to Boyd City to visit a museum or take in a movie. Sometimes they simply grabbed a hamburger before a basketball game.

Claire invited him to a chili supper at her church, and on several occasions he attended church services with her. They were beginning to be known as a couple around the small, cliquish town.

When she remembered how disconcerting his silences had been to her when they first met, she could scarcely believe he was the same person. Now she began to feel as at ease and comfortable with him as if she had known him all her life.

One night toward the end of February he brought her home from the movies and told her about a conference he had to attend for work.

"I leave for Joplin on Thursday afternoon and I'll be gone all weekend, but would you save Sunday night for me? I'll take you out to dinner when I get back."

"You're going to go broke taking me out to dinner, Mr. Meredith. Would you consider taking a risk and eating my cooking for a change?"

"I do have it on good authority that you are an excellent cook," he said mysteriously.

"Where in the world would you have heard that?" She hadn't cooked for anyone in Hanover Falls except—"Ah," she said as the realization came. "Millie."

"You guessed it. She has all kinds of wonderful things to say about you, Claire. If I didn't know better, I'd think she was trying to play matchmaker."

Claire could hear the wicked smile in his voice. Blushing, she groaned. "Just what else has she said?"

"Oh, you'd be surprised," he goaded her.

"Never mind," she sighed. "I don't even *want* to know." Then laughing, she asked, "So can I take that as a 'yes'?"

"Yes, what? I've forgotten what we were talking about."

"Yes, you'll let me cook for you, silly."

"Oh, you bet I will. What are we having?"

"I haven't even thought about it. Probably liver and onions and spinach soufflé."

His comical look of repulsion set her laughing again.

❧ ❧ ❧ ❧

As she did every weekend, Claire telephoned her grandmother on Saturday morning. Sometimes it was difficult to visit with Nana on the phone. The older woman's hearing was not as keen as it had been even a year ago, and sometimes the weariness in her voice seemed almost tangible. But today Nana was in good spirits and very talkative.

She told Claire about a disastrous Valentine's party the activity director at Elmbrook had organized, and Claire had to laugh at Nana's apparent disgust with the woman she called "Matchmaker Mavis."

Nana asked Claire about Michael, and she found herself excitedly telling her grandmother about the supper she was cooking for him the following evening and confiding in her about their growing romance.

"I think one of the things that makes us understand each other so well," she told Nana, "is that we shared some of the same childhood experiences. I don't think Michael has been able to talk about those things to very many people, but I really do understand him because I had kind of a . . . well, a dysfunctional family myself. Present company excluded, of course."

Claire had always been able to talk openly with her grandmother about the hurts of her past. Katherine Anderson had never tried to deny or minimize the shortcomings of her only son. She seemed to understand that it was helpful for Claire to be able to acknowledge and analyze the experiences she had endured in her family of birth.

Now Nana told her, "It makes me happy to see you so happy, Kitty. The good Lord knows it's about time you had some joy in your life," she said, her gravelly voice full of emotion. "I . . . I've wanted to talk to you about some of the things that occurred back then, honey. I know Raymond was never one to talk about such things. Or your mother, either. But I know you must have questions about some of the things that happened when you were small. You know, sweetheart, I'm not going to be around forever."

Claire's voice held an edge of panic as she fairly shouted into the phone. "Nana! Please don't talk that way!"

"Shhh . . . I'm merely speaking the truth, Kitty. I want you to have your questions answered before I'm not here—or able—to answer them anymore."

Claire gripped the phone more tightly in her hand, not liking the direction this conversation was taking.

Nana continued. "Raymond was always so concerned about appearances. Too much so, I'm afraid. And then Myra's problems tested him to his limits. Do you understand the ailment your mother struggled with, Kitty?"

"I . . . I've always thought she suffered from depression. I know she was sick so often, and she always seemed so sad. I guess it was losing the babies?"

"Well, that didn't help matters any, but Myra was . . . ill . . . long before that. Before she and Raymond ever met. I don't know if you are aware of it, honey, but your mother spent several months as a patient—a resident, actually—in a mental hospital before she met your father. I don't know exactly what the diagnosis was. Raymond would never say, but from what I've read, I've always wondered if maybe she was . . . Well, it doesn't matter now," she said firmly. "She was doing so much better after her treatment there. She and your father married and you came along shortly after that. It looked like everything was going to end happily."

Claire heard Nana's familiar little clucking noises and knew she was shaking her head in dismay. How she wished she could be there to hold Nana's hand while they talked.

Katherine Anderson cleared her throat and went on. "When little Michael James died it was a huge setback for Myra. And then they lost the second baby such a short time later. I think it was simply too much. Your mother was never the same after that. And then there was that whole mess with Joseph. . . ." Her voice trailed off.

Uneasy, yet curious, too, Claire seized the opportunity. "Tell me about Joseph, Nana. I've been thinking about him a lot lately since Michael told me that he was adopted. Of course Michael is very close to his adoptive parents. He has a wonderful family, but I think the whole topic of adoption still bothers him a little. What *did* happen with Joseph, Nana? Why did they. . . ?" She had been going to ask why Joseph had been sent away, but suddenly terrified of the territory she was entering, Claire let her sentence drop unfinished.

"Oh, honey, it's a complicated story. I never thought they should have adopted the boy in the first place. Your mother was far too fragile—still recovering from the loss of her babies. They had hoped to adopt an infant, but I suppose your mother's history prevented that. Anyway, when they had the opportunity to take Joseph in, Raymond thought it would be good for Myra. You know, give her something to take her mind off the babies' deaths. And for a time, it seemed that it might be the answer. But Joseph just never bonded with them. Or maybe it would be more accurate to say that they never bonded with him. I think your father truly tried, but Myra's needs were so great. And he let her dictate him so. . . ."

Claire detected an edge of bitterness creep into her grandmother's voice, but she said nothing as Nana continued. "That poor boy. Joseph, I mean. I felt so sorry for him. Rejected by his own mother, shuffled to and fro in the foster care system. It's no wonder the boy had problems."

"I don't remember much about the time Joseph was with us, Nana. I do remember that he was quiet, and he always seemed so sad. He must have been lonely, but he would never talk to me. He always shut himself up in his room. I . . . I really did try to be nice to him." In spite of that awful afternoon by the wading pool, her statement was the truth.

"I'm sure you did, honey. We all did. He just couldn't seem to adjust. Think how difficult it must have been for him to trust anyone after he'd been rejected so many times. And your mother—bless her heart—had her own problems. She simply didn't have the strength to deal with a child as troubled as Joseph was. Still," Claire's grandmother sighed, "I wish it wouldn't have ended as it did."

Claire sat upright suddenly and breathed into the phone, "Nana, do you . . . do you know where he is now?"

"No, Kitty. When your parents turned the boy back over to the state agency, they were denied access to any future information about him. I don't suppose we'll ever know what became of him. I'm not even sure what name he would go by." Nana's voice sounded weary, and Claire had to strain to hear her now.

"For years I prayed for that boy," she whispered. "I was so disappointed in Raymond for what I saw as a terrible betrayal. I understand now that he simply couldn't deal with Joseph's and Myra's problems, too. And, of course, they had you to consider. You were so young and they feared you were being harmed by all the attention Joseph required of them. It was a very difficult situation. In the end, I suppose it was perhaps best they did send him away. I realize that now, but for years my heart was heavy. I thought about the Joseph of the Bible when he was deserted and left for dead by his brothers, and I prayed that the good Lord would redeem *our* Joseph's life as He did the biblical Joseph's. I admit that my prayers have been less fervent as time has worn on, but I still think of the boy now and then and wonder what became of him. It seems impossible that he would be a grown man by now. But then it seems impossible that my little Kitty is a grown-up lady . . . and a school teacher at that!" Nana's voice brightened and Claire willingly allowed her to change the subject.

But when she fell asleep that night, the old dreams crept back into her subconscious and she awoke the next morning feeling sad and depressed.

# Eleven

With Michael Meredith out of town at a conference and Vera Johanssen on a short leave of absence, the mood at Riverview was even more relaxed than the usual casualness of a winter weekend.

On Saturday afternoon the halls were especially quiet, with many of the residents out with their families and others down for afternoon naps. On the north wing two girls from housekeeping folded laundry, speaking rapid Spanish as they worked. A pretty young nurse caught up on med charts and snuck a candy bar at the nurses' station.

Down the hallway in the broom closet, Oliver Moon's mumbling and snorting could be heard, a sound that—to all but the most infrequent visitor—was a familiar, soothing cadence of the everyday workings of Riverview Manor.

Geneva Grayson was the charge nurse on North this weekend. She was never happy about having to work the weekend shift, but it was policy that even those with as much seniority as she had took their turn. It wasn't so bad, really. The time usually went quickly and there were rarely admissions or dismissals to deal with on those days.

Geneva walked briskly down the hallway, her thick-soled nursing shoes barely making a sound on the tile floors. She looked into several rooms as she moved down the hallway, making sure call buzzers were within reach, tucking an afghan around slippered feet here and there. Her true destination was Room N–18. Helga Schultz had taken ill several days ago, and Geneva suspected she had developed pneumonia. It seemed there was a rash of that dreaded disease every winter, and among the elderly it was a killer.

Helga was in the final stages of Alzheimer's disease, and her family rarely bothered to visit anymore. Geneva couldn't blame them, really.

The woman hadn't recognized them for years and lately had been completely bed-ridden. Still, it seemed sad to Geneva to see a human being abandoned that way.

As she approached the room, Ollie came out of the door pushing his cart of cleaning supplies.

"All through in here, Ollie?"

He gave her his trademark grin and nodded.

She entered the room and immediately heard the rattled breathing, which was a tell-tale sign of pneumonia. She'd have to call the doctor and see if he wanted to order any new medications. Unfortunately for Helga Schultz, it probably wouldn't make any difference at this point.

Geneva emptied the woman's catheter and recorded the measurement on the chart on the back of the door. She elevated the head of the bed a bit to hopefully ease the elderly woman's breathing and checked the IV line that provided the only nutrition she could tolerate. The nurse carefully adjusted the drip and smoothed the tape that held the needle in place.

"How are you doing, Helga?" she asked, not expecting an answer.

Even before she had become ill, Helga Schultz would have understood little the nurse said. Since the onset of Alzheimer's disease, the German-speaking woman had lost even the rudimentary English she once knew.

But Geneva prided herself on speaking even to those patients who were thought not to hear or understand. She firmly believed the studies which showed that hearing was one of the last senses to go, and she determined early in her nursing career that her patients would go with a gentle word in their ears.

"Everything's going to be all right now, Helga. You just rest . . . just rest. It won't be long. It won't be long," she told the woman now.

She left the room, pulling the door partially closed behind her. As she headed back toward the nurses' station, she spotted Ollie at the end of the hallway. He was fidgeting with something, mumbling under his breath like always. When he saw Geneva he quickly turned his back to her, and she saw him put something carefully into the pocket of his blue coveralls. Probably a cookie from the cafeteria. She had told him a hundred times not to bring food onto the wings.

Hurrying toward him she confronted him with her suspicions.

"Ollie, please don't tell me you've been eating on the floor again. You know we have a bad enough problem with bugs as it is." She held out a hand. "Give it here, please."

"Nah . . . nah . . . nah foo. Honst."

"What do you have, then?" Ollie wasn't a liar, but he did like his cookies.

Reluctantly, he put his hand in a pocket and pulled out an object, showing it to Geneva.

She stifled a gasp. In his hand was a syringe. *Where on earth had he gotten it?*

She had learned that Ollie upset easily, so forcing herself to speak calmly, she held her hand out again. "Give it to me, please, Ollie."

He dutifully handed over the contraband. "Where did you find this, Ollie?" She had to know.

Without a word, he began to shuffle toward Helga's room. He pushed the door open and went directly to the bedside table. Pointing to the spotless surface, he grunted.

"You found this on the nightstand?" She could scarcely contain the anger in her voice. "Ollie, you know you are not supposed to take things from patient's rooms. There are things here that could hurt you very badly."

Becoming very agitated, Ollie began to circle his hand over the night table, pretending to clean.

Geneva understood. "I know you needed to clean in here, but this is sharp. You could have been hurt." She made her voice as stern as possible. Sometimes that was necessary to make Ollie understand that you meant business.

He began to rub his hands back and forth through his sparse crew cut, obviously distressed. "Nah . . . nah . . . Murrmuff . . . nah," he pleaded with her.

"No. I'm not going to tell Mr. Meredith, Ollie, but so help me, if I ever, ever find you with something like this again, I won't have any choice but to report you. And that goes for cookies, too. You keep them in the cafeteria. Do you understand?"

Ollie nodded vigorously and gave the charge nurse a weak smile.

"Go on now," she told him affectionately. "Get back to work— and stay out of trouble."

Ollie shuffled back toward the broom closet with his cleaning cart, muttering all the way. Sighing with barely concealed relief, Geneva wrapped the syringe carefully in paper toweling and discreetly disposed of it in the sharps container.

ॐ  ॐ  ॐ  ॐ

The conference room had grown stuffy with the warm bodies of more than a hundred health-care professionals who had crowded in to hear a lecture on the philosophy behind the hospice movement. The acrid smell of stale coffee and the faint odor of cigarette smoke drifting in from the hallway made Michael Meredith feel desperate for fresh air.

He loosened his tie and inconspicuously began to gather his notebooks and briefcase. When the speaker broke into a question and answer session, he quietly excused himself and wound his way through the linen-covered tables toward an exit at the back of the room. He walked through the lobby of the hotel and out to the covered courtyard near the swimming pool, now abandoned in the frigid winter air.

He took a deep breath and moved back a few steps to position himself downwind from a small group of businessmen who were smoking at the edge of the courtyard.

The conference had been interesting. Besides gleaning much helpful information from the workshops and lectures, the program had allowed him to fulfill a continuing education requirement. But it had been a long three days and he still had the drive back to Hanover Falls ahead of him.

He filled his lungs with another gulp of the brisk February air and turned to go back up to his room to pack his bags. As he passed the restaurant just off the lobby, two men emerged from the bar, drinks in hand.

Michael slowed his pace to let them go ahead of him. Suddenly, the older of the two men looked up, recognition dawning on his face.

"Michael Meredith!"

Michael suddenly realized why the man knew him. It was his predecessor, Gerald Stoddard. The stocky man extended a hand in greeting and Michael shook it warmly.

"Well, hello there, Mr. Stoddard. I didn't expect to run into you here. I thought you'd retired."

"Well, so did I. And so did the wife," he laughed.

Gerald Stoddard's words were slightly slurred and Michael

smelled alcohol on his breath when the man thrust his face close to Michael's.

"Hey," said Stoddard, "that sittin' around stuff just wasn't for me. I'm doing consulting work now. Get to set my own hours."

"I see. That must be nice."

"Oh, it is. It is." Suddenly remembering his dinner partner, Stoddard turned and introduced him to Michael, then urged his friend not to wait for him. "You go on, Merle. I've got some catching up to do with this young man."

Gerald Stoddard motioned toward a lounge area in the lobby and, without waiting for Michael's assent, steered him to a deep corner sofa. Stirring his drink with a pudgy finger, he motioned for Michael to sit down.

"So how are things at Riverview?"

"Well, things are busy," Michael said, sitting tentatively on the arm of the sofa. "I can say that for sure. My assistant administrator has gone back to school, so I'm putting in quite a few more hours than I'd really like."

"Don't I remember." Stoddard laughed derisively. "They'll work you to death there if you let them."

Michael was uncomfortable with the bitter edge in Stoddard's voice. He liked his job at Riverview and had never felt taken advantage of. He stood and edged toward the main lobby, anxious to extricate himself from the conversation.

"Hey, tell me something, Meredith," the less-than-sober man asked before Michael could free himself.

"Yes?"

"There still a nurse there by the name of Harper? Cynthia Harper?"

Curious and a bit startled, he nodded a reply.

"She still strange as a three-legged duck?"

"I'm not sure what you mean."

"Ha! You must not know her very well." Michael said nothing and Stoddard rambled on. "I didn't know the woman either when we hired her. Oh, did I ever get into it with Vera Johanssen over that one. Is Vera still there?"

"Yes," Michael answered, inwardly impatient for the man to get to the point.

"I tell you . . . that's only one of my regrets from my stint at Riverview. But it wasn't like I had a choice. It was coercion, if you ask me. No, I never should have let that one fly."

Michael was more than curious now. "What do you mean, coercion?"

"Cynthia Harper." Stoddard waved his vodka glass in the air, sloshing the last drops out onto his suit. "Her old man—he's dead now—but the family owns half of Thomas County. There's just the one sister left now, Cynthia's aunt. Seems she planned to leave a nice chunk of land or money—maybe both—to the manor. Nita Dalhardt's her name. Kind of a recluse—still lived alone on the family place out by the lake last I heard. Anyway, the board didn't want to do anything to make her change her mind. It was never really said, but I got the message that if I knew what was good for me, I'd convince Vera to hire that crackpot."

As much as he hated to stand here and take the words of an inebriated man to heart, he had to ask. "Why do you call her a crackpot?"

"That woman has some strange ideas in her head. Strange ideas about life." Stoddard, his tongue loosened by the liquor, was wound up now. His voice rose a pitch. "I suppose she was a decent enough nurse if you could overlook her strange ways, but how she's managed to succeed in her career, I don't know. It makes you wonder."

Stoddard shook his head and went on. "She cornered me more than once and went off on a tangent . . . some fool thing about her husband being an angel. I don't think she meant it figuratively," he sneered. "How he didn't deserve to suffer the way he did and she hoped, wherever he was, he was getting rewarded for all the pain he went through."

"How did her husband die?"

"Long and slow, to hear her tell it," Stoddard said sarcastically. "I really don't know. Cancer, I assume. I never knew him—I think his name was James—but I can't imagine anyone staying married to a loony like her. I always thought she and Ollie would have made a good couple." He laughed derisively and then said, "I suppose ol' Ollie's still there. He's a character, isn't he?"

"Yes, Ollie's still at Riverview. We wouldn't know what to do without him," Michael replied, trying to give the faithful employee back some of the dignity Stoddard seemed to have taken from him with his boorish comments.

Michael had heard enough. This whole conversation was bringing back doubts that he had hoped to put to rest. To make things worse, his source was conceivably credible because of his past connection to Riverview and to Cynthia Harper, but at the same time quite suspect because of his questionable state of sobriety and his admitted resentment toward the board of directors over the alleged incident with Harper.

Michael looked pointedly at his watch and eased toward the elevators across from the lounge. "Well, I really need to get packed and out of here, Mr. Stoddard. It was good to see you again."

"Yeah, you too. You take it easy now."

Stoddard headed back toward the restaurant, weaving slightly as he disappeared into the bar.

As Michael drove home that night, he mulled over the things Gerald Stoddard had told him. His comments about Cynthia Harper were particularly unsettling to Michael. The only contact he had personally had with the woman was the brief interview before Christmas when they had questioned her and several other nurses about Frederick Halloran's files. Michael remembered that Harper had seemed somewhat socially inept and nervous. But certainly that was understandable under the circumstances. However, if it was true that she had been hired because of her connection to one of the center's main benefactors, the fact lent one more edge of credibility to Vera's misgivings. He wondered if Vera knew about the connection. Surely she would have said something had she known.

Stoddard's affirmation that Cynthia Harper was at least a bit odd was disconcerting. Still, none of the things Michael had heard offered a genuine reason for him to take action. *Besides*, he reassured himself, *the man was drunk*. Still, he wanted to talk to Vera about this disturbing encounter.

As he drew closer to Hanover Falls, he convinced himself that Gerald Stoddard's babblings had been just that. Babblings. He forced himself to think about other things.

One pleasant realization made it easy to put the nagging concerns out of his mind. Tomorrow night he would see Claire again.

# Twelve

*C*laire went to early services Sunday morning and hurried home to tidy the house up a bit before she got busy in the kitchen. Afraid to risk trying a new recipe, she made the same chicken dish she had served Millie. *Why mess with success?* she thought as she assembled the ingredients. She baked banana bread and an apple pie, all the while blessing Nana for passing down her culinary skills.

While the pie was in the oven, Claire went for a short walk, relishing the brisk winter air and daydreaming about the evening to come.

Once home she took a quick shower. When her hair, damp and unruly from the shower, wouldn't cooperate, she plaited it into a neat French braid. She brushed a touch of pale blush on her cheeks and glossed her lips. Peering critically into the mirror, she saw tendrils of hair had already escaped the braid, and she wished for the thousandth time that she had been born with smooth, straight hair. But a glance at the clock told her she didn't have time to worry about her hair.

She set the small kitchen table with her best dishes, put classical music on the stereo, but decided against candles, fearful that they might seem too much an attempt at romance.

By the time the doorbell rang at six o'clock Claire was a bundle of nerves, but the casserole was cooked to perfection, her hair had settled down a bit in the dry heat from the fireplace, and the house was fragrant with the scent of apples and cinnamon and woodsmoke.

She took a deep breath and opened the door.

"Hi, Michael."

"Hi." He gently turned her around for inspection. "Your hair looks really pretty like that."

His tender touch, the warmth of his hands on her shoulders affected her deeply, but she laughed nervously at his comment. "Oh, if only you knew how I agonized over this dumb naturally curly hair, you'd know how sweet it is of you to say that. Thank you."

"That doesn't smell like liver and onions to me," he said, changing the subject and sniffing in the direction of the kitchen.

"I changed my mind. It's a chicken recipe I got from Becky. I hope you like it."

"If it tastes as good as it smells, I'll love it."

"Well, let's go find out. Oh, I'm sorry. Here, let me take your coat."

He shrugged out of the heavy overcoat and she hung it in the hall closet, then led the way to the kitchen.

Supper was a huge success. Michael ate everything with gusto, including two slices of apple pie. She would have to remember to send some of it home with him. She'd never be able to finish it herself.

When the second piece of pie had disappeared from his plate, he leaned back in his chair and groaned miserably. "Oh, Claire, I'm afraid this was a big mistake."

"Why?" she asked suspiciously, recognizing his prelude to a joke.

"I'm never going to want to take you out to eat again now that I know we can get the best meal in town right here."

"Maybe I *will* make liver and onions next time, just to be sure you don't take advantage of my culinary talents," she shot back.

"Okay, okay, you win."

"Also," she said with a gleam in her eye, "at Claire's Restaurant you have to do your own dishes."

"Lady, you are one tough taskmaster. Well, let's get it over with."

He pushed away from the table and started to clear away the dishes. Laughing, she followed suit, and when they moved into the living room half an hour later, the kitchen was spotless and a triangle of foil holding three generous slices of apple pie for him to take home sat waiting on the still-warm stove top.

In front of the dying fire, they sat at opposite ends of the sofa, Claire's stockinged feet curled up beneath her. She asked Michael about the conference.

"It was interesting," he told her. "I think I learned some very helpful things."

He was silent then and she sensed his thoughts were distracted.

"Anything wrong?" she ventured, not wanting to lose him to the silence.

"Huh?" He brought his eyes into focus on her face, seeming almost surprised to see her there. "I'm sorry, Claire. I was just thinking about some problems at work. I have a situation I'm not sure how to deal with and . . ." His voice trailed off, the sentence unfinished.

"Do you want to talk about it?" Claire prodded.

He seemed to weigh his options but finally told her, "Thanks for asking, but it's really not something I can discuss right now. I'm sorry." He formed his hand into a Boy Scout's pledge of honor. "I promise I'll put it out of my mind for the rest of the evening."

Claire laughed and was relieved when he changed the subject and became lighthearted again. They joked and laughed together for an hour, but when the subject drifted to their high school days, Michael became serious again, making a reference to his rebellious teenage years.

"Were you really that rebellious, Michael? The more I get to know you the more that wild image just doesn't fit the person I know as Michael Meredith."

"Claire, let's just say that if any child of mine ever gives me as much trouble as I gave Mom and Dad, I'll . . . I'll . . . I'm not sure *what* I'll do."

Claire thought perhaps he was trying to make light of the subject, but one glance at his face told her that he was very serious, even emotional. "I started drinking my sophomore year in high school," he went on hesitantly, "and within a few months I was running around with the 'druggies.' It's a miracle I didn't get killed—or kill somebody—while I was doing drugs. Even though I don't actually remember it because I was so strung out most of the time, my friends told me that I could be pretty mean. I guess I punched a couple of guys out for no good reason."

"Why?" she ventured. "The whole rebellion, I mean. Was it just to fit in, or do you think you were having some sort of identity crisis?"

"Probably a little of both. I just felt so rejected, Claire. By everyone. Even as much as Mom and Dad loved me—and I see now how very much they *did* love me—but back then all I could see was that they couldn't possibly love me as much as they loved their 'real' kids. I didn't like myself a whole lot. I know the drugs were partly just to escape that. I don't have much memory about things that happened while I was on drugs. Maybe that was the point—to just forget everything for a while."

"I sometimes wonder what kept *me* away from all that," Claire said. "I guess I was in my own little world of denial, so maybe I didn't need drugs or alcohol to 'forget.' I never thought that much about it when I was growing up. I think maybe we all take the family we get for granted . . . and assume that everyone else's family is like our own. But I know now that I grew up in a very—well, *strange* family. I suppose we were what nowadays they would call a dysfunctional family," she said with a wry smile. "It was Nana who helped life finally make sense to me. I would never have done anything to disappoint her."

"Grandparents. What a gift from God," he said with awe in his voice. "It was my grandparents who helped me to finally realize that I was worthy of having *anyone* love me. I remember my grandpa came and got me at a party one night. I was so drunk I couldn't even walk, but he carried me to the car and put me to bed that night. And believe me, that was no small task. I was almost as big as I am now, and Grandpa probably didn't weigh a hundred and fifty pounds soaking wet. I remember he sat on the side of my bed and prayed for me. I could just cry when I think about that, Claire. That he would love me that much, that he would be so . . . so patient and compassionate toward the jerk that I was back then." Michael shook his head in apparent disgust at the memory.

Claire sat in silence, waiting for him to go on.

"Claire, my childhood was not a very pretty picture. A lot of it was spent in the inner city of St. Louis. When I look back, I truly wonder how some of the homes I lived in were ever approved to take in foster children. Oh, sure, there were some good ones. But even though I'm sure I've suppressed a lot of the memories, I do remember being beaten until I was bruised. And being locked in a room without food or water. I think one of the things that hurt the most . . ." He had been recounting his story rather matter-of-factly, as though he had told it many times before, but now he swallowed hard and his voice rose as though his disbelief was fresh again. "I was called some of the vilest names imaginable. I think that was the hardest, being ridiculed for things I . . . I didn't even know that I'd done! But for some reason, I believed the things they said. I truly thought I was worthless and lazy and whatever else they called me. In one place the other kids in the family were fed at the table, and I was allowed whatever might be left over. It seems impossible when I think about it that such things could go on here in America. But I was there, Claire. It happens. It happened to me. . . ."

His voice had dropped to a whisper, and Claire sat spellbound, horrified by the things he was telling her, not knowing quite how to respond.

"Anyway," he continued with an obvious attempt to lighten the mood, "it took me a while to believe it, but Mom and Dad were different. I'd been rejected so many times it was hard to trust anyone. But they weren't giving up on me no matter what. It seemed like every time I did some stupid, hateful thing, they just loved me all the more. And believe me, I put them to the test. Oh, they disciplined me, too, but it was their love that finally won me over. I finally came to realize that the God to whom they had entrusted me was real, and that He loved me enough to die for me."

His voice was ragged, but he cleared his throat and continued. "Claire, I don't have any way to prove it, but I know without a doubt, that a miracle—a *real* miracle—happened when God's love was able to break through all the armor I had put on. I can still remember the very minute it happened."

Claire didn't want to spoil the beauty of his testimony with words, so she simply reached out and touched his arm, encouraging him to go on.

"It was during Christmas, my senior year in high school," he said, gazing into the smoldering fire, remembering. "We were all sitting around the living room opening presents. Grandma and Grandpa were there, the whole family together. And all of a sudden, I could *feel* the love. I could just feel that I *belonged* to these people. I hadn't even known what that felt like before—to belong. But somehow I recognized it immediately."

Michael had been staring into the fading embers as he spoke, but now he turned and looked at her. "I guess it doesn't sound like such a big deal, but it changed my life. Not instantly, of course. It was a rough year of disentangling myself from a lot of bad friendships and situations. But if I ever, ever doubt God's hand on my life, all I have to do is look back to that one moment and I'm blessed and reassured all over again."

She just looked into his eyes, enthralled with his story.

"You know," he went on, "statistically I should be in prison or strung out on drugs . . . or dead. I know I still carry some scars, Claire, from all the rejection of my childhood—those first years without any real guidance or any *love*. But I consider myself a walking miracle. Wounded maybe, but a miracle nonetheless."

"Oh, Michael, you don't have to convince me. Your life is the proof. *You* are the proof. I can scarcely believe that the little boy you keep talking about is the same man who's sitting beside me tonight telling me this story. It *had* to be a miracle."

He reached for her hand and took it between his large, warm hands. "Thank you for understanding, Claire. You don't know how much that means to me."

He squeezed her hand and leaned across the sofa and kissed her gently. A thrill went through her and she shivered involuntarily, wondering at these feelings that were so new to her.

He stood up. "It's getting late, Claire, and we both have to work tomorrow. I'd better get out of here," he said quietly. He reached again for her hand and pulled her up beside him. "This was a wonderful evening. It's good to be back."

The smile he gave her melted her heart, and in a joyful daze, she went to the closet for his coat. Remembering the pie she'd wrapped for him to take home, she went to the kitchen for it.

Back in the living room, he put on his coat in silence, but in the dim light of the entryway, their eyes locked and he took her by the shoulders and kissed her again, his lips soft and warm on hers. Then he took the still-warm package from her hands and was gone.

❧ ❧ ❧ ❧

At the office the following day, Michael told Vera about his encounter with Gerald Stoddard in Joplin.

She expressed surprise that Stoddard was doing consulting work. "I understood that he had retired."

"Apparently not." Without mentioning Stoddard's accusations about Riverview's board of directors, Michael relayed the former administrator's comments about Cynthia Harper. "Do *you* see Harper as strange?" he asked.

Vera sighed heavily and seemed hesitant to answer, then plunged in, prefacing her remarks with, "The last thing I want to do is spread gossip, Michael. And I truly hope I'm not imposing my own prejudices on this, but . . ."

He waited.

"What do you know about Cynthia Harper?" she finally blurted out.

"I'm not sure what you mean."

"Well, there's certainly no law against being . . . well, different. But if you ever spent much time around her, I think you'd find that she holds some rather strange ideas about life."

An alarm went off in his head as he heard Vera echo Stoddard's comments almost verbatim. "Can you give me an example?" he asked, struggling to keep the edge from his voice.

"That's just it. It's nothing I can really put my finger on. She's just . . . very different." She thought for a moment. "This might sound silly—and really, it has nothing whatsoever to do with her nursing skills—but for instance, she doesn't believe in banks."

He looked at her askance. "Banks? You mean as in First National?"

"Yes. She cashes her paycheck at the grocery store and pays for everything with cash."

"She told you that?"

"It's common knowledge."

He shrugged. "That *is* rather unusual. But then, a lot of people don't trust banks. Most just don't go so far as to act on their distrust. So do you think she has a mattress stuffed with cash at home?" he asked, attempting to inject some levity into the conversation, though inwardly he was disturbed that Vera seemed to be confirming Stoddard's assessment of Cynthia Harper.

Vera didn't smile. "I know that must sound petty and irrelevant to you, Michael. But it's a lot of little things like that which make me wonder." She threw up her hands in frustration. "I admit I am operating almost solely on intuition or . . . whatever you want to call it. But I can't help—"

"No, Vera," he interrupted, sorry he had made light of her comments. "I trust your judgment. You couldn't have held this position for as long as you have if you weren't a good judge of character. But you know as well as I do that we can't very well let an employee go on the basis of somebody's intuition."

"I know. I probably should never have even brought it up. You're right, it's not relevant." Again Vera hesitated.

"What is it, Vera? Please speak freely."

She sighed and plunged in. "This will probably sound like sour grapes, but when Cynthia applied for this job several years ago, Gerald hired her against my recommendation. At the time, I just did not feel she had the stability nursing requires. She was newly widowed then and, in my opinion, seemed not to be handling her grief well. And frankly, her references from hospice tended to back up my judgment."

"Why do you think Stoddard was so insistent on hiring Cynthia?" He didn't mean to bait Vera, but he was curious.

"Well, as long as we're being very frank, Michael, I'll just tell you that I've always thought it was a bit of a power play. Gerald tended to enjoy throwing his weight around. And I think you could find more than one employee here who would back me up on that." Vera shook her head scornfully, remembering. "He didn't take kindly to being disagreed with, and I was pretty adamant in expressing my reservations about hiring Cynthia. It was a very unpleasant scene."

Her answer surprised him. Michael thought for a minute. Should he tell her about Stoddard's implication of the board? He felt strongly that he could trust his director of nursing, but he was hesitant to draw her needlessly into the controversy.

Finally he asked, "Vera, just how strong are your feelings about this whole situation?" He took a deep breath, feeling as if he were about to walk through a door through which he might never return. "Does this have any reflection on the situation that made you suspicious in the first place, Vera? On Frederick Halloran's death? If there's a possibility we are talking neglect or foul play, or if you believe there might have been something suspicious about Frederick Halloran's death after all, I need to know why."

Vera rubbed her hands together, her distress obvious. "I don't know, Michael. I have nothing concrete to go on whatsoever. It was a gut feeling. Maybe I was wrong to even question things. I can't deny that Cynthia has turned out to be a very capable nurse. She is extremely compassionate. And very efficient. I can't fault her nursing skills at all. And that *is* what she was hired to do here."

"That's a good point," he conceded.

He told her then of Stoddard's claim that he had been pressured by the board to hire Harper against Vera's objections.

"I had no idea Cynthia was a niece of Nita Dalhardt," she said.

"She's never mentioned it. I guess I was so angry with Gerald for what I thought was another instance of throwing his weight around that I didn't think about any other possibilities. I never dreamed that he might be getting pressure from the board. It just doesn't make sense. None of this does. I know most of the board members personally, Michael. Maybe I'm too naive, but I simply can't believe they could be bought like that."

"Well," Michael told her, "I honestly can't put much stock in anything Stoddard said that day. He was far from sober."

Vera raised her eyebrows in surprise. "Gerald was drunk? Are you sure? That doesn't sound like him, Michael. I admit I didn't care much for the man, but he was always pretty straight and narrow."

Michael assured her that there was no doubt that Stoddard had been intoxicated that night.

Vera shook her head in disbelief, but she agreed with Michael that Stoddard wouldn't have had any reason to make up such a story. But even if the things Stoddard had said *were* true, it didn't negate the fact that Cynthia Harper had turned out to be a capable and caring nurse. The alleged incident with the board had not happened on Michael's watch. The monies for the senior center had come through on schedule, and *if* there had been strings attached to the donation, Cynthia Harper had apparently upheld her end of the bargain. There seemed to be no reason to dredge up the past. And for that, Michael was grateful.

He stood and turned toward the door. "I almost hate to ask, but did anything happen around here while we were gone that I should know about?"

"Nothing earth-shattering. It looks like we're starting our winter plague of pneumonia. Helga Schultz on North died Sunday morning, and they took Ben Watson to the hospital last night with the same thing. I doubt he'll be coming back."

"I'll be glad when spring gets here," he sighed.

"You and me both."

# Thirteen

$C$laire went through the next week in a kind of stupor. While teaching long division in the morning, and mindlessly reading a book aloud to her class late in the afternoon, she relived the evening with Michael and every word of their conversation over and over again.

She didn't dare voice it, but she thought perhaps she was in love. Michael Meredith was becoming very dear and special to her. And she felt certain that he was beginning to feel the same about her.

"Oh, thank you, Lord. *Thank you*," she whispered into the silence of her car on the way home that night. A veil of wet snowflakes had begun to cloak the streets. Ordinarily, Claire would have been depressed at the deepening of winter. But now the heavy flakes seemed to dance with a joy that matched her own.

So this was how it felt to fall in love, to have someone in your life who was the most special person on earth—and to whom *you* were most special. Oh, what a wonderful idea romance was! The thought had sounded sappy to her before, but suddenly she understood how love prompted symphonies to be composed and poetry to be written.

She and Michael talked on the phone every night that week, sharing the simplest events of their days, laughing together over almost nothing, taking joy in the very sound of each other's voice.

Saturday morning, the first day of March, the phone woke her before nine o'clock. She rolled over and groped on the nightstand beside her bed. Finally, she found the phone and lifted the receiver.

"Hello," she croaked.

"Hey, sleepyhead. Wake up."

"Aargh!" she groaned, blinking against the glare of sun filtering through the curtains at her bedroom window. "What time is it anyway?" she asked sleepily.

"Time to get up."

"Michael, don't you know it's Saturday?" she whined.

"Look out the window."

"What?"

"Get your lazy bones out of bed and look out the window."

She sat up in bed, rubbed the sleep from her eyes, and parted the curtains from the window by her bed. The ground outside her window was thick with snow, and a few gentle flakes were still floating down. "Wow!" she whispered into the phone.

"Beautiful, isn't it?"

"Oh, it is. But it's almost spring!"

"Apparently not," he laughed. "Now wake up. I'll be over to pick you up in forty-five minutes, so don't you dare go back to sleep."

Silence.

"Do you hear me, Claire? I'm not kidding. Claire?"

His boyish tone was hard to resist. "Okay, okay," she giggled, throwing back the quilts. "I'm up."

"Good girl." And he hung up on her.

By the time she heard his truck pull into the driveway, she was dressed in jeans and a thick turtleneck, her hair pulled back in a low ponytail. A fresh pot of coffee perfumed the kitchen. On tiptoe, she peeked out through the fanlight window in the front door and watched him jump out of the pickup and go back to steady an old-fashioned wooden sled that was propped in the back of the pickup.

She ran out on the porch before he could ring the bell.

"Hi! Are we going sledding?"

"That's the plan," he said, rubbing the top of her head with his knuckles as though she were one of his little nieces.

She reached up and reciprocated, making him laugh and duck out of reach.

"There's a great hill over in the band shell park," he told her.

"Sounds like fun. Do you want some coffee first? It's already made."

"Do you have a thermos?"

She nodded.

"We could take it with us. It might be nice to have something hot to drink later on at the park."

"Good idea," she agreed. "I'll go get it ready. Have you had breakfast?"

He shook his head. "I'm not really a breakfast person. You?"

"I had a piece of toast. That'll get me through."

"Maybe we can go out for pancakes later on."

"Sounds great."

The park was spread with a powdery white quilt of snow feather-stitched with the footprints of early sledders who already crowded the slope. Claire followed Michael to the top of the rise and plopped cross-legged on the front of the sled.

With hands on her shoulders he leaned above her and yelled over the din of shouts and laughter. "Ready?"

"Ready!"

With a grunt he gave the sled a shove and hopped on behind her, his long legs straddling her, his feet on the steering mechanism at the front of the sled. Claire had not been on a sled since she was a child, and the exhilaration of the ride caught her by surprise. She squealed and screamed as Michael steered clear of a huge dog chasing behind its master's sled. He leaned heavily to the left, taking Claire with him as they tipped precariously on one runner. The sled finally righted itself midway down the slope.

At the bottom of the hill stood a thick stand of fir trees, each needled branch drooping under a heavy load of fresh snow. Their sled had picked up speed and Claire saw that they were heading swiftly for the hedge of evergreens.

"Michael!" she screamed. "Michael Meredith, stop this sled this minute!"

"I can't find the brakes!" he shouted back, laughing.

As the hill leveled out, the sled slowed to a coast, but not before they had crashed underneath the lowest snow-draped branches of a huge fir. Like a slingshot, the branches sprang back releasing their ammunition of wet snow.

Claire screamed again as the cold powder fell on her head. Michael was not immune to the onslaught, either. Jumping off the sled and stomping on the ground in an effort to shake off the snow, Claire caught a glimpse of him through wet eyelashes. Snow clung in wet clumps to his head, giving him the very undistinguished look of a blue-jeaned English courtier, complete with powdered wig.

She collapsed on the ground in laughter while he bent at the waist and tried to dust the wet stuff out of his hair.

"Very funny," he said, smiling down at her as she lay on the ground, trying to catch her breath between giggles.

He pounced on her then and force-fed her a snowball. Squealing, she struggled to her feet and fled across the field to the protection of the band shell that towered at one end of the park. He followed in hot pursuit, but when she reached the shelter and dared to look behind her, she saw that he had taken a detour to his truck.

She climbed up on the low stage and, after dusting the remaining snow off her clothing, huddled against the wall of the old band shell. The plastered walls were cracked and the sky blue paint was peeling off in large patches. As far as Claire knew, the bandstand had not been used for years by anyone other than starstruck little girls pretending to be movie stars on summer afternoons. Now it provided shelter from the wind and dry ground on which to sit.

A few minutes later, Michael strode toward her bearing an old wool army blanket, the thermos of coffee, and two styrofoam cups.

"A peace offering," he intoned with a gleam in his eye. He poured a cup of the amber liquid and held it out to her.

The steam rose invitingly in the brisk air. She held the cup close to her lips, letting its warmth thaw her hands and face before she took a sip.

Michael then spread the blanket out on the concrete floor, and they sat in amiable silence, leaning against the back of the band shell. The pale blue cave of the bandstand reflected the sunlight and warmed their faces.

"Mmm," Claire sighed lazily as she drained her second cup of coffee. "I think I could almost fall asleep here." Yawning, she gave him a sardonic sidewise glance and added, "*Somebody*—not to mention any names—got me up just a tad bit too early this morning."

"Come here," he said, smiling and holding out an arm for her to snuggle against.

She scooted along the wall until she was in the circle of his arm and leaned her head on his shoulder. This was where she belonged— by his side.

They sat that way for a long time, laughing over the antics of sledders in the distance, talking quietly, enjoying each other's company.

Finally Michael looked at his watch. "Are you hungry? It's almost two o'clock!"

"No wonder my stomach is growling!"

"Still want pancakes?"

"Sure. Sounds great."

He pulled her to her feet and they walked arm in arm to the truck.

❧   ❧   ❧   ❧

After a leisurely afternoon "breakfast" at a popular truck stop on the highway just outside town, Michael talked Claire into another round of sledding. Back at the park—after Claire made him cross his heart and hope to die that they would *not* run into the snow-capped evergreens again—they spent the afternoon on the hill sledding.

A group of Claire's third-graders showed up late in the day, and she introduced them to "Mr. Meredith."

Hands on hips, little Brianne Sizemore and Mimi Harrold watched Michael haul Claire up by the hands after a spill. Brianne eyed them suspiciously. "Are you guys married?"

Claire blushed and saw Michael's head cocked in amusement, waiting to see how she would answer.

"No, Brianne, we're just good friends," she said with what she hoped was teacherly dignity.

The children attached themselves to Claire and Michael for the remainder of the afternoon, and she was surprised to see his winning way with her students. She watched with amusement as Brianne stared at Michael with a lovesick expression on her pudgy face. And she laughed uproariously when a couple of the young boys piloted a sled with Michael aboard into the same trees he had steered her under that morning.

By the end of the afternoon they were soaked to their skin, hungry, and exhausted. But Claire decided it had been the most wonderful day of her life.

The children began to straggle home for supper, and she and Michael loaded the sled into the bed of the pickup and walked back to the band shell, neither wanting the day to be over.

They sat down on the floor of the stage where they had sat that morning, and Michael put his arm around her.

"Are you warm enough? Maybe I should get you home so you can get into some dry clothes."

She was cold, but not cold enough to risk ending their day together. She shook her head and snuggled closer. "I'm fine . . . really."

They began to talk quietly, daring to voice the new emotions they both were feeling.

"Maybe it's because you had a lonely childhood, too," he told her, "but I . . . I've never known anyone who seemed to understand the hurts of my past the way you do, Claire. And to understand without pitying me. I feel like I've known you forever. I don't know why that is, but I like it. I've never *wanted* anyone to know me so well before. But with you, I find myself wanting to tell you everything. I want to trust you with all my secrets."

She gave him a little smile and, unexpectedly, her eyes filled with tears.

"Are you crying?" He sounded amused.

She shrugged, embarrassed. "I can't help it. Oh, Michael, I feel the same way about you. What . . . what does that mean?"

He smiled and swiped at a tear on her cheek with a gloved finger. "I have a couple ideas."

"Tell me," she risked.

He pulled her closer and bent to look into her eyes. "Claire, for a long time now, I've been praying that God would put someone in my life. Someone who would understand what my life has been and love me anyway. Someone I could love who would love me unconditionally in return. Maybe it's too soon to be saying this, but I'm beginning to believe you are the answer to those prayers, Claire. And I'll tell you what else . . ."

The mischievous close-mouthed grin that she was beginning to know so well played on his lips, and she waited in suspense for him to finish his sentence.

"I *really* underestimated God," he finally said, looking her over appreciatively and breaking into a wide smile.

She laughed with joy at the compliment. "Oh, Michael. I hope you're right. I hope this was meant to be."

He took her face in his hands and looked into her eyes. His voice was low and earnest as he told her, "I think I just might be in love with you, Claire Anderson."

"Michael, I . . . I think I'm falling in love with you, too."

Her heart soared with joy as he held her close to him, kissing her hair, tenderly tracing the contours of her face with one slender finger.

In a way, she hadn't been completely honest with him. She didn't just *think* she loved him. She knew it. Knew it now as certainly as she had ever known anything in her life.

He tightened his arm around her. "I could get used to this, Claire."

"This has been such a great day, Michael. I feel like I'm dreaming. It . . . it almost scares me." He pulled back to look at her face, and she read surprise in his expression.

"Why does it scare you?"

"I don't know. It's just that . . . Well, I wonder if maybe my parents felt this happy together at one time in their lives. And look how that turned out."

She told him then of her fears that she might somehow be susceptible to the depression that had plagued her mother.

He sympathized, but he told her, "You're forgetting one important thing, Claire. From what you've told me, your parents didn't have a strong faith to get them through the tough parts."

Not wanting to spoil the day with too-serious talk, she lightly said, "You're right, of course. Come to think of it, are you *ever* wrong, Mr. Meredith?"

"Well, let's see. I think there was one time back in 1985. . . ."

She punched him playfully in the chest. They wrestled affectionately and he pulled her to her feet and led her to the front of the stage where the last patch of winter sunlight warmed the concrete. They plopped down and sat there together dangling their feet over the edge.

"No, I'm serious, Michael," she said after a while. "You seem to . . . I don't know . . . you seem to have it all together. For everything you've been through, you seem so sure about life now. I don't know. Maybe it's *because* of all you've been through?"

"Claire," he said with mock sternness. "I do *not* have it all together. I have insecurities, and I have doubts. It scares me a little for you to think that I don't. I am human, after all. You'll eventually be disappointed if that's what you think about me." His voice had lost its teasing timbre and she heard the seriousness there now.

"Oh, I know you're not *perfect*, Michael, but I envy your optimism, your faith that everything will always turn out right in the end."

"Well, for me it has, Claire. But it was a long time coming. I don't want to sound like a martyr, but I went through a lot of agony to get where I am today. Believe me, it was no picnic being tossed from home to home, wondering if this would be the one, if these would be the people who would finally *want* me."

"Well," she said too lightly, "at least you always had a family along the way."

He stiffened and his expression changed abruptly.

"Michael, I'm so sorry. I don't know what made me say that. I . . ." She was close to tears, truly not knowing what had possessed her to make such an insensitive remark.

For the first time in many weeks, the darkness clouded his face again. And seeing it, knowing she was the cause, a chill not borne of the winter air ran down her back. He narrowed his eyes and almost glared at her. And when he spoke, the coldness in his voice frightened her.

"You don't know what it was like, Claire, to be shuttled from house to house, family to family. Never knowing how long I'd be there, knowing that I wasn't really a part of *any* family."

He took a deep breath. "I've never told you this, Claire. I've . . . I've wanted to forget it myself. But . . . ."

He paused and looked at her, his voice softening a bit. "I don't want there to be any secrets between us, Claire. I want you to know everything about me—even the hard stuff."

"What, Michael? What is it?" She felt deeply ashamed of her flippant remark earlier. If only she could take it back. What other horrors could this man she loved have suffered? He had shared so many hurtful things from his childhood with her. What other dark secrets haunted him? She was truly frightened now, afraid to hear what he might tell her. Yet she was more afraid *not* to know.

"Tell me, Michael," she repeated, putting a hand gently on his back, coaxing him as she would one of her reticent third-graders.

He stared straight ahead and his voice came out in a low monotone that she had to strain to hear.

"Once . . . once, when I was seven or maybe eight—I'm not sure—a family in St. Louis adopted me. *Legally* adopted me. I was so excited, Claire, that I would finally belong somewhere . . . finally have someone to love me like a real son. It wasn't like I thought it would be, though. They didn't love me. I couldn't seem to do anything right. They even hated my name and forced me to go by a different one. The woman—the mother—seemed to hate the sight of me. I don't know why. I don't remember much else, but I knew that place would never be home—even before . . . before they sent me away. They didn't even tell me . . . not until the day SRS came to get me. They just packed my bags and stuffed me in the car and sent me back where I came from."

Her mind registered that Michael's cheeks were wet, and a strange, incongruous thought crossed her mind. *What if the tears freeze on his face?* It was a thought designed to deny the dawning reality of what she had just heard him say. Claire felt separated from the scene suddenly, as though she watched him from someplace above. And though he refused to look at her, seemingly attempting to hide his tears, he couldn't hide his heaving shoulders or the guttural sob that escaped his throat.

"I was there maybe a year and then they sent me away. Just like all the others. I didn't think you could do that. I didn't think you could adopt a kid and then just . . . just throw him away," he spat out in a voice she didn't recognize. Now he turned to look full into her face. "But they did it. They sent me away, Claire. I was so ashamed, as though I had done something terrible. I still feel it sometimes. . . ." He looked away, unable to go on.

Claire felt dizzy, as though someone had cut off her oxygen supply. Shapes and colors swirled before her like colorful shards in a kaleidoscope: the flat geometric shapes of the playground equipment, yellow-brown rectangles of grass where picnic tables had intercepted the snow, the blue arc of the band shell against a graying sky—all shifting and changing in front of her eyes.

She longed to reach out to him, longed to soothe this deepest pain of his past. But as the awful truth washed over her, she was paralyzed, powerless to comfort him.

Her voice finally came as through a tunnel, sounding hollow in her own ears. "Oh, Michael—oh, dear God . . . Michael . . . no! No! It . . . it can't be!"

And with terrible clarity, Claire heard her brother's defiant voice, a wrenching echo from her childhood. "My name is not Joseph! Stop calling me that! My name is Michael. It's Michael . . . do you hear me? *My name is Michael.*"

She knew then—knew with certainty—that Michael Meredith *was* Joseph Anderson. The man she had grown to love with the deepest part of her heart was a ghost from her past. No, more than a ghost:

the very incarnation of the terrible secret that had haunted her.

She slid off the stage and stumbled across the park toward the street. The late afternoon sun on the band shell, the warm glow of their growing love, the shelter of Michael's arms—all evaporated, and she was overtaken by a biting cold that originated in her very bones.

She ran blindly, clapping mittened hands over her ears as his confused questions rang after her.

"Claire, wait! Come back. What's wrong? What. . . ?"

His cries were lost to the chill March air.

# Fourteen

Claire ran blindly in the direction of her house. Avoiding the main streets, she cut through alleys and side streets, praying she wouldn't meet anyone. The evening shadows fell quickly, and by the time she reached her street, the sky was black with night. Her heart beat painfully in her ears, making her face feel swollen and hot. Some tiny, sane part of her knew she was running from a truth so awful that she wasn't ready to hear it yet. *Couldn't* hear it yet.

But that truth followed her relentlessly, dogging her until she collapsed on the snowy lawn in front of her house. There, on her knees, unable to get back to her feet, she let the sobs come. They rose from deep within her, wracking her body with soundless, painful shudders.

Finally, she came to her senses enough to know that she would freeze if she remained outside. She struggled slowly to her feet and staggered to the door, fumbling with the key in the lock. Inside, she shed her wet coat and boots, leaving them in a soggy heap in front of the door.

She went to the bathroom and hung over the sink, afraid she might be sick. But her stomach finally settled and she splashed warm water on her face and examined herself in the mirror. Her eyes were swollen and red, but her face did not betray the truth she half expected to be painted there like some obscene graffiti.

Like a dream, a disjointed scene from her childhood taunted her— a memory long forgotten or maybe never recalled until this night.

She saw her father's too-bright smile and heard him telling her about the brother who would soon come to live with them.

"And we're going to name him Joseph," Daddy was saying, "Joseph Matthew Anderson."

"He's eight years old and he doesn't have a name yet?" She was incredulous.

Her parents both laughed nervously.

"No, no, darling," her father said. "Of course he has . . . had a name. But we . . . we wanted him to have a new name. A new name to go with his new life. It will be our first gift to him."

"And don't you think Joseph is a beautiful name?" her mother asked.

She only nodded. She didn't think she would like it very much if someone took her name away and gave her a new one. Sometimes when she played house with her best friend, Gretchen, they gave each other pretend names. Claire always became Veronica. It was a beautiful name—elegant and foreign, prettier than Claire and infinitely more grown up than Kitty. But that was pretend. Claire didn't especially like either of her names, but they were as much a part of her as her strawberry blond, naturally curly hair or her hazel eyes. She wasn't sure she would like it if someone chose a new name for her without even asking.

In her mind's eye, Claire saw the little girl she had been, reliving again the confusion and the turmoil of that time. Like a drowning swimmer, she struggled to come to the surface of the present. And then, as though she had broken through the murky water and into the light, the truth began to assemble itself in her mind. Michael Meredith was the Joseph of her past. *I've fallen in love with a man who once, long ago, was my brother!*

All the things this truth implied circled her mind in a frenzy, waiting to be sorted out and comprehended.

The house was cold and Claire began to tremble from the frigid air and the icy truth she had just learned. Like an automaton she threw a log on the grate and lit some kindling. She sunk to the floor in front of the fireplace, her back against the sofa, and hugged a plump cushion to her chest to try to ease her trembling. The flames crackled and spat with a dissonant absence of rhythm that mirrored her confusion.

*I knew him before!* No wonder the photograph in the newspaper had looked familiar! No wonder the stark sadness in his eyes had made her vaguely uncomfortable in the beginning. *I knew him before!*

And poor Michael. It was *her* parents, *her* family who had done this to him. They had caused him this awful pain. *She* was partly responsible for Michael's agony. How could he ever forgive them, forgive her? And why would he want to? She was nothing to him—nothing more than the embodiment of a painful memory, of a hurtful past. She was a hated sister in a family who had abandoned him like so many others. A sister whose lie had robbed him once more of the chance to belong.

A frightening thought came to her. *I'll have to tell him.* Already she had rejected him, running out on him as she had at the park. He would not know why she had fled, would possibly think that she hadn't been able to accept him once she knew his shameful secret. He had made himself utterly vulnerable to her, and she might as well have slapped him in the face.

Her head pounded with guilt and regret and confusion.

The telephone rang again and again before it registered with her. Knowing it would be him, she picked up the receiver, her hands shaking.

"Claire? What . . . what happened? Are you all right?"

She could hear the alarm in his voice, knew he feared her further rejection.

"Oh, Michael." She couldn't say more for the tears that threatened to choke her words.

"Claire, what is the matter? What is it? Please, tell me."

She heard the garbled sounds that came from her own throat and knew that they were unintelligible, yet she was powerless to emit one syllable that made any sense.

"I'm coming over, Claire." The line went dead.

She sat like a statue at the desk in the dining room, her hand still on the phone, her eyes unfocused and glazed over, waiting for him.

A few minutes later he let himself in through the unlocked front door.

"Claire!" he called into the living room, urgency in his voice. "Claire!"

"I'm here," she squeaked.

He came to where she was sitting, took one look at her, and pulled her into his embrace.

"Claire, what is it? I drove all over town looking for you. Where did you go? What happened? You have to tell me. I . . . I don't care what it is. I can take it."

She felt her strength returning at his touch, at the sound of his voice, and felt compelled to give her burden to him, to be strong enough to get this over with, to finish it.

"Michael, I can't believe this. You're . . . you're Joseph!" she finally spat out.

"What?" He looked as though he truly did not understand.

Choked with remorse, she told him what she knew. "The family who gave you up—the family in St. Louis—Michael, it was mine! It was us . . . my mother and father and me! We're the ones who . . . Don't you understand? Don't you remember? You are Joseph," she repeated in a dead whisper, trying to make him comprehend.

She then saw recognition dawn in his eyes, and as the news soaked in, revelation registered on his whole countenance.

"You're . . . you're *Kitty* Anderson?" he choked out, using the name he had known her by as a child.

She nodded miserably and broke down, bitter tears her only reply.

"Oh, dear God," he said, incredulous. "I don't believe it. . . ."

He reached out and tipped her chin toward the light of the desk lamp. But there was no tenderness in his touch, and she knew that he was trying to find the face of the little girl she had been. The girl who had betrayed him.

"I don't remember, Claire. I don't remember what she . . . what *you* looked like. Are you sure? Are you sure about this?"

"Of course I'm sure," she spat at him. "Of course I am. Who else could know this? What else could it be?" She sank back into the chair at the desk. "And I . . . I *do* remember you," she told him. "I thought you were familiar the first time I met you . . . even before, when I saw your picture in the paper."

"Then . . . then you . . . we are brother and sister?"

"Oh, Michael!" She felt sick to her stomach.

"Claire, this is too much. This is going to take some time. . . ." He touched her shoulder tentatively, woodenly, and then took a step backward. All the comfort and rightness they had known in each other's touch was gone now, evaporated in the wake of their discovery.

"I have to go now. We have a lot to think about. I have to sort this out, Claire."

"What are you feeling, Michael?" she pleaded.

"I don't know what to feel." The warmth had gone out of his voice. "I need to go now. I need some time to . . . to . . ."

He moved toward the door, his sentence hanging unfinished in the air. She had to fight the urge to run after him, to beg him to stay, to hold him in her arms, to find the tenderness they had known with each other only hours ago, to pretend this never happened.

At the doorway he turned and gave her a sad smile. "Good-bye, Claire."

He didn't say, "I'll call you." He didn't say, "We'll get through this together." Just "good-bye." And she wondered if it was good-bye forever.

# Fifteen

*C*laire sat in front of the fire through the remainder of the night. She had not eaten since their feast of pancakes that afternoon, and she was aware of a gnawing hunger in her belly. But she couldn't find the strength to get up and fix herself something to eat. As she watched the clock on the bookcase move slowly toward dawn, she wondered how she would ever get through the coming day.

Finally, with a desperate prayer, she forced herself to get off the sofa and fill the bathtub. She eased into the scalding water and tried to wash away the tears and the sorrow of the day. She remembered thinking only hours ago that this day was the most wonderful of her life. Now she was certain it was the darkest.

She shampooed her hair and rinsed it under the shower. Then she stepped out of the tub and wrapped herself in a thick towel.

She went into her bedroom and slipped into a nightgown. Crawling under the blankets of the unmade bed, she remembered how happily she had been awakened from there by Michael's phone call not twenty-four hours ago. Numb of any emotion, she pulled the blankets up around her damp head and burrowed into the pillow.

The next awareness she had was of the alarm clock blaring on her bedside table. She reached over and turned it off, startled to see that it was ten o'clock. In a moment of panic she threw back the covers, thinking she had overslept on a school day. Feeling disoriented, she rubbed her forehead trying to remember what day it was. Slowly it dawned on her that it was Sunday.

She crawled back into bed, knowing she couldn't face anyone this morning. She lay there reliving the events of the day before, unable even to shed tears for all she felt she had lost in that one awful moment of revelation. With a heavy feeling of hopelessness, she drifted back to sleep.

Claire slept most of the day, ignoring the telephone, barely nibbling at a few crackers and some cheese.

Late in the afternoon, she got up and went to the living room to sit in front of the fire. Staring blindly across the room, her eyes suddenly focused on the oak bookcase she had bought. There on the top shelf were two thin photo albums—the only record her parents had left her of her early life. Claire seldom opened the albums because the photographs brought back too many difficult memories. But it dawned on her now that these pages might hold some hint of the connection she had to Michael.

Lifting the windowed door and taking the unwieldy books from the shelf, Claire carried them to the dining room table and began to leaf through the yellowed pages.

There were her parents on their wedding day, stiff and formal, posing for the camera. A much younger Nana and Claire's grandfather, who had died before she was born, smiled beside a sleek forties model automobile. Claire looked carefully at each picture, but it soon became apparent that every vestige of the year Joseph Anderson had shared their home had been removed. It was as though—for them—he had never existed.

She paged back to a photograph of herself as a kindergartner, the age she was when Joseph had been with them. She searched the face of the little girl in the picture. She wore a pale blue dress and a shy smile. Claire ran her hand over the faded picture trying to remember the day. Her fingers detected a thickness of the paper, and she realized that the photo, which rested in the crease of the page, had been folded over. Carefully, she peeled it from the album, the brittle paper and dried glue coming away with it. She turned the picture over in her hand and unfolded it.

There he was standing beside her in front of the house on Madison Street. The glue had obliterated much of the image, but the face was there, faded but not distorted. It was Michael's face. The deep cleft in his chin, the dark hair curling around his ears, the steel gray eyes—smoldering even then—were unmistakable.

It tore at her heart to see the sadness in the little boy's eyes. She looked at the image of herself standing beside the boy she would come to love as a man, and she was struck again with amazement that they should ever have met again, let alone fallen in love.

Numb, she tucked the picture back in the page, replaced the album on the shelf, and went back to sit by the fire.

When evening finally came it was a relief. But when she crawled back into the rumpled bed, slumber eluded her. She lay on her back, staring wide-eyed into the dark shadows a waning moon cast on the high walls and ceiling of her bedroom.

Over and over she replayed her conversation with Michael, remembered the coldness that had crossed his face when he realized the truth. Oh, how deeply it had hurt her to feel his warmth for her depart. What must he be feeling toward her now? Surely he must feel betrayed and rejected. And who could blame him? And whom could *he* blame but her?

The deepest longing she had ever known gripped her, and she ached with a physical pain, wanting to hold him in her arms, to comfort him. She thought of the young Michael and the anguish he must have felt as he was rejected time after time. It was still difficult for her to incorporate the truth that she had *known* that young boy. In her mind, she carried two very different pictures of young Michael and young Joseph. She could not integrate the two, for in her mind the Michael she knew and loved was far removed from the sullen boy who had lived in her parents' house so long ago.

Renewed by the things she had learned last night, a bitter anger burned in her, an anger directed at her parents. How could they have allowed this? How could they have done this to Michael? *How could they have done this to me?*

In the deepest black of the night, in the most anguished throes of her turmoil, she suddenly realized she was needlessly bearing her agony alone. Ashamed, she tried to pray. Yet, not having the faintest inkling *how* she should pray, it seemed at first that her artless attempts were met with silence.

She began to weep great wracking sobs that shook her to the very core, and she found there was cleansing and release and a tentative peace in those tears—tears of prayer. Suddenly she knew she was not alone. There was a sweet solace in the knowledge that the same God whose grace could comfort her was infinitely able to comfort Michael as well. She prayed that it would be so.

She slept deeply for an hour before the alarm clock woke her to the reality of a Monday morning. For a brief moment she thought about calling Marjean and telling her that she couldn't come in today, but she knew she couldn't stay locked up in the house another minute. Yes, she needed time to try to make sense of all that had happened, to discern where she should go from here. But now she felt almost compelled to go to the school and make this day as normal as possible in the face of her horrible new knowledge.

She combed out her still-damp hair, not caring anymore whether it frizzed or tangled. She then tried to hide the dark circles under her eyes with makeup, which only seemed to make them more noticeable. She threw on a turtleneck and a long corduroy jumper, grateful for their warmth. She knew she should eat something, but a glance at the clock told her that she'd be late if she didn't leave the house that very minute.

She drove zombielike, following the familiar route without thought. When she walked into her classroom, she could scarcely remember how she had come to be there. Taking a deep breath, she shook her head to clear the cobwebs of confusion that clouded her mind. It would not be fair to the children to allow her mood to rob them of a sharp and alert teacher.

She prepared a table for a science experiment and greeted her students as they began to straggle in from the hallway. The roomful of third-graders provided a welcome distraction from the raw grief she had been feeling earlier, and she set about the business of being a teacher.

She almost broke down when Brianne Sizemore reminded her, "Hey, I remember! You were at the park! That man who's just your friend is nice."

Claire choked back the emotion that rose within her and replied with false cheer as an attempt to change the subject. "Yes, Brianne. It was a good day for sledding, wasn't it? Looks like we're going to have another day of sunshine today. Maybe we'll finally get to go outside for recess."

Later in the teacher's lunchroom, Becky Anderson did a double take when she saw Claire.

"Are you feeling okay, Claire?"

"Oh . . . I just didn't get much sleep last night." She attempted a smile.

"Ah-ha!" Becky said with a wicked grin. "Did that gorgeous man keep you out too late?" Claire had confided in Becky about her blossoming friendship with Michael.

From the corner of her eye, Claire could see that several other teachers were listening with interest to their conversation. With the slightest shake of her head and a narrowing of her eyes, Claire begged Becky not to pursue the topic. Her friend caught on immediately and changed the subject.

After school Becky appeared in the doorway of Claire's classroom. "Hey," she said sympathetically. "Do you want to talk about it?"

Claire bit her lip and shook her head.

"Is everything okay, Claire?" Becky pressed.

"Oh, Becky . . ." Claire's eyes brimmed with tears, and she swallowed hard, unable to go on.

Becky's face reflected her deep concern and she reached out and put a manicured hand on Claire's arm. "What is it? Claire, what's wrong?"

Her friend's sympathy brought on more tears and she could only shake her head and wave Becky away.

"Let's go to my house for a while," Becky said in her most motherly voice. "Randy is picking the boys up at daycare, and nobody will be home for an hour or so. Okay?"

Claire just nodded and followed Becky to the deserted teachers' lounge for their coats.

They drove the short distance to Becky's house in silence. Tricycles and forgotten mittens littered the Andersons' driveway, and inside, the kitchen bore similar evidence of the youngest occupants of the house.

Claire had been to Becky's house on several occasions, and she was struck again by the homey clutter that pervaded the decor.

"Please excuse this filthy house," Becky apologized.

The refrigerator was cluttered with childish art projects and fingerprinted with smudges of grape jam. The remains of breakfast were still on the table, and down the hallway Claire could see the rumpled, unmade bed in the master bedroom. The house wouldn't be featured in an upscale decorating magazine anytime soon, but Claire found it charming. This wasn't just a house, it was a *home*. And the warmth it exuded began to comfort Claire immediately.

"Do you want something to drink?"

"Maybe something hot. Thanks."

"Here, let me take your coat and then we can go into the living room where it's not quite such a pigsty."

Becky turned on the burner under the tea kettle and then ushered Claire into the large, cozy living room. Claire took the proffered seat on the sofa in front of the window. Becky sat down beside her.

"Talk to me, Claire."

"Becky, I don't even know where to begin."

"Is it Michael?"

"Yes. I . . . we made a terrible discovery Saturday."

Becky waited in silence for her to continue, but her curiosity was unmistakable.

"You know that I had . . . well, a rather lonely childhood?"

Becky nodded.

"Well, there was—there's always been this secret hanging over my head. I've never told anyone, Becky—not a soul—because it was something we just didn't talk about in my family." She paused, not sure how to go on. She had never even hinted to Becky about this part of her family's story.

"For heaven's sake, Claire. What is it?" Becky's curiosity finally became too much for her to contain.

"Oh, Becky, you won't believe this. Michael was . . . he was my brother."

"He *what*? Claire, you're not making any sense."

Claire hesitated a moment, then began to pour out the whole strange, terrible truth.

Becky was stunned. "This is just unbelievable! I mean, what are the chances? Never in a million years . . ." she stuttered, shaking her head in disbelief. Finally, she seemed to remember Claire's anguish, and her voice turned sympathetic. "Oh, Claire. What are you going to do? Do you . . . do you still love him?"

"I don't know what I feel for him now, Becky. It's like he's become two different people in my mind. Oh yes, I still love the Michael I knew before Saturday. I love him even more, if that's possible. But I don't know if that man even exists anymore. I keep getting Michael and Joseph all mixed up in my mind. I don't know how to separate them."

Then she voiced her greatest fear. "Oh, Becky, I'm so afraid he will hate me for this. How can I ever be anything to him but a reminder of the worst thing that ever happened to him? If I were in his shoes, I'm not sure I'd ever want to see me again. But, Becky, I don't want to lose him." She paused, then whispered again, "I don't want to lose him."

Becky put her arm around Claire and let her cry. After a while she slipped quietly into the kitchen and came back with two steaming mugs of tea. Claire took a sip and felt the hot liquid sear her throat and spread warmth throughout her body. She took a ragged breath and, wiping her eyes, looked over at Becky. "Thanks."

Becky put an arm around Claire's shoulder, and what she did next, Claire would never forget. Crying along with her friend, Becky began to pray aloud for her. No one—not even Nana—had ever prayed for Claire like this before. The act was all the more precious because it came at a time when Claire's prayers didn't seem able to reach the heavens themselves.

"Oh, dear God," Becky began, her voice echoing Claire's anguish, "Claire is hurting so badly, Lord. I don't even know how to begin to help her. But you do, Father. You know exactly the 'why' and the 'how' of this whole thing. Please, God, show her what you want her to do, how you want her to respond. Make it clear if she should go to Michael. And, please, be with Michael, too. He must be hurting as deeply as Claire is. I know how much you love them, God. Both of them. You're so much wiser than we are, Father. We trust you to give Claire the answers she needs."

Becky spoke naturally, as though God were sitting there in the room beside them. Claire marveled that her friend spoke to the God of the universe as though they were personal friends. She had never heard anyone pray aloud in such a casual conversational tone, and yet it seemed so very right. Claire raised a tear-stained face to her friend's glowing smile, and she felt such a sweet love for Becky. How strange that in the midst of the deepest grief of her life she could be learning about God's goodness, His intimate care for her.

She leaned over and gave her friend a hug. "Thank you, Becky. It's such a relief to talk to somebody about this. It's so good to have somebody praying for me when I can't seem to get through myself. You . . . you make it seem as though God is right here with us."

Becky laughed. "But He *is* right here with us, Claire. And I won't stop praying for you. I wish there was more I could do. I wish I knew what you were supposed to do. But I don't. All I *can* do is pray—and trust that the Lord will show you the answer."

"Just letting me talk it out helped more than you can know. Thank you so much."

Becky offered to drive Claire back to the school to get her car, but Claire told her she preferred to walk. "I need time to think," she said.

She left her friend's house and walked slowly back toward the school. Her path led her through modest neighborhoods where children played on lawns patched with melting snow. But she scarcely noticed her surroundings. As she walked, she thought over and over about Becky's prayer and the intimate relationship—it almost seemed to be a friendship—that Becky shared with God. It was a new understanding of God for Claire. And she realized with awe that true to His promises, God was revealing himself to her even in her deepest anguish.

That night at home she was again overwhelmed by sadness as she thought about Michael and the abrupt rift in what had seemed such a promising friendship and romance. But slowly, things were beginning to sort themselves out. Claire was starting to make this thing that had happened between her and Michael become real in her mind. Slowly, she was turning and separating the pieces of the puzzle so she could begin to fit them together in a way that made sense.

# Sixteen

*T*he week wore on, and with each day Michael didn't call, Claire's spirits floundered a little more. Still, she found comfort in learning to pray more freely, knowing now that God didn't expect fancy words or *Thee*'s and *Thou*'s. He simply desired a conversation with her. Slowly, she was learning to listen to God's side of the conversation—His Word. The Scriptures comforted her as they never had before. Passages that had once seemed inconsequential now became alive and full of meaning.

A curious solace in the whole ordeal was that since the disclosure of her past relationship to Michael, Claire had not had even one of the nightmares that had haunted her sleep before with such predictable frequency. Most nights she fell asleep with a prayer on her lips. She wondered fleetingly if the two were related.

Though her prayers did not seem to bring her any closer to an answer, it was a comfort to be able to confide her fears in One who truly understood and cared. If not for that, she would have drowned in her heartache.

᙮   ᙮   ᙮   ᙮

Since the confrontation with Michael, Claire had avoided calling Millie Overman, fearful that the woman would press her for information about her relationship with Michael. Millie had closely followed Claire and Michael's courtship and fancied that she herself had played a part in their romance, since she had introduced them.

Fearful that she would run into Michael, Claire also avoided visiting Millie at her Riverview apartment. She dropped her landlady a short note saying simply that she'd been thinking of her, and letting her know that Smokey was doing fine. She hoped the postcard would allay Millie's curiosity, but it proved to accomplish the opposite.

Millie called, concern in her voice. Claire deliberately kept the conversation light and almost managed to avoid the topic of Michael altogether. But as they were saying their good-byes, the old woman asked, "What do you hear from Michael Meredith? I haven't seen him around here lately."

"I . . . I haven't talked to him for a while, Millie."

"Well, he must be out of town or something. I haven't seen him around here all week. I thought maybe you two had run off together."

"No, I don't know where he's been." She tried desperately to keep her tone nonchalant.

"Aren't you two still seeing each other?" Now Millie sounded genuinely concerned.

"We're just friends, Millie. He doesn't report his every move to me." She knew she sounded overly defensive.

"Now, Claire, you don't owe me any explanations, but I hope you know by now that you can talk to me about anything. I may be an old woman, but I'm not so ancient that I don't remember what it was like to have a young lovers' spat."

Claire remembered the warmth of Millie's concern and friendship the night she had invited her for supper. No, she didn't owe the woman an explanation, but she suddenly felt that Millie would be her ally in this. She tried to think of how she might give her some hint of the situation that existed between herself and Michael without revealing too much. "Millie, we did have a . . . a misunderstanding. I'm not sure if we'll be seeing each other again, but it's all right. It's not the end of the world." She wished she believed her own statement.

"Well, don't worry about it, honey. If it was meant to be, it will all work out."

"I know you're probably right. But, Millie, please don't say anything to Michael if . . . if you see him." She was dangerously close to tears, and Claire knew the emotion in her voice wouldn't be missed by her landlady.

"Honey, do you want to tell me about it? Sometimes it helps to have a sympathetic ear."

"Thank you, Millie. I do appreciate that, but I don't think I'm ready to talk about it yet."

"That's all right. You just remember, though, I'll be here when you are ready."

"Thank you. That means a lot to me. It really does."

She hung up and let the familiar, cleansing tears come again. It touched her that Millie seemed to genuinely care for her. It was almost like having Nana in Hanover Falls.

Nana. Ordinarily, she would have called her grandmother and cried "on her shoulder" long distance long before now. But Nana was too closely tied to the whole situation with Michael. Claire knew it would break her grandmother's heart to discover that the awful mistake her family had made regarding Joseph had followed Claire into adulthood, had tracked her to Hanover Falls, and robbed her of the only taste of true happiness she had known. No, she could never let her beloved grandmother know her anguish. She had to find a measure of peace for herself in this revelation of Michael's identity before it could be anything but a burden to Nana.

However, it filled Claire with a bittersweet satisfaction to know that some day, when the time was right, she would be able to tell Nana that she had found Joseph. "Your prayers were answered, Nana," she would say. "He is doing well and he knows the Lord."

᷈᷈᷈   ᷈᷈᷈   ᷈᷈᷈   ᷈᷈᷈

Late in March, Claire went to church for the first time since she had found out the truth about Michael. She felt like an impostor standing in the overflowing sanctuary of her church singing hymns of victory when she felt so defeated.

She sat in a pew near the back, and when morning worship services were over, she hurried out to her car, desperate to avoid answering any well-intended questions. She backed her car out of the stall in the crowded parking lot and waved with false gaiety to Jarrod Hamilton, who was escorting his younger sisters to the family van.

At home she decided to go for a walk before lunch and went to change into jeans and sweatshirt. Smokey was curled up in a comatose ball at the foot of her bed. When the cat heard the closet door open, he stretched and opened his jaws in a wide yawn, then tucked a gray paw under his chin and went back to sleep. Claire shoved him aside with misplaced irritation and sat down on the end of the bed to put her tennis shoes on.

The weather had been cloudy and drizzly for almost two weeks, but now brilliant sunshine streamed between puffy cumulus clouds. She set off with a growing feeling of hope, suddenly refreshed at the mere sight of the sun.

Almost against her will, her path led her past Mario's pizza place and the band shell park where children's laughter rang out just as it had the day she and Michael had sledded there. Finally, circling home, she walked by Riverview Manor and near the apartment building where Michael lived. She rued the many miles she had walked with Michael around the small town because now, no matter how she tried to shake thoughts of him, everything she saw, every sound she heard reminded her of him—and of the sweet romance they had begun.

She had not seen him for almost a month now, and no one seemed to know where he was. She had inquired discreetly of their few mutual friends to no avail and had finally stooped to allowing Becky Anderson to call his office on the guise of civic club business. Becky had been told by a secretary that Mr. Meredith was on vacation and that he would return the following week.

Claire suspected that he had gone to see his family in Springfield. It hurt her deeply that he had not told her he was going away. And yet, how could she blame him? He owed her no explanations. He owed her nothing.

Claire moved woodenly through the rest of the day. Sadly, she realized that the deep joy she had felt in her new life in Hanover Falls was gone. The cozy house in which she had taken such satisfaction no longer offered the warm refuge it once had. Smokey had become an annoying responsibility. Even the smiles of her students couldn't evoke the happiness they once had. It seemed that every vestige of joy had been stripped from her life on that cold night.

# Seventeen

The night following Claire's revelation, Michael tossed sleeplessly in his bed. Wielding denial like a shield, he deflected the stinging questions that assaulted him from every direction. He could not allow them to penetrate his mind because he had no idea how to answer them.

Through a long night of turmoil, he had finally reached a place of accepting Claire's awful words as the truth. He knew in his heart that she *was* Kitty Anderson from the family in St. Louis, but he was still grappling with the reality of what it all meant for him—for them.

How would it change his life? How could he remain in this town where he might run into Claire at any moment? He had come to love her deeply. Was that now to be denied him? And if so, would he be forced to move away from the place that had finally become home to him? Would he have to quit the job in which he was just now beginning to feel confident? What would he tell his family? Could his spirit survive another devastating blow like this? What choices did he have?

He went through the next two weeks in a fog, short-tempered with his co-workers, unable to make a sound decision, feeling completely unorganized and incompetent.

Beth VanMeter, his assistant administrator, had a much lighter class schedule this semester, and her presence at the manor took a great deal of pressure off of him as far as the actual work load. But at the same time, it meant that he had to work closely with her. Had she still been spending much of her time away from the office, he might have been able to make himself scarce, might have been able to hide the despair he was feeling. But Beth picked up on his distress immediately.

She had shown unwavering patience with his moodiness for the first few days, but finally she had apparently had enough. Never one to defer to him as her superior, she confronted him one morning after she had repeated a simple question for the second time without receiving even an acknowledgment that he had heard her.

"Michael, I'm not sure what it is that's bugging you, but don't you think it would be wise to take some time off and just get out of here for a while?"

"What?" He stared at her as though she were speaking a foreign language, then shook his head to bring her face into focus. "I'm sorry, Beth. What did you say?"

She laughed hollowly. "You are obviously somewhere far, far away. Why don't you just go. Get out of here. Take a week of vacation. Heaven knows you've got it coming with all the extra time you put in while I was carrying a full load last semester."

He knew she was right and he didn't have the strength to argue with her. Later that afternoon he checked the manor's schedule against his own calendar and pulled himself together enough to have an informed discussion with Beth about the things that would need to be taken care of while he was gone.

On the office calendar he penciled in his impromptu vacation for the following week and went to talk to Vera Johanssen to see if she had any concerns that needed to be dealt with before he left.

"Good for you, Michael," Vera told him with motherly concern when she heard about his upcoming vacation. "It's about time you took a break. And don't you worry about a thing here. Everything is under control."

"Thanks, Vera. By the way, is everything okay with the . . . uh, the issue we discussed a few weeks ago?" He was speaking in code because they were at the nurses' station where several aides were hovering. In truth, in the wake of Claire's revelation about their childhood connection, he had nearly forgotten his conversation with the former administrator, Gerald Stoddard, that had caused him such deep concern at the time.

Now he sensed the slightest hesitation in Vera's demeanor. But her voice was light when she told him, "Nothing that can't wait."

Michael was alarmed and it showed in his face. "Has . . . has something else happened?"

"Just more things to file in the 'flaky' category," Vera assured him.

She caught his skeptical look and laughed. "Seriously, forget I said anything. Go on, get out of here." She shooed him toward the elevator, laughing.

When Michael had reopened the subject of Cynthia Harper with Vera after his encounter with Gerald Stoddard in Springfield, they had agreed there wasn't enough evidence to warrant an investigation. The issue had seemingly died then. But now, even the slight hesitation in Vera's voice troubled him. He wished he didn't trust her discernment so much. It would be much easier to write off his growing apprehension to a slightly paranoid director of nursing.

Nevertheless, he let the older woman's assurances now persuade him. He knew she would have told him if it was anything truly urgent.

≈ ≈ ≈ ≈

As soon as Michael had convinced himself he could afford to take the time away from work, he had known he would go to Springfield. To his family—to the parents who loved him, the sisters who could console him as no one else could. For a wistful moment, he longed for the sage advice his grandparents might have offered.

He had not told anyone he was coming. He didn't trust his voice on the telephone. The hurt was still too raw, the wound too tender.

He wasn't yet sure what he would tell them when he got there. Perhaps he wouldn't have to say anything. Perhaps he just needed to be with them, to bask in an atmosphere of unconditional love, and then the answer would come. God would reveal what his next step should be.

He drove on, deliberately recalling everything Claire had told him about himself . . . everything about the part of his past that inexorably connected him to her. Strange that such a profound bond was ripping them apart instead of knitting them together.

This forced remembrance of his childhood dredged up other painful memories. Murky recollections of a dark-haired woman lying on a dirty couch. He tried to wake her. He needed her for something— he couldn't remember what—but she wouldn't wake up. She rolled over and turned her back to him, and when he persisted in trying to shake her awake, she shoved him roughly to the floor muttering foul, slurred words under her breath.

He remembered a parade of first days in new schools. It was always the same. An overly cheerful teacher bringing him to the front of the classroom and introducing him while he stood there, his cheeks hot with embarrassment. Evasive explanations to the other children about where he lived and why he had moved to this school. And always, always, just when he had begun to make friends, when he had begun to settle into a family, being wrenched from everything familiar to start the agonizing process all over again.

He tried in vain to think of some happy memory from those days. But it was too painful. Every happiness, he realized, was painted over with loss, negated by good-byes that had separated him from the source of that brief happiness.

He had dealt with all of this before—even the ultimate rejection he had suffered in St. Louis at the hands of the Andersons—when he had gone through the drug and alcohol rehabilitation programs in his teens. And he thought he had put it behind him. No one could take away the assurance he had of the love the Merediths had offered. Or the love God had shown him. He knew with certainty that he *was* a different person, a new creation. Yet here he was, nearing the beginning of his thirtieth year, and it seemed his childhood was still condemning him.

All these thoughts roiled in his mind, threatening to pull him under in a maelstrom of doubt as his truck ate up the miles between Hanover Falls and Springfield. By the time he drove into the city limits of Springfield, he was emotionally spent. He turned, as though on automatic pilot, toward Sarah's house.

When he pulled into the Iverson's driveway, he spotted his sister in the side yard, helping the children lift the cover from their sandbox. She looked up at the sound of his motor, and joyful recognition came to her face.

Brushing the sand from her hands, she spoke quietly to the children and hurried through the gate to greet him.

"Michael! What on earth are you doing here?"

Like a vulnerable little boy, he fell into her embrace, towering over her petite figure but finding ample strength there. "I needed to see you," he said quietly.

"Oh, Michael. What's wrong?" She pulled away to look into his face, as though she might find the answer there. "Come on . . . let's go inside."

"I should say hi to the kids first," he protested half-heartedly, motioning to where the three young children played, bundled in jackets and caps, unaware of his arrival.

"They're not going anywhere. It's the first time they've been able to play outside in ages."

Grateful for the reprieve, he followed her into the house. She started a pot of coffee and came to sit beside him in the spacious family room where they could look out on the yard where the children were. She looked at him and her expression revealed her deep love and concern. He knew she would wait until he was ready.

Finally he began to speak, telling her in hushed tones of his love for Claire, his growing belief that she had been God's answer to his prayers. And then of his terrible discovery on that night three weeks ago, of his doubts and agony since then.

Sarah sat in stunned silence, taking in every word, compassion in her eyes and in her murmurs of disbelief and empathy. Finally, when he had said all he knew to say, she asked gently, "Do you still love her, Michael? Has this changed your feelings for Claire?"

"I don't know, Sarah. I feel . . . numb. I don't know what I feel anymore."

"Are you angry with her . . . for what happened back then?"

His answer was immediate. "No! How could I be angry with Claire? She was just a child. It wasn't her fault."

"Have you told her that?"

He shook his head. "We haven't spoken since that night . . . when I went to her house. I'm not even sure what I did say to her then, Sarah. I was in shock."

"I can imagine how you must have felt, Michael. I feel as though I'm in shock, too. It's unbelievable this could have happened . . . that you would meet again like this."

She shook her head and hesitated, seemingly gathering her thoughts. Then she ventured, "I'm just thinking out loud here, but my first thought is 'what has really changed?' If you truly love Claire, Michael, this shouldn't make any difference at all. You were both victims of circumstance. You're not related—not even legally now. I'm sure the adoption was annulled. It would have to be, wouldn't it—in order for Mom and Dad to legally adopt you? This shouldn't make any difference," she repeated with conviction.

He knew Sarah was right. Long ago he had offered blanket forgiveness to all the people who had hurt him in his childhood. That included the Andersons.

Yes, he *had* forgiven. But had Claire? He remembered her excuses for her parents' sins—before she had known how irrevocably their sins had affected him. If Claire had forgiven, as she claimed she had, it was apparent that she had not forgotten. Her anguish that night in the park had made that quite clear.

Sweet Claire. How she must be suffering over this. He believed she had come to love him. And suddenly, he knew.

"Oh, Sarah, I do love her still. Of course I do. You're right. Nothing has changed, not really."

A horrifying thought struck him. He truly did not have any clear memory of Kitty Anderson. She was an obscure face among a string of foster sisters and brothers. But Claire had told him she *did* remember him. Of course she would remember him! He had been her only living sibling. He hadn't bothered to ask exactly *what* she remembered about him. What if he had hurt her? He had a cruel streak in those days. He knew that. He had been sent to a principal more than once for fighting, for mean-spirited pranks.

He told his sister his fears, realizing aloud, "Sarah, I have to talk to Claire. I have to know. . . ."

"Good, Michael. I know you'll work things out. I know you will." She patted her brother's arm reassuringly.

❧    ❧    ❧    ❧

Michael spent the week in Springfield, shuttling between his parents' and Evan and Sarah's houses. He had long conversations with Sarah and his mother about his childhood and the issues with which he still sometimes struggled. He spent carefree afternoons with his nieces and nephews and with another sister, Mindy, who came from nearby Billings when she heard Michael was in Springfield.

It was a time of healing, a time of calm reassurance that he was indeed firmly rooted in a family who would love him for all time.

At week's end, he knew he would go back to Hanover Falls. He would go to Claire.

# Eighteen

Claire was washing up the few dishes that had collected throughout the day when she heard Smokey meowing to go out the front door. She walked through the living room and absentmindedly opened the door. The gray cat darted out onto the front lawn and Claire looked out to the street, surprised at how much light still remained. The house had grown dark and she had not yet turned on the inside lights. Outside it was apparent that already the days were lengthening toward spring. March would soon turn to April.

Claire was about to step back inside when she noticed a familiar figure walking along the sidewalk in front of her house. His head was bent against the brisk evening air, his hands buried deep in the pockets of his jacket. But Claire knew that posture, knew the strong line of that jaw.

She stood in the doorway, afraid for him to see her standing here as though she had expected him; more afraid to go inside and risk he would just walk on past. As he came closer, he turned up her driveway toward the house, then looked up and saw her standing there.

"Hello, Claire," he said softly. His voice sounded sad, weary, and yet it was beautiful in her ears.

"Hi." She suddenly felt shy.

"Could we talk for a little while?"

"Yes, of course. Come in."

Her heart beat faster at his nearness. What had been going through his mind these weeks since they had parted?

He stepped into the living room, and Claire reached for a lamp and turned it on, bathing the room in rich golden light. She motioned toward the couch and he sat down heavily. Sitting on the opposite end, she curled her legs beneath her. The silence was dense and uncomfortable between them.

The room was warm, and Michael pulled his gloves off and unzipped his jacket but didn't remove it. Finally he spoke. "How have you been?"

She shrugged. "I'm okay."

"I . . . I took some vacation time off. I went home . . . to Springfield. I'm sorry. I should have told you. I had to get away to think."

"And what have you been thinking?" She was trembling visibly—with fear at what his answer might be, with intense emotion at being near him again, realizing anew how deeply his presence stirred her.

He took her hand and closed the distance between them on the couch. "Claire, this whole thing has . . . well, it's opened up a wound I thought had healed long ago. . . ." His voice trailed off.

Shame overwhelmed her and she put her head in her hands and wept bitterly. "Oh, Michael, I'm so sorry. I am so very sorry."

He seemed shocked at her outburst. "Claire, it wasn't you! *You* have no need to apologize. It's okay. It's all right."

She had to know. "Michael, do you remember that day we had your birthday party? In the little swimming pool?"

He narrowed his eyes and she knew he was trying to recover the memory.

"I . . . I sprayed you with the garden hose," she prompted.

She saw recognition come into his eyes as though he was remembering for the first time. "I cut you, didn't I? Trying to grab the hose away. I hurt you."

He squinted, trying to remember again. "Claire, I've tried so hard to put you in my memories of that time—as Kitty, I mean. I can't make you and her be the same person. I scarcely remember, but it's so hard to believe that was you."

"I know," she said, amazed that he had felt the same confusion in trying to meld the small shared part of their childhoods with the present.

"I remember he—your father—was so angry. But I . . ." His gaze was far away. Then, as though a thought suddenly came to him, he took her forearms in his hands and turned them first one way, then another. In the yellowish light from the lamp, the long, thin white scar showed faintly on her bare right forearm.

"Oh, Claire, I did hurt you. I'm so sorry." He traced the scar gently with his fingertip.

She grabbed her arm away and rubbed at it as if to erase the scar. "No! No, Michael. It's . . . it's nothing—*nothing!* I didn't bring it up because you hurt me that day! It was nothing," she repeated. "It didn't even need stitches."

She shook her head violently, then dropped it to her chest in shame. "You don't understand, Michael. The whole thing was all my fault. I lied. *I* started the whole thing. You were just defending yourself, but I told Daddy it was you. I told him you hurt me for no reason. And he believed me—and you were the one who got punished. They . . . they sent you away after that." Her words poured out in a torrent.

"They sent me away because of that?" It was becoming obvious that her memory of the event was much more vivid than his own.

"Yes. It was my fault, Michael." Her voice dropped off.

"Claire, you were a little girl. Sending me away wasn't your decision. You can't really believe that?"

She just shook her head hopelessly, not knowing what else to say. They sat together in silence for a long minute.

Finally he spoke, his voice almost a whisper now, as though a memory had just dawned. "Claire, I remember your Nana! I do remember her! She used to play games with us—dominoes and . . ."

Claire nodded as though to affirm that Michael's memories were accurate.

"Your grandmother was always very nice to me. I liked her," he finished simply.

"She prayed for you, Michael. For years." Claire's expression held amazement as she realized for the first time how miraculously God had answered Nana's prayers for the young boy. "Nana told me just this past Christmas how she always thought of the Joseph of the Bible when she thought of you. She prayed that God would redeem your life as He did Joseph's."

"Does she know? Have you told her about me?"

Claire shook her head. "I can't. Not yet, Michael. It's too . . ." She let her voice trail off, not knowing how to express her anguish to him.

"I think her prayers have been answered, Claire," he said quietly.

There was much in their discovery about which to be amazed. If she thought too long about it, it overwhelmed her that she and Mi-

chael should ever have met again this way. It seemed almost provi-
dential. And yet . . . could a loving God be the author of the sorrow
and confusion they both were feeling now? Why would God have or-
chestrated this strange reunion between them?

Now she asked him, "But have they, Michael? Have Nana's
prayers really been answered? You say the wound has been opened
again. Will it ever truly be healed? I'm responsible for that, Michael.
I am guilty for so much of what you went through. You can't ever
forget those things. Don't tell me you can."

"Shh . . . Claire." He hushed her with a gentle smile and a finger
to her lips. "Let me finish. Let me tell you what I've been thinking
these past weeks."

She waited in anguish.

"Claire, I don't know why everything has happened as it has. I
talked for hours to my sister about it. Sarah thinks maybe in some
ways it has helped me to be confronted all over again with all the rejection of my life—and especially with that one horrib—" He stopped
abruptly.

Claire knew what he had been about to say. She closed her eyes
and cringed inwardly as he confirmed what she already knew. He
could never forget.

But he ignored her and continued. ". . . with that rejection. Sarah
helped me to realize that if I had never met you, maybe I would never
have come to terms with the most painful rejection of all. Maybe it
would have gone on haunting me without my even realizing it. I
thought I *had* dealt with it. But even that night in the park when I
told you about it, I knew then that it still had some kind of hold on
me."

He looked her in the eye and told her bluntly, "It hurt, Claire. It
changed my life. I won't lie to you about that. But I honestly don't
blame you—or even your parents. I know from what you've told me
that they had their own problems apart from me. And I know I wasn't
an easy kid to get along with. I had problems of my own." He attempted a grin. "But I think I have put it behind me now. And I want
to go on. I don't want this same issue to ruin my life all over again.
After all, Claire—and I don't want to offend you by saying this—but,
if your parents hadn't sent me away, I never would have become a part
of the family I have now. Do you understand what I'm saying?"

She nodded. It did hurt to have him say those words. In spite of her family's problems, she felt a certain loyalty to them. And yet, she could never defend what they had done to Michael. Yes, it hurt. But at the same time she was grateful that he could look at it this way, that he could see the good that had ultimately come of their rejection. She wished she could feel the same.

"Claire, I want things the way they were before. We . . . I think we had something wonderful between us. I didn't misread that, did I?"

She shook her head.

"I've missed that, Claire. I've missed *you*. Us. Couldn't we start over again?" he asked abruptly. "Do you think we could do that?"

She couldn't give voice to all her fears. Part of it was simply being afraid of starting their relationship anew only to have it blow up in her face again. She was frightened that no matter what he said now, he would—somewhere down the road—come to blame her after all. Such a deep hurt couldn't be healed quickly. And it could never be forgotten. She couldn't be certain beyond all doubt that he could look at her and not think every time he did of the role she had played in his painful past.

And then there was the other issue. Michael was her brother—or had been once. Surely they could not pretend that it had never been so. The feelings they had just begun to acknowledge for each other were certainly not those of brotherly love. What were the moral implications of those feelings in light of the relationship they'd had as children?

She dared to broach that subject with him now. "Michael, how do you see our relationship—I mean if we 'try again,' as you say?"

"What do you mean?"

"Would . . . would it be as friends? Or . . . as a brother and a sister?"

He looked downcast and his voice was tinged with frustration. "Is that how you see us now, Claire? As a brother and sister?"

"Oh, Michael, I don't know. I'm so confused. . . ."

He took her hands in his again, gripping them tightly. "Claire, you surely know that it was more than a platonic love that I felt . . . that I *feel* for you. I love you, Claire." His words were ragged with emotion.

In spite of her caution, her heart soared at his words. And yet her joy at hearing him declare his love with such feeling didn't change anything. Not really.

"Michael, I don't know what to say. I can't . . . I just don't see how it could ever work between us." She heard the words come from her mouth and immediately wanted to snatch them back. She wished she could fall into his arms and pretend none of this had ever happened. But she didn't. Instead, she steeled herself and repeated the words woodenly, as much for her own benefit as for his. "I don't think it could ever work between us."

Michael slowly loosened his grip on her hands, placing them purposefully back into her lap. Standing, he zipped his jacket and shoved his hands back into his gloves, then covered the distance to the front door with long strides. With his hand on the knob, he turned and looked deeply into her eyes.

"I can't force my love on you, Claire. I can't force you to love me back."

His voice held no anger, but to her it seemed cold and abrupt. He opened the door and was gone.

*But I do love you, Michael. I do love you,* her thoughts pleaded.

She went to the window and pulled back the curtain. Numbly, she watched as he disappeared into the encroaching shadows of dusk, remembering another day long ago when she had peered through a curtain and watched him go away, out of her life. She sank to her knees and wept.

# Nineteen

Michael returned to work Monday morning. The events he had been forced to relive over the past days and weeks—and then Claire's rejection of him—had taken a heavy toll. He was confused and depressed, still not able to understand why things had happened as they had. Yet, physically and emotionally exhausted as he was, he knew it would be better to go on with his life—to maintain his regular work schedule, to continue the activities in which he normally participated—rather than seclude himself in his grief. And it was, he realized, grief. That had always seemed such a strong word, reserved for death. Yet the numbing disbelief, the physical ache in the pit of his stomach, were no less real than the pain he had felt after his grandfather's torturous death.

Seeing Claire again had made him realize how deeply he did love her. He wasn't sure he could ever see her as Kitty Anderson. And wasn't that a good thing? The Claire he loved was the shy, sweet, thoughtful strawberry blonde who laughed at his jokes, who sometimes seemed to understand him better than he understood himself, who took delight in the smallest pleasures of life: sledding on a snowy hillside, a game of Scrabble, a shared cup of cocoa. The Claire he loved was the woman whose touch thrilled him, whose hand fit so perfectly in his own. *Not* the little girl whose face he could scarcely recall. That dim memory from the past had nothing to do with them—with Claire and him.

He had held such hope for a future with her. He had felt they belonged together. How could he have been so wrong? It was unimaginable to him that this was happening all over again, just like it had happened countless times in his childhood. Just like it had happened with Michelle back in college. Like a drowning animal, he clawed desperately to find a foothold, to find again the peace he had known when Michelle had told him she loved someone else. His mind knew that peace had been real, but deep in a secret place in his heart anger rose up to strangle him.

Did God not want him to be happy? Was He some cruel trickster who sat up in heaven and held out enticing bits of hope in human packages, only to grab them out of reach just when he opened a trusting hand to accept the gift?

In the dead quiet of his apartment the night after he left Claire's, he raised his fist and shouted at the ceiling. "I don't understand, God. I don't get it. Why are you doing this to me again? Haven't I suffered enough?"

He ranted and wept. And then it came. Not an answer, certainly. Not an overwhelming peace. But in the silence after the tears and questions, a simple assurance. A knowledge that said, *I have everything under control. It's not for you to try to understand. Only know that I am here. And I will never leave you.*

He would pray for Claire every minute, but he could not allow himself to fantasize about a future with her. If God's plan for Michael Meredith's future did not include Claire Anderson . . . well, he couldn't let himself think about that now. He would have to be content to live each day as it was given to him.

In the way that it was a relief to resume a routine after a funeral, it felt good to walk through the doors of Riverview Monday morning. It didn't change the fact that something terrible had happened, but there was comfort in the familiar after the foreignness of tragedy. Getting back into the schedule of work would keep him focused on something other than his problems, on something other than Claire.

After sorting through the mountain of mail that had accumulated on his desk in his absence, he walked over to the residential apartments. He took a quick tour through the hallways, stopping off in the central lobby to visit with the residents who gathered there for coffee each morning. Everything seemed to be running smoothly. He was even able to joke and banter with an elderly couple who had taken a particular liking to him. He was struck once again by how much he enjoyed this part of his job. These people were the reason he found such fulfillment in his work, he reminded himself. In spite of his loss, there were still small joys to be found in life.

With a lighter step, he headed back toward the nursing-care unit where his office was located. As he passed the construction site where the new senior center was rising from the earth, he noticed how much had been accomplished in his short absence. In just a week's time, the exterior work had been nearly completed and there was a beehive of activity inside the building as workers began to lay the flooring and prepare to do the finishing work.

He resisted the temptation to go inside and take a closer look. Beth VanMeter would be in the office around nine, and he was anxious to talk to her and Vera Johanssen to find out how things had gone while he was away. After his time in Springfield, he felt ready to take on the challenges of this job anew. He prayed it would offer distraction and consolation.

❧   ❧   ❧   ❧

The weeks went by quickly and Michael was busily occupied with the activities surrounding the completion of the senior center. One entire week was spent moving in and rearranging furniture and equipment between the old fellowship room and the new center.

A dedication and open house were scheduled for a Sunday afternoon late in April. It took a hectic pace to finish everything on time, but the day turned out to be a huge success. A record number of visitors toured the facility, and the reaction of the public was more favorable than Michael could have hoped for.

By the time he got home after the clean-up Sunday evening, he felt he might sleep for a week. He did, in fact, sleep late the next morning. It was almost nine when he arrived at the office. He headed down the hallway to Vera Johanssen's office, anxious to revel with her in the success of the weekend's event.

Vera looked up from her desk as he walked through the door, and he knew from her face that something was wrong.

"Michael, thank God you're here."

"What is it, Vera?" He felt bile rise in his throat. *Please, God*, he thought, *not now*.

Vera picked up a narrow advertising flyer from her desk and handed it to him. He glanced at the pamphlet and back at Vera, questioning her wordlessly. He held in his hand an announcement of a lecture to be given in St. Louis by a member of the Hemlock Society, an organization that actively promoted euthanasia. Even a cursory scan of the flyer revealed the society's radical agenda for promoting assisted suicide and what they termed "death with dignity."

"Ollie brought that to me first thing this morning," she explained.

He turned the paper over in his hands, willing himself to stay calm. "Would Ollie understand what this was all about, Vera?"

She shook her head. "I'm not sure. I know he reads a little bit, and I know he comprehends more than you might think, but . . . not this. I don't think this . . ."

"Did you ask him where he got it?"

"No. I'm afraid I intimidated him with my reaction. He became very upset, and after that I couldn't make any sense of what he was saying."

"Have you talked with any of the nurses who worked last night?"

"No. I wanted to talk to you first."

"That was probably wise."

He skimmed over the flyer again and threw it on his desk in disgust. "I can't believe anyone would bring something like that to work."

He shook his head in dismay, then mentally checked himself. It wasn't fair or rational to jump to conclusions. "Of course, it's entirely possible that whoever brought this in was just as appalled by the subject as we are. Anyone could have picked up this type of brochure. It doesn't necessarily mean anything . . ." He let the sentence drop unfinished.

"No, it could be perfectly innocent," Vera admitted, but her voice was devoid of conviction.

"But you don't think so?"

Vera shook her head.

"How would Ollie have gotten hold of it?" He thought for a minute. "I suppose I should try to talk with him."

Vera nodded. "I think he's working on the east wing today."


Oliver Moon was washing windows in the day room on the east wing. His back was turned to the wall, so Michael stood out of sight and watched him for a few minutes.

Meticulously, the diminutive man ran a squeegee down each window, then took a chamois from the pocket of his coveralls and polished each pane of glass until it sparkled. The entire time he worked, he muttered and mumbled unintelligibly to himself.

There were only three residents in the day room, but one began to complain loudly about the "racket" Ollie was making when she saw Michael. "It's bad enough we have to sit in this drafty hole all day," Ethel Manning screeched. "Do we have to listen to his jibberty jabber, too?"

Ignoring her, Michael cleared his throat and approached Ollie.

The man turned, seemingly startled.

"Hello, Ollie. Could I talk to you for a minute?"

Immediately Ollie began wringing his hands. "Ar sorr . . . Ar shu-up . . . Ar sorr . . . Murmuff . . ." he mumbled.

Michael realized that Ollie thought he was being reprimanded for disturbing Ethel Manning. Putting a hand on his shoulder, Michael steered him into the hallway and out of hearing of the day room.

"No, Ollie. You don't need to apologize. I'm not upset with you." Michael cocked his head toward the day room. "I'm sure Ethel would find something to gripe about even if you didn't say a word," he said conspiratorially.

The nearly toothless mouth split into a broad grin, and Ollie's rounded belly shook with silent laughter.

Michael smiled and motioned toward the corridor. "Let's go down to the cafeteria. It'll be quieter there. I have something I want to talk to you about."

Ollie merely nodded and shuffled obediently alongside the administrator.

True to Michael's prediction, the cafeteria was deserted at this hour between coffee breaks and lunch. He pulled out a chair and motioned for Ollie to sit down. Michael sat across from him at the small table.

"Are you a coffee drinker? Can I get you a cup?"

Ollie shook his head.

Slipping the pamphlet from his suit pocket, Michael laid it on the table in front of the older man. In the gentlest voice he could find, he said, "I want to talk to you about this, Ollie."

Oliver Moon hung his head as though ashamed.

Michael put a hand on the narrow shoulder. "I'm not angry with you, Ollie."

"Ver. Ver," he said, wagging a finger, pantomiming what he perceived as Vera's scolding.

"No. I just talked with Vera and she's not angry, either. She just had some questions. I need to ask you some questions about this paper. Do you know what this writing is about?"

Silence.

"Where did you get this, Ollie? Did someone give it to you?"

Slowly the white-blond head wagged back and forth.

"Can you tell me where you got it, Ollie?"

The little man became agitated. Stuttering more than usual, he finally spat out, "Shar . . . shar . . . charner . . ."

"I'm sorry, Ollie, I don't understand. Sharpener?"

He shook his head adamantly. "Uhnn," he grunted. "Charners . . . mah sacks. Mah sacks . . . ners . . ." He made a vigorous motion with his hand as though he were throwing something on the floor.

"I'm sorry, Ollie. Are you saying *nurse*? Did you get this from a nurse? Can you tell me which nurse gave it to you, Ollie?"

"Nah. Nah. Charp-ner," he repeated, growing more distressed. "Mah sacks. Aarp-ners," he tried again, complete with the hand motions.

It was obvious that Oliver Moon knew he had not made himself understood clearly, but Michael felt he was too distraught to take any more questioning. He pushed back his chair and stood up.

"Thank you, Ollie. I appreciate your help."

Ollie seemed near tears.

"Hey, you didn't do anything wrong, all right? Everything's okay. Thank you for your help. Do you mind if I keep this?" he asked, pointing at the brochure.

Ollie pushed it across the table toward Michael as though it were a hot potato.

※ ※ ※ ※

On a whim, Michael stopped off at the Hanover Falls Public Library after work that evening. Sitting down at a computer, he pulled a notepad and pen from his briefcase and waited while the computer searched the word he keyed in: EUTHANASIA.

The screen came up and he saw at a glance that there were several volumes on the topic in this library. He was surprised to see that nearly half of them were currently checked out. He jotted down the catalog numbers of the selections that were available and exited the screen.

He found the nonfiction section in a poorly lit room at the back of the library. He waited for his eyes to adjust and began to scan the shelves, looking for the titles he'd written down.

Feeling strangely deceitful, yet not wishing to arouse curiosity or suspicion by checking out such books in this small town—where everyone made it their business to know everyone else's business— he took the books to a secluded study carrel and thumbed through each one. Most were thoughtful exposés or compilations of essays on medical ethics. One publication was an autobiographical account of a woman who had helped a terminally ill parent commit suicide. Another unapologetically promoted legislation that would make euthanasia an accepted option, sighting the Netherlands' supposed "success" in ushering in legal physician-assisted suicide.

Michael leafed through one book and was shocked to find that it was virtually a handbook of various methods of "self-deliverance," as the volume referred to suicide and euthanasia. The book was complete with lists of lethal dosages and methods—legal and otherwise— of obtaining sufficient quantities of the necessary drugs.

Why would anyone in a town like Hanover Falls desire to read such a book? He certainly didn't condone censorship, but surely library funds could be put to better use than on material that seemed to Michael to be indefensible. He supposed there might be a logical explanation for the other books on the subject being checked out: school reports, information on other areas of medical ethics, and so on. The topic had been discussed in some of the college courses he had taken toward his degree in social work. And of course, many of the continuing education seminars he attended offered a workshop or lecture on euthanasia. But never had Michael seriously thought that he would face the question head on in this quiet, conservative midwestern town. After all, euthanasia was illegal.

Frighteningly, voters in the state of Oregon had ratified a decision to legalize physician-assisted suicide, and the topic had actually reached the Supreme Court. A Michigan physician known as "Dr. Death" had attended and assisted in numerous suicides, apparently immune to the law. But regardless of those threatening inroads, for the vast majority of the nation, euthanasia and physician-assisted suicide remained against the law.

Michael struggled to remember the details in the medical files of Frederick Halloran that he had destroyed. Was there a connection? Had Vera Johanssen been right all along? Was there something suspicious about that patient's death? If so—if there was even a remote possibility that someone at Riverview had acted on the beliefs espoused in these books and in Ollie's pamphlet—those actions went far beyond the prevailing definition of euthanasia. Evil though it was in his eyes, physician-assisted suicide did at least purport to require the consent of the patient involved. Frederick Halloran had never been in any condition to make a rational decision concerning his own death. Halloran had been out of his mind, his cries for help a visceral reaction to unrelieved pain. If his death had been hastened, it could not be labeled anything other than murder. The thought chilled Michael.

He made copies of a few pages he wanted to study further, returned the books to their proper place on the library shelves, paid for the copies, and gathered his briefcase and jacket. He drove home slowly, deep in thought . . . and deeply disturbed.

# Twenty

The following morning found Michael in Vera's office telling her what he had—or hadn't—learned from Oliver Moon.

"You know how hard it is to understand him," he told the director of nursing. "I feel sorry for the poor guy. He gets so frustrated trying to get the words out. All I could make out was what sounded like 'sharpeners' and something about sacks. Does that mean anything to you?"

Vera shook her head slowly, thinking.

He thought for a moment, then abruptly asked, "Vera, would Ollie know the difference between a registered nurse and an LPN or an aide?"

"Oh yes," Vera replied with a low chuckle and an adamant nod of her head. "Oliver Moon knows exactly whose orders carry the most weight around here."

"You know, I wonder if he might have been trying to say '*charge* nurse.' Sharp-ners? Charge nurse?" He tried out the syllables.

Vera looked up, startled. "Michael, Cynthia Harper was transferred to East Sunday night because we were short-handed."

"I'm not sure what you're saying."

"Ollie worked the east wing that night."

"But Cynthia's not a charge nurse, is she?"

"She was on Sunday night. Or at least Ollie would have interpreted it that way. Betty Holland called in sick at the last minute, and Cynthia was the most senior nurse on the wing. But even if Ollie didn't realize that, might he have been saying 'Harper'?"

Michael let the implication soak in.

"I am at a complete loss as to how this should be handled," Vera said, sounding almost panicky. "We can't very well single out Cynthia or make accusations against her, but if we go asking questions of the entire nursing staff, then they will know that we have suspicions. And that would scare off the person we most need to talk to."

"*Do* we have suspicions, Vera? You seem to think Cynthia has something to do with this." He glanced down at the pamphlet that he had placed on Vera's desk.

Vera came around from behind her desk and closed the door to her office. She took a seat in front of the desk beside Michael.

"Michael, I didn't want to say anything because I am getting different stories from both sides, and frankly, until now, it sounded like another ridiculous argument. But . . ."

Vera began to shake her head in disbelief even as she spoke, as though she was just beginning to realize what her words implied. "Geneva Grayson—the charge nurse on West—told me a couple days ago that Cynthia Harper informed her that she had been instructed by—" Vera swallowed hard, as though the words were distasteful. "By an *angel* to keep a close watch over Margaret Wallace."

"What? Margaret Wallace? From the apartments?" Michael was confused. He knew Maggie Wallace well. She lived next door to Millie Overman in the manor apartments. He had spoken to the friendly old woman many times as she strolled the hallways of the building. But what connection did she have to Cynthia Harper? And an *angel*?

"Maggie was transferred to the nursing unit over the weekend," Vera explained. "She's been failing quite rapidly, and the doctors feel certain her cancer has recurred. She is scheduled to go in for tests sometime this week, but she has been so confused and is in such terrible pain that they want to stabilize her before they move her again. You wouldn't recognize her, Michael. She looks terrible."

Michael felt truly sorry to hear the news. Maggie brought a spark of life to everyone she touched. But his disquiet over the things Vera had just told him overpowered his sadness at the news.

He tried to make sense of what he had learned. "Wait a minute. How is this? Cynthia claims an angel told her to watch over Maggie?" He shook his head. "This is getting too strange, Vera."

"Yes, it is very strange—especially if what you think Ollie might have been trying to say is true. Of course, I asked Cynthia about the statement and she flatly denied it, Michael. That's why I didn't say anything to you before. It's no secret that Cynthia and Geneva have never seen eye to eye on anything. I'm forever mediating their differences."

His mind was churning with the bewildering possibilities. "Vera, is it possible that Geneva Grayson is the charge nurse Ollie is referring to?" he ventured.

Vera was obviously taken aback. "I don't think so."

"I don't know either of these nurses well, Vera. Is it possible Geneva is trying to stir up trouble for Cynthia? Why would she make up something like that? *One* of them isn't telling the truth."

Vera thought for a minute. "I don't know. Geneva can be . . . I guess 'overbearing' is the word. But she is a very good nurse, Michael. She might be rather dogmatic, but I don't believe she's vindictive. And besides, like you said, there just isn't any reason to make up something like this."

Michael was alarmed. He picked up the pamphlet. "Do you honestly think there could be a connection between this flyer and this . . . this angel thing, Vera?"

"I don't know." Vera sighed heavily. "I'm trying to think what else Geneva said. She said that Cynthia was going to ask to be assigned to the wing where Maggie is. But Cynthia never approached me about it. Of course if she had, I—"

Michael jumped up, interrupting Vera. "She what? Vera, something is very wrong here!" he exploded. "I want Cynthia Harper dismissed!"

Vera replied with a seemingly forced calm. "Michael, wait a minute. Like I told you, Cynthia has completely denied making any such statement. In fact, when I asked her about it she laughed in my face like she thought I was joking. When I pressed her, she said, 'Yes, of course I believe in angels.' She also said she had no idea where Geneva might have gotten that idea. I don't know who to believe, Michael. It's Cynthia's word against Geneva's, and I for one wouldn't want to be the one to decide who is telling the truth. If either one of them *is* implicated, there is not one piece of evidence I could cite that would indicate it. Nothing that would give me grounds to dismiss either one of them. Geneva Grayson has performed her duties flawlessly for more years than I can count. Cynthia Harper is efficient and compassionate and dependable."

"I don't care. I am not comfortable with that woman working

here. If there is any chance that she has made these statements about angels—"

"Michael, I understand your alarm. I'm concerned, too. But you know as well as I do that you cannot dismiss a nurse because she believes in angels! For heaven's sake, half the world believes in angels. You and I believe in angels!"

"This is different and you know it, Vera. Believing in them and having conversations with them are two different things."

She gave a deep sigh. "Michael, we don't even know if that's true. Even if Geneva is telling the truth about Cynthia's statement, nothing came of it. No harm has been done. If we fire Cynthia now, with nothing to go on, we would have a lawsuit to end all lawsuits on our hands. How do you think a judge would view this?"

She looked up at Michael, and her eyes were lined with deep fatigue. She sighed heavily. "Don't you see, Michael? It would be ludicrous to try to base a charge on things we merely have a hunch about. It would be seen as a witch-hunt when we don't have one shred of evidence to prove . . . prove what? We don't even know exactly what it is we suspect. By every indication Cynthia Harper is, granted, a rather queer duck—but nevertheless an exemplary nurse."

"Then I want her watched like a hawk. I don't want her in a room alone with a patient. I don't want her near the meds. I don't want her so much as dispensing an aspirin."

Now anger tinged Vera's voice. Because the director of nursing was twenty years his senior, and in truth, far more experienced in the health-care industry, Michael had always bowed to Vera's knowledge and wisdom. He allowed her the tone of authority she took with him now. "And exactly how are you going to explain this demotion to her? Michael, you can't limit a nurse's access to her patients without just cause. And *I* certainly can't follow her around the halls every minute of the day. We don't even work the same shift," she reminded him.

Michael slammed his fist down hard on the desk. Seeing Vera's shock at his violent reaction, he quickly regained control. "I'm sorry, Vera. I know I'm being unreasonable, but I feel like my hands are tied. How can we just go on as though there's nothing amiss?"

Vera shook her head. "I don't know, Michael. I just don't know. It's entirely possible there *is* nothing amiss."

Michael stood and paced the length of her office. "We have a board meeting next Thursday night. I would do anything in my power to keep from opening this can of worms, but if I have to, I *will* bring this before the board, including what Gerald Stoddard told me about the board's role in hiring Cynthia Harper.''

"Michael, you know that would mean that this whole thing will go public.''

"I know. It will also mean a full-scale investigation.'' He sat down again, defeated. "Vera, I am not ready to drag this institution through the mud, and I'm certainly not ready to falsely accuse an innocent woman, but something is not right and somehow we have to find out what it is. We can't just sit here and do nothing!''

Vera looked at him hard. "Do we have a choice, Michael? Do we have any choice at all?''

⁊⁊    ⁊⁊    ⁊⁊    ⁊⁊

The school year was quickly winding to a close, and Claire was finding teaching to be a blessed distraction from her thoughts about Michael Meredith.

The warm spring weather had the students in a less than studious state of mind. Like impatient race horses, they chomped at the bit for recess time to arrive, and when it was over, it took them half an hour to settle down to their classwork. Claire found herself growing short-tempered and crabby with them, and yet she understood their impatience for summer to arrive. She was growing tired of being cooped up in the classroom herself.

One afternoon, in a fit of spontaneity, she herded the entire class out to the playground where they sat cross-legged in the grass and practiced for the upcoming all-school spelling bee.

Claire was delighted with her students' progress. After working with them for almost an hour, she turned to take in the whole cluster of children sitting on the sparse new grass in front of her.

"I am impressed!'' she told them sincerely. "You guys get better every time we do this! Remember what I told you way back at the first of the year?''

"Practice makes perfect!'' they all chimed together.

"See! I was right, wasn't I?''

Eighteen heads nodded proudly in unison.

"Okay, extra recess for you guys! Go!''

They jumped up and ran, squealing and crowing, to various corners of the playground. Claire dusted the grass and sand off her slacks and gathered up her spelling charts with a sigh. Only two more weeks of school! Where had the time gone? And just when she felt she was beginning to make progress with some of these children. It was rewarding and frustrating all at once. Next year she would turn these children over to someone else and begin all over again with fifteen or twenty bright new little faces. It made her tired just thinking about it.

She walked to the rear entrance of the school building. As she reached for the door, Brianne Sizemore and Talisha Jackson untangled themselves from the knot of children at the edge of the playground and ran toward her. Brianne's pale freckled hand was knit tightly with Talisha's ebony one, each girl holding her opposite hand secretively behind her back.

"Wait, Teacher. Wait. We've got thumthing for you," Brianne said mysteriously, her lisp still charmingly evident despite hours spent with the school's speech therapist.

"For me?" Claire bent down to the girls' eye level and scratched her head, playing along with the guessing game. "Well, now, what could it be?"

"Ta-da!" Simultaneously, the pair presented already-wilting bouquets of bright yellow dandelions to their teacher.

"Oh! How pretty!" Claire sniffed the pungent bouquet, stifling a sneeze. "You know what? These are the very first flowers I've gotten this spring! Let's go inside and find a vase."

The two girls skipped through the door ahead of their teacher, obviously proud to have pleased her, and Claire felt the first whisper of contentment and joy she had known since Michael Meredith walked out of her house on that cold night in March.

❧   ❧   ❧   ❧

Final parent/teacher conferences and plans for last-day-of-school festivities kept Claire busily occupied during the following weeks.

One especially busy day she ran to the post office after school to buy some stamps and mail a package to her grandmother. As she was coming out, a tall figure, partially hidden behind the stack of heavy boxes he was carrying, approached the door from the outside. Smiling politely, she held the door open for the man.

"Ah, thank you," the masculine voice said. "I wasn't sure how I was going to manage that."

Immediately she knew. As the form entered the building and pivoted so that their eyes met, Claire's heart began to pound. It was Michael. She had not seen him since the night she had told him good-bye. Now she felt faint and feared he would see the way her hands were shaking.

"Hello," he said. It was as though he was a polite stranger. There was no hint of a smile on his lips. She could read nothing in the gray eyes that had always held such deep expression.

"Hello, Michael."

She felt near tears. Mercifully, the lobby was crowded, and it didn't seem overly awkward for her to hurry out of the way of the other customers.

She unlocked her car and hurriedly turned the key in the ignition. She was trembling almost too violently to drive safely, but she couldn't risk him seeing her this way when he emerged from the building. She drove several blocks and pulled off onto a side street. She sagged over the steering wheel and sobbed.

She hadn't expected his presence to affect her the way it had. She had been doing so well. She had immersed herself in the other activities of her life and thought she was getting over him. But now she felt the wound of their rift afresh.

She told Becky Anderson about the encounter that evening when they straightened up their classrooms after an evening of parent conferences. Becky was a sympathetic listener, letting Claire cry on her shoulder and allowing her to voice the same thoughts and fears again and again, rarely offering advice, merely being a sounding board. Claire treasured their friendship . . . especially now.

৯৫    ৯৫    ৯৫    ৯৫

One Sunday, toward the end of May following a week of rain and cool temperatures, the thermometer soared into the seventies, and Becky invited Claire on a picnic with her and the boys. Randy, Becky's husband, was out of town on business for the weekend, as his job often required him to be. Becky confided to Claire that she dreaded spending a long Sunday cooped up with her two lively pre-schoolers, and Claire gladly accepted the invitation. It would be nice to have some company and nice, too, to get out of the house and enjoy the sunshine.

Moments after Claire got home from church, Becky's van pulled into the driveway, horn blaring. Claire hurriedly changed into jeans, and leaving her dress in a heap on the bed, she ran out and climbed into the van.

Claire deftly directed Becky away from the town's larger park where the band shell and the sledding hill held too many poignant memories. Instead, they drove to Hanover Falls' smaller City Park on the outskirts of town. They spread a blanket on the greening field near the circle drive, which served as both entrance and exit to the park.

Becky's small boys gobbled down peanut butter sandwiches and ran off to play on the jungle gym nearby. The two women sat cross-legged on the blanket, savoring the simple lunch and basking in the warmth of the sunshine. They chatted idly and laughed at the boys' antics.

Claire was telling Becky about an incident that had taken place in her classroom the previous week. As she spoke, she spotted a freshly washed green pickup out of the corner of her eye as it pulled slowly onto the circle drive. Realizing that it was Michael's, she stopped mid-sentence, panic on her face.

"What's wrong?" Becky asked with alarm. Becky had her back to the driveway so she could keep an eye on the playground. Now she looked at her friend with genuine concern.

Claire struggled to regain control. "Nothing . . . it's just . . . Michael's truck just pulled in over there."

Instinctively, Becky turned to look. "Are you going to talk to him?"

"I can't, Becky. I just . . . oh good," she sighed with relief. "He's leaving."

The truck drove slowly on around the circle, apparently headed back to the main road, but as the passenger side came into clear view, Claire saw that Michael was not alone. A head of smooth, blond hair, a coquettish smile, and slender fingers gesturing animatedly to the driver were all Claire could see of the woman seated beside him in the truck. A stab of jealousy went through her, and she felt the blood rush to her face, hot and pounding.

Becky saw the woman at the same moment. "Ooooh . . ." she

said, uncharacteristically at a loss for words, but empathy in her low murmur.

Claire fought for composure. "Hey, don't worry about it. It's no big deal."

Becky found her tongue and, in the straightforward way that Claire ordinarily appreciated, said, "If it's no big deal, then why are your cheeks so red? And why did you have that look on your face when they first drove in?" She sat with a smug grin on her face, waiting for Claire to defend herself.

Tears sprang to Claire's eyes, and she fought to hold them back. "Okay, okay. I guess I'm not quite over it."

"Oh, Claire, I'm sorry. I didn't mean to tease you. I . . . I know it still hurts." She leaned over and put a consoling arm across Claire's shoulders.

"Why can't I just forget him?" Claire cried with self-disgust.

"Why can't you just admit that you love him?" Becky countered.

"Even if I did, what difference would it make, Becky? It would never work. There would always be that . . . that *thing* between us. Besides, he was my brother! I can't just ignore that fact. That couldn't be right, could it?"

Becky had heard the whole story and more than once had given Claire her vehement opinion. The past was the past and true love could forgive anything. Now she spoke boldly. "Claire, the only thing between you and Michael is your own stubbornness. And you are not related by blood! I don't see how living in the same house for a year when you were kids could possibly make having a relationship with him wrong. You've told me that he's willing to work things out and go on from there. Now you need to either face the fact that you still care for him and tell him that, or you need to get over it and forget about him. You're making yourself miserable. And Michael, too."

"He didn't look too miserable just now," Claire reminded her friend with a wave toward the empty drive.

"You're jumping to conclusions. For all you know that was a client."

Claire couldn't help but laugh. "Becky! He works in a nursing home. His clients are little old ladies!"

"Well, maybe it was just a friend," she retorted. "And even if it was a date, that doesn't necessarily mean anything."

"Oh, Becky, how can you be such an optimist all the time?"

"Sorry, sweetie, it's just the way God made me."

"Well, don't ever change," Claire said with genuine affection. "I feel better already. In spite of how it might seem, I do take everything you say to heart. It's just . . . it's all so confusing."

"I'll keep praying for you, Claire." There was deep sincerity in her statement.

"I know. I know. I'm sorry if I ruined your afternoon."

"Hey, what are friends for?"

It truly did help to have someone in whom to confide, someone she knew was faithfully and patiently praying for her. Claire's spirits lifted and she slept that night blanketed in the tentative, familiar peace that she had stopped trying to understand.

# Twenty-one

*T*he month of May left on warm breezes and the promise of the summer to come. The grass grew lush and green, and flowers began to bloom all over town. But Claire tasted none of the joy she usually felt in the season.

For her, the last day of school was a bittersweet mixture of sadness and elation. She was astonished that the year had gone by so quickly. It seemed like such a short time ago that she had stood nervous and inept in front of these children she now knew intimately. They had come so far together.

Brianne Sizemore had taken top honors among third-graders in the county spelling bee, and Claire couldn't help feeling deep pride in the little girl's accomplishment.

Jarrod Hamilton and Will Frederick had formed an unlikely and sometimes stormy friendship in the wake of the incident with the smashed thumbnail. She felt partially responsible for that success story as well.

All of the children had become her own in a sense, and she couldn't think of them moving on next year—to another classroom, another teacher—without tears springing to her eyes. She consoled herself with the knowledge that she would see them in the hallways and on the playground when school started again, but she knew it would never be quite the same. They would grow as close to their fourth grade teacher as they had been to her, and that was as it should be. Still, it was hard to let them go.

Underlying her melancholy was the realization that the summer would leave her with hours on end to fill. She had budgeted her money carefully so she wouldn't need to take a summer job, but now she wondered if it might be wise to do just that.

She had promised her grandmother she would spend two weeks of the summer in Kansas City, and she was looking forward to that. That still left many empty days ahead with too much time to brood.

Claire got through the last day of school without a tear—at least in front of her students. The halls echoed with a hollow emptiness, as if the corridors themselves somehow knew they would be barren for months to come.

She dreaded the following week of teachers' workdays in an empty classroom, but they turned out to be rather enjoyable. She slept late and brought breakfast with her to the school. Jeans and sweatshirts were the accepted apparel, and most days found a lighthearted group of teachers heading out for a late lunch at McDonald's or some other eating establishment.

The first Monday morning of her summer vacation Claire rose early. She was determined to have a productive summer. She refused to spend her free time brooding, wishing for things she couldn't have.

She cleaned the house from top to bottom, rearranged the furniture, and hung freshly laundered curtains at the front windows. By evening she was exhausted, but after a hot shower, she sat on the sofa admiring her handiwork. Candles flickered on the coffee table, Mozart played softly on the stereo, and Claire reflected on how special this little house was to her. It had truly become home.

She thought of Millie Overman, who had spent most of her adult life in the embrace of this house. Realizing she had all but ignored the older woman during the busy last weeks of school, Claire was now anxious to see her and to make up for her neglect. She invited her landlady to supper for the following Sunday night.

They spent an enjoyable evening together, but Millie seemed more feeble than Claire remembered. And though Millie rarely complained, Claire suspected that the occasional grimace which crossed the old woman's face reflected severe arthritic pain.

When the evening ended, Claire drove Millie back to her apartment. They ambled slowly up the walk toward the entrance, Millie clinging tightly to Claire's arm. As they neared the door, it opened, and Michael Meredith walked toward them. Claire's heart began to pound.

Appearing distracted and distant, Michael spoke solemnly, avoiding their eyes. "Hello. How are you?" It was a mere formality, not a question genuinely asked.

Without another word he hurried purposefully past them, seemingly agitated, not even glancing Claire's way.

"Well, what's wrong with him?" Millie wondered.

Claire felt as though she had been slapped. His apparent blatant disregard of her hurt deeply. Her face grew warm, and she prayed Millie wouldn't notice the color that rose to her cheeks.

She walked Millie safely to the door and quickly made her exit, then drove home with a knot in the pit of her stomach. Though she knew she had no one but herself to blame, it still hurt.

She lay in bed that night wondering how she could face any more painful encounters with Michael. She knew she had hurt him by breaking off their romance, but couldn't he understand her reasons?

She drifted into a fitful sleep, resolving to leave for Kansas City sooner than she had planned. And she would stay as long as Nana would have her. Perhaps if she could find a place to stay, she could afford to remain for several weeks.

*Yes*, she thought with a heavy sigh, *maybe I just need to get away from Hanover Falls.*

ॐ    ॐ    ॐ    ॐ

Claire awoke early the following day, her resolve only growing stronger with the morning light. She called Nana as soon as she knew she would be awake and felt satisfaction in her grandmother's excitement over her plans to extend her visit.

Claire took a mental inventory of the things she would need to bring with her from Hanover Falls. After some searching and a dozen phone calls, she found a small apartment near Elmbrook that the owner agreed to rent by the week. It was a bit discouraging to think that for several weeks she would be gone from the house she had worked so hard to make hers. Yet she knew for certain she had to get away from this town that was full of memories everywhere she turned.

The week before she planned to leave, she made hasty arrangements for one teenage neighbor to feed Smokey and another to mow the lawn while she was gone. She was almost afraid to tell Millie she would be leaving Smokey alone for such a long period of time, but since the weather had gotten warm, he had been spending most of his time outdoors, anyway. Jennifer Baker, the bookish fifteen-year-old across the street, promised she would give the cat plenty of love and attention along with his daily food and water.

Claire dreaded the afternoon she had planned to inform Millie of her trip, especially in light of Smokey's "situation," but the landlady surprised her by agreeing that it was probably a good idea for her to get away before the start of a new school year. Claire didn't tell Millie the full extent of her reasons, but she suspected Millie knew that Michael was a large part of it. Since the encounter with him on the sidewalk that Sunday night, Millie had been strangely silent on the subject of Michael Meredith.

Claire spent the next days getting the house in order, cleaning out the refrigerator, stocking up on supplies for Smokey, and trying to decide what to bring with her to Kansas City.

She spent one evening crunching numbers in her bank accounts, trying to decide how she would make ends meet. If she used the full limit of her credit card and drained her savings account, she could probably afford to stay for three or four weeks. And while she didn't relish coming back with a depleted savings and a large debt besides, staying in Hanover Falls all summer simply wasn't an option for her. Besides, she couldn't disappoint Nana now.

❧   ❧   ❧   ❧

When the middle of June rolled around, Claire said her good-byes, promising to keep in touch with Becky and Millie. She had gone over every detail a dozen times. Now she was anxious to be gone.

She pulled out of the driveway and looked back at the reflection in her rearview mirror. There sat her house, so contented-looking on its summer green lawn. She had found refuge here and a place to belong. Hanover Falls had been good to her in many ways. But now this place held too many memories, too many opportunities for chance meetings that would tear at her heart.

She drove north out of the village and found herself wondering if she would ever come back.

# Twenty-two

C laire arrived at Elmbrook, Nana's apartment complex in Kansas City, at three o'clock on a hot afternoon in the middle of June. She spent the first night on the sleeper sofa in Nana's living area but left early the next morning to move the few belongings she had brought with her into the apartment she had arranged to rent during her stay in the city. After the Hanover Falls house, it was difficult to muster much excitement about the tiny rented space in the city suburb. But she knew that, despite Nana's protest, it wasn't feasible for her to spend several weeks on the sofa in Nana's one-room apartment.

She unloaded her belongings from the car and stacked the boxes and bags in the small front room. The studio apartment was one large L-shaped room with a kitchenette and bathroom in the short end of the L and a living area with a shabby daybed in the long end. The large window in the living area offered an uninspiring view of a parking lot and the street beyond. Fortunately, the window was covered with thin cream-colored draperies that let in enough light to prevent the room from being dreary. The walls had been freshly painted in the same off-white as the drapes, and brick red countertops in the kitchen provided a splash of color. It was a far cry from her cozy little house, but it was clean and livable. And it was far away from Hanover Falls— and Michael Meredith.

❧   ❧   ❧   ❧

On Claire's second Saturday morning in the city, she decided to take her grandmother for a drive, since the weather was glorious and she was already beginning to feel smothered by the city around her.

Even though Elmbrook was in a relatively uncrowded suburb of Kansas City, it was a far cry from the rural atmosphere of Hanover Falls, where Claire could view acres of plowed fields and forestlike groves of trees just a short walk from her front door.

Apparently Nana had felt the same sense of confinement. Again and again as they drove along the four-lane highway that led out of town, she exclaimed, "Oh my, but it's good to get out!"

Claire deliberately headed north toward Richmond. Within an hour they were driving along a quiet rural highway flanked by ripening fields of wheat and green pastures dotted with cattle. As she drove, Claire commented that the countryside reminded her of home—Hanover Falls.

Nana turned to Claire and said candidly, "I must tell you, honey, I was a bit surprised you would leave this wonderful life you keep telling me about. All I ever hear when you phone me is how lovely your little town is, how amusing the cat you've adopted, how bright your students are . . ." She paused and gave her granddaughter the searching look Claire had come to love and dread at the same time. "And how charming a certain young man . . ."

Claire drove on without acknowledging Nana's insinuations, grateful that it was necessary to keep her eyes on the road.

Nana waited for Claire to respond, and when she was met with only silence, she put a frail hand on her granddaughter's arm. "Has something gone wrong there, my dear?" she asked gently. "I haven't heard you speak of him since your arrival."

"Oh, Nana. I suppose I'm running away from my problems." Then, afraid her grandmother might misunderstand, she quickly added, "Not that I'm not thrilled to have this time to spend with you. It's just that . . . well, Michael and I aren't seeing each other anymore. I needed to get away."

"Oh?" Nana arched an inquisitive eyebrow, waiting for Claire to explain herself.

"It's a long story, Nana."

Katherine Anderson chuckled her deep, rich laugh. "Well, dearie, I've got all the time in the world, so you just start talking." She looked to Claire expectantly.

But Claire could not bring herself to open the old wounds again—for her own sake and for her grandmother's. Instead, she made feeble excuses and forced herself to laugh away Nana's questions, pretending that her rift with Michael didn't bother her at all.

They stopped for lunch in a small town and then, because Claire could see that Nana was tiring, she headed back toward the city.

By the time they got back to Elmbrook it was nearly three o'clock. Nana retreated to her room, complaining of a headache.

"Do you want me to get you an aspirin?" Claire asked.

"Oh no. I just need to take a rest. It'll be gone when I wake up."

She reclined in her chair and fell asleep almost immediately. Claire skimmed the day's newspapers and dozed on the sofa for a few minutes herself. Nana was still sleeping when Claire woke, so she left a brief note on the end table for her grandmother and went out to the courtyard for some fresh air.

The courtyard was crowded with elderly residents and their visitors. Claire didn't feel like conversation, so she decided to take a short walk in spite of the sweltering summer heat. She followed the meandering sidewalk to a gracious old neighborhood in the Kansas City suburb. The tree-lined streets offered respite from the blazing sun and Claire walked on, enjoying the manicured lawns and flowers and the architecture represented in the huge old Victorian houses.

Triggered by her conversation with Nana, thoughts of Michael Meredith crowded her mind as she walked. It seemed ironic that she had come to Kansas City to forget the man. Yet even here, the very sidewalks reminded her of the pleasant strolls she and Michael had taken together. Reluctantly, she gave rein to the thoughts.

She could no longer deny that she felt for Michael an emotion she could only identify as love. And upon frank examination, she found her love for Michael to be pure and selfless—truly wanting only what was best for him and what was right in God's eyes. But she knew, too, that love didn't always justify a relationship. Weren't many illicit affairs rationalized by love? Even true love? No, love alone was not reason enough for a relationship to exist.

With Michael, there had been larger issues to explore: the disturbing fact that he had once been her brother; her fear that he would subconsciously associate her with the deepest hurt of his life; the knowledge that she hadn't yet fully forgiven her parents—or herself—for the ways they had hurt Michael. No, she decided, she had made the right decision concerning Michael. Now she would learn to live with that resolve.

Claire looked up, realizing she had walked farther than she intended. Glancing at her watch, she was surprised to see how late it was. Nana would surely be awake by now and wondering what had happened to her. She hurried back to Elmbrook and entered through the front doors, her mind still foggy with thoughts of Michael. Distractedly, she turned toward the east wing where Nana's room was.

She rounded the corner and was jolted out of her reverie by a commotion in the hallway. All along the east corridor, doors were open and elderly residents peeked curiously into the hallway. Several nurse aides stood in a doorway at the far end of the hall, and a woman Claire recognized as the head nurse issued orders in a sharp, clipped staccato. Claire's heart leapt in her chest as she started running toward the knot of nurses even before she was fully aware that Nana's room was the focus of all the turmoil.

Speechless and out of breath, she neared the doorway still running. Two of the aides closed the space between Claire and the doorway with long strides. Gently they took her by the arms and steered her to one side of the hallway.

"Miss Anderson, you had best wait out here for a while."

Trembling, Claire managed to squeak out a question. "What happened?"

"We're not certain, but Mrs. Dixon thinks your grandmother suffered a stroke."

"No, no!" Claire put her face in her hands and slumped against the wall. The two older women tightened their grip on her, letting her lean against their strong bodies.

"Is . . . is she going to be all right?"

"I don't know, Claire." The honest reply came from Deanne Waverly, an aide who often worked the east wing and had become Nana's friend, and thus Claire's. "She's unconscious now but breathing on her own. We'll have to wait and see."

"What happened?" Claire asked again, her voice rising to a high pitch. "She was fine when I left her. She was fine."

Guilt flooded her. This day had just been too much of an exertion for Nana. She should have known that when her grandmother complained of being tired, of having a headache, she shouldn't have left her side. Surely there had been a sign, some indication that this stroke was imminent. But she had been too preoccupied with her own selfish thoughts to notice.

Mrs. Dixon, the head nurse, was directing traffic with authority, clearing the hall for the ambulance attendants who hurried down the hallway from the main entrance.

When the EMTs had carried their equipment into the room, Claire stepped cautiously into the doorway, still supported by the aides. She watched through a haze of emotion as her grandmother was deftly transferred from her bed to the hospital stretcher.

The old woman's skin was ashen and Claire heard her shallow, labored breaths even above the commotion. She backed away to clear a path and looked on in shock as the metal cart carrying the only family she had left in the world was maneuvered out the doorway and wheeled down the hall and out to the waiting ambulance.

# Twenty-three

*D*espite the protests of the nursing staff at Elmbrook, Claire insisted on driving herself to the hospital where Nana had been taken. Deanne Waverly thrust a scrap of paper bearing a crude, hastily drawn map into her hand and Claire ran to the parking lot.

Fortunately, the hospital was only a short distance away, and rush hour traffic had peaked an hour earlier. Claire parked the car illegally along the circle drive of the hospital's main visitors' entrance and ran inside the building.

There she was directed to the third floor, where a young nurse showed her to a small waiting room and assured her they would let her know the minute there was any news.

Claire had been there only a short time when a doctor appeared in the waiting room. His silver hair and sun-crinkled face gave him a venerable air. His eyes were kind and searching and Claire trusted him immediately.

"Miss Anderson?"

"Yes." Claire jumped up from the shabby upholstered chair and stood silently in front of him.

"Katherine Anderson is your grandmother?"

"Yes. Is she going to be okay?"

He gestured toward the row of chairs along the wall in the dimly lit room. "Please, sit down."

She did as he asked.

After they were seated, he extended a hand and introduced himself. "I'm Dr. Graham."

She nodded wordlessly.

"We still have several tests to run, but all the preliminaries indicate that your grandmother has had a stroke."

He looked at her as though to assess her reaction to the news. Claire nodded weakly to show that she understood and he continued.

"She is conscious and breathing on her own now, but we will want to watch her closely over the next twenty-four hours or so. I'm concerned that we're having trouble getting her blood pressure stabilized, but that is certainly not unusual in the case of a stroke." Dr. Graham put a large, warm hand over hers. "If you wait for twenty or thirty minutes, you can go in to the ICU to see your grandmother for a short while."

᪅  ᪅  ᪅  ᪅

Claire kept watch at her grandmother's bedside for the next hours, scarcely taking a moment to stretch her muscles or use the ladies' room. She did find a pay phone just outside the ICU and called Becky in Hanover Falls to explain what had happened and to ask her to pray for Nana and to pass the news on to Millie Overman.

Nana's condition had improved markedly by the following evening. She had been moved out of the ICU and was sitting up in bed and able to swallow a few clear liquids. Though her speech was slurred and she was very weak, she was able to make herself understood. It was clear that she knew where she was and what had happened. To Claire's great relief, her grandmother did not seem to be confused or disoriented.

Dr. Graham stopped by the hospital room that evening and, after examining Mrs. Anderson, motioned for Claire to step into the hallway with him.

"Your grandmother is a strong woman, Miss Anderson," he told her. "I think it's safe to say that given time, she will recover from this episode. However, she is going to require around-the-clock care. I don't know exactly what your situation is, but I think it would be wise—and in the best interest of both you and your grandmother— to try to get her settled in a nursing facility a bit closer to where you live. That's Hanover Falls, right?"

Claire nodded.

"Are you familiar with the facility there? Riverside, I believe."

"Riverview," Claire corrected him. "Yes, I know it well. It would be wonderful to have Nana there. How would I go about making those arrangements?"

Dr. Graham gave Claire information on how to expedite the transfer and told her that he would approve Katherine Anderson's release from the hospital as early as the following afternoon.

"Of course, there may be a wait to get into Riverview. I hate to move her any more than necessary, but ordinarily the insurance won't cover a longer stay in hospital," he continued. If there is a waiting list at Riverview, she could go back to Elmbrook. I assume they are holding her room there."

When Dr. Graham left, Claire went to a pay phone to call Riverview to find out if there was an opening available. When she told the receptionist why she was calling, she was transferred directly to the administration office. Claire was surprised and a little disconcerted to hear Michael's voice.

"Michael Meredith here. How can I help you?"

"Michael, this is Claire. Claire Anderson."

"Claire. Hello." It was difficult to read his voice. Uncertain, perhaps. Curious, understandably.

"I'm in Kansas City with my grandmother, Michael. She . . . she's had a stroke."

"Oh, I'm so sorry to hear that, Claire. Is she going to be all right?" The concern in his voice warmed her.

"She's doing better each day, but the doctor says she will need to be in nursing care. . . ."

"And you want her closer to home?" he guessed correctly.

"Yes. Are there any openings there right now?"

"There will be within the week. Our social worker is on another line right now, but I'll explain things briefly and then transfer you when that line is free. Mrs. Janzen can help get you set up for the evaluations."

The conversation became very businesslike as Michael explained the procedure for admission. Claire was disappointed to realize that it might be two weeks or longer before the move could actually take place. But Michael and, later, the social worker assured her that it was in her grandmother's best interests that the thorough screening process be followed. This would provide individualized care for all her needs: physical therapy, nursing care, speech therapy, and any number of other services that might help her to regain as much independence as possible.

It was enlightening for Claire to see Michael in the new light of his professional side. He was extremely sympathetic and helpful, seeming to understand that Claire had no idea what was involved in making this type of arrangement and explaining everything in terms she could easily understand. The social worker was equally helpful, and Claire hung up feeling encouraged about her grandmother's situation and about the way her conversation with Michael had gone. It was a small light in the darkness of her grandmother's illness to have had a positive conversation with Michael.

She spent the next afternoon making the necessary phone calls, signing the papers releasing her grandmother from the hospital, and arranging for skilled nursing care back at Elmbrook until the admission to Riverview was approved.

❧   ❧   ❧   ❧

Claire stayed in Kansas City for two more days, making certain that Nana's condition was stable and that the transfer back to Elmbrook went smoothly. She then made arrangements for Nana's furniture and other belongings at Elmbrook to be shipped to Hanover Falls.

After explaining to her grandmother the arrangements she had made, Claire drove to her temporary apartment one last time and loaded her belongings into her car. She went to the office and settled with the landlord, growing ever more eager to be heading back home.

She drove into a quiet Hanover Falls while the afternoon sun was still high in the sky. Though Claire had been away scarcely two weeks, summer had engraved its changes on the face of the village she'd left seemingly a lifetime ago. She drove through the familiar streets and realized with utter contentment that she *was* home. Especially now that Nana was on the mend and would soon be living nearby, she, who had always struggled for a sense of belonging, had truly found a home in this little town nestled in the Ozarks.

She pulled onto the narrow driveway of the house on Brookside Drive and parked the car near the back door. Millie's four-o'clocks were just opening up, and the pungent citrus scent of geranium leaves drifted to her on the slight breeze. The grass was tall, and here and there a dandelion threatened to invade, but the potted flowers she had hastily set out before leaving were beginning to overspill their pots and seemed well cared for. The flagstone patio desperately needed sweeping and the cracks were filled with tiny weeds, but it all seemed to her an inviting challenge.

She stretched her arms over her head and breathed deeply, then set about unpacking the car. As she reached the back door with her first load, Smokey sauntered around the corner of the house, meowing loudly.

"Smokey!" She set her burden of boxes and bags on the patio and stooped to pet him. He was fat and sleek, and he'd been rolling in the dirt under the lilac bush. She brushed the worst of the dust and debris from his fur.

"You silly old cat. Can't you find another place to play? Did you miss me, boy?"

He purred loudly in reply and leaned deeper into her fingernails as she scratched under his chin.

She unlocked the back door and set the things she had been carrying on the kitchen floor. The house was warm and the air smelled stale. She walked through the kitchen to the living room. The drapes were drawn and the room was dark. The furniture was covered with a fine layer of dust, but like the weedy patio, the dust seemed a friendly demand for her attention.

Feeling renewed, she hurried back through the kitchen to finish unloading the car. Smokey trotted back and forth with her as she carried in the rest of her boxes and bags. The large cat threatened to send her sprawling as he rubbed against her legs, purring and meowing as though to scold her for abandoning him. She groused at him good-naturedly and left him in the garage after the last box had been brought in. Tonight she would let him sleep on her bed and get his fill of pampering, but until then, she had work to do and she didn't need any interference. If she hurried, she could be settled in before she went to bed.

☙ ☙ ☙ ☙

Two weeks later Claire borrowed Becky's van and a wheelchair and made the trip to Elmbrook to move Nana to Riverview. The prospect of taking charge of her grandmother's fragile health for the journey was daunting, but Nana's insurance did not make provision for the transfer, and Claire's own resources were depleted after the expense of staying in Kansas City.

Though it was exhausting for Katherine Anderson, the trip proved uneventful. Claire helped her grandmother settle into the room at Riverview, and by week's end she was satisfied that the move had been a wise one.

Nana seemed to have weathered the trip from Kansas City well and was slowly adjusting to her new surroundings. Her belongings had arrived safely from Elmbrook, and Claire moved a few of her things into the room at Riverview. This room was smaller and more hospital-like, so it was difficult to make it seem homey and cozy like the apartment in Elmbrook had been. But Claire added some personal touches, making the best of the situation.

As she was able, the older woman began to receive more extensive physical therapy, and Claire thought she could see her grandmother improve almost daily.

🙦   🙦   🙦   🙦

As the days went by, Claire fell into a routine, spending the mornings—when Nana was fresh and alert—at Riverview, and the afternoons working on her lawn and flowers. By mid-summer, however, there was little left to do in the yard besides the weekly mowing and watering, and again, Claire found herself with too much time on her hands.

While visiting Nana one morning, she noticed an advertisement posted on the hallway bulletin board asking for volunteers to read to residents whose eyesight no longer allowed them to read for themselves. Claire was immediately drawn to the idea. It would be a way to fill her time productively and to give something back to the place where Nana was being cared for with such devotion. Besides, she loved to read, and here would be an opportunity to share that joy with someone else, as well as strike another title or two from her "must-read" list. She decided to inquire about it that very morning and stopped at the front desk, where she was directed to the personnel office.

Lana Welbourne, the Director of Human Resources, told her that the volunteer program was just getting off the ground, but if Claire was willing, she could unofficially begin her service the next day.

"In fact," Ms. Welbourne told her, laughing, "we have a gentleman who would drag you down to read to him this instant if he knew you were in my office. His name is Robert Tripleton," she explained. "He's a temporary resident in our respite care program—a rather unconventional resident, I might add. He's recovering from a serious car accident. He very nearly lost his sight and recently had a second surgery on both his eyes. Unfortunately, the surgery wasn't as successful as they hoped, so he is here until he regains his health and hopefully his eyesight. I'm afraid Mr. Tripleton is going crazy with boredom. He says the books-on-tape we've recommended are 'totally unsatisfactory—too impersonal.' " The woman lowered her voice, apparently attempting to imitate Mr. Tripleton's tone. "And he can't abide the television. He was a college professor," she added, as though that explained his loathing for television. "I'm sure he would be delighted if I could tell him you'll read for him tomorrow."

"Well, if I can read to suit him, I'd be glad to," Claire told the woman with only partly feigned apprehension. "What time should I come?"

"You're volunteering, Miss Anderson—may I call you Claire?"

"Of course."

"Well, Claire, you tell me what time. As long as it's not too early in the morning or too late at night, the man will simply be grateful you've come at all."

They agreed that Claire would meet Mr. Tripleton the following day at four and decide how to proceed from there. Claire left Ms. Welbourne's office with a feeling of satisfaction and anticipation.

# Twenty-four

"S ee you tomorrow, Nana." Claire leaned down and kissed the proffered cheek, then glanced at her watch. "Oh, goodness. It's nearly four now. I don't want to be late my first day!"

"Go then, dearie," Nana said, shooing Claire away with an awkward wave of her hand. Katherine Anderson was sitting up in a chair near her bed and looking very well, in Claire's estimation.

Claire had come to Riverview today with a double sense of purpose. Nana needed her less and less as she improved each day, and Claire was anxious to begin her volunteer work reading to residents of the manor. Afraid she would be late, and not wanting to make a bad impression her first day, she hurried down the hall, quickly deciphering the cryptic signs at each hallway intersection.

Robert Tripleton lived on the north wing and Claire, now more familiar with the layout of Riverview, hurried around a corner. As she did so, she nearly collided with Michael Meredith. They both laughed nervously and he stepped aside.

"I'm sorry," Claire blushed. "I must have been exceeding the speed limit."

He held out his hands in surrender. "Then I plead guilty as well." Then, with concern in his voice, he asked, "How is your grandmother getting along, Claire?"

She had been in Michael's office twice since Nana moved to Riverview, signing one paper or another, and their encounters had, by unspoken agreement, been polite, if rather formal. Their near collision now seemed to have lightened the mood, and Claire felt more comfortable in his presence than she had in a long time.

Sensing his genuine interest, she told him, "I just came from Nana's room. She's doing remarkably well, thank you. The physical therapy has made a tremendous difference."

"I'm glad to hear that," he said warmly. Their eyes locked and for a few seconds they were silent. Suddenly looking uneasy, he glanced at his watch. "Well, it was nice to run into you . . . quite literally."

She laughed. "You too."

He started down the hallway, but Claire, feeling unaccountably brave, called after him.

"Michael?"

He turned toward her, his expression open and curious.

She moved toward him, suddenly overwhelmed again by the way he made her feel. Her heart raced and she felt her palms grow clammy, but she had started this and she wasn't about to back out now.

"Michael, I . . . I wonder if you'd like to meet Nana? Sometime. Not right away of course, but—" She cut her sentence off, longing for a sense of how he was receiving this invitation. She had been thinking about the possibility ever since Nana had been moved to Riverview.

Now his eyes held hers with a warmth she remembered from their first meeting. "I'd like that, Claire. I'd like that very much." He hesitated. "Does she know . . . who I am?"

Claire shook her head. "I haven't told her yet. She knew about us—" Claire swallowed hard. She hadn't counted on the memories this invitation would evoke. "She knew about us before, but I haven't told her that you were Joseph. I always meant to tell her, but after the stroke, I . . . I was afraid it would be too much."

"I understand. I know you have her best interests at heart. I would like to meet her, Claire."

"I think she's strong enough to know the truth now," she told him, even as she realized that it was she who was finally strong enough. "I want a chance to tell her everything before you meet her."

"Whatever you think is best. Let me know when you think the time is right."

"I will. And thank you, Michael." The lump that had formed in her throat threatened to choke her. It was so good to be standing here talking with him again. So good to be able to refer to their past without accusations and tears. Maybe this was the closure she had longed for. No, *not* a closure, she realized. Instead, a promising beginning to a new bond of friendship with Michael. It was still difficult to be in his presence without stirring up the old feelings. But she knew it wasn't right to feel so awkward and uncertain every time they ran into each other. Christian love surely allowed them to be on friendly terms. She wanted to do her part to permit that to happen.

Michael looked at his watch again. Smiling warmly, he made excuses. "Well, I'm going to be late for a meeting if I don't get going. I'll see you around, I'm sure."

"Yes," she said simply. As she watched him hurry down the hallway, an old, unwelcome sensation tugged at her insides. *Why does he have to be so handsome? Why do his gentle ways have to melt my heart so?*

Mentally chiding herself, she turned on her heel and directed her attention to finding Robert Tripleton's room. She slowed her pace, checking the number on each room, nervously smoothing a hand over her hair and straightening her clothing as she approached the door.

She knocked quietly and, hearing a gruff, muffled reply within, cautiously opened the door to the private room. The gentleman seated in the large recliner at the window couldn't have been more different than Claire had expected.

Though he wore a neck brace and a thick bandage on his left hand, not a wrinkle marred the dark olive complexion, and a head of thick brown waves nodded for her to enter. If Robert Tripleton was a day over forty, he had discovered—and drunk often from—a fountain of youth.

Claire was left speechless. She was grateful for the dark glasses he wore, for they served to remind her that the man was—at least temporarily—legally blind and hopefully unable to detect her surprise.

"M-Mr. Tripleton?" she stammered.

"Yes. That's me."

"I'm Claire Anderson. They sent me to read for you. Do you have something you'd like me to start with? Is this a good time?" Suddenly flustered, her voice squeaked out of control.

She had carried a vague picture of this Mr. Tripleton in her mind: a picture of a very wizened, feeble, ancient person. And now here the man sat—dark, good-looking in a rugged, outdoors way, and seemingly far too young for a place like this. She wondered what his story might be. What tragic circumstances had decreed that a man so young and seemingly vital recover from his accident in a nursing home?

He was neatly dressed in tan slacks and an open-collared oxford cloth shirt. His smooth-shaven face—and a tiny scrap of tissue covering a razor nick—attested to the recent use of a spicy masculine shaving soap, the scent of which hung faintly in the air of the room.

"Ah . . . so they finally sent you," he said, not impolitely.

"Yes. Do you have something in mind you'd like me to read today? Or is there something I could bring you from the library?" Claire asked, regaining her composure.

He fumbled for a well-worn volume on the table beside his chair. "I was in the middle of this when I was"—he searched for a word—"sidelined by this." He touched the dark glasses gingerly.

"Do you have any sight at all?" Claire ventured.

He was very matter-of-fact. "I can make out light and darkness—some vague shapes if the light is right. It seems to be a bit better day by day, but the doctors are not promising that I'll be able to return to work anytime soon."

"And what is your work?" Claire asked, making conversation.

"I teach—I taught," he corrected himself, "at the college in Mullinville. English literature."

"Oh, how awful!" Claire cried reflexively.

"Teaching English literature? It's not all that terrible." In spite of the confining neck brace, Robert Tripleton laughed heartily at his deliberate misinterpretation of her remark.

His genial laughter put her more at ease. "No, I meant . . . well, it must be terribly difficult to lose your sight—especially in your profession."

He turned serious again. "It's not been easy. But I am looking at this as a very temporary condition. And I do thank you for your offer to read to me. I will appreciate it more than you can know." As though dismissing any further sympathy, he handed her the book. "I believe my place is marked."

She took the book from him and turned the brittle pages to the place marked with a folded sheet of writing paper. She was dismayed to see that the volume was an early copy of Tolstoy's *Anna Karenina*.

"I thought you said *English* literature," she commented, hoping he could detect the smile in her voice.

"Ah, but I much prefer the Russians. This is not my classroom reading. *This* is for pleasure."

"I remember reading this book in college, but I don't recall finding much pleasure in the reading. I seem to recall it as very dreary and depressing and *long*."

"Are you aware that many scholars believe this to be the greatest novel ever written? It is a tragedy, but it has a very profound message."

"Which is?"

He turned his head in the direction of her voice, a skeptical grin on his lips. "But I thought you read the book, Miss Anderson. You didn't perchance just read the Cliffs Notes version, did you?"

In spite of the fact that he could not see her face, she blushed. "It's possible," she admitted, smiling sheepishly. Then changing the subject, she smoothed her hand over the frayed book cover. "This is a wonderful edition. It looks very old."

"It was my grandfather's. Look inside. I think this copy was published in the early part of the century."

She leafed back to the front of the book. "Oh, this *is* old," she whispered almost under her breath.

Handling the volume on her lap gingerly, she told him, "I hardly feel qualified to read a book like this aloud. I admit I came in expecting to read a light mystery novel or maybe a biography. But I'll do my best. Would you mind filling me in on what has happened to this point?"

"Why don't we just start all over at the beginning. I could make an honest student of you yet."

Claire laughed, feeling much more at ease in the man's presence. But she protested, "You don't need to start over on my account."

"No. It's been so long since I began the book"—he cleared his throat deliberately—"my third reading, I might mention—that I would benefit from starting over at the beginning anyway."

"Well, if you're sure."

Claire opened the book and cleared her throat. At first the words and phrases of the great novelist seemed difficult and foreign to her, but as she became involved in the story, the characters began to come to life and she found herself lost in the drama of the unfolding story.

" 'Happy families are all alike; every unhappy family is unhappy in its own way,' " she read thoughtfully. "Oh, how true!" she interjected, almost involuntarily. "Oh, I'm sorry, I promise I won't comment on every sentence. It's just that that statement struck me as so timeless." She read another paragraph and started to read on, but he lifted a bandaged hand and interrupted her.

"You sound as though you know something about unhappy families," he broached cautiously.

She sighed, caught off guard by the gentleness in his voice. She started to reply, then felt embarrassed that she had been about to confide in a complete stranger—and one to whom she was supposed to be providing help, not the other way around.

"No more than many people, I suppose," she hedged.

"I wonder if an unhappy family is preferable to no family at all," he said pensively.

"And I sometimes wonder the opposite," she said with more candidness than she intended. Then, partly to deflect the attention from herself and partly because she sensed that his remark had been a hint at his own situation, she asked, "Do you have a family?"

In a straightforward manner, as though he had answered the question many times, he told her, "I was born when my parents were in their forties. They died within a few months of each other the year I turned twenty-five. So to answer your question, my childhood was spent in quite a happy family, but I have been alone for many years. Nine now . . . no, nearly ten." He seemed surprised by the realization.

Claire did some quick math. So he was, indeed, in his thirties. She was struck by his genteel, old-world manner. In spite of his youthful appearance, his refined speech and dignified bearing—made more pronounced by the brace that held his neck high—caused him to seem older than his years.

"And you have no other relatives?" Her question sounded blunt in her own ears.

"No. I doubt that I would find myself in a place such as this had I any family at all." It was the first time she had heard the least hint of bitterness in his voice.

"I'm sorry," she said simply. "It must be terribly difficult."

He forced a smile and waved her sympathies aside. "Well, it's not your fault. Let's get back to the story."

"You'll remember that you were the one who interrupted that time," she teased, trying to lighten the moment and feeling bold, perhaps because he couldn't see her.

"Touché," he laughed. "Read on, Miss Anderson."

Disregarding the fact that he couldn't see her smile, she grinned at him and began reading where they had left off.

She read for an hour, until her voice became hoarse and she could see that he was growing weary.

"That's the end of the chapter. Shall we quit for today?"

"Yes, but don't wait too long to come back. We're just getting to the good part."

"Oh, I'll be back tomorrow if that's all right with you. You see, my grandmother is here recovering from a stroke. I teach here in Hanover Falls, but during the summer my days are free."

"That's good news. So you're a teacher too?"

"Well, yes, but just elementary school. Third grade."

"Oh, now don't sell yourself short. I should rather teach a thousand college students than one third-grader. It's a high calling—to teach a young child."

"Well, I do love teaching." His comments made her feel as though she had been fishing for a compliment and yet she basked in them. Suddenly self-conscious, she looked at her watch. "Well, I really should be going. I'll see you tomorrow—at the same time if that suits you."

"I'll look forward to it. I do thank you so much for volunteering your time. You have a very pleasant reading voice."

She blushed, embarrassed at the compliment. "Well, I don't know about that, but thank you."

"No. Thank *you*. I don't think you have any idea how much this means to me. I do thank you." The sincerity in his voice was charming.

As she closed Robert Tripleton's door behind her and met two nurses in the hallway, she had to conceal a smile. What an interesting encounter this had turned out to be. She found the man utterly enchanting and so easy to talk to that it was tempting to confide too much. She would have to guard herself against being unprofessional. Even though this was a volunteer position, it was an assignment she had taken under the auspices of Riverview, and she wanted to do it with propriety.

On the way home she stopped at the library and checked out a copy of *Anna Karenina* and a biography of its author, Count Leo Nikolayevich Tolstoy.

She read until late into the evening, and she dreamed that night that she walked along the shadowy streets of nineteenth-century Moscow, escorted by a handsome man who wore a neck brace and dark glasses. But when the man in her dream turned stiffly toward her, it was Michael Meredith's face that smiled above the brace.

# Twenty-five

*T*he door to Robert Tripleton's room was open, but Claire rapped quietly on the door jamb to announce her arrival.

"Is that my story time lady?" a deep voice joked.

"'Tis I," Claire played along.

She made herself comfortable in a straight-back chair in front of his recliner and took the book he held in her direction.

"I did a little research last night and borrowed a biography of Tolstoy from the library. It's a lot more interesting than I thought it would be."

"You're certainly taking this assignment seriously," he said somewhat smugly.

"Well, you made me feel so guilty I started to fear my degree might be revoked if I didn't make up for my indiscretion back in Literature 101."

"And it might yet be if you don't get busy reading."

Claire loved the easy repartee they had quickly established. Laughing, she opened to the place she had marked and began reading.

᷍ ᷍ ᷍ ᷍

Claire read to Robert Tripleton every afternoon during the week, and in the evenings she waded through the biography of the great Russian author. Though much of it was interesting, especially in light of the novel she was reading, there were dry passages and information that didn't interest her a great deal. Still she was determined to finish both biography and novel—word for word. Not the Cliffs Notes version this time.

❧   ❧   ❧   ❧

Michael Meredith strode purposefully out the door and down the sidewalk toward the newly finished senior center. The building was operating at full tilt now, and overseeing its maintenance and activities was just another thing to keep him busier than he thought possible.

He made a quick tour through the main activity room, stopping to chat briefly with the residents who had gathered there to work on a quilt, play cards, or just to visit. As always, he was greeted warmly, and his attention was eagerly sought by the elderly residents. Michael was flattered to be a favorite of these people, and he intended never to forget that they were the reason he was here—not the buildings or the money or any of the other things that tended to steal so much of his time from the things he felt to be truly important.

But this morning it was difficult to focus his attention. He knew that his preoccupation was apparent to his elderly friends. After only a few minutes of visiting, he headed back to his office.

With a sinking feeling in the pit of his stomach, Michael thought about the things he had learned yesterday. The suspicions Vera had voiced weeks ago never completely died, but Geneva Grayson and Cynthia Harper seemed to have mended their differences and each continued to perform her duties with efficiency and compassion. Though hard to ignore, Cynthia Harper's eccentric ways had been, for the most part, overlooked. Margaret Wallace had recovered sufficiently to move back into her apartment for a short time, though recently she had taken another turn for the worse and was back in the skilled-nursing unit. Cynthia reportedly claimed it was her prayers that were responsible for Margaret's recovery. While Michael certainly would not deny the power of prayer, he was mostly relieved that there had been no more mention of conversations with angels, nor had any other suspicious literature materialized.

But today the doubts loomed large and, in fact, seemed to be mushrooming far beyond vague suspicions.

The latest incident was more worrisome than anything that had come before, and Michael knew that he could no longer pretend that something was not terribly wrong. He also knew with certainty now that Cynthia Harper was somehow implicated.

A young nurse aide, new on the job, had come to Vera that morning telling of an alarming conversation she had had with Harper. According to Melissa Warrington, Harper had told her an impassioned tale of her husband's death three years earlier.

"Mrs. Harper told me that her husband—Jimmy was his name—was in such pain that she couldn't even stand to be in the room with him. She said the strongest pain medications didn't seem to phase him, and when he finally died, he had been driven all but mad by the pain." The story had poured out of Melissa in a frightened whisper as she sat in Vera's office.

"The thing that scared me more than anything," the young girl told Vera, "was when Mrs. Harper told me that he shouldn't have suffered that way. She said, 'I should have ended his suffering. There are things I could have done.'"

"Did she explain what she meant?" Vera had coaxed.

Melissa nodded and plunged in. "She got this funny look in her eyes and started rambling on about the government and something about the Netherlands—how they have it all figured out over there so that everyone is allowed a compassionate death, and no one has to suffer needlessly. I may not have much of an education, Mrs. Johanssen, but I know enough to realize that she was talking about supposed mercy killing. She . . . well, she almost looked crazy when she was telling me all this. Her eyes were . . . it was so weird—really creepy. I just thought I should tell you."

When Vera related the incident to Michael that morning, she reported that the young aide had actually shivered involuntarily when she told the story. He immediately called Beth VanMeter into Vera's office for a solemn meeting.

"We can't sit on this for another minute," he told the two women. "Something is seriously wrong here, and we had better get to the bottom of it before someone gets hurt." *If they haven't already*, he thought with a sinking feeling, remembering Frederick Halloran's death ten months before.

The three had agreed that in light of an incriminating statement from a second source—completely unrelated to Geneva Grayson's earlier accusations—Harper must be questioned and the board of directors be informed that an in-house investigation was underway. Michael headed back to his office intent on arming himself with as much evidence as possible before he confronted Harper. And the first person he intended to talk to was Gerald Stoddard.

He searched through the files until he found the information he was looking for, Stoddard's forwarding address and phone. Dialing the Texas number with determination, he tapped his fingers on the desk, listening as the phone rang on the other end.

"Hello?" a cheery middle-aged voice answered.

"Gerald Stoddard, please."

"May I ask who's calling?" There was casual caution in the voice, as though the woman were screening out a possible sales call.

"Yes, this is Michael Meredith with Riverview Manor in Hanover Falls."

"Yes, of course, just a moment."

Michael heard a muffled conversation over the wires, and then the feminine voice was on the line again, this time sounding agitated. "My husband isn't able to come to the phone just now. Could I take a message?"

"Yes. Please have him call me at his earliest convenience. This is somewhat of an emergency. I need to ask him some very important questions."

"May I tell him what this concerns?"

Michael had the impression that her questions were being prompted. He thought of referring to the conversation he and Stoddard had at the conference in Joplin, but he feared the man had been too drunk to remember. Finally he said, "Just tell him that we need some information about a nurse he hired shortly before he left his position here. It's very important," he repeated.

"I'll tell him."

Michael gave her the number. "Thank you, Mrs. Stoddard."

He pushed the button for a dial tone and began to call the members of Riverview Manor's board of directors.

❧   ❧   ❧   ❧

The air in the boardroom hung heavy with curiosity. In his two years at Riverview, Michael Meredith had never called a special meeting—most certainly not an emergency meeting—and the members were naturally inquisitive about what had precipitated this gathering.

As the last stragglers filtered into the room and found seats around the large table, Michael brought the meeting to order.

"I know you are all busy and I'm sorry to have to take up your time, but something has come up and I need your input. I feel this is something that cannot wait, something on which we need to take immediate action."

He turned to Vera, who sat beside him at the head of the table. "Over the past several months, several questionable incidents have been brought to our attention, but until this morning we did not feel we had any valid reason to take action in the matter." He went on to briefly review the significant events that had transpired.

"Vera and I have interviewed Cynthia Harper," he concluded, "and while she categorically denies any wrongdoing, Mrs. Johanssen, Ms. VanMeter, and I agree that in light of our recent observations and statements made by at least two other employees, Nurse Harper does not seem to have the stability necessary for the extreme responsibility she holds in her position." He took a deep breath. "As of this morning, Cynthia Harper has been suspended from employment at Riverview, and I am requesting that an in-house investigation begin immediately."

A collective gasp rose from the table.

"Do you think this is wise, Michael?" Jack Braverman posed. "You hold to this suspension and we're liable to have a lawsuit on our hands. You said yourself she denies the accusations!"

There were assenting murmurs.

Michael held up a quieting hand. "Yes, Jack, that's true. But we have two unrelated sources attributing some pretty incriminating statements to Cynthia. In light of the information we have, I don't think it would be prudent to do anything less than dismiss her. This is only a suspension, of course, until we have solid proof of anything. Hopefully our investigation will answer all the questions we have, and we will be able to dissuade any legal action for the time being."

He cleared his throat and addressed the room again. "As administrator of this facility, I am bound by law, and certainly by ethics, to report any legitimate suspicions of abuse or foul play—anything whatsoever that would put our residents at risk. And while it's true that we don't have solid proof of anything at this time, I don't think there is any doubt that this situation has come dangerously close to warranting a report to the health department. I'm sure I don't have to tell you what that kind of investigation would mean for this facility."

Several of the board nodded knowingly. Mildred Swafford took her reading glasses off her nose and let them dangle on the chain around her neck. "While I do understand your concern, I wonder why the board wasn't consulted on this *before* action was taken."

Vera came to Michael's defense. "Mildred, we have never required board approval to dismiss an employee who was not performing to expectations. That has always been an administrative decision."

"Yes, Vera, but *Cynthia?* Surely there was some other more . . . diplomatic way to deal with this." The matronly woman glanced in Jack Braverman's direction as though he were a conspirator in some secret.

Her action gave Michael courage to broach the subject that he dreaded. "I understand that Cynthia Harper is somehow related to Nita Dalhardt?"

His question was met with silence, except for a nervous clearing of throats. Nita Dalhardt was the main benefactor of the new senior center and a long-time contributor to many manor building programs. It was her name that Gerald Stoddard had invoked as his reason for being pressured to hire Harper, even against Vera's objections.

"I've heard some disturbing rumors about the circumstances under which Cynthia Harper was hired in the first place," he said now, his growing anger giving him courage. "If I think for a minute that her relationship to Nita Dalhardt is influencing your reaction to this decision, I will have no choice but to turn this whole mess over to an unbiased agency for investigation."

He felt sick to his stomach. He made such a threat because he was convinced that the opposition he was facing had *everything* to do with Dalhardt, the philanthropist. For him to make good on his threat was tantamount to professional suicide. Scrutiny by an outside agency would irreparably damage the pristine reputation of Riverview, and certainly his own professional reputation. Even if his suspicions about Cynthia Harper ultimately proved to be unfounded, by then it would be too late.

Apparently the board took his threat seriously. Jack Braverman looked around the table and spoke, presumably for the entire board. "We'll stand behind you, Michael. Let's do everything possible to keep this quiet and to clear Cynthia's name as quickly as possible."

The meeting was adjourned and the boardroom became a hive of activity as the attendees broke into groups of two and three, discussing the situation in hushed whispers as they edged toward the door.

Michael sought Vera out in the hallway and together they and Beth VanMeter walked back toward the building that housed their offices.

"You were wonderful in there," Beth told him. "Talk about a rock and a hard place."

"Well, thank you, Beth. I loathe having to make threats, but I felt I had no choice."

"What are you thinking, Vera? Did I do the right thing?"

"I think you did the only thing you could do at this point, Michael. But . . ." Vera stopped abruptly and shook her head, as though she'd decided not to say more.

"What? Please, Vera. I'm certainly open to any advice."

"It's just that I don't think there's any way we're going to keep this quiet. This is a small town, Michael. I have a feeling you'd better be preparing your statements for the six o'clock news."

# Twenty-six

*A*s the days progressed, Claire felt almost guilty at the benefit she was receiving from her volunteer work. Unable to resist playing the professor, Robert Tripleton was making Claire's reading sessions an enlightening experience. Every few paragraphs he would stop her and challenge her with a question or an observation. When he pointed out the correlation between events in the story and those in Tolstoy's life, Claire was pleased that, because of her reading of the biography, she was able to add to his observations. Soon she became comfortable asking him to explain a difficult passage or define a word. He was making the book come alive for her, and she relished the feeling of accomplishment it was to tackle a literary work such as this. She was beginning to see why certain works became classics. And although the story still seemed rather depressing to her, she saw that it had spiritual dimensions she might not have perceived without the guidance of her "tutor."

One afternoon she had asked a question about the story, addressing him as always as Mr. Tripleton.

He answered her with an amicably mimicking "Yes, Miss Anderson." Then, suddenly serious, he asked, "May I call you Claire?"

His sudden change of tone surprised her but she replied in the affirmative.

"And please, even my students call me Rob. I'd appreciate it if you'd do the same. I feel enough like an old geezer in this place as it is. It doesn't help to be addressed as *Mr. Tripleton*." He lowered his chin into the neck brace and spoke the title in a mockingly formal baritone.

"Okay, Rob." She tried out the informal label, then wrinkled her nose. "Oooh . . . that's going to feel strange after all this time. Rob," she repeated firmly, as though to commit the change to memory.

"Claire," he reciprocated, sounding satisfied. "And while we're at it, Claire, would it be too personal if I asked you what you look like?"

She was taken aback. "Does it matter?" she asked tentatively.

He flashed a grin in her general direction and goaded, "I have this picture of you in my mind. I'm curious how accurate it is."

"Let's hear your preconception first," she said with feigned suspicion.

"Well . . . Oh, I'd guess about four hundred pounds, a big wart on your nose, frizzy gray hair—"

"Hey! Wait a minute! Okay, okay, I give," she laughed. But suddenly she felt terribly self-conscious. She realized that she cared very much what he thought about her. But how did one describe oneself to an attractive man?

She thought for a minute. "Well, you're right about the frizzy hair. But it's reddish blond, not gray. I'm about five-seven, my eyes are hazel. And I don't *quite* weigh four hundred pounds. Not yet, anyway."

Rob spoke in a tone that suddenly unsettled her. "How old are you, Claire?"

"I'm . . . I'm twenty-six."

"And I'll bet you're beautiful."

She started to protest, but he cleared his throat and shook his head as if to clear away some disturbing thought. "Well, we'd better read on."

Claire found the place they had left off and read in a quiet voice, but she looked up at him surreptitiously between paragraphs and sensed that if he had had his sight she would have caught him staring at her.

Claire tried to eschew the undercurrents she felt flowing between them. This feeling—a tenderness that seemed too intimate even though it remained unspoken—made her uncomfortable and yet it intrigued her too.

She finished the chapter and said her good-byes, but conversation was awkward between them now, and she feared she had somehow allowed things to become too personal.

The following day, however, Rob greeted her with his usual joking manner. Their discussion of the book resumed its scholarly feel, and by the time she left that afternoon, she wondered if perhaps she had imagined the—were they romantic?—undercurrents.

Claire had asked for and been assigned two more residents to whom she began to read. Guiltily, she found herself cutting her sessions with these two elderly women short and saving her voice and her time for Rob. She thoroughly enjoyed his company, and day by day she grew to know him better.

Though they had each shared personal stories of their lives and had seemingly mutually come to view their relationship more as that of equals than of student and teacher, or invalid and "nurse," they still deftly skirted around any straightforward discussion of their friendship.

Claire thought about Rob as she drove home one afternoon after spending an hour reading and visiting with him. Since the day they had come to be on a first-name basis, she had tried to ignore the decidedly romantic undercurrent she had sensed early on. She simply didn't need that complication in her life. Yet when she carefully searched her heart, she knew that the feelings she held for Rob were beginning to go deeper than mere friendship.

She began to wonder if their friendship might blossom into something more if she permitted it. Perhaps the easy, comfortable friendship she shared with Rob held more of the kind of emotion that made for a good lifetime relationship than the roller-coaster feelings she had for Michael Meredith. Maybe the emotions she felt for Michael were based more on sympathy than on true love. Yet she had to admit that if anyone deserved to have her sympathy, it was Rob. But she felt none of that for him because he didn't ask for it and wouldn't have allowed it.

Still, if her friendship with Rob was to lead to something more, she knew she would feel more than mild disappointment that there was not the "electricity" that she always felt in Michael's presence. Perhaps she was too hung up on romance. She shook her head to clear away the confusing thoughts and turned her attention to the traffic in front of her.

❧   ❧   ❧   ❧

As the upcoming school year drew near, Claire found it more and more difficult to find time to spend with Nana. She had learned that a major change in curriculum—which unfortunately, included her grade level—would need to be reviewed and her lesson plan adjusted accordingly. It was a frustrating undertaking for a second-year teacher. In addition were the hours spent each week with Riverview's volunteer reading program. She had warned Lana Welbourne that she would have to cut back drastically during the school year, but she had committed to the summer and was determined to fulfill that promise.

Nana was doing well, growing stronger each day, and seemingly very happy at Riverview. But the combination of her physical limitations and her newness to the Riverview "community" had curtailed the active social life she had experienced at Elmbrook. This meant that for now, Claire *was* Nana's social life. Claire felt sure things would change as Nana became more mobile, but for now, it put an extra burden on her.

Though Nana didn't seem the least confused or disoriented, Claire found it rather disconcerting that since the move, the elderly woman seemed to be dwelling on the past—almost reliving her life aloud to her only granddaughter. Most upsetting to Claire was the fact that Nana seemed to have Michael—though of course she spoke of him as Joseph—on her mind often.

On a Saturday afternoon when Nana had brought up her worries about Joseph yet again—wondering aloud what had become of him— Claire decided that perhaps now was the time to reveal the truth about Michael's identity. Nana seemed to be emotionally strong, and Claire felt certain that now that she herself had come to a tentative peace about what had happened with Michael, the knowledge of "Joseph's" whereabouts and well-being would give her grandmother peace as well.

Walking together in the hallway, Claire followed slowly beside Nana. The stroke had left Katherine Anderson unable to walk unaided. Now she used a walker, taking frail, halting steps and barely managing to keep her balance as she pushed the metal framework along in front of her.

"I just pray that we might yet know what became of your brother, Claire."

Claire cringed inwardly at Nana's reference to Joseph—Michael— as her brother. "Nana," she finally said, "let's sit down for a bit."

Gathering her wits, she steered her grandmother to a quiet window seat at the end of the hallway.

"You have something on your mind. Tell me, Kitty."

Claire hesitated for the slightest moment, then plunged in. "Nana, I have something I want to tell you. This is going to come as a shock to you. It still doesn't seem possible to me but—well, I *do* know where Joseph is." She let the revelation soak in and was surprised by the emotion that rose within her as she prepared to speak the profound words. Taking her grandmother's hand tightly in her own, she spoke quietly. "Nana, you remember my friend, Michael Meredith?"

"Well, of course I do. Oh, Claire. Are you seeing him again? I know how much you liked that young man."

Claire bit her lip. "No, Nana. It . . . it turns out that Michael was . . . Michael *is* Joseph, Nana."

The smile faded from her grandmother's lips, and the blood drained from her face. "Michael Meredith? Your young man? I don't understand. What are you saying, Kitty?"

"Nana, when Dad—when we sent Joseph away," she said gently, "he was adopted by another family—the Merediths—and he took his real name back and . . . then we met and . . ." Claire felt her eyes well with tears and she struggled to keep her composure. "We were talking one night—Michael and I—about our childhoods. One thing led to another, and suddenly we realized that we had known each other before. Michael is the boy we . . . the boy Mother and Dad adopted, Nana. He remembers you," she said, trying to give some fragment of happiness to her grandmother. In spite of her attempt to keep the revelation upbeat, a sad smile crossed Claire's face. But it turned into a frown of concern as she saw the sum of this information register as shock on her grandmother's face.

"Nana, are you all right? Nana?"

"It's just so unbelievable, that's all," the old woman said, her voice quavering. For a moment, her words seemed slurred as they had right after the stroke. But when she spoke next, Claire was relieved to hear her enunciate clearly as she had learned through many sessions of speech therapy. "To think that it would turn out this way," she said slowly. A faraway look came to her eyes and she whispered to no one in particular, "Joseph. Joseph. I always wondered . . ."

Returning to the present, she gave Claire a searching look. "How long have you known this, Claire? Is Joseph all right? Is he. . . ?" She couldn't seem to find the words.

"He's fine, Nana." Claire patted the frail hand, concerned that the news had been more of a shock than she had foreseen.

Trying to reassure her grandmother, she went on. "The family Michael has now is wonderful. It's obvious that he loves them very much. It hasn't been easy for him, but he has a strong faith—a very real faith—and his life is good now. Remember I told you he's the administrator over all of Riverview Manor," she told her grandmother proudly, as though she held some claim to Michael's success. She brightened for a moment just thinking about him. "He is wonderful with the older people here, Nana. He really has made a successful life."

"Joseph . . ." Nana whispered, still shaking her head at the shocking news.

"Nana," Claire asked suddenly, "why would Mother and Daddy have changed his name? He was eight or nine when he came to live with us, wasn't he?"

Nana nodded, a faraway look in her eyes. "His real name was Michael—but of course you know that. Michael, just like Raymond and Myra's first baby. Your mother simply couldn't abide the boy having the same name as her firstborn son, so they decided to change it."

Claire was stunned. "I never knew that."

"No. There was much you weren't told, Kitty. Of course, you were young yourself."

Claire let the revelation soak in, imagining how confusing it must have been for Michael trying to adjust not only to a new life and a new home, but even a new name. For the first time she was almost able to picture young Joseph as Michael Meredith—the wounded little boy who had grown into the man she loved. And her heart broke for him.

Unbidden, his name escaped her lips. "Oh, Michael," she whispered, tears springing to her eyes.

"You still love him, don't you, Kitty?" Nana said bluntly, not needing an answer.

"Oh, Nana, I do feel love for him, but . . . I don't think I'm *allowed* to love him the way you mean. After all, he was my brother. And I . . . we hurt him so. . . ." She let her words hang in the air.

"I certainly hope he doesn't hold against you the choices Raymond and Myra made for him," Katherine Anderson said defensively.

"He says he doesn't, Nana, but I know I must be a constant reminder to him of the worst time in his life . . . the worst thing that ever happened to him." She spoke the words almost as a question, perhaps subconsciously hoping her grandmother could dispute what she feared to be true.

Instead, Nana asked her again, "Do you love him, Kitty?"

"I *can't* love him, Nana. Not that way. I don't have that choice."

"Well, darling, I'm not sure we *choose* whom we love—whether it's allowed or not. But I can't believe that it would be wrong for you and Michael to have that kind of a friendship—a romantic one, I mean—if you are both agreed. After all, you're not related by blood."

"I'm just so confused, Nana. One minute I don't think I can live without him, and the next minute I realize it couldn't possibly work between us."

"Does he return your love?" Nana asked.

"He did. Once." She shook her head quickly. "But not anymore."

"I'm sorry, Kitty. Maybe it will still work out. Only the Lord knows what is right for the two of you," Nana said quietly, patting Claire's leg softly. "If it was meant to be, it will be."

A gleam came to the aged eyes. With some effort, she reached up and put a withered hand on Claire's arm, and with a hint of mischief in her voice she told her only granddaughter, "If an old woman could put in a word though, it certainly does not seem to me that the Lord would forbid two innocent young people love simply because they had been thrown together as brother and sister for one ill-begotten year of their lives."

Nana's words confused her and put a terrible seed of hope inside her. Claire couldn't let this conversation continue. She had already worked this out in her mind. She and Michael had only recently come to the place where they could be friends again. She didn't need to hear this. She couldn't allow herself to think this way.

Quickly changing the subject, she broached the real reason she had been wanting to discuss this matter with her grandmother. "Nana, I've been wondering. Would you . . . would you like to meet Michael?"

"Oh, Kitty. Do you think he would be willing to do that?"

Claire smiled. "I know he would, Nana. I've already talked to him about it."

"It would mean more to me than you can imagine."

"I'll invite him for a visit as soon as possible."

Nana reached up and put a frail hand to her head, finger-combing the yellow-white curls. "Oh now, Kitty. Please try to arrange it for late in the week. They come to do my hair on Thursdays. I don't want to scare him off with this mop."

Claire laughed and squeezed her grandmother's shoulders. "You always look beautiful, Nana. But I'll make sure it's after Thursday."

🐝　🐝　🐝　🐝

The corridor was wrapped in a cloak of midnight silence. Only the soft whir of air conditioners and the drone of the computer at the nurses' station broke the perfect stillness. The lone figure padded softly down the tiled hallway and slipped unobserved through the door to Margaret Wallace's room.

Maggie had finally ceased the tossing and moaning that had tormented her earlier in the day. Now she lay exhausted, barely conscious, in the bed. She did not hear the door open, nor did she see the slight figure lean over her bed.

Hands sheathed in sterile surgical gloves reached out and patted her emaciated shoulder with great tenderness. A deep intake of breath could be heard and then the instrument of mercy, a small syringe, was withdrawn from a pocket and uncapped. It took only seconds to inject the contents into the IV line.

As silently as they had come, the footsteps retreated down the hallway and descended the stairwell, out into the sultry night air.

# Twenty-seven

*L*ate Sunday afternoon Claire left her grandmother's room and headed down the corridor toward the main entrance. She was still excited about her conversation with Nana the previous day, pleased that her grandmother was so open to meeting Michael. She would try to speak with him about it tomorrow. After his positive response the first time she had mentioned the possibility, she felt certain Michael would be happy to know that Nana felt ready for such a meeting. But she didn't want to talk to him in front of the other office staff. Perhaps if she came later in the day she could catch him alone.

Preoccupied with trying to think of what she would say to Michael, she almost didn't notice the disassembled trash receptacle in the middle of the main hallway. The lidded top piece was lying upside down on one side of the hallway, and on the other side Oliver Moon was cursing—at least the inflection in the unintelligible words sounded profane—at a large plastic trash bag, attempting to secure it inside the container, which was almost as tall as he. Beside him lay the overflowing bag he had just removed.

Just as Michael Meredith had promised Claire when she first moved to Hanover Falls, she had quickly come to know Ollie as one of the town's eccentric characters. Everyone seemed to agree that Ollie was harmless, and most spoke of him with deep affection. But though she would never have admitted it, the man made her very uncomfortable.

The first time she had run into him in a hallway at Riverview, she had asked for directions, not knowing that a serious speech impediment was part of Ollie's "charm." She could not make head nor tails of the garbled instructions he gave and had finally thanked him

abruptly and headed in the last of the six different directions he had
pointed. The encounter had embarrassed her and since then, though
she felt guilty about it, she often went out of her way to avoid Oliver
Moon if she could.

Unfortunately, it was too late for that now. She would have to step
around the mess he had strewn across the hall.

Avoiding his eyes, she eased past, stepping over the full bag. However, as she did so, the heel of her shoe caught a corner of the bag,
causing her to lose her balance. She managed to remain upright, but
in doing so, she dragged the bag several inches across the floor. Paper
cups, soda cans, a half-eaten apple, and various other garbage scattered across the tile.

Ollie clicked his tongue and wagged his head back and forth, but
he was uncharacteristically silent, staring at the mess she had created.

"Oh, I'm so sorry," Claire said, heat rising to her face. She
stooped down and gingerly picked up a half-empty fast food drink.
Ollie squatted beside her and began scooping trash into a heap.

Claire stood up and used the toe of her shoe to push the less offending trash into the heap, while Ollie started stuffing things back
into the bag. Expertly sorting through the debris, he spotted a red-
and-white drinking straw and cleverly slipped it into his pocket. Like-
wise a plastic spoon.

Claire never saw the spoon in Ollie's hand, but she did see his
hand go into his pocket. Thinking nothing of it, she picked up another piece of trash. But when she looked back at Ollie, what she saw
in the hand that had just come from his pocket was an unsheathed
plastic syringe.

Her alarm must have registered on her face, because when Ollie
realized that she had seen him with it, he began to jabber incoher-
ently.

"Nah my . . . nah my . . . uh-uh . . . uh-uh . . ."

*Oh no*, she thought. *What ever could he be doing with a syringe in
his pocket?*

By this time, Ollie had thrown the offending instrument into the
trash bag and had backed as far away from it as the wall would allow.
He swatted at the air in the direction of the bag and continued his
garbled diatribe.

Thinking quickly—and not caring if she offended Oliver Moon—
she reached into her handbag for a tissue, carefully extracted the sy-

ringe from the trash, wrapped it in the tissue, and hurried to the parking lot.

ॐ    ॐ    ॐ    ॐ

Michael felt as though he was being hounded by an invisible menace. Vera's prediction about the media picking up the story of Cynthia Harper's suspension had not yet come to fruition, but he jumped every time the phone rang and decided he might as well be stalked by the papparazi, vulnerable as he felt.

Sunday night he turned on the television and was watching the evening news, half expecting to see a blurb about the brewing scandal at Riverview, when Vera called.

"Michael, I thought you'd want to know that Maggie Wallace died this morning."

Michael truly felt sad to learn of the sweet old woman's death. "I'm so sorry to hear it, Vera."

"Don't be, Michael. It was a blessing. I don't know if you'd seen her recently, but she was in terrible shape. In great pain and, unfortunately, very much alert and aware." Vera gave a sad, cynical laugh. "I guess we needn't have worried about Cynthia's so-called angels after all. The night shift found Maggie on their rounds early this morning. She apparently died very peacefully in her sleep."

Michael was silent on his end, wondering suddenly what Cynthia Harper's reaction would be when she heard the news. He had been told that Harper had called the floor several times since her suspension, asking about Maggie's condition.

Finally Vera said, "Maggie was quite a lady, wasn't she? You know, she would have turned ninety-six next week."

"Yes, she was quite a lady," Michael agreed. "Thank you for letting me know, Vera. I assume there will be a memorial service at the manor chapel?"

"I would imagine so, although her family lives out of state. I'll let you know as soon as I hear the details."

Michael hung up the phone, feeling depressed. Life was strange. Even though Maggie had lived nearly a century—and he knew she'd had a strong faith and was rejoicing in heaven this minute—still it saddened him to realize that on this earth there would forever be good-byes. And in the profession he had chosen, he would have more than his share of them.

As she did so often, Claire Anderson came to his mind now. Claire was the only one who had ever seemed to understand his sorrow over the solitary nature of this life. He had seen the sadness that shadowed her face after her grandmother's stroke, and he understood that Claire was only too aware of how little time was left before she would be completely alone in the world. They had shared the despair of those feelings during the long talks they'd had back when romance had blossomed between them.

Lately he had been so overwhelmed and burdened by the problems at Riverview that he didn't have time to dwell on the abrupt ending of his romance with Claire. Now that Katherine Anderson was at Riverview and he and Claire saw each other more often, they seemed to have formed a tentative friendship. For that he was grateful.

He had been heartened the day she told him she wanted him to meet her grandmother. She had said nothing further about it since then, but he felt that very soon she would. Despite the fact that things were less awkward now, something still felt unfinished between them. Maybe meeting Mrs. Anderson would bring closure for him.

When he thought of Claire, it was hard not to remember how wonderful it had been to have someone in his life with whom to share his doubts and fears, someone who was a willing recipient of his love. He remembered most of all how she had given him a growing hope that true happiness and healing from his past were possible. With Claire there had been such a feeling of oneness. It was like nothing he had ever known before.

He wasn't sure he could ever truly accept a mere friendship with Claire. She had meant too much to him. And yes, he believed he still loved her—even after all these months. There was no other way to explain the powerful feelings that came over him whenever he was near her. When she was near, he wanted only to take her in his arms and hold her close. He wanted to touch her hair and look into her eyes and whisper his love. But he had no outlet for his emotions.

He was glad, of course, that now he could run into her unexpectedly and not feel the agonizing pain such meetings had brought at one time. But that didn't mean it was easy. The pain was still there, though now it was less intense—a dull ache in the region of his heart. He wasn't sure what he would do when he heard that Claire had found someone else—as a beautiful woman like she surely would.

Reluctantly, he realized that perhaps it had happened already. His heart sank as he recalled a day just last week when he had seen her in the courtyard with the new patient in respite care, Robert Tripleton.

Michael had seen Claire's name on the list of manor volunteers and knew that Tripleton was one of those she had signed on to help in the new reading program. It was only natural that Claire would be drawn to the personable newcomer. Michael had met the man when he first arrived and had found him to be intelligent and likeable. It was quite an oddity for Riverview to have someone as young as Tripleton even in the respite-care program, but apparently this man had no family to take him in.

Then it struck him. Tripleton was alone in life. He would have the same things in common with Claire as Michael had had. It all began to make sense now.

He replayed the day in the courtyard over again in his mind. What he had seen that day hurt deeply. There was no denying that there had been more to what he witnessed than a volunteer reading to a patient. Claire had not spotted him as he walked by some distance away, headed for the retirement apartments. Her eyes had focused completely on the good-looking man in the dark glasses sitting beside her. Michael had heard the easy laughter between them, and his heart had sunk with sadness and jealousy as he realized that the playful music of her laughter was for someone else now. The few brief seconds he watched them as he passed by were enough to discern that there was very little reading going on. He had seen that look of attentiveness and concern in Claire's eyes before. But then, it had been directed at him. His heart ached as though he had lost Claire all over again. And yet a part of him was happy for her . . . glad to see her smile again, to hear her laughter.

*Oh, if only it could have been for me.*

❧   ❧   ❧   ❧

Michael was sitting at his desk Monday morning, mulling over the disturbing events of the previous week when the telephone rang.

"Michael?"

It was Claire and she sounded upset.

"Hello, Claire," he said uncertainly. "What can I do for you?"

"I'm not quite sure where to begin, Michael. There's something I think you should know about. I tried to call earlier, but I got your answering machine and I didn't want to leave a message."

In a faltering voice she went on to tell him about her encounter with Oliver Moon the day before, ending by saying, "I have the syringe, Michael. I . . . I sort of panicked and carried it out of the building with me. But I thought—well, I thought the syringe might be some kind of evidence or something."

"What do you mean?" he asked, suddenly defensive.

"Well, surely that man shouldn't be walking around the halls with sharp needles? I thought you might need it as evidence against him."

"You're certain there is still a needle in the syringe?"

"Of course I'm certain," she said, sounding irritated and defensive herself.

"I can't imagine what Ollie would have been doing with a syringe, but I don't think you need to worry about it. If you don't mind, though, I would like to have you bring it in to the office. We'll need to talk to Ollie about this, and sometimes it's easier to communicate with him when we have—well, for lack of a better term—a visual aid in front of us."

"I hope I haven't caused any trouble. But the more I thought about it, it just didn't seem right that he would be carrying something like that around." She hesitated for the slightest moment before giving what seemed to be her final contention. "It seems like this is something that needs urgent attention. I hope you agree."

Michael didn't like her accusing tone, but he realized that he had overreacted with his defensiveness. Forcing himself to calm down and attempting to appease her, he told her, "You were right to call, Claire. Ollie definitely shouldn't have had the syringe. Thank you for letting me know."

Sounding somewhat mollified, she said, "I'm running a little late for school this morning, but if I bring it in when I come to see Nana this afternoon, would that be soon enough?"

"That'll be fine. And, Claire . . . be extremely careful. The needle could be contaminated."

"I know. I will."

Michael hung up the phone, puzzled. This just didn't make sense. As he had told Claire, he truly had no idea why Ollie would have been carrying around a syringe. And why would he have taken it out of his pocket in Claire's presence?

He called Vera's office, and not getting an answer, he went looking for her. He finally tracked her down on the north wing, where she and Geneva Grayson were at the nurses' station discussing a patient's chart. The floor was quiet for a Monday morning.

"Good morning, ladies."

"Hi, Mr. Meredith."

"Hello, Michael," Vera said with a look and tone that said she knew he'd had a rough weekend.

Michael lowered his voice. "Would either of you happen to know—Oliver Moon's not diabetic is he?" he asked, the possible explanation coming to him suddenly.

Looking puzzled, they both shook their heads.

"Well, at least I don't think he is," Vera said. "Why do you ask?"

"A visitor on the north wing saw him take a syringe out of his pocket yesterday. The needle was still intact."

The blood drained from Geneva's face, and she let out a seemingly involuntary gasp.

"What's wrong?" Michael and Vera asked in one voice.

"I . . . I caught Ollie with a needle too. It was quite a while back—last winter, I think. I know I should have reported it, but I didn't want to get anyone in trouble. Sherry Kensington had just started working here, and she apparently left the syringe on the nightstand after she gave an injection." Geneva was speaking rapidly now, trying to explain herself. "Ollie found it when he was cleaning the room. I was certain he hadn't stuck himself or anything and . . . well, I just . . ."

Geneva's voice rose as she tried to defend her actions. "Sherry was doing her best and having such a rough start. I did speak to her privately about her carelessness, but I should have reported it, I know," she repeated. "I don't know what to say. I am sorry."

"Well, that doesn't explain where he would have found the syringe he had yesterday," Vera said sternly, ignoring Geneva's apologies. "Has Sherry or anyone else done this again since that day, Geneva?" she asked.

"Oh no. Never. In fact, now that I think of it, Sherry denied having left it out. She felt certain she had properly disposed of the syringe she used in the sharps container."

"Do you remember the details, Geneva? What floor were you on when this happened? Who was the patient? We'll need to document all of this."

"Well, let's see . . ." The nurse thought for a minute. "It seems to me that I was working the east wing that day. Oh, I remember. It was in the room of that German-speaking woman. What was her name? Schultz . . . Helga Schultz. I remember because—Oh!" Geneva gasped, a hand to her mouth in alarm. "Helga Schultz died the next morning. It was the beginning of that siege of pneumonia we had last winter. Don't you remember?"

"You surely don't mean that Ollie could have. . . ?" Michael couldn't finish the horrible thought.

"Oh no, Michael. No." Vera's voice was a hoarse whisper.

Michael's head was spinning as a labyrinth of possibilities assembled itself in his mind. Ollie had been discovered with a syringe in his possession twice now. He was the one who had produced the pamphlet touting euthanasia. *Maggie! Claire had found the syringe in Ollie's hands the day after Maggie Wallace died.* Was Ollie behind all this? Was it possible that this five-foot-two simple man was capable of such things? Had he fooled them all? The man had been at Riverview for almost thirty years. Had he been quietly ending lives under their very noses all this time? But how could he have obtained the means to carry out such things? Did he have an accomplice? Or was *he* someone else's accomplice? Michael had to admit that explanation seemed more plausible.

No. There had to be some mistake. Oliver Moon wasn't capable of such evil. There had to be another explanation. Suddenly he remembered that Claire had the syringe in her possession. If they could determine what it had contained, maybe it would give them some answers.

Leaving the two nurses gaping after him, he ran down the hall toward his office.

As he ran, a horrifying thought struck him. Had Cynthia Harper been falsely accused? The statements she had been purported to make were frightening, to say the least. But what if the suspicions they'd had—beginning with Frederick Halloran's death early in Michael's tenure—pointed not to Cynthia, but instead to Oliver Moon?

Either way, it seemed clear now that the unthinkable had happened. No longer suspicion or a nagging intuition, it had become reality. Suspicious deaths had occurred during his supervision, and Michael knew that a formidable time of investigation and placing blame lay ahead of them. How could any of them—the residents, the nursing staff, the families involved . . . indeed, the entire community—ever recover if he had allowed such a tragedy to happen?

Light-headed and out of breath from more than his dash down the hallway, he closed the door to his office and dialed Claire's number.

# Twenty-eight

C laire still shuddered when she thought about her encounter with Oliver Moon. More than the incident itself, she was embarrassed and discomposed by the fact that she had left the building with the syringe in her possession. What had she been thinking? It had been a foolish, foolish thing to do. Beyond the fact that she could have stuck herself with a contaminated needle, she also could have destroyed or damaged important evidence.

She found small comfort in the fact that Michael didn't seem to feel it was a serious matter. She found it hard to understand how it could *not* be serious to have an employee like Oliver Moon in possession of such an object. Perhaps her prejudice against this disabled man was coming through too frankly. As Michael had explained when he called her back Monday morning asking her to bring the syringe by immediately, it was possible that Ollie was diabetic and gave himself insulin injections. Michael had seemed rushed and distracted when she spoke with him then, but apparently the center was going to send the syringe to a lab to find out just what it had contained.

At any rate, Claire scarcely had time to think about the incident with all the preparations to be made for the new school year. In addition, with Nana to be looked after, yard work, and her volunteer hours at Riverview, she fell into bed each night exhausted.

In spite of her hectic schedule, reading to Robert Tripleton had become the highlight of Claire's days. They had finally finished *Anna Karenina*, and to Claire's surprise, Rob had chosen a popular new mystery for their next book. There was far less to discuss in this fast-paced novel and they finished it in a few days.

As Claire's friendship with Rob grew and as she learned more about him and revealed more of herself to him, she began to suspect he held deep feelings for her. Her feelings for him grew ever deeper, as well. She supposed she did love him in a way. But was it the love that lifetime relationships were made of? She was confused about the nature of love after everything that had happened with Michael Meredith.

She couldn't deny that the age difference concerned her more than a little. Rob was almost ten years older than she. Yet it certainly did not prevent them from having much in common and a seemingly endless supply of topics on which to converse. More and more, Claire found herself wondering if Rob might be the man God wanted in her life. Of course, she had thought that about another man not very long ago.

Michael was rarely on the floors of the nursing unit where Nana and Rob resided, being more involved with the apartments and the senior center. Still, Claire couldn't avoid running into him occasionally when she visited Millie. They had developed a polite, rather serious way with each other, speaking briefly, warmly, yet about nothing of consequence. And yet she always felt a sense of excitement in his presence. It was disturbing. If her friendship with Rob was becoming closer and more intimate—if indeed, she was growing to love Rob—why were thoughts of Michael never far from her mind?

Claire knew that Rob had met Michael several times during his stay at Riverview. Once, when he mentioned Michael's name to Claire, she gave him the briefest information about her relationship to Michael, telling Rob simply that they had dated for a short time and were friends. She had confessed her unhappy childhood to him and even told him about Joseph, but she didn't tell Rob the profound connection between Joseph and Michael. It somehow seemed that to do so would have been a betrayal of Michael's trust.

Rob seemed to be making progress in recovering from the surgery, and his injuries—except for his loss of vision—were virtually indiscernible now. The bandage and neck brace were gone, and though he still wore the dark glasses, he claimed to be seeing more clearly, now able to make out smaller shapes and even to distinguish some colors. Claire could see that he now seemed to be looking directly at her when she spoke. She often felt self-conscious when she caught him squinting in her direction, as though he were attempting to make out her features.

Often Claire would walk with Rob, guiding him to the courtyard to sit for an afternoon of reading and conversation. The hot days of summer seemed to linger, and they often sought the shade of a bench on the east side of the courtyard. Here a row of Bradford pear trees bolstered a leafy canopy over the bench, and a choir of wrens and robins blended with the rustling of leaves to provide soft background music for their reading sessions.

It was in this serene setting that Rob first saw Claire's face.

He had asked her to read his mail to him. She was reading a dry description from a university course catalog when she heard his sharp intake of breath. Looking up from the booklet, she saw that he had taken off the dark glasses and there was a look of astonishment on his face.

"What? What is it, Rob?"

"Claire! I . . . I can see you. More clearly than ever! I can see even the color of your eyes—they *are* hazel! And your hair . . ." He reached up in amazement and touched a wayward curl.

His excitement was infectious. "Oh, Rob! That's wonderful! I'm so happy for you!"

Suddenly tears sprang to his eyes, and he covered his face in a futile effort to hide his emotions. Then he began to weep openly. "Thank you, God. Oh, thank you," he prayed through tears.

In spite of the fact that she shared his joy and gratitude, Claire felt uncomfortable at his ardent expression of emotion.

She sat in silence, her head down as he wept. When at last she heard him quiet, she looked up into eyes that undeniably *saw* her—scrutinized her.

"Oh, Claire. I . . . ." He stretched his arms out in front of him and waved his hands slowly from side to side, testing. "Things are still fuzzy peripherally, but when I look straight ahead, I see unbelievably more clearly than I did even yesterday." His voice turned to a whisper. "You are as beautiful as I imagined, Claire. *More* beautiful."

"Please, Rob . . ." Struggling to escape the seriousness of his declaration, she laughed artificially. "You make me doubt that you truly have your sight back."

Immediately she was sorry she had made light of his comment. She was allowing her unease with his genuine compliment to overshadow the miracle that had seemingly taken place.

Trying to make up for it, she told him, "Let's walk back to your room and see how it is out of the sunlight. Don't you think you should contact your doctors?''

"Yes!" He stood and, declining the offer of her arm, held his hands out in front of his body and began walking slowly toward the entrance.

✿   ✿   ✿   ✿

Michael Meredith felt guilty at his unintended eavesdropping, but he could not make himself walk away from the window. Taking a quick stroll through the assisted-living wings as he often did on his way back to his office from staff meetings, he couldn't help but hear the sweetly familiar voice that floated through the open window from the courtyard outside.

The dense foliage that grew up between the building and the yard prevented him from seeing the source of the sound, but there was no mistaking Claire Anderson's gentle voice. Some acoustical peculiarity of the narrow passageway carried crystal clear snippets of the conversation through the open window. It didn't take long to surmise that Claire was speaking to Rob Tripleton. The tender expression and the gentleness of her words caused him to stop abruptly.

In spite of the rather unpleasant exchange they'd had the week before when Claire had called to tell him about finding Ollie with the syringe, Michael found that hearing her speak now moved him deeply. Feeling almost paralyzed by the melody of her voice, he wasn't sure he could have walked away had he wanted to.

"Oh, Rob, I'm so happy for you," she was saying. They were obviously celebrating some wonderful news.

What Michael heard next, however, cut at his heart. Robert Tripleton was telling Claire how beautiful she was. The deep, emotion-filled voice conveyed much more than simple admiration. Michael realized that he had unintentionally intruded on a romantic interlude between two people who were obviously falling in love. He half feared that he might do something foolish—that he might race out the door and attempt to talk some sense into Claire's head. How could she even think of loving someone else when he still loved her so deeply?

He forced himself to turn away, to put his mind back on the responsibilities, the pressing problems he had here at Riverview. But the significance of the exchange he had just heard left him feeling chilled.

He walked on, his heart sinking as their words of affection echoed through his head like a baleful warning bell.

🙞 🙞 🙞 🙞

Rob's sight improved rapidly over the next few days. Though his peripheral vision remained blurred, and it was virtually impossible for him to read any but the largest print, by week's end he was making plans to move back to his apartment. He even voiced his hope that he might be able to return to teaching.

"Of course it's too late for this semester. And I'd need someone to read research papers and test essays to me so I could grade accurately," he told Claire, "but with the help of a graduate assistant I know I could do it. I know the material I'd be teaching like the back of my hand. The classroom wouldn't be a problem at all."

The enthusiasm in his voice made him sound like one of his young students. It was so different from the formal, dignified manner Claire had grown accustomed to.

"Rob, I'm so excited for you. It really does seem like a miracle."

"It *is* a miracle, Claire. Whether it was performed by God himself or by the hands of doctors He created and guided, I won't call it anything but a miracle."

They were sitting in the shade on the same bench where they had sat when Rob's sight had returned. More and more often the intention of reading books had gone by the wayside in favor of these quiet conversations.

Rob turned to her now. "Claire, you are so dear to me. You've made this whole ordeal bearable." He touched his eyes gingerly as though remembering the pain of his accident. "You . . . well, you're a very special woman. There are so many uncertainties in my life right now. I don't have much to offer, Claire, but I hope we can continue to . . . to be friends. I don't know if I'll be able to go back to teaching, if I'll ever be able to drive a car again. The doctors aren't willing to make any promises about how much more of my sight I'll get back, but . . . well, I just hope you'll give me a chance." His voice was taut with emotion, revealing that he wasn't speaking lightly.

Claire's heart filled with love for Rob. He *was* a dear friend and a special man. They shared a special relationship, and she would always have warm memories of this summer. But Claire knew she didn't love

Rob in the way she was afraid he was hoping for. Perhaps their friend-ship would grow into something more . . . maybe someday it would.

Gently, she tried to put him off. "I know you can't think too far into the future right now, Rob. We both need time—"

He held up a hand. "I know. I understand. We'll take it one day at a time. I'm not asking for more than your friendship right now."

She reached over and hugged him. "You know you have that."

Today, for the first time, Claire let herself think about what Rob's newfound independence and his moving back to Mullinville would mean for their friendship. Neither of them had ventured to speak of how his leaving would change their relationship. She supposed they were both pretending that nothing would change. But she knew that was a supposition born of denial. Until Rob had begun to speak of leaving Riverview himself, Claire had been able to imagine that her times with him would continue indefinitely.

Rob's friendship and flirtatious attentions had filled a void in her life, taking her mind off the turmoil of the past months. He had given her fascinating, inspiring stories to think about and discuss, and Claire appreciated how they understood each other. But no matter how she tried, she could not deny the deep feelings she still held for Michael Meredith. How did one know what love was? Did she love either of these men? Both of them?

The questions monopolized her thoughts as she walked with Rob back to his room.

If he sensed her preoccupation, he said nothing. Claire told him good-bye at the doorway, no longer needing to help him find his way around the room.

❧    ❧    ❧    ❧

School started in the midst of record-breaking high temperatures. Without air-conditioning, the classroom was an oven, and in spite of her excitement at beginning her second year of teaching, Claire found herself crabby and impatient with her new crop of third-graders. She had forgotten what a struggle it was to learn twenty new names and faces and to establish a routine and a sense of discipline that fit this particular mix of personalities.

She couldn't help but feel a bit sad when she saw her students from last year's class in the hallways and realized they would never again share the bond that had been so special. And yet she trusted that soon the same bond would endear her to the unfamiliar faces in the desks before her, and that just like that first year, she would come to know and care for these children almost as if they were her own.

As the time for Rob Tripleton's departure from Riverview drew near, Claire found herself pensive and downhearted, wondering what would become of the friendship they had established and had been such a blessed distraction for her.

Sometimes she felt they were meant to be together. But at other times she couldn't begin to imagine a life with Rob apart from Riverview. It startled her to realize that their entire relationship had developed on the grounds of the nursing facility. She had never once seen him in the "outside world." She wanted to talk with him about these things, wanted to explore the feelings they had for each other. But Rob had so much on his mind, so many decisions to make about what he would do after he left Riverview. He was still adjusting to the remaining physical handicaps from his accident, and she didn't want to burden him with another emotionally charged matter.

Sadly, the possibility of losing Rob's friendship caused her to think more than ever of Michael Meredith.

More than two weeks had passed since Claire had spoken with her grandmother about meeting Michael. Nana had mentioned it once or twice, and Claire had told her the truth.

"Nana, I haven't been able to talk to him. I'm not sure what's up, but there seems to be something going on in the administration department."

"Something going on? What do you mean?"

"I'm not sure. There have been a lot of people in the office—people I've never seen here before. The employees seem on edge."

"Probably just the health inspectors. I know the nurses at Elmbrook used to get antsy whenever they knew the inspectors were coming."

"That must be it. I keep thinking I'll ask Michael about it, but every time I see him he's either with one of these inspectors—or whoever they are—or he's in a hurry and doesn't have time to talk. He seems very preoccupied."

The worry that tinged Claire's voice was because she feared something more serious was happening at Riverview. Michael had indeed been preoccupied—almost to the point of being rude—and the expressions on the faces of the official-looking strangers she had seen him with were grave and stern.

Worse, Claire hadn't seen Oliver Moon on the floor since the day she'd taken the syringe.

Nana misinterpreted Claire's wrinkled brow.

"Are you still mooning over Michael Meredith?" she asked her granddaughter gently.

Claire shook her head. "No, that's not it. I was just—"

"Kitty, I want to say something to you," Nana interrupted, ignoring her protests. "You are not responsible for what happened to Joseph—to Michael. From what you've told me, it sounds like Michael Meredith understands that fact better than you do. What happened was unfortunate. It was tragic. But it is in the past and it had nothing—nothing whatsoever—to do with you."

Assuaged as she was by her grandmother's words, Claire knew that Nana wasn't making her judgment with all the facts. Nana didn't know the role Claire *had* played in having Joseph sent away. And that made all the difference.

Now, with her heart pounding in her chest, she said what had to be said. Choking on her own words, she managed, "Nana, they . . . they *did* send him away because of me." There. It was out.

"Kitty, why would you think such a thing?" Nana was incredulous.

"Because . . . because he . . . he cut me with that stick. Don't you remember? You were there—at his birthday party just a few weeks before they took him away. We were playing in the wading pool, and he cut my arm with a stick. It wasn't that bad really. It didn't even need stitches." Instinctively, she looked down to where her short-sleeved blouse revealed the pale scar. "But Daddy was so angry, and after that I heard Mother and Daddy arguing about sending him away."

"Oh, honey. Of course it wasn't your fault."

Claire began to cry, feeling the shame of the little girl again. "It *was*, Nana. Oh, Nana. I lied."

"What? Whatever are you talking about, Kitty?" her grandmother muttered, obviously not understanding Claire's distress.

"I lied . . . that day it happened. I told Daddy that I didn't do anything, but it was a lie. I started the whole thing. I sprayed Joseph with the garden hose. He was just trying to make me stop. He didn't mean to hurt me. I honestly don't think he did it on purpose. But I didn't say anything. I just let them go on believing that he had done something terrible. . . ." She couldn't go on for the tears that welled in her throat and burned hot behind her eyelids.

Nana put her hand on Claire's knee and let her cry. "Kitty, it *wasn't* your fault." Enunciating her words carefully and speaking in the stern voice Claire remembered from Nana's scoldings when she was little, Katherine Anderson told her only granddaughter, "Your mother had made up her mind long before that day that she wanted Joseph sent away. Perhaps she used that incident as an excuse to sway Raymond's thinking and get her own way, but *no*, darling. It was not your fault. You put that thought to rest this minute."

"You're sure? Do you know that for certain, Nana? For absolutely certain?"

"Claire Marie Katherine, you surely know me well enough by now to know I wouldn't say it if it weren't so."

"Oh, Nana. All this time I've thought . . ." Claire leaned her head on her grandmother's shoulder and let cleansing tears flow.

So the incident that day hadn't been the catalyst for Joseph's exile after all. She wasn't trying to excuse her lie. It was wrong, and she had faced that fact and confessed it long ago. But a burden was lifted to know for certain after all these years that her actions hadn't been the thing that sent Joseph—that sent *Michael*—away.

Claire sat beside her grandmother, the afternoon sunshine warming their backs, love filling her heart. No gift her grandmother could have given could have been more treasured. It was a peace of mind that no one else on earth could have granted her. In this simple conversation, Nana had given her a sense of God's offerings of healing and forgiveness—and a deeper understanding that the problems of her family had been greater than she could possibly have understood or been responsible for as a child. There was liberation in learning that Joseph would have been sent away regardless of her childish lie and the incident that provoked it.

But had anything really changed? It didn't change the fact that Michael's memories of her and her family were ones of torment and rejection. She could understand that Michael might be able to forgive her for the hurts of his childhood. But he would never truly be able to forget. She knew only too well what that required. As much as she had tried to forgive her parents for the sadness in her own childhood, the memories still cut deeply, and she knew that a part of her would always—on this earth anyway—carry the scars of those wounds.

And after all her turmoil, had she come to this place of peace only to find that it was too late for her and Michael? Painfully, she remembered the blonde she had seen him with that day at the park. He seemed to have put their romance behind him. He was getting on with his life.

Why couldn't she do the same?

# Twenty-nine

Michael left the administration offices and headed for his car. The events of the past two weeks had taken their toll on him. Now he was confronted with one of the most difficult challenges he had ever faced.

The tests from the lab had come back today, and they confirmed Michael's worst fears. The syringe Claire had found in Ollie's possession contained traces of morphine. This very afternoon, Oliver Wendell Moon would be charged in the wrongful deaths of Helga Schultz and Margaret Wallace. Margaret Wallace's body would be exhumed immediately, and Michael felt depressingly certain that the coroner's findings would be the proof needed for a conviction.

He took little comfort in knowing that it was unlikely Ollie would be sent to a state penitentiary. To the smiling, simple little man who had lived the whole of his life in Hanover Falls, the strange confines of a mental institution would be prison enough.

Though it seemed impossible that Oliver Moon had done the horrible things of which he was being accused, Michael had to admit that the evidence pointed overwhelmingly at Ollie. If it were somehow true, Michael felt sure that Ollie did not understand the gravity, the finality of his actions. The burning question for Michael was: *Where* had Ollie obtained the drugs? It was inconceivable that any pharmacy would have filled a prescription for the toothless, mumbling, obviously disabled man. And surely he wasn't capable—mentally or physically—of stealing them or buying them off the street. Riverview's drug supply had been carefully monitored and investigated, and everything seemed to be completely in order.

The only explanation that seemed remotely possible to Michael was that Ollie had merely been mimicking the actions of the nurses he had watched every day for thirty years. It was possible that his childlike mind connected the syringes and medications with the compassionate relief of pain. But even that didn't explain where he got the drugs or how he had learned to administer them. Vera felt certain that any nurse at the center would have detected the bruising or swelling from an ineptly administered injection. And no one seemed to recall such an occurrence.

Michael slowed the car and craned his neck to make out the numbers on the row of dilapidated houses on Murdoch Street. There it was. Four-thirteen. The house where Ollie lived was scarcely more than a shack, but the yard was neat and the tiny front porch was lined with blooming, overgrown pots of flowers.

Michael had already visited Ollie in the county jail where he was being held for questioning. Since his confinement the previous day, Ollie had been distraught and depressed, but Michael promised to bring a change of clothing after managing to make out Ollie's one simple request: "keen corr-alls"—clean coveralls.

Michael now opened the door—unlocked, like most doors in this small town—and waited for his eyes to adjust to the darkness. The air smelled stale and musty, but the room was tidy and clean. In contrast, the tiny bedroom at the back of the house was piled high with boxes and bags. There was a rickety chest of drawers in one corner of the room, but to get to it, Michael had to move several brown paper grocery bags. The first bag he lifted was surprisingly light. Michael looked inside and was puzzled to see hundreds of plastic drinking straws. The bag beside it was equally light and equally full of plastic cafeteria spoons. Increasingly baffled, he began to examine the contents of the dozens of bags stacked around the room.

Each one held a spotlessly clean collection of seemingly worthless junk—pull tabs from soda cans, tiny plastic rectangles that had once contained a single-serving of jelly or jam, convenience store coffee stirrers by the thousands—all carefully sorted and separated. In a far corner were several plastic grocery sacks tied in loose knots. Michael opened one to find rubber-banded stacks of meal selection menus carrying Riverview's logo. Another bag contained a seemingly mismatched assortment of medical pamphlets and brochures.

Excitement rising in him, Michael opened another sack: a cache of tiny, neatly stacked plastic cups. Michael recognized them as the type of containers that were used to dispense medications at Riverview.

The nurses had said they often caught Ollie rummaging through the trash. Of course! He was looking to add to his vast collections. His sacks! That was what he had tried to tell Michael. The euthanasia flyer was for his sacks! And might not a syringe have looked like an equally promising bauble to add to his collection?

Michael could have cried with relief as he realized the ransoming truth. Oliver Moon was a collector! A simple-minded, snaggle-toothed, harmless collector of junk.

☙　　☙　　☙　　☙

Vera Johanssen wiped the perspiration from her brow and looked at the calendar on the desk in her office. Idly, she flipped through the pages. It was the middle of September, and the month didn't seem to be offering an ounce of relief from the August she had just endured.

She couldn't remember a more difficult time in her professional career. She was too old to be dealing with this kind of stress. Maybe Harv was right. Maybe it was time to think about retiring. She loved her job, and her husband had always supported her in her desire to work, but she knew that Harv's patience was at its limit with the current situation. She had been unable to leave her worries at the office. She knew she had been cranky and irritable, taking her frustrations out on her husband.

Poor Harvey. He was a saint to have put up with her for so long. But lately, his hints had been more adamant. He was older than Vera by several years. He'd been retired for over a year now. His company had a good pension plan and they had managed to save a nice little nest egg. They had always planned to travel together once the kids were grown. Well, the last of those kids had been gone from the nest for over ten years now. Their oldest was beginning to see her own teenagers fly the coup. Maybe it was time. Maybe—

Before Vera could complete the thought, Geneva Grayson, the charge nurse on duty, appeared in the doorway, out of breath and looking flustered. She rapped on the jamb of the open door.

"Sorry to bother you, Mrs. Johanssen, but Ethel Manning is having another one of her spells. We're a little short-handed on the floor today. Would you mind helping me for just a minute?"

She was already up and moving toward the door. "Sure. Do you want me to cover the floor or talk to Ethel?"

"Would you handle Ethel? She seems to respond better to you. I'm afraid I might kill the woman if I have to walk into that room again." Instantly, she clapped her hand over her mouth, looking sheepish. "That was a *poor* choice of words. I'm sorry."

Of course everyone in the nursing facility was aware of Cynthia Harper's suspension. In spite of the increasing likelihood that Oliver Moon, not Harper, was responsible for the deaths at Riverview, it had been decided that the LPN's statements were incriminating enough to warrant continuation of the in-house investigation that had been underway at the time Ollie was taken in for questioning. Many of the nurses who had worked with Cynthia had been interviewed, and privately, Vera had been very candid with her charge nurses about the concerns the administration had over the situation.

Now Vera laughed half-heartedly and sighed at Geneva's thoughtless comment. "Don't apologize, Geneva. I know you don't mean it literally." She sighed, thinking that she well understood the charge nurse's feelings about Ethel Manning. The cantankerous old woman was famous at Riverview for her hysterical outbursts. She had a voice that could wake the dead, and she wasn't afraid to use it when she felt she wasn't getting the attention she deserved.

Vera followed Geneva down the corridor and could hear Ethel's ravings even before they turned the corner onto the east wing, where the woman's room was.

"Do I pay good money so you wretched people can treat me this way?" the high-pitched voice bellowed. "I want my pills, and I want them now!"

Vera waved Geneva on and, taking a deep breath, stepped into the room.

"Good morning, Ethel. You're looking nice this morning. You must have had your hair done yesterday." She had learned that a little flattery and a soft voice went a long way to appease Ethel's moods.

"Hah! That crazy beautician can't do my hair right to save her soul," Ethel stated, beginning another tirade.

Vera could tell, however, that she was soaking up the attention. It wouldn't be too difficult to get her calmed down today. She sat deliberately in the chair beside Ethel's wheelchair, knowing it would communicate to the woman that she intended to spend some time here. They visited for a few minutes, Ethel pouring a laundry list of complaints in Vera's lap, Vera listening attentively, but commenting little. Ethel berated each nurse in turn.

"The only decent people in this place are that new little girl on the day shift . . . what's her name? Hillary? And then Cynthia Harper, and she got fired."

"Who told you that, Ethel?" Vera asked, trying to keep the anger from her voice. The nursing staff had been given strict instructions not to discuss Cynthia's dismissal with the residents.

"Why, she told me herself."

"Cynthia told you? When was that, Ethel?"

"Let's see. It was on a Saturday night. Two weeks ago. Yes, I'm sure that's right, because it was the first of the month and that good-for-nothing son-in-law of mine had been in to have me sign a check. He thinks I don't know what he's up to but I'm not blind—"

"So Cynthia was *here?*" Vera interrupted, trying to steer Ethel back to the subject at hand. When Cynthia Harper had been suspended in August, a preeminent condition of her suspension was that she stay off the premises of Riverview Manor.

"Yes. It was late at night," Ethel told her now. "Long after the late news. I couldn't sleep for wanting to give my son-in-law a piece of my mind. When I saw Cynthia out in the hall, I called to her. I hadn't seen her for a while, and I wanted to talk to her. She was in uniform, so I thought she was working a different shift. That's when she told me about getting fired. She said she was just visiting."

Abruptly, Ethel shook an accusing finger at Vera. "Now *she* was a nice nurse. I don't know why you people always get rid of the nice ones. Anyway, we talked for a while, and then she said she had to go."

"You're sure it was only two weeks ago, Ethel? That would have been . . ." She did some quick figuring. ". . . September first."

"Of course, I'm sure. I told you it was the first of the month. That's when he always hits me up for cash."

Though Ethel Manning's body was frail and she was in need of full-time nursing care, her mind was sharp as a tack. Vera knew she would not be mistaken about the date.

Not caring that sudden desertion might set Ethel off again, Vera said a hasty good-bye and all but ran down the hall to the nurses' station.

She picked up the phone and punched in a number.

"Michael, it's Vera. We have to talk. Now. Cynthia Harper was on the east wing the night Maggie Wallace died."

Michael heard Vera's words, but it took a moment for their meaning to soak in. When it finally did, he could only whisper in horror, "Oh, dear God. Please . . . help us."

He picked up the telephone and dialed the emergency number. When the dispatcher connected him with a police officer, he explained the situation in detail and was assured that officers were enroute to pick up Cynthia Harper for questioning. He didn't hang up the receiver until he had also been assured that Oliver Moon would be released immediately and delivered to his own front door on Murdoch Street.

Michael hung up the phone and put his head in his hands.

             ❧     ❧     ❧     ❧

Claire was with her third-graders in their afternoon reading circle when she was paged by Marjean Hammond.

"You have a phone call, Claire." Concern colored her voice, even over the out-of-date intercom system, as she told Claire, "It's Riverview. On line two."

Claire turned the book over to Megan Leads, the best reader in the class, and hurried to the telephone in the hallway.

The manor had never called her at school. Trembling with apprehension, she picked up the receiver and pressed in the extension. "Yes? This is Claire Anderson."

"Claire, this is Geneva Grayson at Riverview. I'm so sorry to have to tell you this, but you're grandmother has taken ill. We've been in contact with Dr. Bricker, and he agrees with us that she's probably had another stroke. It . . . it doesn't look good, Claire. Could you—"

"I'll be right there," Claire interrupted, tears springing to her eyes even as she spoke.

She went back to the classroom for her purse, stopped by the office to ask Marjean to cover for her, and hurried to her car.

Geneva Grayson was in the room with Nana when Claire arrived. The charge nurse explained what had happened as Claire stood over her grandmother's bed, stroking the frail, unresponsive hand.

Her grandmother was lying amid a tangle of IV tubes attached to her body and to the bed with various straps and white surgical tape. Her eyes were closed, but Claire sensed she was not sleeping.

"Nana?" she said, emotion making her voice a whisper.

Her grandmother's head stirred on the pillow, and the paper-thin eyelids fluttered open, though seemingly unseeing. Her dentures had been removed, and her cheeks appeared sunken and hollow. She moved her mouth as though to speak, but the sounds that came forth were garbled and broken. Claire thought she saw panic in the vacuous eyes.

Suddenly knowing she needed to be strong for her grandmother, Claire forced herself to smile and willed reassurance into her voice. "It's all right, Nana," she said, stroking the soft, pallid cheek. "I'm right here. Don't try to talk. You've . . . you've had another stroke. You . . ."

Claire's voice failed her, but she found her grandmother's hand again beneath the snarl of tubes and wires and took it gently in hers.

An hour later a nurse came in to take Nana's vitals again. It seemed obvious that Katherine Anderson had lost consciousness. Her skin was pale, her breathing shallow. Taking the stethoscope from around her neck and folding it carefully into her pocket, the nurse simply shook her head.

"I'm so sorry, Claire. I'm afraid it's just a matter of time now. Would you like us to call an ambulance to transport your grandmother to the hospital?"

"Is there anything they can do for her there?"

"Nothing that couldn't be done right here," the older woman told her. "We will see to it that she's made as comfortable as possible. But it's your decision. Some people feel more comfortable in a hospital setting. Others would rather be in familiar surroundings. You just let us know what you prefer. She patted Claire's hand sympathetically.

"She would want to be here, I think," Claire told the nurse quietly, still not believing this could be happening.

"We're going to change the IV now. You might be more comfortable waiting outside. I'll let you know as soon as you can come back in," she assured.

Claire stood in the hall across from the room and watched in a daze as nurses and medical equipment came and went from her grandmother's room.

When she had waited for fifteen minutes, a young nurse touched her arm lightly. "It might be a while, Miss Anderson. If you want to go get some coffee or sit in the waiting room, I'll come and get you just as soon as your grandmother is settled."

Claire turned without answering and trudged to the tiny lounge at the end of the corridor.

True to her word, the young nurse came for Claire after half an hour. Claire sat at her grandmother's bedside for the remainder of the afternoon, watching her fade with each minute. Toward evening, Nana began to moan and to struggle against the oxygen tubes the nurses had taped securely in place. With a strength that belied her frail skeleton, Nana tossed fitfully in the bed. Afraid that she would pull the IV tubes out, the nurses loosely restrained her arms.

Claire stroked Nana's forehead and spoke quietly to her. She felt self-conscious in the presence of the nurses who came and went from the room, but a feeling of urgency overcame her uneasiness. She didn't know if Nana could hear her, but there were things she needed to tell this woman who had given her so much, who had been her only source of happiness for much of her life.

Through tears, Claire whispered her love and gratitude. But the woman's breathing became more labored, and she seemed to be in pain.

Several nurses assured Claire that her grandmother was not really aware of what was happening to her, but Claire was terrified that Nana was frightened and hurting. She tried to reassure her, whispering comforting words in her ear. Nana seemed not to hear. Her only response was to groan and fidget even more. Finally Claire could stand it no longer.

She ran from the room and fled to the same waiting area where she had spent the afternoon. Sinking down onto a hard vinyl-covered sofa, she put her face in her hands and wept.

She didn't know how long she had been there when a gentle hand reached out and touched her arm. "Don't cry, honey. Can I do anything to help?"

Claire brushed her cheeks with the back of her hands and looked into the kind, gentle face of a middle-aged nurse. She thought she had seen the nurse here a few times before when she had come later in the evenings.

"You're Katherine Anderson's granddaughter, aren't you?" the nurse asked, as though just realizing to whom she had been offering comfort.

"Yes, I'm Claire Anderson," she gulped, trying hard to control her emotions.

"Has something happened?"

"You haven't heard? My grandmother had another stroke."

"Oh, Claire," the nurse said softly, using Claire's name as though she had known her forever. "I'm sorry to hear that. Are they taking her to the hospital?"

"No. I . . . I think she's dying." The reality of her words hit hard, and she began to sob. The nurse simply sat at her side, patting her arm gently, waiting for her to calm down.

Claire felt the comfort of the woman's touch and began to pour out her fears. "I'm so afraid . . . so afraid. . . ."

"You'll be all right, Claire. You'll get through this."

"No. You don't understand. I'm not afraid for my self. It's Nana. I'm so afraid that she's hurting . . . and frightened. I tried to explain what was happening, but I don't think she could hear me. But . . . she's moaning and—"

"Hush, hush now. There's nothing to be afraid of. We won't let your grandmother suffer. There is no reason for her to suffer. There are plenty of things we can give her to be sure she doesn't feel any pain."

"How . . . how long do you think it will take?" Claire asked. "I want to be with her, but I can't bear to see her like that."

"It won't be long, Claire. She'll be at peace very soon. I'll see to it myself. I know you love her very much. I can see that you only want what is best for her."

"Yes, oh yes." Claire nodded vigorously, grateful that Nana would soon be given something to ease her pain.

Claire sat alone in the waiting room for a few moments after the nurse had left. She was feeling calmer now. It still seemed unreal that this moment could have come—that Nana might truly be near death.

She glanced at her watch and realized she had been gone from her grandmother's room for almost half an hour. Feeling a strange urgency to get back she stood and started down the hallway. The charge nurse, Geneva Grayson, was coming toward Claire. As they met, Claire reached out a hand and stopped her.

"Excuse me. They gave my grandmother some pain medication a few minutes ago. Do you think it will have taken effect yet?"

Nurse Grayson looked puzzled. "I'm not sure what you mean, Claire."

"The nurse told me she would be giving Nana something for the pain. I . . ." She dipped her head in shame. "It's so hard for me to be with her when she's hurting. I just wondered if the medication would have taken effect by now."

"I don't think your grandmother is in great pain, Claire. Fighting against the tubes and restraints is an instinctive reaction. I'll check, but I don't believe the doctor has ordered anything new for your grandmother."

"But the nurse told me she would give Nana something right away," Claire protested, disturbed by the conflicting information she was receiving.

Geneva Grayson looked doubtful. "Well, I'll look at her chart, but I don't think so. Which nurse told you this?"

"I don't know her name, but I've seen her here before. She's probably around forty-five or fifty, petite . . . short blond hair with gray streaks in it."

"That doesn't sound like anyone on this floor."

Claire struggled to think of any other distinguishing characteristics. "She's very soft-spoken."

Suddenly Geneva gasped and took off running down the hall toward Katherine Anderson's room.

# Thirty

*C*laire stood in the middle of the hallway, too stunned to move. When she finally came to her senses, she realized there was a commotion in the hallway outside her grandmother's room. She stumbled toward it, terrified of what she might find there.

A young nurse aide met her a few feet from the door. "Your grandmother is fine . . . everything's all right." She motioned toward the door, then stopped, seemingly at a loss for words. Finally she breathed out, "Please don't worry. Everything is under control." Then she rushed toward the nurses' station.

Claire followed behind her, not willing to leave until she saw with her own eyes that Nana was safe, but feeling, too, that she needed to get out of the way.

The aide was speaking into the telephone in a barely controlled voice. She hung up and, without explanation, went quickly back down the hall toward Nana's room.

Claire thought she would go crazy wondering what was happening.

After almost ten minutes, the elevator in front of the nurses' station opened and Michael Meredith hurried out. At the same time, two police officers came through the door to the stairwell. Michael spoke with them briefly and directed them down the hall.

Then he saw her.

"Claire."

She burst into tears. "What's happening, Michael? What's going on?"

He put a steadying hand on her arm. "I can't explain right now, Claire, but I promise you your grandmother is okay. I'll tell you everything as soon as I can." He looked at her as if to assess her mental state. "Are you all right?"

She forced a nod, sensing he was needed more desperately down the hall.


When Michael walked into the room, he was met by a strange scene. Katherine Anderson lay peacefully in the bed, her breath coming in slow, even whiffs. At the back of the room, Geneva Grayson knelt on the floor against the wall, cradling Cynthia Harper in her arms.

Harper was sobbing uncontrollably. Her hushed words were nearly lost in tears, but Michael strained to hear.

"I had to do it. I had to. Don't you understand. I promised him. I promised him. . . ."

Geneva spoke in a controlled voice, trying to draw the distraught woman out. "Who did you promise, Cynthia? Tell me." She waited, and when no answer was forthcoming, she prompted again, "Tell me, please."

"Jimmy. My Jimmy. He made me promise I would never let anyone suffer the way he did. Don't you understand? I was helping them. I made it easier for them. All of them." She dissolved into tears again.

The room held its breath as Geneva asked quietly, "How many were there, Cynthia?"

"I . . . I'm not sure. Hank was the first one. That was the hardest. . . ."

"I don't remember Hank, Cynthia. Do you know his last name?"

"It was . . . it was Henry, really. His first name, I mean. We just called him Hank. Hank Burton. Yes, that was it. Burton. And then there was Virginia. That was in November. Two years ago. I remember because it was Thanksgiving Day."

"And then what?" coaxed Geneva.

"Then it was a long time before it happened again." The nurse spoke as if in a trance. The tears ceased and her quiet voice grew more confident as she recounted her missions of mercy and compassion. She admitted with pride that she had carefully stored up medications obtained with her husband's prescriptions—some legally before his death, some fraudulently, at a pharmacy in another town after he died.

In spite of his horror at the awful truth, Michael was impressed with the way Geneva was handling the woman. The others in the room—the two police officers, another nurse, and the young nurse aide—stared transfixed as the charge nurse drew from Cynthia Harper a full, detailed confession.

❧  ❧  ❧  ❧

During the following days Claire sat at her grandmother's bed-side, the previous events still begging to be made sense of in her mind. Michael had explained everything as best he could, and the local newspapers had carried the story the following evening. ANGEL OF MERCY GOES TOO FAR, the headline read; the sub-head confirmed that Harper was being held for the death of Maggie Wallace.

It still frightened Claire to think that she had trusted Cynthia Harper so completely. She shuddered to think what might have happened had she not run into Geneva Grayson in the hallway that night. Grayson had gone to the room and caught Harper red-handed, injecting Katherine Anderson's IV with a deadly dose of morphine. They had been able to remove the IV before the poison entered the old woman's bloodstream, and she was now in stable condition, apparently unaffected by the incident.

How Michael must be agonizing over these events. Claire's heart went out to him, knowing he was carrying a heavy load of guilt for all that had happened. Though from what she could understand, it certainly seemed he had done everything possible given the knowledge he had. Still, she knew him well enough to realize that he would take this very personally. She prayed fervently he would not be too hard on himself and that the legal aspects would be quickly resolved without Michael being implicated in any way.

Claire had given much thought to Cynthia Harper's actions. A part of her felt deep sympathy for the woman. Claire felt certain, after reliving her conversation with Harper, that the nurse had acted out of genuine—though tragically misguided—compassion. Without stretching too far, she could understand how the argument for "death with dignity" could seem sensible and humane. She remembered her own anguish at Nana's suffering and how she would have done almost anything to prevent it. Yet Claire believed within the deepest part of herself that man dare not make such a profound decision.

The following days demonstrated the truth of her convictions in a beautiful way.

☙   ☙   ❧   ❧

Claire kept a vigil at her grandmother's bedside, leaving only to grab a sandwich or to run home for a quick shower and a change of clothes. As she waited, her thoughts churned wildly between scenes of the terrifying ordeal Cynthia Harper had provoked and happy fragments of memories from her grandmother's life.

What she wouldn't give for just one more chance to tell her grandmother how much she loved her, how deeply grateful she was for all Nana had given her.

She and Nana had shared a rare and dear relationship. In many ways, Nana had been Claire's best friend—best friend and sister and mother and father and grandparent all wrapped into one. And she had played each role brilliantly.

Examining her heart, Claire realized she had always been reluctant to allow herself to love anyone too deeply—perhaps because it seemed that everyone she loved had let her down or been taken away from her. Nana was the exception. Claire had loved her fully. And now, with her death imminent, Claire realized there was something good and right about having allowed herself to become vulnerable to someone she loved. She suddenly realized she had known that sweet vulnerability only one other time in life. With Michael Meredith. She had felt—truly *experienced*—the varied emotions of life more deeply in this past year than she ever had before, and she was amazed to realize how much more richly textured her life had become when she allowed herself to laugh and cry, rejoice and agonize with her whole being.

Sadly, she began to understand why her parents' deaths had left her numb and unfeeling. For many complicated reasons, she had never allowed herself to fully love them. She vowed to never again make that mistake. To ache so deeply now for Nana gave the older woman's life profound meaning. It was a privilege to mourn such a loss because it meant you had loved and been loved.

The hours wore on and as Claire sat at her bedside, Nana seemed to stabilize and even improve a bit. Nurses and doctors came and went from the room, offering brief explanations to Claire, assuring her that they were doing all they could to see that Nana was comfortable. They didn't offer her hope, but neither did they deny it.

Michael Meredith stopped by each morning to see how things were going and to offer a brief word of encouragement. If Claire had one regret, it was that Michael and Nana had never had the privilege of meeting each other. Claire had promised her grandmother she would arrange a meeting, but before that could happen the tragedy had begun to unfold at Riverview, and then Nana had the second stroke.

Feeling awkward, but also feeling an urgency to keep her promise, she had made a one-sided introduction one day when Michael stopped in to check on Claire. Of course, Nana hadn't known he was there.

Claire sensed that Michael carried a burden of responsibility for Nana's situation because of the terrible things that had happened under his administration. Claire wished she knew how to ease his guilt, but she simply couldn't find the words nor the strength to utter them.

❧   ❧   ❧   ❧

On the morning of the fourth day, Claire was dozing in the chair, her hand—as always—on Nana's arm across the bedsheets. In the fog of half-sleep, she became aware that Nana was stirring restlessly in the bed. Instinctively, she began to pat the bony arm and whisper soothing words. She put her hand to Nana's cheek, and the paper-thin eyelids fluttered and then remained open.

The rheumy eyes seemed to focus on Claire, and then it was obvious that recognition dawned.

"Nana?"

The old woman opened her mouth as if to speak, but the words wouldn't seem to form.

"It's okay, Nana. Don't try to talk now." Claire was having trouble speaking herself, her throat was so full. "Just rest. I'm right here."

She arranged the light blanket tenderly around her grandmother's shoulders and pressed the call button.

Nana came and went from consciousness over the next three days. She called Claire's pet name distinctly several times and was able to answer questions with a simple yes or no, but otherwise she seemed to be barely cognizant.

Late on Monday afternoon, one week from the day of her second stroke, Katherine Anderson raised her head from the pillow and called out for Claire in a loud, gruff voice.

Startled at the strength in the voice, Claire went to the side of the bed and took her grandmother's hand. "What is it, Nana? Can I get you something?"

"Sit down and talk to me."

Claire was amazed at the flow of words from the mouth of this woman who had been silent for so long. "Oh, Nana. How . . . how are you feeling? Do you want a sip of water?"

"No, Kitty. I want to talk to you." The words were only slightly slurred.

"I'm right here, Nana."

"I'm going home soon, honey."

At first Claire thought her grandmother was confused, but as Nana continued, Claire realized that she was entirely coherent and that the home she spoke of was heaven. Claire squeezed the blue-veined hand and gulped back her tears. "I know, Nana, I know."

"Now, I want you to cry a little for me, Kitty." A faint smile, a shadow of Nana's mischievous side, played on her face, then faded as she turned serious. "And then I want you to wipe your tears and make a wonderful life for yourself."

Claire swallowed the huge lump that had formed in her throat. "I love you, Nana. I love you so much."

"I know that, Kitty. You've never left me any doubt. And I love you dearly." Nana cleared her throat and struggled to raise herself in the bed. Claire gently lifted her grandmother's head and shoulders, shocked at the feathery weight of the frail body. She plumped the pillows behind Nana's back.

"You made a promise to me, Kitty." The strength was fading rapidly from her voice. "I want to see Jo—I want to see Michael before I die. I . . ." She closed her eyes and Claire waited for a long minute, but Nana was silent, her energy apparently spent.

Claire smoothed the wrinkled brow. "I'll bring him, Nana. I promise."

"Bring him now," the old woman ordered.

Claire's heart was pounding hard and fast in her chest as she hurried down the hallway to the offices. "Oh, God, please . . . please let him be there."

The administrator's office was empty, but the receptionist told Claire that Michael hadn't yet left for the day.

"I can page him if you like," the woman told her, undisguised curiosity on her face.

"Please. It's important."

She paced the hall outside his office until five minutes later, Michael was walking toward her, his expression unreadable.

"Hi, Michael. I'm sorry to bother you, but—" Unable to hold it back another minute, she burst into tears.

He put a consoling arm around her. "Is it your grandmother?" She nodded.

He squeezed her shoulder. "I'm so sorry, Claire."

As she realized that he had misunderstood, she forced herself to regain her composure. "No . . . no, Michael. She's awake and she's asking for you. Could you please come and see her—meet her? Please?"

"Oh, of course. Of course." She could hear the relief in his voice.

They walked back to the wing, Claire leading the way into Nana's room. Nana appeared to be asleep when Claire reached her side. Gently, she began to pat her grandmother's arm.

"Nana. Nana, Michael's here."

The old woman opened her eyes, closed them, then opened them again. It seemed a supreme effort. "Hello."

Claire glanced over at Michael, who stood near the door, looking uneasy. With her eyes, Claire motioned him to the bedside. She willed her voice to remain strong, willed herself not to break down. "Nana, this is Michael Meredith."

"Hello, Michael."

Claire stepped back as Michael put a hand on the bed rail and leaned down to Nana's eye level. "Hello, Mrs. Anderson. I'm honored to meet you."

Katherine Anderson attempted a smile. "I'm not a formal person, Michael. And I don't have many words to waste."

He nodded, deferring to her with a faint smile.

"My Kitty tells me you are happy?"

"Yes, I'm happy," he said simply, reaching through the rail to touch her hand briefly.

"Good," she said with an affirming dip of her chin.

"Thank you . . . thank you for your prayers."

His voice was so low Claire had to strain to hear him.

"Claire told me that you prayed for me."

Nana clutched at the air over the blankets, seemingly searching for Michael's hand. He seemed to understand and caught her hand. Large, strong fingers swallowed frail, emaciated ones as Michael enclosed her hand in both of his. Nana's chin quivered and a tear slid down her temple and dampened the pillow beneath her head. Michael's shoulders shook with emotion, and the silence between the man and the aged woman became sacred.

Claire watched the tender reunion with tears streaming down her face, touched beyond words at Michael's openhearted emotion, her own heart overflowing with gratitude that they had been allowed this precious time.

After a while, Nana looked past Michael and whispered, "Kitty? Where is Kitty?"

"I'm right here, Nana." She wiped her eyes and came to stand beside Michael at the bed rail.

Slowly Nana looked from one to the other, then told her granddaughter, "I'd like a word alone with this young man, sweetheart."

Startled, Claire nodded and backed out of the room.

As she stood in the hallway outside her grandmother's room, she marveled at the moment that had just occurred. If she had known on that day long ago when Joseph Anderson was taken away that this reverent reunion would one day take place, how different things might have been. Her awe at the remarkable events that led to this moment overshadowed her curiosity about Nana's private conversation with Michael. It truly seemed a miracle had occurred.

After a few short minutes, Michael emerged from the room. He tipped his head and gave Claire a curiously searching look, then, seeming to shake off a disquieting thought, he told her, "She's asking for you again, Claire."

She put a hand tentatively on his arm as the tears threatened to escape again. "Thank you so much for coming, Michael. It meant so much to Nana to be able to see you . . . and . . . and . . ."

"Thank *you*, Claire." Again, his eyes held hers with a question she couldn't read. She opened her mouth to ask what he was thinking, but he continued.

"You'd better go to her."

"Yes."

He turned and disappeared around the corner.

Claire watched the empty corridor for several minutes, wondering at the unreadable expression his eyes had held, and reliving the bittersweet reunion she had witnessed between Michael and Nana. She was overcome with sorrow as she realized the finality of their exchange.

Hanging by a thread of emotion, she fought to compose herself, then walked back through the door. She stood beside Nana's bed, silently waiting for her to speak.

The sunken eyes were closed, but Claire saw Nana's lips tremble, and she knew that her grandmother, too, was struggling to gain her composure.

Finally Nana spoke, her voice calm and gentle. "Thank you, Kitty. Thank you for bringing him to me. I am at peace about his life now." Beneath hooded lids she studied Claire's face with startling intensity. "He seems a very nice young man."

"He is, Nana. He is very nice." She looked at the floor, suddenly fearful of her grandmother's scrutiny.

Nana was not fooled. "Look at me, Kitty."

Obediently, Claire looked into the liquid eyes.

"It is plain for anyone to see that you love this man." Nana raised a crooked finger and shook it weakly at Claire. It was a tenderly familiar gesture. "Don't let your stubbornness get in the way of love, Kitty. You know I would never tell you what to do, but for heaven's sake, don't close your mind to what God might have for you."

As Nana reached for her hand, Claire was aware that she deliberately softened her scolding tone before she spoke again.

"I know you've been hurt, Kitty, but open your heart to love, sweetheart. Let God show you what is right. Don't try to figure it out for yourself."

"I *can't* figure it out, Nana. I've tried."

"Exactly my point." Nana wet her parched lips and squeezed Claire's hand. "I know you'll do just fine in this life, honey." The ragged voice cracked and Nana spoke her final words of blessing with deep emotion. "God be with you, Kitty. You have been the joy of my life."

Claire stroked the soft, ashen cheek tenderly, unable to speak as tears coursed down her own cheeks.

# Thirty-one

On the twenty-eighth day of September, Katherine Jayne Anderson slipped quietly into a coma.

In these final hours of waiting, Claire found it a privilege to watch and wait with this woman whose life was so precious and meaningful to her. Though her grief ran deep, she trusted that a timing more perfect than she could begin to fathom was in operation. These moments spent waiting for Nana to be ushered into the presence of God were sacred.

Her eyes rested on her grandmother, the thin form in the bed seeming to grow smaller by the hour, her breathing barely perceptible. A strange mixture of calm and disbelief filled her as she watched Nana's life ebb away.

Memories of their happy times together paraded before her eyes. She remembered their laughter around the dining room table, always set with a Scrabble board or a domino game. She saw her grandmother's slender hands stained with juice from the cherries they picked together every summer in Nana's backyard in Lee's Summit. She heard the rich voice of a younger Nana as she brought storybook characters alive for the curly haired granddaughter on her lap.

There didn't seem to be any pain now. Nana did not struggle against death. She simply took one ragged breath and then another, and finally no more.

Claire took the thin, lifeless hand in hers. Trembling, she said her last good-byes. And as she sat beside the still form, the profound sorrow in her heart was slowly, surely transcended by a sweet knowledge that the shriveled body on this hospital bed no longer contained all that was Katherine Anderson, beloved Nana. Somewhere, at this very moment, a joyous reunion was taking place.

An hour later, Claire walked numbly out to the parking lot. The weather was hot and gusty—a Missouri Indian summer. The leaves on the myriad trees in these foothills were beginning to emerge as blazing orange and crimson tongues of fire, and under the conductorship of the wind, they murmured a haunting hymn of grief. It seemed impossible to Claire that the world could continue to breathe and live in Nana's absence. And yet it endured. She endured.


She drove home from the hospital and, as though in a trance, parked the car in the garage, and went into the dark, quiet house. Scarcely able to fathom what had occurred, she changed out of the clothes she'd worn for two days and fell into bed, exhausted.

The next morning, she awoke to the sound of faraway thunder. For a moment, she lay in bed and listened to the eerie cadence of the distant rumble. Then, the realization washed over her. Nana was gone. Gone.

Numb, she crawled out of bed, showered, and dressed mechanically. She had a sense that she was using every ounce of her will to hold her emotions in check, to keep from falling apart. There was business to be taken care of—funeral arrangements, moving Nana's things from Riverview, closing Nana's bank accounts, canceling insurance, calling Becky. . . . Until those things were dealt with, Claire needed to remain strong and in control.

She spent the morning on the telephone, handling as many details as she could by phone. Nana had a funeral plot in Kansas City beside the grandfather Claire had never known. She called the chaplain of Elmbrook and was pleased that he remembered her. He graciously agreed to perform the graveside service. They discussed arrangements for the short service, and the chaplain assured Claire that he would coordinate things with the funeral home in Hanover Falls.

Finally, when she could put it off no longer, she got in her car and drove back to Riverview. It was difficult to walk through the front doors of the building knowing that Nana wasn't there anymore. The nurses' station in the main hall was empty, so she walked down the east corridor and slowly opened the door to the room that had been Nana's.

The bed was made up with sterile white sheets, the corners mitered hospital-style. The colorful quilted comforter Claire had brought back with Nana from Elmbrook, and which she had carefully spread over the bed each morning, was gone. All of Nana's personal items had been removed from the room. The bathroom was immaculate and smelled of antiseptic. The room did not at all resemble the cozy little space that had become Nana's home for these short months.

For the first time since she had gotten the call from Geneva, Claire allowed herself to fall apart. She slumped in the chair by the window where Nana had always sat. The large padded chair was the only thing left in the room that conjured a remembrance of her grandmother. Tomorrow she would bury the last member of her family and begin to learn to live alone in the world. She covered her face with her hands and wept bitterly.

As Claire prepared to leave Riverview Manor, she decided to stop off to see the two women to whom she had been reading as a volunteer.

Gladys Armond and Nina Garcia had become special to her, and though she had explained to them that she wouldn't be able to continue full-time with her volunteer work now that school had started, she wanted to let them know she thought of them often and that she intended to visit whenever she could.

She knew they would have been told of her grandmother's death, and she was tempted to avoid the emotional condolences she knew would come from these dear women. But she found to her surprise that their gentle coddling consoled her greatly, and she was glad she had made the effort to visit them.

Impulsively, she decided to make a quick stop by Rob's room. She knew the staff had probably told him about Nana's death as well and that he would have heard the media accounts of the events which had transpired at Riverview the past week. Still, it had been several days since she had seen Rob, and she wanted to let him know that she would be going to Kansas City for the burial and would be away for a couple more days.

She walked down the familiar corridor of the north wing where the respite-care unit was located and knocked on his closed door.

"Come in."

"Hi, Rob," she said quietly, sticking her head in the door.

He was standing over a suitcase, opened and empty on his bed, with piles of folded clothing stacked all around it on the narrow mattress. The dark glasses were gone and Robert Tripleton looked as though he needed the services of a place like Riverview Manor about as much as Claire herself did.

He turned at the sound of her voice, happy surprise in his expression. It was obvious his once nearly blind eyes now took her in quite clearly.

"Claire! I've missed my story time lady." The tenderness in his voice was unmistakable.

She nodded toward the bed. "Are you packing already?"

"I leave tomorrow." His statement was devoid of emotion, and Claire thought he sounded very tired. But there was new warmth in his voice when he told her, "I'm so sorry to hear about your grandmother, Claire. Are you doing all right?"

She nodded. "I'll be okay. It's . . . it's just hard to believe she's really gone." She knew she didn't dare say more or she would break down.

Rob came toward her, and for the first time since they had known each other, he put his arms around her. "I'm sorry, Claire. I know how much you loved her—how much you must miss her. Is there anything I can do?"

She stepped back. "Thank you, Rob, but I don't know what it would be. I'm . . . I'm hanging in there. I'm coping better than I thought I would."

She looked around the room again at the signs of his imminent departure. "I just can't believe you're going home so soon."

He laughed softly. "Well, it doesn't seem so terribly soon to me."

"I'm sorry. I didn't mean it that way. It's probably seemed like forever to you. It's just that . . . well, it seems like we just met."

Suddenly she felt self-conscious in his presence. Her voice trembled as she tried to wish him good luck. She felt as though her emotions were hanging by a delicate thread and that at any moment it would snap and she would come undone.

Rob seemed to sense her fragility. "Sit down, Claire," he said with a stern authority. She was grateful for the order and sat heavily on a chair beside the bed.

Carelessly, he tossed the stack of shirts he had been folding into the suitcase and came around to stand in front of her, putting his hands on her shoulders.

"You don't have to be strong for me, Claire. You've lost someone very dear. It's okay to fall apart."

Rather than causing her to crumble, his permission somehow gave her strength. She smiled crookedly up at him and let the cleansing tears flow unchecked.

"Too many good-byes," she told him, sniffling and motioning toward the suitcase and bags on the bed. "It seems like every time I feel I've gotten a solid footing somewhere, it crumbles beneath me."

Rob sank to his knees and then sat down on the floor beside her chair, leaning an elbow on the end of the bed. "I do know a little how you feel, Claire. It gets easier as time goes on. We're not ever really alone."

Claire accepted his words, allowed them to comfort her, because she knew that he, of all people, did know what it meant to lose the only real family you had. And hadn't he made a life for himself despite his situation? She could do the same. Rob was right. She would never truly be alone as long as the Lord was with her. But could God fault her for longing for a human touch, longing to be the *most* special to someone? Was it wrong to yearn for that?

"Thank you, Rob," she told him finally, "for helping me through this. You've been a dear friend."

He waved her comments away. "It's the least I can do after everything you've done for me, Claire."

Now it was her turn to shun the compliment. "Rob, I didn't do anything—"

"You just don't realize how much you've done, Miss Anderson," he interrupted. "You saved my life."

"Oh, for heaven's sake," she laughed. "That's more than a slight exaggeration."

"No, Claire, it's really not—"

She started to protest again, but he rebuked her.

"Claire, just let me finish what I want to say here, will you?"

She bowed her head in deference.

"I have dearly loved our time together here. It's given me hope and . . . well, something constructive to do while I recovered. Claire, you've probably guessed that my feelings for you are—"

"Please, Rob. Don't." She was close to tears, not wanting him to say the words, not knowing how she could answer him.

"Claire, you must know that I've hoped that there could be something . . . something serious between us."

"Rob—"

He held up a hand, silencing her. There was a tinge of regret in his voice, a sadness that cut Claire deeply because she knew she was responsible.

"Don't worry, Claire. I know you don't return my feelings. I realize things are different now. . . ."

He looked down at the floor and scuffed at the carpet with the toe of his shoe. When he looked up, there was a sad smile on his face. "Let's just say that my eyesight has never been so clear as it was the afternoon I saw you and Michael Meredith together in the hallway. It is quite obvious that you love him very much. You love him the way I had hoped—" His words came out as an accusation, and he seemed to be struggling to compose himself.

Claire's throat swelled with unexpected emotion. She momentarily put aside Rob's assumption concerning her feelings for Michael and recognized she did love Rob. He was precious to her. But precious in the way that Becky and Millie were precious to her. She knew she couldn't offer him more.

"I'm . . . I'm sorry, Rob. I want you to know how much I've appreciated your friendship. The time spent reading with you has made this whole summer special. I don't know what I would have done without you."

"But now the summer's over, and you've found someone new." There was an edge of bitterness in his voice.

"No, Rob." She couldn't begin to explain her feelings for Michael to Rob, but neither could she deny that she loved Michael.

Rob closed his eyes and shook his head contritely. "I'm sorry. That wasn't fair." He met her eyes and waved a hand. "Never mind me. You caught me in a rotten mood. I'm sorry, Claire," he repeated. "I don't want to make this difficult for you. I should be thanking you for everything you did for me. It made a difference. It really did." He attempted a grin, suddenly looking more like a little boy than a dignified college professor.

They sat there reflecting sad smiles to each other until, feeling awkward, Claire deliberately looked at her watch. "I really do need to be going, Rob."

She rose to leave, and Rob got up and walked with her to the door.

"Well, so long," she said lightly, backing out of the doorway. "Good luck with your move."

He raised a hand. "I'll be thinking about you this week, Claire."

"Thank you, Rob."

"Keep in touch."

It was the phrase of polite company—something people said to keep from saying good-bye. But she let it go. She'd said good-bye too many times this week. God had allowed their lives—hers and Rob's—to touch for one brief season of time, and she would always be thankful for that.

She waved back at Rob with false cheer and stepped into the hallway. And she knew in her heart she might never see him again.

Claire then walked back to the front desk and arranged to get Nana's things out of storage. There was a small bag of clothing and a box of books and personal items, along with some framed photographs. It took Claire and a nurse aide two trips to load the entirety of Nana's earthly belongings into her car.

She dropped her grandmother's things off at the house, packed a small bag, and set out on the drive to Kansas City.

It was after dark when she checked into a hotel. She fell into the strange, hard bed with the knowledge that tomorrow would be a difficult day.

# Thirty-two

*C*laire slept late and awoke in a cheerless hotel room to a cloudy, sultry day. She was startled to hear a radio weatherman announce that the day marked the beginning of October. She had taught only two weeks of the school year before everything had fallen apart. Marjean Hammond had assured her that everything would be fine in her absence and encouraged her to take as much time as she needed. The previous weeks seemed lost in the chaos and trauma surrounding Nana's illness and death.

Somehow it seemed fitting that Nana should be buried on a day of a new beginning. Claire knew she would always look back to this day as a marker in her life. This was the day she would begin her life alone.

She made coffee in her hotel room and later stopped at a small café for a roll and juice, but her appetite seemed to have left her. She drove to the cemetery, arriving twenty minutes before the services were to begin.

Nana had left a written request for a simple graveside service. "*A service that clearly gives the message of Christ's salvation and not one that eulogizes this old woman,*" Nana had penned in her shaky handwriting. Claire had smiled when she read the words on the folded sheet of paper Geneva Grayson had handed her the day Nana died. She could almost hear Nana speaking the words. It touched her that her grandmother had left instructions for this day. It made it easier, knowing she was doing things as Nana wanted them done.

She parked the car at the edge of the drive and walked across the grass to the area where the mortuary had set up a funeral tent. The simple casket was already in place over the open grave, perched firmly on the metal framework of the lowering device.

Reverend Crighton, the chaplain from Elmbrook, crossed the lawn to meet Claire with outstretched arms.

"Hello, Claire. How are you doing?" he asked warmly.

"I'm fine, thank you." In spite of her sadness, she truly did feel strong and at peace.

He led her to a row of chairs beneath the canopy and she sat there, prayerfully remembering her grandmother.

Several minutes passed before she became aware of hushed voices approaching. She turned and saw her principal, Marjean Hammond, and fellow teacher Norma Blair. She rose and started forward to greet them when she spied another car—an older mini-van—pull up beside Marjean's car. Randy and Becky Anderson stepped from the van and started across the lawn.

At the sight of her friends, Claire broke down. She had felt so calm and in control, but this outpouring of love and concern touched her deeply. She tried desperately to collect herself as she walked toward the little knot of people who were gathering for her sake.

She reached Marjean and Norma first.

"Thank you so much for coming." She accepted their embraces and sympathetic words, then turned as Becky approached, arms outstretched.

Claire fell into her friend's arms, experiencing an emotional tug-of-war between the joy of seeing Becky here and the sorrow of Nana's death. The two friends dissolved into tears, words unnecessary to convey their emotion.

When Claire could finally speak, she thanked Randy and Becky for coming, and Becky told her of the other teachers and friends from Hanover Falls who sent their condolences.

Claire introduced her friends to Reverend Crighton, who ushered the small group to the grave site.

Claire sat in one of the chairs, while the others gathered around, standing beside or behind her and placing their hands on her shoulders or the back of her chair. At first she felt awkward being the focus of everyone's attentions, but soon she allowed the warmth of their touch to comfort and minister to her.

The message Reverend Crighton delivered was indeed one of redemption and victory, and Claire knew that Nana would have approved wholeheartedly.

When the brief service ended and she had told Marjean and Norma good-bye, Claire walked with Becky to her car.

"Becky, you just can't know how much it means to me that you and Randy drove all this way today. Thank you so much."

She gave Becky a spontaneous hug and was surprised to sense in Becky's demeanor that something was amiss. She held her friend at arm's length and looked questioningly into her face.

"Becky? Is something wrong?"

Becky bit her lower lip and a brief smile played on her lips. "Claire, do you know that Michael is here?" Her gaze traveled to the opposite side of the cemetery, behind Claire. Claire turned and followed Becky's line of vision to a narrow road at the far end of the grounds.

There, parked in the distance, was a familiar green pickup, and standing solemnly beside it, Michael Meredith.

Claire took in a sharp breath. "Oh, Becky. He came."

"He's been here the whole time, Claire. He wasn't sure you'd want him here, but he wanted to be near . . . just in case."

Becky put her hands on Claire's shoulders and pleaded. "Go to him, Claire. Please. Just talk to him. Please," she begged, sensing Claire's hesitancy.

"Will you wait?"

Becky looked anxiously toward the driver's side where her husband sat waiting. "We left the boys with Randy's mom. We really do need to start back. But I'll see you back home," she promised. "You'll be coming back soon, won't you?"

Becky's simple question sparked a thought of such clarity that it almost took Claire's breath. Suddenly she knew that what she was yearning for—*aching* for in her loneliness—was not some elusive, imaginary thing. She was homesick for Hanover Falls, for the friends she had made there, for the home on Brookside Drive that waited to wrap her in its comfort, for the children at the school who loved her and needed her—even for a silly gray tomcat to warm her lap.

And yes, she ached for Michael's touch. Perhaps that desire was one she would ultimately be denied, but she couldn't deny the truth of her longing for him and for what they so briefly had together. Suddenly she could scarcely wait to see him, to hear his voice again.

She pulled Becky into a final hug. "I love you, Becky. Thank you. Thank you for everything."

Becky gave her a playful nudge. "Go. Go on. I'll see you in a few days."

Claire turned and started across the grass, forcing herself not to run.

He met her halfway, eyes downcast, seemingly unsure of how she would receive him.

"Claire, I'm so sorry about your Nana," he said sincerely, almost shyly.

Her heart warmed at his use of her pet name for her grandmother. Looking uncertain, he attempted a smile. "I . . . I hope you don't mind that I came. I wanted to be here . . . for her. And for you."

"Oh, Michael. I'm so glad you're here!" The words came out in a sob. She wanted to throw herself into his arms, but instead, she stood unmoving in front of him, taking in the contours of his face, the sun on his dark hair, the warmth in his eyes. *How she had missed him!*

"Your grandmother was one of the few bright spots in my childhood, Claire. I'm realizing that I need to acknowledge that there *were* some good things about those years. She was a wonderful woman. I wanted to pay my respects."

Claire shook her head. "Thank you. Thank you for coming. I could use a friend right now."

"Do you want to walk for a while?"

She nodded and they set out down the gravel drive toward a hedgerow at the back of the cemetery grounds. A hot sun had broken through the haze of clouds, and the afternoon humidity felt more like July than October. Michael loosened his tie and rolled up the sleeves of his dress shirt before turning to her again.

"Are you doing okay, Claire? Really?"

Her eyes welled again and hot tears mingled with the perspiration that beaded her temples. "I'm crying a lot," she said, smiling in spite of the tears.

"You need to," he said simply. "It's healthy."

"Well, then, I should be the picture of health."

He laughed gently, and reaching for her hand, he steered her toward the shade of a long row of giant cottonwood trees. In the distance she saw Randy and Becky's van pull out of the entrance. She was overwhelmed again with how much it had meant to her for these people to have been here on this difficult day. She tried to explain it all to Michael.

"As hard as it's been to lose Nana, I've just been . . ." She paused, groping for the right word. "I've been *surrounded* by love. I know now what the Bible means when it says that His grace is sufficient, that His peace passes understanding. It's all so true."

"I know, Claire. I've felt it myself through the whole ordeal at Riverview."

"I've thought about you so much these past days. I know this whole thing has been awful for you."

"It has been awful. But I'll get through it. Don't worry about that."

"I guess the important thing is that it's over now. The . . . the killings, I mean."

He shook his head. "I'm not sure if I'm ready to look at it quite that way yet, Claire. Three people lost their lives in the care of an institution that was under my administration. I carry full responsibility for that."

"Do you . . . is there a chance that there will be legal action against you?"

"It's possible."

"Are you scared?"

He looked directly at her. "I'm not, Claire. I suppose I should be, but I know that God knows my heart and knows that my intentions were pure. I trust that He'll take care of me—whatever happens."

Claire was silent, thinking over this frightening possibility.

"I'm just so sorry this whole thing had to involve you, Claire. With your grandmother, I mean."

"Maybe I'm still in shock. Maybe it'll all hit me later, but somehow I don't think so. I guess in some ways I've been preparing myself for Nana's death for a long time now . . . as much as you *can* prepare yourself for something like that. The circumstances don't really change the fact that she's gone—and I'm alone now."

He seemed to sense she was thinking aloud, and he let her go on without reply.

They walked in the shade, talking and thinking, Michael holding tightly to her hand while the giant cottonwoods whispered over their heads.

She began to share her memories of Nana with him, laughing over some of them, brought to tears by others.

After a while she fell silent and he ventured, "I hope your grandmother knew how fully her prayers for me were answered. I . . . I never really told her the whole story. There . . . there wasn't time to say everything I wanted to say that day in her room."

Claire nodded her understanding.

"I've been overwhelmed lately to think that she prayed for me all these years," Michael continued. "I just hope she knew."

Claire squeezed his hand and smiled up at him through tears. "She knew, Michael. She knew."

They circled back to the place where the fresh grave of her grandmother marred the earth. The canopy and grass carpet were gone now, the casket forever buried under the mound of pungent black earth. The wind had toppled over one of the huge funeral sprays that had been placed at the foot of the grave. Michael stooped and reverently set it aright.

They stood silently together as Claire said her final good-byes, then he walked with her across the lawn to where his truck was parked.

He put down the tailgate, improvising a bench. They sat in companionable silence. Claire found such comfort—such belonging—in his presence.

"How did you know where the funeral was?" she finally asked, already suspecting the answer.

He grinned impishly. "I have quite a network of informants," he told her.

"Becky."

"And Millie, and the kid who mows your lawn, and . . ." He pretended to count off a lengthy list on his fingers.

"The boy who mows my lawn! You are pitiful," she laughed.

"Claire?" He turned to her, suddenly serious. "You might as well know that nothing has changed in the way I feel about you. This isn't the time to pressure you—I know that. We both have a lot of things to work through, but I have to know if I have even a prayer with you. . . ." He shrugged his frustration.

She shook her head slowly. "Michael, I thought I could run away from my feelings for you. I've tried. I've tried everything I know to forget you, but you've haunted me everywhere I go."

"Claire." He reached up and tenderly brushed a strand of hair from her forehead, then stroked her cheek with the back of his hand.

"I love you. I *still* love you, Claire."

To hear her name on his lips, to feel the warmth, the tender touch of his hand on her face made her realize beyond a doubt that her love for him had never dimmed, was stronger than ever if that were possible. But were all the worries, all the fears that had caused her to run from his love of her own imagination? Or were there valid reasons to be cautious?

She didn't know, but of one thing she was certain. She loved this man, loved him in a way she had never loved before. Sitting beside him in the quiet of the cemetery, she sought to examine that love—to hold it under the microscope of God's truth and to see if it would be allowed her.

*Lord*, she prayed in the quietness of her heart, *I so want to be in your will. I truly want to do what is right. I don't want to make a mistake. Most of all, I don't want to hurt Michael. He's been hurt so deeply already. With your help, he's overcome so much, and he deserves some happiness now. Could I ever possibly be part of that happiness?*

Joy surged through her being as the sudden realization came. What she felt for Michael was not merely an infatuation or a romantic love, though the thrill of those emotions was undeniably there. But suddenly she knew why Michael's grief had touched her so deeply, why the sorrows of his childhood wounded her as though they had happened to her. Her love for Michael was pure and right! The emotion she felt for him was the selfless love of which the Scriptures spoke—the love that caused one to seek the other's well-being above one's own and to be joyful in the sacrifice. She knew now that she would be willing to stand beside him no matter what the future brought.

As all these thoughts bombarded her, Michael sat silent beside her. Now she turned to him. "Michael, I have never stopped loving you. If we go slowly . . . if there's no doubt in either of our minds that God is blessing our relationship, I'm willing—oh, I'm so willing—to see where He leads us. I do love you."

He took her hand in his, and Claire saw that his eyes brimmed with tears. "She told me you did."

"What?" Claire was confused.

"Your grandmother . . . when she asked you to leave the room that day. She told me that you still loved me."

Claire looked at him, startled. "Nana told you that?" she asked, then started to cry as he put his arm around her.

"She couldn't have given me a greater gift, Claire."

She leaned her head on his shoulder and they sat that way—thinking, talking, praying—side by side on the tailgate of a green pickup truck, until the sun was low in the sky of a dying Indian summer.

When evening shadows began to fall on the cemetery, Michael walked Claire to her car. He offered to take her out for dinner that night, but she told him honestly that she was exhausted.

"It's sweet of you to offer, but I'm afraid I'd fall asleep in my soup."

"I'll be driving back tonight then," he told her. "You'll be home tomorrow?"

"I hope so. I have so much to do before I go back to school Wednesday. I still have a few loose ends to tie up here, too."

"Anything I can do to help?"

"Thank you for offering, but it's mostly things I have to do myself. I want to make arrangements to have the date put on Nana's gravestone. And I still have to sign some papers at the insurance office. . . ." She was thinking out loud. She rubbed her temples wearily and turned to him. "There are so many things to think about. I never realized how complicated it is to die."

He touched her cheek. "You'd better get back to the hotel and get some sleep. I'll see you when you get back. You're sure you're okay?"

She nodded.

He turned and started back toward his truck but she called out to him.

"Michael."

He turned around, questioningly.

"I'm so glad you came."

He smiled and saluted playfully in answer. She watched him walk away until his strong, lean figure disappeared over the crest of a hill.

# Thirty-three

On the second day of October in a drenching rainstorm, Claire loaded her suitcase into her little car and pulled out of the hotel parking lot.

She was still reeling from the loss of her only living family member. She missed her grandmother sorely, feeling the loss as a physical pain in the pit of her stomach.

She truly had no ties to this city of her childhood now. She was returning to Hanover Falls alone, and a feeling of great loneliness washed over her. She wondered if she would ever truly be free of that ache.

She drove on in the downpour, the windshield wipers marking a staid cadence with her mournful thoughts. Yet as the road signs began to measure the distance to a little village called Hanover Falls, Claire couldn't help but feel the hint of a promise well up in her spirit. *Ninety-eight miles to Hanover Falls. Sixty-five miles to Hanover Falls. . . .*

She was going home. She was going to Michael. And he loved her. He still loved her. Excitement rose within her with each passing mile. The rain had let up slightly, and all around her the countryside gleamed from the cleansing shower. She drove through one small town and smiled to see five or six young children playing in the shallow pools of water that had collected at the curbs. They splashed and squealed, carefree and full of delight. She caught some of their joy.

Ten miles outside of Hanover Falls the sun broke through the clouds, and Claire began to feel a sense of anticipation she had experienced only a few times in her short life. How beautiful it was to have *hope*.

Yes, she had suffered a grave loss with Nana's death. But Nana had lived long and enjoyed good health—and a generous measure of happiness and fulfillment. She had been ready to die, and in spite of the frightening attempt by Cynthia Harper to circumvent the natural course of things, Katherine Anderson had been ushered into heaven at a divinely appointed time. There was peace in that knowledge.

Claire's mind filled again with dear memories of her grandmother, and she suddenly understood that those precious remembrances were a gift and a legacy.

Her mind turned to the promise the year ahead held for her: the anticipation of the school term now underway and the special children, barely known to her yet, but who would capture her heart as surely as Lucas and Jarrod and Brianne and the others had.

She thought warmly of her friendship with Millie Overman—a friendship she suspected would take on new significance now that Nana was gone.

The Lord had filled her life with special friends. Millie and the others at Riverview. Becky. And yes, there was undeniable excitement in the hope of a renewed friendship with Michael. She sent up a prayer that Michael would be given strength to face the difficult legal proceedings that were sure to be brought against Cynthia Harper. She begged God that He would not allow Michael to come under criticism himself.

The things that had taken place at Riverview still seemed unbelievable. She knew it would cause Michael deep heartache as he sorted out his own feelings of guilt and grief and as he tried to rebuild the community's trust in Riverview. She prayed that she could be a support and encouragement to him as he dealt with the aftermath of the tragedy.

She wished for just a moment that she could know just how the story would end but wistfully decided that some things were better left unknown and in the hands of God.

Claire passed a highway marker announcing that Hanover Falls was seven miles ahead. It seemed as though she had been gone for a year, and yet only yesterday she had made this same trip in reverse. The countryside began to look sweetly familiar. Her car crested a steep hill, and the old water tower in City Park came into view, its huge silver belly emblazoned with faded letters that spelled out the town's name. Her heart beat faster and she realized with elation that she was nearly home. *Home*. The word had tripped from the tongue of her mind as though it were true!

She slowed down as she entered the city limits. Though summer seemed reluctant to take its leave, autumn was waiting in the wings, and the air was alive with the spiraling waltz of a million golden leaves.

She turned onto her street and gave a sigh of satisfaction. She was almost there. And tomorrow night she would see him. There was so much to be said, so very much. But those words needed to be spoken face-to-face. She couldn't wait to be with him again.

🙚  🙚  🙚  🙚

Claire smoothed her hair nervously and hurried to answer the doorbell.

"Hi, Michael. Come on in."

He greeted her with a warm hug. "Welcome home," he said lightly. He held her away from him and his eyes held hers as he asked, "Are you okay, Claire?"

She sighed. "I'm okay. I'm glad to be home."

He smiled and took her hand. "It's so good to have you back—in Hanover Falls, I mean. Did everything go okay at school today?"

"I'm still learning names, but yes, I feel like I'm getting back in the routine." They both seemed to be trying desperately to recapture the light, carefree way they'd known with each other, but their conversation was stilted and awkward. She loosed her hand from his, then sat down on the couch.

"Is something wrong?"

"I . . . I'm just not sure how to be with you now, Michael."

"It's kind of awkward, isn't it?" he acknowledged, sitting beside her.

She nodded.

"Claire, I've been thinking that it wasn't fair of me to tell you all the things I did knowing you were still trying to deal with your grandmother's death. Not because I didn't mean them," he added quickly. "It's just that I realize now that it wasn't the best time for you. I know you must still be sorting out your feelings about so many things. Your grandmother, and the whole thing at Riverview . . . not to mention everything that happened between us before. I hope it didn't seem like I was pressuring you, Claire. I guess I got overly anxious."

"Michael, it didn't take much sorting out to know that I love you with everything that is in me. It's just that I want to be sure. I want to know for certain that we're not acting only on our feelings."

"There's a lot to talk about, isn't there?" He smiled.

"So much I don't know where to begin," she said, feeling a familiar anxiety rise within her.

"We have a whole lifetime, Claire. Let's not hurry it one bit." He reached for her hand again and rubbed his thumbs across her fingers, as if to knead the tension out of them. "I won't rush you, Claire. I promise you I'll give you all the time you need."

The tender honesty of his words began to take their effect on Claire. She willed herself to relax and to embrace the gift of being here beside him, of being loved by a man like Michael. She leaned her head against the back of the sofa and closed her eyes. He left her to the silence, stroking her hand, waiting on her.

Then the words emerged. Slowly at first, then a trickle, then a torrent. And as Michael filled her in on the happenings in his life while they had been apart, and as she told him of her feelings and doubts and of all that happened in her life since they had parted—even of her friendship with Rob—little by little they began to find an easiness with each other again.

"So just how serious was it with you and this Rob fellow?" he wanted to know.

She tried to keep her answer light, yet truthful. "Rob is a wonderful guy, Michael. We became very close friends. We both had kind of a tough summer, and we helped each other through."

"Did . . . did you love him?"

"Not the way you mean. For a time I thought I might, but it was always you, Michael. It was always you." She shook her head slowly and smiled up at him.

He smiled back, seemingly satisfied. "Okay . . . just wondering."

Sheepishly she ventured, "All right, while we're on the subject, just how serious was it with you and that blonde?"

"What blonde?"

"Don't play dumb," she teased. "I saw you driving around with some gorgeous blonde."

He cocked an eyebrow at her and shook his head. "You must have me confused with somebody else."

"Yeah, right."

"No, seriously, Claire." His defensiveness seemed genuine. "Believe me, I would have remembered driving around with a gorgeous—o-o-oh," he said, a light obviously dawning. He began to laugh. "*That* gorgeous blonde. Claire, I have to confess. I *was* driving around with a gorgeous blonde and I . . . I have loved her since I was ten years old." He strung out his words, obviously relishing her open curiosity.

Skeptical at his laughter, she shot him a questioning look. She was not sure she liked the direction this conversation was taking.

He burst out laughing. "That was my *sister*, you silly goose! You know, Sarah—Eli's mom."

She punched him in the arm and laughed at her own suspicions, trying not to analyze the deep relief she felt at his answer.

Slowly, as they shared their hearts, the deep emotion she had always felt in his presence welled up within her, and she experienced anew the happiness she had known with him before.

"Oh, Michael," she whispered, her head cradled on his shoulder, the pain of a lifetime of hurts draining from her. "How could we be so blessed? To have another chance like this. . . ." She couldn't go on. Her heart was too full.

"I love you," she said finally.

His kiss echoed the simple, joyful words back to her.

They sat together on the sofa, not noticing when October's light faded, casting the living room walls in shadow, then darkness. It didn't matter that they each had to work the following day, that the harsh realities of all that had happened would accost them just beyond these walls. For now they were together. For now, the love they shared was enough. And tomorrow, with God's help, they would face the future together.

# Thirty-four

O ver the next weeks, Michael poured out his heart to Claire, and they both experienced many conflicting emotions with all they had gone through.

Claire's own emotions had run the gamut from elation to anguish. Her heart ached at the loss of her grandmother, and she found herself in tears at the slightest provocation. To have no one who shared her family history, no one to whom she was connected by the ties of blood, felt desolate.

Yet from the depths of that desolation, she had climbed to the heights of joy at her unexpected reunion with Michael. It still seemed too wonderful to be true—that he loved her, that she could finally love him in return.

As for Michael, the tragedy at Riverview had shaken him deeply, and Claire sensed he was feeling a terrible guilt for what had happened.

"I keep thinking back to the time when Vera and I first started feeling that something wasn't quite right," he told her one chilly night as they walked near the park together. "There was honestly never anything concrete we could point to, yet we both had this nagging feeling. I have to wonder now if it was God's prompting, and I was just too involved in my own little world to listen." He shook his head sadly. "I don't want to make that mistake again, Claire. The stakes are too high."

She didn't understand everything that had happened, but she told him, "I think you're being too hard on yourself, Michael. The newspapers quoted several of Cynthia Harper's co-workers and neighbors as saying they would never have guessed her to do something like this in a million years. If even the people who knew her well would say that, how could you have possibly known? And besides, some of the stories said the former administrator was being questioned. At least two of the people died while he was at Riverview."

"Yes. That's true," he said. "I have a feeling some very unpleasant things are going to come out when they talk to Gerald Stoddard. It appears that the board pushed him to hire Cynthia Harper over Vera's objection, and when that comes out, I'm afraid it's going to get ugly."

Claire shook her head, still unable to believe the tragedy that had happened in their quiet little town. Silently, she worried that Michael would still be implicated somehow. She knew he was innocent, but she also knew that *someone* would shoulder the blame for all that had happened. She kept her fears to herself though.

"I know one thing," Michael told her now, "there has to be a better way to help those patients who are in pain and dying. Cynthia was right about one thing. No one should have to die alone and in pain. There just has to be an alternative to this . . . this so-called mercy killing. I'm frightened by the articles that newspapers and industry journals are running. It seems impossible this could happen in America, but unbelievably, the tide seems to be turning slowly in favor of legalized euthanasia."

"I don't understand how people could fall for that rationale—" Claire stopped short, remembering guiltily how she would have done almost anything to spare her grandmother the pain she had seemed to suffer. She told Michael of the thoughts that had gone through her mind then, and they agreed that without belief in an omnipotent God, without believing that there was something—*Someone*—bigger than man, euthanasia *did* seem a compassionate act.

"What sets us apart is our personal relationship with the living God and our faith in the fact that only He should decide when our time on earth will end. Until people understand that, it won't make sense to them."

Suddenly he turned to her, his voice impassioned. "I want my experience to make a difference, Claire. To really count for good. I don't think I could carry on if those people died in vain."

"I know you will make it count for good, Michael. I know you will." She had every confidence in this man she loved.

❧ ❧ ❧ ❧

As winter settled on Hanover Falls, the scandal of the tragedy that had drawn unwelcome attention to the quiet midwestern community diminished in the minds of the people.

Cynthia Harper's first court date had been set, and there were lawsuits pending against Gerald Stoddard and two members of the current board of directors for their roles in hiring the nurse. Claire knew that Michael would be required to testify at each of the hearings.

Though it was too early to be certain, it appeared that none of the families of the deceased patients were intent on filing charges against Riverview. Out-of-court settlements were being negotiated, and for all intents and purposes, it looked as though Michael would not be implicated in any of the lawsuits. The board had asked him to stay on, and thus he faced the daunting task of rebuilding the reputation of Riverview.

One night Michael and Claire walked together near the park, as had become their habit, and he told her that, much to his dismay, Vera Johanssen had turned in her resignation that morning. Vera had assured him that the scandal had not soured her, merely prompted her to do what she should have done long ago. "It's time, Michael," she had told him. "Be happy for me."

Oliver Moon was back at work, taking his duties more seriously than ever. Geneva Grayson reported that she hadn't once had to reprimand him for sneaking cookies onto the nursing wings. Claire had been touched to learn that Michael had bought the childlike man a dozen large laminated storage cartons for the safekeeping of his precious collections. Michael had delivered the boxes to Ollie's house soon after the man's release from the county jail, and Ollie had proudly traded him a small collection of paper cups for the shiny new boxes.

Best of all, Claire was getting to know Ollie during her volunteer time at Riverview. She still had trouble making out his jumbled words, but she was learning to interpret his own special dialect of sign language, and his nearly toothless grin was a ready reward for her efforts.

Michael's testimony in the first court date went well. He told Claire that it helped him to see the crimes of the people involved recognized as such. She knew that he still felt a twinge of guilt for the small part his naivety and inaction had played in the tragedy, but he was spending his energy developing a support group for terminally ill patients and their family members. He confided that he eventually hoped to have a full-blown hospice program operating under the auspices of Riverview Manor.

ॐ   ॐ   ॐ   ॐ

Claire had her hands full with an unusually bright but undisciplined group of third-grade students.

In particular, she was struggling to know how to handle one student who had established himself as chief troublemaker in the classroom. Storm Waymire seemed determined to live up to his unique name, and nothing Claire tried seemed to have any effect on him.

She shared these thoughts with Michael one night as they drove to the apartments to pick up Millie. They had invited their mutual friend for an early Christmas dinner at a new restaurant in nearby Boyd City.

"I could just kick myself sometimes for being so impatient with him," she told Michael, bemoaning her most recent episode with the mischief-maker.

"It sounds to me like he had it coming, Claire. I think you handled the situation just about right."

"I'd be more likely to agree with you if I saw any results whatsoever, but if anything, I'm afraid he's getting worse. I'm at my wits' end to know what to do next. I really don't want to have to call in Marjean. Maybe it's pride, but I think I should be able to handle this myself without getting the principal involved—at least not yet."

"Well, taking it from someone who was somewhat of a 'storm' myself at that age, sometimes a higher authority is what it takes."

She looked at him thoughtfully. "Do you remember what went through your mind when you were acting out back then?"

His brow furrowed, and she saw a shadow of the sadness that had so distinctively marked his eyes when she first met him. But the look passed and he turned to her, appearing more puzzled than disturbed.

"I honestly don't remember, Claire. I have vague memories of sitting in a principal's office—more than one principal, probably—but what I hoped to accomplish by my behavior back then I truly don't know. As I got older I can remember thinking that everyone was against me. I suppose I had what you'd call a victim mentality. 'Why me? Poor me.' " He shrugged. "I don't know. I guess if I were more analytical, I'd want to figure it out, but I'm content just knowing that boy isn't me anymore. I wish I could help you get inside this kid's head." He shrugged an apology.

She waved it off. She had nearly forgotten about Storm and the challenge he presented. Instead, she was hearing Michael's words with a clarity she couldn't ignore. *I'm content just knowing that boy isn't me anymore,* he had said. And somehow she knew his statement contained a truth more profound than any advice he could have provided concerning Storm Waymire.

It was true. Michael truly was a new creation in Christ, not at all resembling the troubled, disturbed child he had been. His past no longer had a hold on him. And she knew then that he truly had forgiven the wrong her parents had done him. It no longer had any hold on him. He had tried to tell her this. Why had she not been able to see until this moment how certainly Michael Meredith's life reflected this truth? If he could forgive so wholly, be changed so utterly, what did she have to fear? And how could she do any less?

They picked Millie up and the three of them spent a pleasant evening together, visiting and enjoying a delicious meal, but Claire found herself struggling to remain attentive to the conversation. She was preoccupied, mulling this new thought over in her mind with a growing sense of joyous expectancy for what it meant for her.

On the trip home Claire sat in the backseat of her car while Michael drove, and Millie chatted in the front beside him. Tonight Claire was grateful for the older woman's presence and especially for her talkative nature. It gave her time to think again about the things Michael had said earlier. Claire realized that whether he knew it or not, his simple words had been spoken for her benefit. She had held on to the bitterness, had even hated them—her mother and her father—for the way her life had turned out. But now she was ready to let go. She wanted a taste of the simple peace Michael had found in forgiving. Forgiving and forgetting. It had eluded her for so long and yet, it flowed so simply from Michael's mouth, as though he had no idea what a profound secret he had disclosed. With tears flowing silently, Claire sat in the dark warmth of the backseat. Oblivious, Michael's laughter mingled with Millie's in the front of the car while Claire prayed the very simple words heaven had been waiting to hear. "Father, I forgive them. They didn't know what they did. But you knew, and you took care of it all at the Cross. I *am* a new creation in you. Thank you, God. Oh, thank you."

After they dropped off Millie at her apartment, Michael invited Claire to his place for coffee.

"You're awfully quiet," he observed as he measured coffee grounds into the filter. "Anything wrong?"

"No, I'm just thinking about the things you said tonight." Not quite ready to share how deeply she had been touched on this night, she gave him a hint of the direction her thoughts had been taking.

Together they sat at the tiny table in his kitchen, talking, drinking too much coffee, not willing for the evening to end. Finally Claire looked at her watch. "You'd better get me home, Mr. Meredith, before I turn into a pumpkin."

He was looking at her with a strange expression on his face. "Before you go, Claire, I want to tell you something. This isn't a question. I don't want an answer—not tonight."

He reached across the table for her hand. "Claire, there's something that I'm having trouble keeping from you, and I don't want there to be any secrets between us. That's gotten us in trouble before."

She looked at him, curious, not able to imagine what he was about to reveal.

"I promised you I wouldn't rush you, and I meant that. But I know tonight, Claire, beyond a shadow of a doubt, that I want you to be my wife."

She started to open her mouth—to say what, she hadn't the faintest idea. But he put a gentle hand to her lips and shushed her, childlike tenderness in his deep voice. "Shhh . . . I'm not asking you, Claire. This isn't a question to be answered right now. I just want you to know where I stand on the subject of us. I have loved you almost since the moment I first laid eyes on you. We've weathered some incredible storms together and *still* I love you. I know now that won't ever change. So when you're ready—when you feel as sure as I do of our love—I want you to know that I will be waiting, very patiently waiting, for your answer."

Tears of joy filled her eyes and again she opened her mouth to speak, but he leaned across the table and silenced her with a slow, playful kiss.

"Shhh . . . I *said* I don't want an answer tonight."

# Thirty-five

*E*arly in December Claire tackled a task she had deliberately put off for weeks. Nana's belongings from the Elmbrook apartment had sat in boxes in Claire's closet since the day she had moved into Riverview. Claire tried to ignore the bulky cartons whenever she came across them while hunting for a seldom-worn pair of shoes or jacket. She knew she couldn't put off the matter of sorting through her grandmother's things forever, but she also knew that it would be very difficult to face the memories and relive the sorrow of Nana's death all over again.

Now, on a cold, cloudy Saturday afternoon, she came across the boxes while rummaging for her Christmas decorations. Before she could talk herself out of it, she lugged the two larger cartons out onto the floor of her bedroom and went for the scissors to cut through the sturdy packing tape.

The first box contained the knickknacks and various decorative items that had adorned her grandmother's dresser and end tables at Elmbrook. Claire smiled as she unwrapped newspaper from a pair of ceramic candlesticks shaped like playful kittens. Nana had loved cats and there had always been two or three in residence when she lived in the Lee's Summit house. Katherine Anderson had always said her greatest regret at moving into Elmbrook had been that she couldn't bring her beloved cats with her.

Claire dug farther in the box and unearthed a familiar table lamp and Nana's much-used magnifying glass. Tears came to her eyes as she remembered her grandmother's veined hands holding the glass over the worn pages of her Bible. Tears moistened Claire's cheeks, and yet she was surprised to realize that the emotion she was feeling was

# PORTRAITS

far from sorrow. Instead, the objects Claire had feared would bring her such pain brought her joyful memories instead. It would be a comfort to have and use these things that had been Nana's. They would be dear reminders of a precious part of her life.

Swept away in nostalgia, Claire opened a smaller box, one of several that had been given to her at Riverview after Nana's death. This one was filled with Nana's books. Claire lifted each one reverently from the box and thumbed through them, trying to decide which ones she would like to keep.

Tucked away to the side of the carton—as though it had been the last thing packed before the box was taped shut—was Nana's Bible. Its leather cover was worn almost bare in spots, and its frayed edges testified to decades of use.

She opened the cover and read the neatly penned inscription: *To Katherine Anderson, presented on the occasion of her sixtieth birthday with love from Raymond, Myra, and Claire Marie Katherine.* Claire recognized her mother's handwriting and was shocked to realize that the date was more than a quarter of a century ago.

She leafed through the thin, almost translucent pages. Many paragraphs were heavily underlined, and there were copious notes scrawled in the margins. Old church bulletins tucked into the pages contained more scribbled notes and sermon outlines. Claire leafed unhurriedly through the Psalms, thrilled to have this unexpected access to her grandmother's thoughts and spiritual insights.

She read with fascination for half an hour. She was about to tuck the book away when one of the pages yielded a new-looking envelope bearing her name.

Eagerly, Claire unsealed the envelope and brought out a thin sheaf of paper dated several weeks before Nana's death. She unfolded it and brought it close, trying, through tears, to decipher her grandmother's feeble, shaky handwriting.

> My Dearest Kitty (I'm sorry, my dear, but I cannot think of you as "Claire" any more than you could think of me as "Katherine"),
>
> If you are reading this letter, it means that I have gone home to be with the Lord. It grieves me to think of you all alone in this world, Kitty. And yet in these past few weeks I have seen that you are a strong young woman—strong in your sense of what is pure and right, and strong in your faith in our Lord. That comforts

me greatly as I live out my last days upon this old earth.

Kitty, I want you to know what a dear, dear treasure you have been to me every day of your life. As we have already discussed, your childhood was certainly not one I would have chosen for you, but I have all faith that the Lord will use (and perhaps already has used) even that part of your life to His glory.

I know that you have suffered in this life, Kitty—perhaps more than your share. I have come to believe that suffering is an integral part of the life we are called to live on this earth. I believe that as you grow in your faith you will come to see, as I have, that our response to suffering can give meaning and purpose to our lives. Through suffering I have experienced the depths of sorrow, but had I not plumbed those depths, I would not have known the great heights of joy God had to offer through His gift of hope. I pray you might find such a hope in this truth.

On another matter, Kitty, I hope you can forgive an old woman for meddling, even from the grave as this will seem to be; but I feel compelled to share with you a passage that the Lord showed me in my prayer time this evening. It is frightening to dare to speak for the Lord (so I won't), but I have a strong impression that these verses will speak to you concerning Joseph—Michael Meredith. They are beautiful verses, Kitty. They offer such hope and restoration. Please let God speak to you through them however He wills. I trust that He will show both of you—you and Michael—what is right.

"And I will restore to you the years that the locust hath eaten . . . and ye shall eat in plenty, and be satisfied, and praise the name of the Lord your God, that hath dealt wondrously with you; and my people shall never be ashamed."

I love you, my dearest granddaughter. I pray you find God's blessing in all you do and all you are.

With love,
Nana

Claire put her head in her hands and collapsed in sobs. She knew within her spirit that this was the confirmation for which she had longed. It had been here, concealed in a box in her closet for all these weeks. Yet Claire knew that she had not been ready to receive it even two weeks ago. She had needed this time to think things through, to come to know Michael more intimately, to search her heart and God's Word for direction and assurance.

Slowly, she had begun to feel all the markers pointing her toward this minute, this sure knowledge. But the confirmation—from a source so sweetly improbable—had come in a timing so perfect that it could have only one Source.

Claire read the letter again and again, with a dawning of truth. Yes, the "locust" had eaten away many years of her life and of Michael's. And yet, she and Michael had faced the deepest secret of each of their lives and had been offered a healing so creative it was unfathomable. How wonderfully God had chosen to restore those years! Now when Claire looked into the very face that represented the ghosts of her past, she saw instead the face she loved most dearly in all the world. And she knew it would be the same for Michael.

Tomorrow she would go to him in joy, knowing that God had granted the blessing she coveted to be upon their love.

🙢   🙢   🙢   🙢

The snow had fallen silently in the night, making fools of Missouri's meteorologists, most of whom had predicted "possible light flurries overnight." Now every lawn, every sidewalk, every tree and any vehicle unfortunate enough to have been left outside was buried under six inches of "light flurries."

Claire dusted the white powder off her jeans and leaned the heavy broom she'd been using to clear the walk against the gnarled trunk of a tree. Sighing with happy exhaustion, she peeled off her gloves and examined the blisters on her palms.

From across the lawn came the voice she loved. "Hey! Don't quit on me now. We're almost done." Michael Meredith leaned on his shovel and looked at her accusingly. "You're not wimping out on me, are you?"

"Michael, look at this," she whined, only half joking. "My hands are one big blister." She held out her palms for inspection.

They had been working for half an hour, two narrow paths on the driveway and the sidewalk in front of Claire's house testifying to their joint efforts.

Now he let the shovel fall to the ground and covered the distance between them in long strides. "Let me see," he said with mock impatience, taking her hands in his.

He brought one reddened palm to his lips and in none-too-sympathetic baby talk kissed each blister. "Oh, my poor wittle Claire. Did her get a bwister?"

"Cut it out!" she laughed. "They hurt!" She rubbed her palms together gingerly before pulling her gloves back on.

"Come over here," he said, totally unsympathetic. "I've got just the thing for those blisters."

He put an arm around her shoulders and escorted her to the edge of the yard where snow had drifted deeply against the fence. Positioning her strategically in front of the white mound, he gave her a gentle shove.

She fell backward into the soft cushion of white. Sputtering and squealing, she came up clutching a handful of snow. She packed it into an ill-formed snowball and tossed it in his direction, barely grazing his shoulder.

"Oh, now you've done it," he threatened as a brisk gust of wind scattered the snow in a mini-blizzard. "You will be eternally sorry you did that, Miss Anderson," he announced through clenched teeth, barely concealing the laughter in his voice.

"You started it," she dished back playfully, cowering by the fence as he started toward her.

He dived into the drift beside her and held her arm to prevent her from gathering any more ammunition.

"Ouch! Uncle! Uncle!" she cried, slipping out of his grasp and scrambling out of reach.

He lunged and tried to tackle her again but dissolved in laughter before he could get a firm hold on her. They chased each other across the yard, wrestling playfully, leaving a lawnful of disheveled, half-formed snow angels in their wake.

Finally, breathless and cheeks red from the cold, Michael pulled Claire to her feet and held her wrists, forcing her to look into his face. The rippling sound of her laughter was muffled by his kiss.

Suddenly serious, he took her face in his hands and, looking into her eyes, whispered her name. "Claire." His breath hovered in steamy plumes between them.

She swallowed her laughter, her heart beating faster at the lovely sound of her name on his lips. Tenderly, he brushed away a bit of snow that had stuck in her hair and pushed a wayward curl off her forehead.

She had wanted to wait until tonight, but suddenly, she knew that this was the time, the perfect moment. She had never been more sure of anything in her life, yet she began to tremble, nervous and excited with the joy of what she had to tell him.

"Are you cold?" he asked, misinterpreting her shivering, apparently unaware of the emotions she was holding in.

"Michael . . . do you remember the question you asked me a few months ago?"

"Question?" Even as the word came from his mouth, Claire saw understanding come to those piercing gray eyes.

"The one you wouldn't let me answer." For one frightening moment she let herself think about the horrible possibility that he might have changed his mind.

But he touched his finger to her nose, utter tenderness in his eyes. "I'm still asking, Claire."

She fell into his arms, her heart overflowing. "The answer is yes! Oh yes, Michael. Yes!"

# Acknowledgments

I would like to thank the following people for their assistance in researching and preparing this manuscript:

Rich Heim, who helped me understand the diverse and important roles a nursing home administrator plays.

Joyce Bedsworth, Kate Dellinger, and Mary Jean Sweigart, for sharing their expertise in the field of nursing.

Debbie Allen, Beverly Bishop, Bev Heim, and Winifred Teeter, for offering encouragement and helpful suggestions.

And as always, my wonderful editor, Sharon Asmus, for her great ideas and unlimited patience. I'll never understand why an editor doesn't share the byline!

With deep appreciation to the dedicated employees and volunteers of the many nursing homes that over the years provided my grandparents with safe and caring homes.

# Books by Deborah Raney

*Kindred Bond*
*A Vow to Cherish*
*In the Still of Night*